*Emperor
and Nation
in Japan*

Emperor and Nation in Japan

Political Thinkers of the Tokugawa Period

David Magarey Earl

Seattle: University of Washington Press

Copyright © 1964 by the University of Washington Press

Library of Congress Catalog Number 64-20539

Manufactured by Vail-Ballou Press, Inc., Binghamton, N.Y.

Printed in the United States of America

Preface

THE PRESENT STUDY attempts to elucidate the development of Tokugawa-period political attitudes, as shown in the writings of the major thinkers of the time and as exemplified in the life of a nineteenth-century samurai, Yoshida Shoin. Particular emphasis is placed on attitudes toward emperor and nation, a subject that also involved the role of the Bakufu, or Tokugawa shogunate government.

The study proper closes with the death of Yoshida Shoin in 1859. This roughly marks the close of the period during which certain concepts were formed and the opening of a period of implementation, beyond the scope of this investigation. Some idea of the importance of this formative period to modern Japan may be gained from the fact that the leading works of many of the writers included in this study, beginning with Yamaga Soko's *Chucho Jijitsu* (originally published in 1669), were reprinted in large quantities by the Ministry of Education for high-school textbook use in the 1930's and 1940's; these may still be readily found in second-hand book stores.

In making this study, all available Western-language sources—English, French, and German—and existing translations were carefully examined, but comparatively little of such material was found to be really pertinent. For example, Van Straelen's monograph on Yoshida Shoin [1] is a useful general introduction to Shoin as teacher, patriot, and writer, but it does not present a detailed analysis of Shoin's political attitudes. Therefore, almost all the actual research has been done on the basis of Japanese publications. Where quotations are given, if the title cited is in Japanese, it may be assumed that the translation is my work; in those cases where I have used previous translations, credit is given in the footnote.

In making translations my goal has been accurate reproduction of the sense, style, and feeling of the original passage, rather than meticulous attention to English style. However, in translating from Japanese into English, the term "accuracy" can have only a relative meaning; if the same person translates the same passage on two separate occasions, it is extremely unlikely that he will produce identical translations. Translating Tokugawa writers presents a further problem, in that each is likely to have personal peculiarities of style and vocabulary, known only to the specialist. I have not hesitated to rely on the advice of Japanese friends and colleagues where necessary; but as I have in each case made the final decision myself, it is possible that some poor or misleading translations may have occurred. After finding what appear to be errors in practically all the Western-language material examined on this subject, I can hardly expect to be free of error myself; my only hope is that actual mistakes may be few and unimportant.

Many standard terms were used by all Tokugawa writers on ethics and government, and for these I have tried to set up standard translations. When such a special sense is intended rather than a simple English word, I have used capital letters—as Benevolence, Loyalty, etc. In some cases where English translations would be misleading or awkward to use in context, I have retained the Japanese or the original Chinese forms. These are explained either by footnotes or by reference to the Glossary of Special Terms (Appendix B). In one case, it has been difficult

[1] H. J. J. M. Van Straelen, *Yoshida Shoin, Forerunner of the Meiji Restoration* (T'oung Pao, Monographie II [Leiden: E. J. Brill, 1952]).

to establish a uniform translation: the second Confucian virtue (Chinese *i;* Japanese *gi*) includes in its connotation such concepts as righteousness, justice, and duty. Depending on the context, either Righteousness or Duty may appear as a translation for this term.

Personal names have been written in the normal Japanese style —that is, surname first. During the Tokugawa period it was customary for important men, scholars, and even ordinary samurai, to have several different given names, which might be used at different periods of their life or simultaneously. Ordinarily, not over two of these names are well known for any individual; sometimes only one is commonly used by modern writers. I have tried to choose the best-known name for each man mentioned in this study and have referred to him consistently by that one. Where other names are encountered in the literature, they have been indicated in parentheses when the person is first introduced.

A further problem in connection with Japanese personal names is that they are written with characters that often have several possible pronunciations. This is not considered serious by the Japanese, but it creates difficulties when transcribing into a Western language. Within this general problem, there are two separate aspects: (a) Japanese reading vs. "Chinese" reading for the same characters, as in the case of the last shogun, Yoshinobu or Keiki; (b) alternate Japanese readings, or alternate Chinese readings, for the same characters, as in the case of Sakuma Zozan or Shozan. Since this is an area in which a foreigner hesitates to take sides, I have uniformly followed the usage of the *Nihon Shi Jiten* (3rd printing, 1955), an up-to-date historical dictionary compiled by the Historical Research Bureau of Kyoto University.[2]

[2] The readings "Yoshinobu" and "Keiki" are both familiar in Western-language publication; but the reading "Zozan" seems to have been little used outside Japan. Because of Zozan's importance in late Tokugawa thought, I asked the opinion of Dr. Kumura (see p. viii) on this reading. He informed me that modern Japanese scholarship prefers "Zozan" over "Shozan" on the basis of two items of evidence—an extant manuscript in which Zozan (a famous scholar of Dutch) signed his own name in Roman letters as "Zozan"; and a mountain near his home, from which he apparently took the name, which is called "Zo-zan."

Some work on this study was done at the East Asiatic Library of Columbia University in 1951 and again in 1956–57. I completed the major part of the bibliographical and basic research while teaching at Meiji University, Tokyo, in 1952–54; and the bulk of the actual study was done while I was teaching at Yamaguchi University, Yamaguchi, in 1954–56. In its original form this work was submitted as a doctoral dissertation to the Faculty of Political Science of Columbia University.

Especial gratitude is due Dr. Hugh Borton, who, as Director of the East Asian Institute of Columbia University, guided my early steps in this field and whose suggestions on organization, content, and style added considerably to the value of the manuscript. I also deeply appreciate the comments of Professor Nathaniel Peffer, Department of Public Law and Government, Columbia University.

In Tokyo, the interest taken in my work by the late Dr. Uzawa Fusaaki (Somei), Chancellor of Meiji University and a famous classical scholar, and the advice and encouragement of Mrs. Kenneth E. Colton (Dr. Hattie M. Kawahara), are gratefully remembered.

I regret that I can mention only a few of the many good friends who made of Yamaguchi a second home and provided ideal conditions for research—the late Dr. Matsuyama Motonori, President of Yamaguchi University; Dr. Shibata Kei, Dean of the Faculty of Economics; and Assistant Professor Watanabe Masaharu, who gave up many precious hours to assist me in reading the works of Yoshida Shoin. Above all, there was Dr. Kumura Toshio, Dean of the Faculty of Education and one of the outstanding modern authorities on Yoshida Shoin. Dr. Kumura took a personal interest in guiding the portion of my research that has become Part Two of the present study; he also provided the detailed background information and intangible feeling for the late Tokugawa period that could never be obtained from books. The contributions of all these, and many others, are unforgettable.

DAVID M. EARL

Tokyo
August 1, 1960

Contents

Part One

*The Development of Loyalist
and Patriotic Theories Under Tokugawa Rule*

1

Chinese Thought and Japanese Tradition

WHEN IEYASU, the founder of the Tokugawa shogunate, appointed Hayashi Razan as his personal adviser and official scholar in 1610, he was setting in motion a train of events that would be affecting Japanese ideas on the state and the duties of the subject some three hundred years later. Razan was the outstanding Confucianist in Japan at that time, and with the shogun's encouragement he was to establish the Neo-Confucian philosophy of Chu Hsi as the norm for samurai education. But Ieyasu's motives in giving official sanction to Confucian learning were concerned primarily with immediate practical and political problems. He had only recently succeeded in imposing his rule on the country, after a long period of civil war; now the chief requirement was to encourage the arts of peace and, in particular, to inculcate loyalty to his government.

3

Confucian Ethics and Chinese Learning

The purpose of the ethical philosophy generally attributed to Confucius (551–479 B.C.) had been to counteract social and political disintegration by subjecting all human relationships to orderly regulation, instead of permitting the free operation of human will and emotion. In order that each might know his place in relation to others, Confucian teaching enunciated five fundamental human relationships, and assigned to each a certain quality or characteristic by which it should be distinguished: [1]

Father-Son	Affection
Sovereign-Subject	Righteousness (or Duty)
Husband-Wife	Distinction
Older-Younger (or Older Brother– Younger Brother)	Precedence
Friend-Friend	Faithfulness

In addition, the Confucian system placed great stress on the quality of virtue, which was analyzed into five factors—Benevolence, Righteousness (or Duty), Propriety, Wisdom, and Faithfulness.[2] Benevolence was considered to be fundamental, the essential characteristic of Nature, its practice being the secret of human moral progress.

Among the ethical teachings of Confucianism, those contained

---

[1] These will be cited hereafter as the Five Relationships. In Tokugawa Japan, it was customary to place the Sovereign-Subject relationship first.

[2] These will be cited as the Five Virtues. While such ideals seem to be vague generalizations, it should be noted that in Chinese political science these were technical terms, which acquired definite thought content and clearly defined connotations through many centuries of exposition. The translations into five (or six) English words, while fairly standard, are not the only possible renderings and do not adequately indicate the feeling contained in the Chinese words. On these points see George B. Sansom, *The First Japanese Constitution* (Tokyo: Asiatic Society of Japan, 1938), p. 14.

in the *Great Learning* were thought to be particularly valuable both in China and in Tokugawa Japan. This work expounded the concept that, from the emperor down to the commonest person, the cultivation of character is the chief business of life. Its precepts nominally referred to the process by which the individual, becoming the most virtuous person in the state, achieves the position of sovereign, according to the ancient Chinese idea; but because of its value in teaching morality, this book came to be regarded as the foundation of the whole Confucian ethical structure. Its message may be summed up as "discipline oneself before attempting to rule others."

As for the reasons why Ieyasu selected Shushigaku [3]—the Japanese term for the philosophy of Chu Hsi—from among the many existing schools of Confucianism, at least two factors suggest themselves. In the first place, it was by far the best known in Japan at the time; and, more to the point, Shushigaku seemed to be the form of Confucianism ideal for his purpose:

What Ieyasu sought from Confucianism was not literary or expository investigation, but a treatment of ethics, morality, and loyalty; and for this purpose, rather than the exegetical scholarship of Han and T'ang, the Sung learning, which extolled the traditional Way of the Sages . . . and especially Shushigaku, offered characteristics completely suitable for his patronage.[4]

Chu Hsi (1130–1200) had lived some fifteen hundred years after Confucius, during the Sung dynasty. He had created a new philosophical system so outstanding both in its comprehensiveness and in its idealism that he became recognized as the leading thinker of his age. While this new thought was still Confucianism, it had been transformed into an all-embracing metaphysical cosmology. The ethical standards of original Confucianism were not abandoned or ignored, but they were now part of a much larger whole. The new material was drawn both from Buddhism

[3] In this and similar terms used herein, the word *gaku* (Chinese *hsueh*) is a separable suffix denoting "learning" or "school of thought."

[4] Maruyama Masao, *Nippon Seiji Shiso Shi Kenkyu* (Tokyo: Tokyo Daigaku Shuppankai, 1952), p. 13.

and from Taoist sources (Lao Tzu and Chuang Tzu); pre-Confucian Chinese ideas were also included. The result was a Confucianism more philosophical than had been known previously and possessing a newly spiritual or religious coloring.

In his writings, Chu Hsi singled out for particular attention the principle of fulfilling one's duty or obligation. His argument revolved around the nature of Righteousness, which appeared among both the Five Relationships and the Five Virtues. Righteousness between sovereign and subject, from the viewpoint of the subject, became Duty or the obligation of rendering loyal service to the sovereign. It also demanded, as a prerequisite to this, recognition of one's proper station or rank and a complete dedication to meeting the requirements connected with it. This combination—knowing one's place and fulfilling one's obligation to his sovereign lord—summed up the entire duty, or great Way, to be followed by all subjects.[5]

Such a code responded so exactly to the demands of the new lord-and-vassal, or Bakufu-and-*han*,[6] feudal administrative system set up by Ieyasu, that his decision to choose Chu Hsi's school of Confucianism for the ethical foundation of his new government can be readily understood.

However, the establishment of Shushigaku as the approved or official form of learning in Tokugawa Japan did not mean that only the writings of Chu Hsi were to be studied. Just as a full understanding of the Bible's New Testament requires study of the Old, so the study of Shushigaku necessarily entailed knowing the fundamentals of Chinese learning—the "Four Books" and the "Five Classics." Furthermore, it assumed some familiarity with the mass of related material, which, together with Confucianism in the stricter sense, made up the body of Chinese

---

[5] These principles were expressed in Japanese by the two words *taigi meibun*, which might be used either together or separately. *Taigi* is equivalent to "Supreme Duty (Righteousness)," i.e., the highest of all obligations, that to the sovereign. *Meibun* is an abbreviation of two words meaning "name" and "rank or position in society." *Taigi meibun* indicates that the individual should fulfill the duties proper to his position; or that the nature of duties should correspond to the titles by which they are called.

[6] See Appendix B.

thought and literature. (The "Four Books" included three attributed to, or based on the teachings of, Confucius, and one recording the teachings of Mencius [7]—the *Analects,* the *Great Learning,* the *Mean,* and *Mencius.* The "Five Classics" included four important texts of ancient Chinese history and literature— the *Book of Changes,* the *Book of Odes,* the *Book of History,* and the *Book of Rites*—and, in addition, the historical compilation traditionally attributed to Confucius, the *Spring and Autumn Annals.*)

Out of the immense store of Chinese history and thought, certain theories relating to government were to be particularly significant in Tokugawa Japan, although their interpretations and applications differed from their treatment in China. Among these are the "Mandate of Heaven," the "Way of the King," and the doctrine that the state is based on the people.

The Mandate of Heaven

One of the special characteristics of Chinese thought, long antedating the time of Confucius, was that the ruler (Son of Heaven) held his position by authority of Heaven's command, or mandate. In practice, the mandate was understood as applying to a family or dynasty, but according to the strictest interpretation of the theory it was granted to each individual ruler because of his personal merit. This viewpoint is represented by words attributed to T'ang, who overthrew the last Hsia ruler and founded the Shang dynasty (1766? B.C.)—although the record was undoubtedly written long after the event:

[7] About two hundred years after Confucius, Mencius (approx. 371–289 B.C.) repeated the teachings of Confucianism, with particular emphasis on Benevolence and Righteousness, and gave them practical application in terms of contemporary conditions. Although the philosophy of Mencius cannot justifiably be labeled "democratic" in the modern sense, it is clear that his purpose was to advance the interests of the people rather than the power of the ruler. He represented a liberalizing influence within the Confucian structure. Nevertheless, as his book was included among the basic texts of Shushigaku, during the Tokugawa period it became part of the standard learning for the samurai and contributed one more element to Japanese political thinking.

T'ang said: "This rank of Son of Heaven is to be assumed by one who is a follower of the Way. The realm [*t'ien hsia*] is not the possession of one house; it is the possession of him who is a follower of the Way. Therefore only the follower of the Way shall rule this realm; only the follower of the Way shall reform it; only the follower of the Way may rightfully and permanently occupy this position." [8]

The mandate theory was originally connected with the primitive Chinese belief in Heaven as a personalized supreme deity. Even after the concept of Heaven had become more abstract, the theory was retained as a useful justification for assuming and holding sovereign power. The point of difficulty, which was never solved satisfactorily, was the method by which Heaven indicated the termination of the mandate. Great stress was laid on signs and omens, which might indicate Heaven's approval or the opposite. Natural catastrophes could be taken as proof of the Son of Heaven's failure to regulate the elements. But in the final analysis, at least during the period for which reasonably trustworthy historical records exist, the most positive and practically the only means by which Heaven could make its displeasure effective was to permit the military defeat of one who had lost the mandate. Therefore, it came to be assumed that a victor was such by Heaven's will; and in this way the theory was eventually used to justify both the successful founding of each new dynasty and the preservation of the status quo until it was again violently upset.

The Way of the King

Together with the Mandate of Heaven theory, a belief existed that government in primitive China had been carried on by a succession of "sage-kings," starting with Yao and Shun. The sage-kings were conceived of as holy, perfect, and wise men, who ruled according to the Way of the King (*Wang-tao;* Japanese *Odo*). Despite the highly artificial nature of this theory, it was accepted as the basis for Confucian teachings on government

[8] *I Chou Shu Yin Chu.* Quoted in Nakae Ushikichi, *Chugoku Kodai Seiji Shiso* (Tokyo: Iwanami Shoten, 1950), p. 174.

and thus became the unchallenged ideal, against which the actions of every later ruler could be measured.

The concept of the Way of the King involved the nature of the ruler, the nature of sovereignty, and the method of administration.

Since the sovereign ruled as the representative of Heaven, his personal ideals were nearest to those of Heaven. Therefore he was simultaneously wise and holy. When, by his actions, he had demonstrated that his virtue was superior to that of all others, he received the office of ruler as a natural consequence.

As his possession of office depended upon the will of Heaven, the sovereignty of the ruler had certain special characteristics. In the first place, it was not absolute. From the standpoint of the people, he was a sovereign only so long as he manifested the virtues of a sovereign; from the standpoint of Heaven, his sovereignty might be terminated at any time. Therefore, he had no intrinsic right to use his power for personal advantage nor to transmit it to his descendants. His function was essentially to serve, on the one hand, the "Higher Emperor" (Shang Ti, a concept of Heaven as conscious intelligence or God), and, on the other, the people by enforcing justice and protecting their livelihood.

In the original ideal state postulated by Way of the King theory, the administrative practices were a direct expression of the ruler's personality, and their purpose was the moral perfection of the people. Laws were unnecessary, their place being taken by the educational and reforming influence of the sovereign's virtue ("rites" and "music"). The people, thus trained in their ethical duties, would naturally act in accordance with morality and refrain from evil.

Opposed to this was another theory that gained currency during the late Chou period—that of the Way of the Overlord (*Pa-tao;* Japanese *Hado*). According to the context, this term might mean the rule of a military leader, a noble or prince, or a usurper; in any case, it denoted a rule of force, a theory of practical government to be applied by one who desired to maintain peace and order without claiming to possess the Mandate of Heaven.

The original Way of the Overlord thought is attributed to Kuan Chung (Kuan Yi-wu) (d. 645 B.C.), prime minister of the state of Ch'i about two hundred years before the time of Confucius. Kuan Chung did not base his theory of government on virtuous guidance or reform by example, but on strict control and law enforcement. In his system an absolute ruler established laws and administered justice, receiving the loyalty of his people in direct proportion to his ability to guarantee safety of life and family, permit the acquisition of wealth, and promote the general happiness. The contentment of the people as a whole was to be the chief aim of the ruler.

In this original Way of the Overlord theory, the ruler was assumed to be wise and just. Later, as treated by other thinkers, the theory tended to emphasize force, and the welfare or contentment of the people came to be overlooked. Thus, Confucius spoke approvingly of Kuan Chung's methods of government,[9] but Mencius took the opposite side, saying: "He who, using force, makes a pretence to Benevolence, is an Overlord. . . . He who, using virtue, practices Benevolence, is a King."[10] For this reason, when the term "Way of the Overlord" (*Hado*) was used in Tokugawa Japan, its connotation might be either favorable or unfavorable. When used approvingly, it referred to principles resembling those of Kuan Chung; but when applied in a disparaging sense, it meant the rule of a usurper governing without the Mandate of Heaven and in defiance of the standards of the Way of the King.

Emphasis on the People

Although it was impossible for the people to participate in Way of the King government, their intrinsic importance was not overlooked in Chinese thought. The institution of the Son of Heaven was assumed to be for their benefit; the people existed before the ruler, and they were the foundation of the state. Nevertheless, it would be a serious mistake to interpret these ideas in modern democratic terms. The state was for the benefit

[9] See *Analects,* Book XIV, 17–18.
[10] *Mencius,* Book II, Part I, chap. iii, 1.

of the people, but they were not its masters. They were required to submit loyally to any sovereign appointed by Heaven; the Way of the King theory is completely autocratic and patriarchal in this respect. In the words of the *Book of History:* "That which is to be loved is not the ruler, and that which is to be feared is not the people." [11]

The purpose of this emphasis on the people as the foundation of the state was to make a clear distinction between the people or nation, on the one hand, and the person of the sovereign, on the other. This distinction, implicit in the Mandate of Heaven theory, was given explicit statement in various works.[12] One of its forms was the maxim, "The realm [*t'ien hsia*] belongs to the people; it does not belong to one man." [13] Again, it was expressed briefly as "The realm is [or, constitutes] a public [affair]." [14]

While completely in harmony with the basic Way of the King principles of China, this kind of thinking could be applied in Japan only to the assumption of power by the shogun, and could never be reconciled with the theory upholding the divine authority of the emperor.

Confucianism in Tokugawa Japan

Once Confucianism had been favored with the patronage of the Tokugawa family, it was not long before the *han* governments adopted a similar policy. Education according to the curriculum of Shushigaku thus became the norm for upper-class samurai throughout the country. By the end of the Tokugawa period, Chu Hsi's principles were the universal possession of the

[11] *Book of History,* Part II, chap. ii, "Counsels of the Great Yu," 17.

[12] Among them, the *Liu T'ao,* a collection of writings on military affairs, where it appears in Book I, Part I, 1. A photographic reproduction of a Sung-dynasty copy of the *Liu T'ao* was published in 1929 by the Commercial Press, Shanghai (*Ssu pu tsung k'an* edition).

[13] Literally, "the *t'ien hsia* is the *t'ien hsia* of the *t'ien hsia;* it is not the *t'ien hsia* of one man." As this was repeatedly cited by Tokugawa writers as "Tenka wa tenka no tenka . . ." I will refer to it in the Japanese context as the *tenka no tenka* theory.

[14] *Book of Rites,* Book I, chap. vii, 2, "The Great Way."

samurai class, and even the wealthy townspeople were developing a taste for Confucianism.

Even before the Tokugawa period, scholarship in Japan had meant familiarity with Chinese works. Learned men had sought their criteria in China: when they discussed government, they considered Chinese government; and it was usual for a scholar to be better informed on the history of China than on his own country. Thus, when a conscious effort was made by the government to propagate Confucianism, it was quite natural that its theories should, at least initially, be expressed within the framework of Chinese history and political philosophy, by citing Chinese examples and using Chinese terminology.[15]

However, the process of importing, adapting, and adopting Chinese principles was neither a smooth nor simple one. It was in fact slow and difficult; and part of the unique interest attaching to Tokugawa political ideas lies in the two-hundred-year-long clash and reaction between Chinese thought and Japanese tradition. Some components of Confucianism, such as the emphasis on ethics as the foundation of society, were accepted without question. Others were changed only slightly: loyalty, for example, was at first interpreted in terms of feudalism as due to one's lord or to the shogun rather than to the emperor. But some elements caused bitter controversy, such as the idea that government exists for the benefit of the people, or that persons of the rank of the ancient sages could not appear outside China.

Beyond these points, the fundamental difference between China and Japan, which was never eliminated, touched the very heart of the emperor's position in the state. According to Chinese theory and practice, the sovereign might be removed or the dynasty changed under certain conditions. In Japanese theory, on the other hand, regardless of how unreasonable the sovereign might be, the subjects could never forget their duty to act as

[15] The Chinese influence extended even to the language of literary composition. Just as Latin was the choice of educated men in medieval Europe, Chinese was used in Japan throughout the Tokugawa period. So generally accepted was this practice that scholars who wrote serious works in Japanese were rare exceptions.

subjects. Although this rule was partially violated in practice by forced abdications, there was no recorded instance of *dynastic change* in Japanese history.

The Enduring Influence of Shinto

This peculiarly Japanese way of thinking, which viewed the emperor as a sacrosanct or inviolable personage under all conditions, was based on Shinto teachings as they had been refined and interpreted down through the centuries. Shinto, the ancient "Way of the Gods" of Japan, was undeniably a religion, but the borderlines between religion and philosophy, like those between general ethics and political thought, were not clearly drawn. Certain elements in Shinto belief took on the nature of political principles; and, particularly in the Tokugawa period, many scholars specialized in finding analogies between Shinto and Confucianism.

The basic Shinto teaching affecting attitudes toward the emperor concerned the divine ancestry and confirmation in office of the imperial family. According to this myth or tradition, as found in ancient records such as the *Kojiki* and *Nihon Shoki,* Japan was created in a special manner by the two primeval deities, Izanagi and Izanami, who later appointed their offspring, the Sun Goddess Amaterasu, as its protector and ruler. Amaterasu in turn commissioned her grandson, Ninigi no Mikoto, to leave the heaven-like Takamagahara where the gods were living, take up his residence in Japan, and found a line of imperial rulers who would govern eternally in her name. The first emperor, Jimmu, was considered to be the great-grandson of Ninigi no Mikoto and therefore a lineal descendant of Amaterasu; and all succeeding emperors were the descendants of Jimmu.

As Shinto theory developed before and during the Middle Ages, the additional idea was incorporated that civilization, ethics, and government were due to the instructions of Amaterasu as implemented by successive divine emperors. Thus, by the beginning of the Tokugawa period, a relationship between Shinto belief and the principles of government had been established by several writers.

An early example of this relationship, showing also how Confucianism was used to reinforce Shinto, was the work of Kitabatake Chikafusa (1293-1354), the *Jin-no Shoto-ki* ("Record of the Legitimate Line of the Divine Emperors"), completed in 1339. This book, widely known in the Tokugawa period, was a history of Japan from the Age of the Gods down to the author's own time. Chikafusa wrote it to defend the legitimacy of the Southern Court established by Emperor Go-Daigo;[16] his stress on undeviating loyalty was inspired mainly by his familiarity with the teachings of Chu Hsi. In this work, Chikafusa explained that Japan differed from all other countries in that it was the Land of the Gods, and possessed the Three Sacred Treasures[17] —the mirror, which represented honesty; the jewel, mercy; and the sword, the wisdom that lay in bravery and resolute action. A combination of these qualities was the essential foundation for sovereign authority. Summing up this argument, he wrote: "The Way of government . . . with honesty and mercy as its basis, must have the power of resolute action. This is the clear teaching of Amaterasu."[18]

[16] Emperor Go-Daigo (reigned 1318-39), driven into exile, established a court at Yoshino, south of Nara, which maintained itself from 1338 to 1392. During this time, a Northern Court with a different series of emperors was functioning in Kyoto. Although what power there was had unquestionably remained in the capital, Chikafusa's argument that the Southern Court was the true one was supported on theoretical grounds by many later writers.

[17] The Three Sacred Treasures are the mirror, jewel, and sword. According to Shinto belief, these were bestowed by Amaterasu upon Ninigi no Mikoto when he was preparing to descend to earth, as symbols of the divine authority and perpetual rule of the imperial house.

During most of recorded Japanese history the original treasures or replicas of them have been kept in the following places: the mirror, at the Inner Shrine of Ise (in the modern city of Ise); the jewel, at the Imperial Palace (Kyoto); and the sword, at the Shrine of Atsuta (in the modern city of Nagoya). As physical objects, believed to be proofs of the emperor's exalted position, the Three Sacred Treasures were to take on great ideological significance in Tokugawa political thought.

[18] *Jin-no Shoto-ki*. Quoted in Tanaka Yoshito, *Nippon Shiso Shi Gaisetsu* (rev. ed.; Tokyo: Meiji Shoin, 1943), p. 120. The *Jin-no Shoto-ki*, important from the standpoint of historiography as well as that of political thought, is available in a German translation by Hermann Bohner,

At the beginning of the Tokugawa period, the tendency to accept the simultaneous validity of Confucianism and Shinto was evident in the writings of Hayashi Razan himself and was carried on by many others. While the basic differences between the two systems were denied or intentionally obscured at first, there eventually came a realization that Japan was, after all, not China; that Japan had its own character and history; and that the literal application of Chinese principles as a whole might be neither possible nor desirable. When this occurred, it had a definite effect on the interpretation of such Chinese ideas as the Mandate of Heaven and *tenka no tenka* theory.

The Question of the Shogun's Status

The controversy over the shogun's status, which continued throughout the major part of the Tokugawa period, exemplifies the kind of dilemma that arose when an attempt was made to apply the Chinese approach to Japanese conditions. According to the old Chinese idea of the "rectification of names," which was an essential element of the Chu Hsi system, situations and titles should agree: what then was the correct title for the shogun in terms of Chinese theory? This apparently innocent and basically theoretical question concealed a potential attack on the entire authority of the Bakufu. Regardless of its artificial nature, the question was one that Japanese scholars had to face, particularly since they were all directly or indirectly dependent on the Bakufu for their sustenance.

That the Tokugawa family were the actual rulers of Japan was an inescapable fact. Within one hundred years after Ieyasu had been appointed shogun, the title had lost all relation to its original meaning of "Great Barbarian-Subduing General," and was purely hereditary in nature. Ietsugu, for example (the seventh of the Tokugawa line), became shogun at the age of four and was affianced to an imperial princess before dying at seven. The Bakufu could and did make laws restricting even

Jinnô-Shôtô-Ki; Buch von der wahren Gott-Kaiser-Herrschafts-Linie, with introduction and extensive notes (2 vols.; Tokyo: Japanisch-Deutsches Kultur-Institut, 1935–39).

the daily life of the emperor. But so long as the legitimate imperial line existed, Japanese tradition made it completely unthinkable for the Tokugawa family themselves to assume the imperial title.

The only counterpart for such a situation in Chinese history was during the late Chou period (approximately 700–400 B.C.), when the "Son of Heaven" had lost both power and authority, and princely rulers of individual states were asserting their leadership instead of deferring to the Chou court. However, according to a common interpretation, these defiant princes were usurpers, following the Way of the Overlord, in contrast to the Son of Heaven, who represented the Way of the King.

Under the political conditions existing during most of the Tokugawa period, it was impossible for any reasonable person to view the shogun as a usurper; even up to the very end, since the imperial court never canceled the shogun's appointment, there was no completely satisfactory basis for such an argument. Thus, what started out as a question of semantics ultimately led to serious thought on the true nature of the shogun's relation to the emperor, and before the close of the Tokugawa period, at least four theories on the shogun's status had been developed, based on the Way of the King and the Way of the Overlord:

(a) *Odo* (Way of the King) I: The shogun is the legitimate ruler in his own right; the emperor is above him, to be revered but having no actual connection with the government. This was the theory of Arai Hakuseki, and it became the official Bakufu ideology.

(b) *Odo* (Way of the King) II: The emperor is the true sovereign, but the shogun is his rightful proxy or deputy. This seems to have been the original or basic theory. It was mentioned by Kumazawa Banzan and Yamaga Soko and was later developed by others, such as Asami Keisai. With the gradual weakening of Tokugawa power, it gained eventual acceptance even among most Bakufu supporters.

(c) *Hado* (Way of the Overlord) I: The shogun's rule is based on force, but it is not to be condemned on that account. Force is essential to good government, as the Way of the King is an impossible dream. This was the theory of Ogyu Sorai; it received little approval.

(d) *Hado* (Way of the Overlord) II: The shogun is a disloyal subject, and must be overthrown in order to return the ruling power to the emperor. This theory did not develop until the last decade of Tokugawa rule, when the Bakufu persisted in opening the country to foreign trade in defiance of the Emperor's wish. It then became the inspiration of many who were influenced by the ideas of the Mito school; some, such as Yoshida Shoin, displayed a definite shift in viewpoint from (b) to (d).

2

Some Early Tokugawa Viewpoints

IN CONSIDERING the writers and teachers who made significant contributions to Tokugawa-period political thinking, it is reasonable to start with Hayashi Razan; but other outstanding thinkers emerged during his lifetime. While Shushigaku was readily accepted as the general norm or standard for education as such, before the end of the first century of Tokugawa rule divergent attitudes were beginning to arise on the question of the respective roles of shogun and emperor.

Razan was considered the leading Chu Hsi scholar of his day. But it is noteworthy that he had a firm faith in Shinto as well, and that he devoted much of his scholarly energy to studying and interpreting Shinto tradition. It is obvious that he personally felt no incompatibility between Confucianism and Shinto belief.

During Razan's lifetime, several younger scholars also followed this joint Confucian-Shinto approach, with varying degrees of emphasis on the two components: examples of such thinking are to be found in the writings of Kumazawa Banzan, Yamaga Soko,

18

and Yamazaki Ansai, among others. However, within a few years after Razan's death, some scholars were emphasizing Chinese learning and minimizing or so far as possible disregarding Japanese tradition; among the best known of these are Arai Hakuseki, Muro Kyuso, and Ogyu Sorai. As the Chinese and Japanese viewpoints assumed contradictory positions on the source of the ruler's sovereignty—the divine appointment of an unbroken imperial line, as taught by Shinto, contrasted with the revokable Mandate of Heaven found in Chinese thought—they actually involved distinctly different attitudes toward emperor and shogun. This meant that the more emphasis placed on the validity of Shinto, the greater the respect due the emperor; but if Chinese traditions were to be taken as precedent, the shogun might be considered to have replaced him as legitimate ruler. Thus, as more and more serious attention was paid to this question, those scholars who inclined toward Shinto tended to uphold the idea (designated above as *"Odo* II") that the emperor was the true ruler, while those who accepted the shogun as sovereign (*"Odo* I") necessarily played down or rejected Shinto.

Shogun and Shinto

Hayashi Razan (Doshun) (1583–1657) obtained the favor and personal support of Ieyasu and his next three successors; with such powerful backing Razan was able to found a school that developed into the leading educational institution of Tokugawa Japan.[1]

A man in his position would be expected to employ his knowledge of Chinese philosophy to explain and defend his

---

[1] This school had various designations during the Tokugawa era, but was most commonly called the Shoheiko. Beginning as the private possession of the Hayashi family, it gradually came under Bakufu control and in 1790 was formally taken over by the government, although each successive head of the Hayashi family served as its principal. By training teachers and setting standards of orthodox Shushigaku, the Shoheiko served as the headquarters for ideological support of the Bakufu power until the very end of the Tokugawa period. Still under government control after the Meiji Restoration, it ultimately became one of the forerunners of the present Tokyo University.

patron's right to rule, and Razan did not neglect this duty. On a certain occasion some years after Ieyasu's retirement, the former shogun brought up the question of how one should regard vassals who overthrow their lords,[2] with specific reference to T'ang and Wu.[3] Razan's answer, clearly intended to cover the case of Ieyasu, indicates that he had done careful thinking on the subject:

> Even though T'ang and Wu, accepting the Mandate of Heaven and responding to the will of the people, did conquer Chieh and Chou, since from the first they had no desire to promote personal advantage, but their true intent was solely for the sake of the people to extirpate tyranny and bring relief to the populace as a whole, we cannot consider their action as evil in even the slightest degree.[4]

Later, in recording and commenting on his answer, Razan wrote further: "Only in accordance with the popular will of the whole land is one a sovereign; without this, he is but another common man."[5]

In emphasizing the point that government must be for the benefit of the people, Razan's political thinking actually went beyond what can strictly be called Shushigaku and included the substance of the older *tenka no tenka* theory. Writing on the actions of T'ang and Wu in the light of this theory, he explained in another work that the exile and execution of the former rulers were the unavoidable results of conditions. Furthermore, upon the fall of Chieh, the realm did not pass automatically to T'ang.

[2] An allusion to Ieyasu's own action in violating his promise of allegiance to the young son of Toyotomi Hideyoshi.

[3] T'ang and Wu, who used force to overthrow their lords and establish themselves as rulers in ancient China, were nevertheless considered as sages, due to the fact that they punished the cruelty and tyranny of the former kings. T'ang, the founder of the Yin (Shang) dynasty, drove Chieh, the last king of Hsia, into exile (1766? B.C.); Wu, the founder of the Chou dynasty, killed Chou, the last Yin king (1122? B.C.). The examples of T'ang and Wu, as the archetypes of the enforcement of the Mandate of Heaven, were familiar to all students of Chinese thought, and were frequently mentioned in Tokugawa Japan.

[4] *Hayashi Razan Bunshu.* Quoted in Ono Hisato, *Meiji Ishin Zengo ni okeru Seiji Shiso no Tenkai* (Tokyo: Shibundo, 1944), p. 67.

[5] *Ibid.*

And as for Wu, he purified the land by his virtue, his benefits far and wide were as brilliant as the sun and moon; his assumption of ruling power was not in order to promote his personal advantage, but was rather the natural result of his having received the Mandate of Heaven; and the purpose of his administration was to ease the burdens of the people: ". . . so that even though we may say the realm came into the hands of the Chou family, the realm belonged to the people, and it was not the private property of King Wu alone." [6]

In justifying Ieyasu's seizure of power by indirectly equating him with the ancient sages T'ang and Wu, Razan introduced the Mandate of Heaven theory into the Japanese situation, but applied it to the position of the shogun rather than that of the emperor. While this was logical within the frame of reference of the Bakufu government itself, it left unanswered the question of how to explain the station of the emperor.

Thus Razan turned to Shinto; far from seeing any inconsistency, he held that Confucian ideals and Shinto were identical: "*Odo* in a different aspect becomes Shinto; Shinto in a different aspect becomes the Way; as for the Way, it is what is called Confucianism." [7] Furthermore, despite his loyalty to the shogunate, Razan frequently expressed deep appreciation for the unbroken imperial line. In the first book of his great historical work, the *Honcho Tsugan*, he said: "From the time of Emperor Jimmu, the Imperial line has been one, continuous for one hundred and thirty generations. In China or other countries, however, there is nothing of such eternity. How glorious!" [8]

The Three Sacred Treasures of the imperial house also had great importance to Razan. According to the *Mean*,[9] the sage-kings had governed by means of Wisdom, Benevolence, and Courage. In the *Shinto Denju*, Razan equated these three virtues respectively with the mirror, jewel, and sword, thus proving

[6] *Jumon Shimonroku*. Quoted in Ono, *Seiji Shiso*, p. 68.

[7] *Hayashi Razan Bunshu*, LXVI, 3rd leaf. Quoted in Inoue Tetsujiro, *Nippon Shushigakuha no Tetsugaku* (14th printing; Tokyo: Fuzambo, 1924), p. 84.

[8] *Honcho Tsugan*. Quoted in Mikami Sanji, *Son-no Ron Hattatsu Shi* (Tokyo: Fuzambo, 1941), p. 184.

[9] *Mean*, chap. xx, 8–11.

that the *Odo* followed by the sage-kings was identical with the Shinto taught by Amaterasu. He continued:

Again, the mirror represents the sun, the jewel represents the moon, the sword represents the stars. When these three luminaries are present, heaven and earth are alight. When the Three Sacred Treasures are at hand, *Odo* is supreme.[10]

In going to such lengths to demonstrate the identity of Confucianism and Shinto, Razan was in fact upholding the essential superiority of his own country, and approving the idea of Japan as the "Land of the Gods." In the introduction to his *Honcho Jinjako,* he wrote:

This country is the Land of the Gods. Ever since Emperor Jimmu as the successor to Heaven founded the Empire, the Imperial line has continued in unbroken succession; this was a dissemination of *Odo.* This is the Way bequeathed by our heavenly gods. This is the Way of the Gods. . . .

The Sun Goddess is the sun; because this is the source country of the sun, it is called *"Nihon-koku."* [11, 12]

Razan was able to combine his knowledge of Chinese learning with an equally strong faith in the traditions of Japan, and his example stimulated the Tokugawa-period interest in "Confucian Shinto." [13] However, as the study of Shinto proceeded and its implications became more evident, later Shinto scholars completely abandoned Razan's attempt to attribute the Mandate of Heaven to the shogun.

[10] *Shinto Denju.* Quoted in Iijima Tadao, *Nippon no Jukyo* (Mombusho: Nippon Bunka, No. 16 [Tokyo: Nippon Bunka Kyokai Shuppambu, 1938]), p. 31.

[11] The word *Nihon* or *Nippon* literally means "source of the sun."

[12] *Honcho Jinjako.* Quoted in Tanaka Yoshito, *Nippon Shiso Shi Gaisetsu* (rev. ed.; Tokyo: Meiji Shoin, 1943), p. 136.

[13] A new form of Shinto developed during the Tokugawa period, in which ideas borrowed from Chinese philosophy were used to supplement Shinto dogma. The leading scholars of Confucian Shinto were Watarai Nobuyoshi (1619–90), Yoshikawa Koretari (1615–94), and Yamazaki Ansai (1618–82). For details, see Appendix C.

Emperor and Shogun

A different approach to the reconciliation of Confucianism and Shinto is exemplified in the writings of Kumazawa Banzan (Hakkei) (1619–91), a scholar partly contemporary with Razan but born after the founding of the shogunate. Banzan emphasized Wang Yang-ming's [14] ideas as opposed to those of Chu Hsi; and although he placed great reliance on Chinese learning, he saw it more as a useful supplement to Shinto than vice versa. The distinction between his thought and that of Hayashi Razan is clearly shown by comparing his treatment of the Three Sacred Treasures and the quotation from the *Mean* with Razan's theories mentioned above.

Whereas Razan tended to equate *Odo* and Shinto, according to Banzan Shinto alone was the source of all necessary knowledge:

The Three Sacred Treasures are the "sacred scriptures" of the Age of the Gods. In primeval times there were no writings, there were no letters; and so these objects were fashioned as symbols. The jewel was caused to be the symbol of Benevolence; the mirror, the symbol of Wisdom; and the sword, the symbol of Courage. . . . The letters and language of the Age of the Gods have become extinct and are no longer handed down; these three symbols alone are still extant: supremely clear and simple, they are the fountainhead of morality and learning. Boundless in their wisdom; compelling admiration in their profundity; eternal in their mystery; their endowment is perfect. The standards of personal conduct, government, and learning are not to be sought elsewhere: these are sufficient.[15]

The following passage indicates his attitude toward Confucianism:

[14] Wang Yang-ming (1472–1529) was a Neo-Confucianist of the early Ming period. His viewpoint differed from that of Chu Hsi in several particulars, chiefly in placing more emphasis on action and intuition, less on pure scholarship. These teachings, called Yomeigaku in Tokugawa Japan, were considered heretical from the standpoint of orthodox Shushigaku.

[15] *Shugi Gaisho.* Quoted in Inoue Tetsujiro, *Nippon Yomeigakuha no Tetsugaku* (rev. ed.; Tokyo: Fuzambo, 1928), p. 217.

As a commentary on the Three Sacred Treasures, nothing excels the *Mean*. The sages of China, the god-men of Japan—their virtue was one, their Way was identical. Therefore, their symbols [i.e., of Japan] and their writings [i.e., of China] correspond exactly.[16]

With regard to the question of the true sovereign, Banzan made it clear that for the Japanese, loyalty meant loyalty to the emperor before all else:

Our country, since it is under the control of the Sun Goddess, is called *Nihon*. . . . The origin of all lands, the source of all realms, is our country. . . .

For those who live in a country, to be unaware that there is any lord other than the lord of their own country is the Way of the subject. To respect and serve the Imperial line of our land in deepest reverence is the fundamental Duty.[17]

To explain why the sovereign of Japan in particular must be served with reverent devotion, Banzan argued that Amaterasu, by assuming direct responsibility for ruling Japan, had liberated the people from their state of primitive ignorance:

. . . her virtue in truth is higher than heaven, broader than earth; for this reason, the people-subjects may not forget this benefaction for all time. So long as this country shall exist, her descendants shall be reverently served as lords and sovereigns. For even the shogun to attain the rank of king [*kokuo*] is absolutely impossible. . . . As the Emperors are of one line for all ages, no matter how great the power an inferior may possess, he can never attain to such a position.[18]

---

[16] *Daigaku Wakumon*, chap. xvii. Quoted in Iijima, *Nippon no Jukyo*, p. 45. The *Daigaku Wakumon*, concerned chiefly with economic problems but also including some political thought and other subjects, is one of Banzan's major works. For an English translation by Galen M. Fisher, see "Dai Gaku Wakumon: A Discussion of Public Questions in the Light of the Great Learning," *Transactions of the Asiatic Society of Japan* (2nd series), XVI (1938), 259–356; Fisher's version of the quotation cited here appears on p. 329.

[17] *Miwa Monogatari*, in *Shinto Sosetsu*, comp. Kokusho Kankokai (Tokyo: Kokusho Kankokai, 1911), p. 47.

[18] *Ibid*. Quoted in Mikami Sanji, "Kumazawa Banzan no Chotei ni Tai-suru Kangae," *Meiji Seitoku Kinen Gakkai Kiyo*, IV (1915), 35.

Japan is not like China, Banzan continued. In China, people consider the universe to be their parents, and therefore all are equal; anyone may achieve respect and anyone who takes control becomes sovereign. In Japan, however, the emperor is essentially different from the people:

> . . . in Japan, the Emperor is the descendant of the heavenly gods. The people are completely different in nature. At a time when the people had not entirely left off behaving as birds and beasts, through the divine virtue of Amaterasu, and the virtue of her descendants, the successive generations of Emperors continuing on from Emperor Jimmu, morals were established and they came to know Propriety. For this reason it is said that her benefaction can never be forgotten for all eternity.[19]

In pointing out the special characteristics of the imperial line, Banzan believed that there was a fundamental relationship between the existence of the imperial family and the nature of Japan itself: "The Imperial Amaterasu was not earth-born, and Emperor Jimmu as her descendant continued the heavenly line. . . . If the divine line should be broken, this could not indeed be called the Land of the Gods."[20]

Reverence for the imperial house, combined with his study of history and Chinese thought, led Banzan to develop a theory on the relation between emperor and shogun that is logically more satisfying than Razan's attempt to honor both simultaneously. It was based on the tacit assumption that the shogun acknowledged himself a subordinate of the emperor, which was technically true but in fact a mere formality during most of the Tokugawa era. Although the Imperial Court is without power, Banzan said, it appoints the shogun, who in turn reverently serves the Court; and just as the shogun serves the Court, the various military lords serve the shogun. If the Imperial Court did not exist, after two or three hundred years of rule by military families, Japan might take on the aspect of India or the southern barbarian countries; but as it is, every person in Japan knows

---

[19] *Ibid.,* p. 36.
[20] *Shugi Washo.* Quoted in Fujii Jintaro, *Meiji Ishin Shi Kowa* (4th ed.; Tokyo: Yuzankaku, 1937), p. 34.

the ancient relation of sovereign and subject. As a result, each is loyal to his superior, and the shogun is an example for all: "When they see the shogun acting with such reverence toward an Imperial Court which is devoid of actual power, the daimyos as well as others follow his example and offer their loyalty in the service of the shogun." [21]

If a daimyo or other person might consider plotting against the shogun, seeing the shogun's loyalty to the emperor such a person would reverse himself and become a loyal vassal. On the other hand, if the Imperial Court should assume direct control, this could only be a temporary condition, due to the normal changes of the world, and it would again be subject to failure. As the emperor is not really earth born and the imperial line is eternal, it is better for him to be apart from the actual political power, "remaining gently in a superior position," preserving forever his station as sovereign lord.

If—although it is almost beyond possibility—a military family should attempt to rise to the rank of Emperor, it would be the utmost extreme of treachery; but on the other hand, for the Imperial family to attempt to regain the actual power would be alike impossible. To preserve the present situation of mutual interdependence, paradoxically, is to the best interests of the Imperial family. [22]

Others whose viewpoints resembled that of Banzan included Yamaga Soko and Yamazaki Ansai, who are discussed in separate chapters below. These men were living at exactly the same time, during the reigns of the third, fourth, and fifth shoguns, when the Bakufu was at the height of its power. There is nothing to indicate that these three had any great influence on each other; their significance lies rather in the fact that at a time when the Bakufu was unchallenged as the supreme authority of the land, they were among the first to analyze the relation of emperor and shogun on the basis of Japanese tradition rather than of Chinese theory.

[21] *Ibid.* Quoted in Mikami, *Son-no Ron Hattatsu Shi,* p. 37.
[22] *Ibid.,* p. 38.

Ieyasu and the Mandate of Heaven

Of those who used Chinese learning to bolster the position of the Bakufu, probably the best known today is Arai Hakuseki (1657–1725). Born in the year of Hayashi Razan's death, Hakuseki was destined to become one of the leading Confucianists of the Tokugawa era. He was personal adviser to the sixth shogun and *de facto* regent during the reign of the seventh, who died as a child. During the seven-year period from 1709 to 1716, when he was in a position to influence legislative and administrative policies, Hakuseki strongly advanced his theory on the relationship of shogun to emperor.

Although, according to the literal meaning of its name and its actual historical origin, the Bakufu was a military government, the tendency to de-emphasize its military nature had begun with Ieyasu. The natural effects of a long period of peace, supplemented by the active patronage of scholarship during the reign of Tsunayoshi, the fifth shogun, had in fact changed the Bakufu into a "literary government." Hakuseki wanted to provide a form and theory suited to the changed circumstances. This necessarily involved clarifying rank and precedence and providing suitable titles and etiquette for the outward expression of the relationships.

Hakuseki certainly did not ignore or despise the imperial family. After spending several months in Kyoto studying court ceremonies, he suggested—and the suggestion was accepted—that an additional branch of the imperial family be set up with an independent income from the Bakufu, as a safeguard in case there should be no heir. In one of his historical works he wrote: "Our country surpasses all other countries; the divine Imperial line exists co-eternally with Heaven and Earth." [23] Yet when it came to the question of rectifying procedures, the existence of two rulers created an almost insoluble problem.

The difficulty of precisely defining the shogun's position was

[23] *Koshitsu Wakumon,* in *Arai Hakuseki Zenshu,* III, 325. Quoted in Kurita Motoji, "Arai Hakuseki no Seiji Shiso," *Rekishi to Chiri,* XV (1925), 572.

epitomized in the signing of diplomatic correspondence,[24] and it was in this connection that Hakuseki brought the matter to a head. In the *Shugo Jiryaku* ("Memorandum on the Special Title"), he explained his attitude carefully with references to Chinese and Japanese history. He opposed the use of the word *Taikun* (Great Lord) for the shogun—a usage initiated by Hayashi Razan—as being a superlative arrogation of rank. In China, he said, this was a title of respect for the emperor, but the Japanese divine imperial line had never been broken, and there had never been a case in Japanese history of any person's assuming such a rank on his own authority. Aside from this, the title was being used in contemporary Korea for the Crown Prince. *Kokuo,* on the other hand, would be absolutely correct in its significance. It could cause neither confusion, nor insult to the emperor, as by calling the one *Tenno* (Heavenly Emperor) and the other *Kokuo* (National King), the distinction between superior and inferior would be as manifest as that between heaven and earth. The title *Kokuo* would in this way distinguish the shogun from both emperor and subjects.

Hakuseki's opinion was opposed by many, but he was in a position to have his ideas accepted. In 1711 the official style was changed, and the title of *Nihon Kokuo* was introduced for diplomatic correspondence.[25] Later, after the accession of Yoshimune, the eighth shogun, and the attendant retirement of Hakuseki, opposition to the *Kokuo* title increased; and in 1719 the official style was changed back to *Taikun.* However, the result of the scholarly debate on this subject, which extended over

[24] In practice, this meant correspondence with Korea and Ryukyu. Occasional diplomatic correspondence had been exchanged with several other countries until the closing of Japan in 1636, and with China until the fall of the Ming dynasty (1662), but relations with Korea were maintained throughout the Tokugawa period. The status of Ryukyu was not clear at this time; treated in some ways as a possession of Japan, or as a dependency of Satsuma-*han,* it nevertheless had its own king and maintained diplomatic relations with both China and the Bakufu.

[25] For a translation of the first letter signed by a Tokugawa as "King of Japan" (Shotoku, 1st year, 11th month), see Yoshi S. Kuno, *Japanese Expansion on the Asiatic Continent,* II (Berkeley: University of California Press, 1940), 328–29.

a period of several years, repeatedly set forth Hakuseki's opinion on the true roles of shogun and emperor: that the Bakufu wielded the paramount power, although not for the private advantage of the Tokugawa family; that the shogun, holding the supreme political authority, took all responsibility for the welfare of the nation out of a sense of duty; and that the emperor occupied a superior position, transcending political affairs.[26]

The distinction between the two types of theory designated above as *Odo* I and *Odo* II lies in the location of sovereignty— in whether the people are subjects of the shogun or of the emperor. Hakuseki further clarified his stand on this point in his *Dokushi Yoron*. He wrote that except for the emperor and those members of his court who owed their position to his appointment, all other inhabitants of Japan were under the direct rule of the shogun. This meant that while the emperor was to be revered as holding the highest rank in the country, he was not the ruler; and that the sovereign-subject relationship applied between shogun and people, not between emperor and people.

The opinion that the true ruler was the shogun rather than the emperor was approved by many other scholars of the time. While Hakuseki's support of the Bakufu hegemony was expressed chiefly through the "rectification" of titles and ceremonies, one of his contemporaries devoted especial attention to developing basic political theory that would justify the rule of the Bakufu in terms of the Mandate of Heaven and related Chinese ideas. This was Muro Kyuso (1658–1734), who was already a famous scholar and teacher when in 1711 he received an appointment to the Shoheiko through Hakuseki's recommendation. With the accession of the eighth shogun, whom he served as personal

---

[26] Although Hakuseki lost the argument so far as the title itself was concerned, his view of the shogun's authority became the foundation of Bakufu policy and the orthodox position of the Hayashi or official school of Shushigaku. While the Bakufu and its scholars occasionally mentioned the *Odo* II theory (emperor as sovereign), in practice they acted upon and defended the *Odo* I principle (shogun as sovereign) up to the very moment when Tokugawa power began to disintegrate. An example of this was the attitude of Yamagata Taika in the mid-nineteenth century, described on pp. 154–56.

adviser, Kyuso's authority and influence continued to rise even after Hakuseki himself had lost favor.

Unlike Razan, Kyuso firmly rejected the claims of Shinto; and in contrast even to his friend Hakuseki, he practically disregarded the emperor. While others puzzled over the reconciling of Chinese and Japanese ideas, Kyuso merely ignored the Japanese tradition. Later generations have tended to rank Hakuseki higher as an all-round man of letters; but in their lifetimes, Kyuso's single-minded devotion brought him renown as the greatest "pure Chu Hsi" scholar of the day.

The principle of loyalty was an important element in Chu Hsi's teaching. In the case of Muro Kyuso, there was no question as to the proper object of that loyalty; *taigi meibun* was unfailingly to be directed toward the Tokugawa family and the founder of its power, Ieyasu. Kyuso praised Ieyasu in extravagant terms, not only as a general and an inspiration to his followers, but as the source of government, culture, and peace; all should give worshipful praise day and night for the blessings bequeathed by him; the highest duty of scholars was to transmit and expound his holy virtue.

This attitude was connected in Kyuso's thought with an acceptance of the "state based on the people" tendency in Chinese thinking. For example, he wrote that the principle of the *tenka no tenka* theory "is one which ought never to be forgotten by him who is the lord of the realm; it must be considered as the supreme maxim, undying for all time." [27]

While admitting that even in China, after the Three Dynasties,[28] there was general failure to practice this theory, Kyuso felt that its influence nevertheless endured, and was a strong factor in enabling the founders of new dynasties to gain the

[27] *Shundai Zatsuwa.* Quoted in Sato Kiyokatsu, *Dai Nippon Seiji Shiso Shi,* II (Tokyo: Dai Nippon Horei Shuppan K. K., 1939), 188.

[28] The Three Dynasties were Hsia (2205?–1766? B.C.), Shang or Yin (1766?–1122? B.C.), and Chou (1122?–256 B.C.). Although strictly speaking the Hsia dynasty is primarily a matter of myth or legend and details on administration during the Shang dynasty are a matter of conjecture, the term "Three Dynasties" was generally used in Tokugawa Japan as a reference to a supposed Golden Age when Chinese government followed the theory of the Way of the King.

throne. As for Ieyasu, his exploits were not excelled even by some of these same founders of Chinese dynasties; his heart was an example of the verse "Heaven's will is manifested through man."

In comparing Ieyasu's seizure of power with the operation of the Mandate of Heaven in later Chinese history, Kyuso was following Razan's precedent of equating Ieyasu with the sage-kings T'ang and Wu. Kyuso went even further than this, and on the basis of the *tenka no tenka* principle he developed an original social-contract theory that was unique in the Tokugawa period and strikingly resembled European ideas of the same time. According to Kyuso's argument, men love and follow a great leader for their own advantage and happiness, and he becomes ruler in response to the wishes of the people. Consequently, "the ruler is not an official who causes the people to toil, but he is an official who toils for the sake of the people." [29] But if the time comes when "failing to toil on behalf of the people, he causes the people to toil, disregarding the Way of Heaven and disregarding likewise the hopes of man, . . . [then] the body politic is rent asunder, and he reverts to the status of a solitary individual." [30, 31]

Under these circumstances, the would-be ruler is powerless, and "another person who gains the confidence of the people, unable to stand aloof, administers defeat and punishment on behalf of Heaven." [32] This consequence is inevitable. The new leader does not endeavor to take control of the nation by conquering it; he accepts control "for the sake of the people." Nor does he assume power as a feudal right, but "in response to the desires of the people." In summary, "The state is not bestowed by Heaven, nor is it granted by a lord, nor is it even seized by the individual; but it is only granted by the action of the people." [33]

The rank and power of the ruler should never become the cause of enmity or distrust between him and the people:

[29] *Fubosho.* Quoted in Ono, *Seiji Shiso,* p. 81.

[30] Kyuso uses here a special term taken from the *Book of History,* which carries the connotation of a once-powerful Son of Heaven, rejected by his people as a tyrant, standing defenseless and alone.

[31] *Fubosho.* Quoted in Ono, *Seiji Shiso,* p. 81.

[32] *Ibid.*   [33] *Ibid.*

The ruler is not inherently noble; his nobility is of the same order as that of the people. Because of reverence for the ruler to despise the people, allowing one man alone to wield the sharp-edged sword [34] —this amounts to saying that a setting of one against the other is to be expected, that rising against that man they will utterly destroy his sword; the impropriety of such a policy, to say nothing of its wickedness, is extreme.[35]

The ideal relationship between ruler and people is one of mutual understanding and agreement. As stated from the viewpoint of the ruler, it is as follows: "The people, approaching, request me to serve. I promise to serve. For this reason the people, worshipping, make me ruler. I, becoming ruler, carry out my promise to serve for the sake of the people." [36] The unbridgeable gulf between this thinking and the belief in a divinely appointed and descended emperor whose authority is coeval with heaven and earth is apparent.

Antipatriotism

Another supporter of the Bakufu, contemporary with Hakuseki and Kyuso, was Ogyu Sorai (1666–1728). Sorai was probably the most determined champion of Chinese learning in the Tokugawa period: preferring to write even his own name in Chinese style, he often called himself Butsu Sorai so as to use three characters instead of four. In his desire to restore the original purity of Chinese thought, Sorai rejected much of what was then generally considered Confucianism. His approach toward political theory was practical and utilitarian; the Way, he taught, had no mystical origin but was intentionally constructed by the sage-kings as a device for guiding and ruling the people.

Sorai was neutral to negative toward Japan and its special characteristics. The ancient sage-kings dominated his thought; Japan had never produced men such as Wu's father Wen, Wu

---

[34] Probably an allusion to the "sword hunt" of Toyotomi Hideyoshi in 1588, by which he deprived the people of their weapons. Kyuso frequently attacked the motives and policies of Hideyoshi.

[35] *Fubosho.* Quoted in Ono, *Seiji Shiso,* p. 81.

[36] *Ibid.*

himself, Chou Kung,[37] or Confucius. He accepted Shinto in a sense, but considered it worthy of no special emphasis: all supernatural forces could be called "gods"; the true Way was the same for every country. In an essay of advice to the shogun, he indicated that whatever there was of value in Shinto could be found in Confucianism:

What should be called the Way of the Gods of our country is no more than this: to worship the ancestors and be subservient to Heaven; to consider Heaven as the first ancestor; and to carry out all things whatsoever in accordance with the commands of the gods. Although this came down from a time before it could be transmitted in writing, it is the same as the ancient Way of the Three Dynasties of China. . . . For a person born in a certain country to reverence the gods of his country—this is the meaning of the Way of the Sages.[38]

As for the sacrosanct Treasures to which Japan-centered writers attached such deep significance, Sorai dismissed them as mere superstition: "The Three Sacred Treasures to which Shinto . . . gives particular pre-eminence have resulted from errors in the traditions of later ages. It is clear and manifest that they did not exist in ancient times." [39]

The furthest that Sorai could go in praising the unique institutions of Japan was his somewhat equivocal introduction, written in 1719, to a new commentary on the *Kuji Hongi*.[40] In this, he wrote as follows:

[37] Chou Kung, or the Duke of Chou, the brother of King Wu, was the power behind the throne during the reigns of Wu and his successor. Chou Kung is credited with inspiring the administrative reforms that confirmed the position of the Chou family and were to some extent responsible for inaugurating the longest dynasty in Chinese history. His clarification of the principles of the Way of the King became the foundation for the teachings of Confucius.

[38] *Taiheisaku.* Quoted in Miura Kyo, "Butsu Sorai no Keisei Shiso— oyobi Kumazawa Hakkei to no Hikaku," *Toyo Bunka,* No. 117 (1934), p. 47.

[39] *Ibid.,* p. 50.

[40] At that time, the *Kuji Hongi* was much respected as an authentically ancient historical record, attributed to the Mononobe family. As the outstanding descendant of the family in his generation, Sorai was requested to write the introduction. Modern scholarship considers the *Kuji Hongi* to have been compiled in the Heian period.

We may say that our eastern land has followed the Way of the Gods for age after age. . . . As for the statement that by means of the Way of the Gods, the sages established their teachings,[41] is it not clear and manifest? When "rites" and "music" [42] had been abandoned, the study of "inherent nature" and *li* [i.e., Sung philosophy] began. Those persons say that Heaven is without a heart, that the gods are *ch'i*,[43] that worship is nothing but the application of one's sincerity. These opinions of theirs are as much as to say that the ancient sage-kings deceived us.

As the untalented Sorai was lately born, he is not yet proficient in the Way of our eastern land. Still, to give his personal opinion concerning those who made this land their own, who considered their ancestor to be Heaven and Heaven to be their ancestor, who considered worship to be government and government to be worship, without distinction between things divine and things official; whether gods or men—among the people today there are some who doubt, among the people today there are some who believe—in this way they have been kings for a hundred generations without a change: are they not firm and substantial monarchs? [44] If sages should appear in China in later times, they would unfailingly endorse this alone.[45]

While Sorai gave a certain amount of praise to Japan in the above passage, it is noteworthy that he did so from a Chinese viewpoint; this was implicit from the beginning, where he called Japan an "eastern land" (China being the Central Land), to the end, where he spoke in the name of possible future Chinese sages.

[41] A quotation from the *Book of Changes*. Actually, this is an example of difference between Chinese and Japanese connotations of the same character—Chinese *shen*, "spirits"; Japanese *shin* or *kami*, "gods"—which Sorai chose to ignore.

[42] "Rites" and "music" were the traditional methods of Way of the King theory, by which the ruler controlled his people without need for law. See p. 9.

[43] The terms *li* and *ch'i* (Japanese *ri* and *ki*) represented two of the fundamental metaphysical concepts in the Neo-Confucian system. *Li* may be defined as the fundamental, unchanging essence of the universe; *ch'i* as force or primal motion, the power behind creation, giving embodiment to *li*. *Ch'i* included both *yin* and *yang* (Japanese *in* and *yo*), the opposing active-passive, male-female principles of the physical world.

[44] The word translated as "monarchs" is *zoshin* (Chinese *tsang shen*), taken from the *Book of Rites*, where this term is used in the sense of "sovereign."

[45] *Kuji Hongi-kai Jo*. Quoted in Iijima, *Nippon no Jukyo*, pp. 52–53.

His argument was merely to the effect that early Shinto was in accordance with the teaching of the sages and therefore superior to the corrupt ideas of the Sung dynasty. Although recognizing the continuity of the imperial line, he referred to the emperors in the language of the Chou dynasty, before the institution of emperor existed, and he avoided using contemporary Japanese terms of respect.

When this statement is considered together with his other writings on the question of sovereignty and his categorical approval of the Mandate of Heaven theory, it is clear that Sorai viewed the shoguns as the actual sovereigns of Japan in his day. This attitude is especially evident in the *Seidan,* where he opposed those who would see in the emperor the "true sovereign." In this book, written for Yoshimune, he suggested that the government should be entirely in the hands of the shogun, to be administered at his will. He also supported Hakuseki's idea that the daimyos were vassals of the shogun, not of the emperor, and that a system of ranks similar to that of China should be set up for military lords and Bakufu officials.

Although he considered the shogun the true sovereign, and in his personal relations with him gave him the respect due the emperor, Sorai did not insist that Bakufu power was based on the Way of the King. Rather, his iconoclastic attitude led him to teach that the Way of the Overlord was the only practical form of government. In the *Kenen Yodan,* he wrote that *Hado* (the Way of the Overlord) had been condemned by Hsun Tzu and Mencius, and that since that time scholars generally had praised *Odo* and censured *Hado.* But Confucius himself had approved the doctrine of Kuan Chung,[46] and did not condemn the theory of *Hado;* while the attack made by Hsun Tzu was due to his trying to reform the low moral standards of his own day, his purpose being no different from that of Confucius. *Odo* was in fact an abstract ideal, something apart from the Way itself, worthy of admiration but of no practical use in government.

With this sort of argument, Sorai became the first scholar of the Tokugawa period to attempt to legitimize *Hado.* His intention was to give ideological support to the shogunate, and as

[46] See p. 10.

this was already being done on the basis of the more attractive—because more idealistic—*Odo* theory, his efforts were neither welcomed by the Bakufu nor widely approved by other thinkers. Sorai's theory is interesting chiefly as representing the furthest extreme to which the acceptance of Chinese thought could lead —an extreme that was essentially antipatriotic and would thus serve future generations not as a model to be followed but as the archexample of *Kara-gokoro* (Chinese heart).

3

Yamaga Soko and the Emphasis on Patriotism

AMONG early Tokugawa thinkers who supported both fundamental Confucian ideas and Japanese conceptions of patriotism and respect for the emperor, Yamaga Soko most succeeded in awakening a sense of love for country and pride in the uniqueness of Japan.

In the formative first century of Tokugawa-period thought, Soko played a complex and significant part. As a Confucianist, he initiated a revolt against Han-, T'ang-, and Sung-dynasty Chinese ideas, and led the way in establishing a new, orthodox school of Confucianism opposed to Shushigaku. As a historian, he strenuously maintained the superiority of Japan over all other countries, teaching that its national character and eternal, divine, imperial house were without equal in the world. As a professor of military science, he developed his own school of tactics and strategy, which continued to be taught up to the end of the Tokugawa period. In addition, drawing on his knowledge of Confucianism, Japanese tradition, and military science, he created a new, coherent theory for Bushido, which was to become the standard ethical code of the samurai class.

Of all his diverse interests, Soko's views on Japanese history and his conception of loyalty—that is, the duty of repaying the benevolence of one's lord—were the most significant contributions to political thought.

Soko's Life and Thought

Yamaga Soko (1622–85), the son of a physician, became a pupil of Hayashi Razan at the age of eight. Later, in addition to the standard works of Chinese literature, he familiarized himself with Shinto, Zen, Taoism, Japanese literature, and poetry. Eventually he concentrated upon military science and continued his studies in this field until his thirtieth year.

Soko then became instructor of military science for Ako-*han*, where he remained for eight years. He resigned in 1660 in order to open his own classical and military school in Edo. The next six years were his time of greatest activity as a teacher. In military science, he introduced several innovations: the Yamaga school, which he founded, while not ignoring the Chinese authority Sun Tzu, emphasized the use of European firearms and artillery, the subordination of tactics to over-all strategy, and the Bushido code for the individual soldier.

During this time also, Soko's thought on Confucianism and patriotism was maturing—although the latter aspect was not immediately evident. As he wrote later, from about the age of forty he began to realize fully the worthlessness of foreign scholars' theories and the true value of Japan. With his fresh approach to both classical and military learning, Soko's fame grew until he had over two thousand pupils, including daimyos and members of the *hatamoto*[1] class.

At this point, Soko took a step that affected the entire course of his life. Putting his arguments against post-Confucian Chinese

[1] See Appendix B.

philosophers into the form of a short book, the *Seikyo Yoroku* ("Essentials of the Holy Teachings"), he released it for publication at the end of 1665. But his popularity as a teacher with an unusual viewpoint had already aroused suspicion and enmity in high places. The book was banned, and Soko was exiled from Edo, in the custody of the lord of Ako.

Although officially in disgrace, Soko was in fact still highly respected. He resumed his former duties as teacher to the samurai of Ako-*han* and devoted much of his time to study and writing. Among his new pupils was Oishi Yoshio, then only a boy but later to become the leader of the forty-seven loyal samurai.[2] There is no doubt that the action taken by the men of Ako to vindicate the name of their lord was inspired by Soko's personal teaching of Bushido.

In Ako, Soko's thinking reached its final stage of Japan-centered patriotism, when he turned his attention from the advocacy of pure Confucianism to the analysis of Japanese history. During this period, he began to use the terms *Chuka, Chugoku,*[3]

[2] The loyal samurai of Ako are better known in the Western world as the Forty-Seven *Ronin*. Technically speaking, they became *ronin* with the death of their lord, but as they refused to forget their obligation, they are not generally called *ronin* in Japan. (For the meaning of *ronin*, see Appendix B.)

The events that made the loyal men of Ako the epitome of the Bushido ideal began some fifteen years after Soko's death. The lord of Ako who had employed and befriended him, Asano Naganao, was insulted by a high official at the shogun's castle in 1701. In angrily drawing his sword, the *hanshu* violated the law against unsheathing weapons within the Edo castle precincts, and was sentenced to commit suicide. The forty-seven samurai, by carefully waiting almost two years to avoid any appearance of a plot, were able to avenge the insult to their lord by taking the life of the official who had caused his downfall; but they in turn were sentenced to commit suicide.

The story of the Forty-Seven Samurai is one of the best known and most popular in Japan; usually under the title of "Chushingura" ("A Treasury of Loyal Retainers"), it remains a frequently used theme for stage and screen.

[3] *Chuka* ("Central Culture") and *Chugoku* ("Central Land" or "Middle Kingdom") (Chinese *Chung-hua* and *Chung-kuo*, respectively) are typical of the names by which China has traditionally designated itself. As Japanese patriotism developed, the use of such terms by the Japanese in referring to China became a controversial issue.

and *Chucho*[4] as designations for Japan rather than China. Here he produced what was to be his most famous work, the *Chucho Jijitsu.*

In 1675, Soko was unexpectedly pardoned. Returning to Edo, he lived quietly for ten more years, continuing to write but not engaging in wide-scale teaching.

Theory of Bushido

In the middle of the seventeenth century, Yamaga Soko observed a military class that was for the first time entirely divorced from the soil, living in comfort in a time of continued peace. As he expressed it in the first chapter of the *Shido,* the samurai eats without tilling, uses without making, and profits without buying and selling; there must be some reason for this; he must have some function. This function, as it appeared to Soko, was to be the living expression of Duty (*gi*). In order to provide a practical guide by which the samurai might know his duty, Soko developed his theory of Bushido.

The concept of Bushido, considered as the pride of a warrior class in its own tradition and custom, had existed in Japan from the most ancient times and had flourished particularly in the Kamakura period. However, it was not until the warrior class achieved leisure and culture under Tokugawa rule that an attempt was made to give the term philosophical content.

A short book of ten chapters, the *Bukyo Shogaku,* which Soko wrote in 1656, is considered the earliest actual text on the subject. The title itself, roughly translated as *"Samurai's Hsiao-hsueh,"* is a tribute to the influence that Chu Hsi's *Hsiao-hsueh*[5] (Japanese *Shogaku*) had already achieved in Japan. In choosing this title, Soko indicated that the Chinese work should be replaced with something better suited to the Japanese spirit.

---

[4] "Central Court"; i.e., the Imperial Court of Japan considered as the world's most important center of authority; by extension, Japan itself.

[5] The *Hsiao-hsueh* ("Lesser Learning") was a short work on ethics and personal conduct written by Chu Hsi for the edification of Chinese youth.

Although the topics covered did not go beyond Confucian ethics, the way in which they were interpreted is significant. For example, in the sixth chapter, on material possessions, Soko wrote:

The Way of the samurai is, placing himself under the control of his lord, to follow absolutely unto death. . . . If he cannot give up treasures and finds pleasure in material possessions, then he is necessarily deficient as regards weapons and arms. In time of stress, he will be almost unable to forget his home. If it should happen that he yearns for his home, then abandoning Duty [*gi*] he will evade death; he will be covered with disgrace, and the stain will extend back to his ancestors.[6]

It was this stern manner of treating ethics from the single viewpoint of Duty that set Bushido apart from orthodox Confucianism.

Later, Soko expanded the ideas of the *Bukyo Shogaku,* and wrote the *Shido* ("Way of the Samurai"), his definitive exposition of the subject. Here again, Confucian ethics were made the foundation; Letters and Arms were both praised, but the essence of the teaching was the necessity for individual sacrifice. In discussing the worldly concern with profit and personal advantage, Soko pointed out that the samurai must clearly discern values:

As for what is of greater and what of lesser importance: lord, father, older brother, teacher, and husband are of greater importance to us; retainer, son, younger brother, child, and wife are of lesser importance to us. Country is more important than person; sight, hearing, words, and deeds are less important than inner motivation.[7]

Profit for an individual results from sacrificing the less important to the more important; for the samurai, nothing is more important than Duty. In following its requirements, he will find his

---

[6] *Bukyo Shogaku,* chap. vi, in Tsukamoto Tetsuzo (ed.), *Yamaga Soko Bunshu* (Yuhodo Bunko, XXII [Tokyo: Yuhodo Shoten, 1926]), p. 35.

[7] *Shido,* Part II, chap. i, sec. 6, in Tsukamoto, *Yamaga Soko Bunshu,* p. 60.

true profit; for even if he loses his life, he will leave a good name to his family, something far more valuable than any immediate temporal gain.

Soko's Bushido thought, although inseparable from Confucianism, was nevertheless a distinct approach to social relationships, in which the ideal of the "heroic man" replaced that of the "superior man." This philosophy, growing out of Japanese tradition but refined by Confucian concepts, was to find ready acceptance in Tokugawa samurai society.[8]

Interpretation of History

When, in his later years, Soko directed his interest to the ancient history of Japan, he found that Shinto belief provided Japanese tradition with certain unique characteristics. These, he believed, should serve as a basis for national patriotism.

Shinto in its original form, according to Soko, was very simple: the emperor followed the instructions of Amaterasu, carefully protected the Three Sacred Treasures, and governed with Benevolence, Righteousness, and Wisdom. In this sense, Shinto was equivalent to government; it did not disagree with the Way of the Sages. But in later generations, when the sacred mirror was transferred to Ise, the imperial palace lost its character of a shrine. Gradually, Shinto also lost its true meaning, the people made gods of animals, plants, and evil spirits, and corrupt teachings crept in. Therefore, Shinto should be purified and returned to the original teachings of Amaterasu and the symbolism of the Three Sacred Treasures.

While preaching "pure Shinto," Soko also claimed to be remaining true to pure Confucianism. In this, his approach was quite distinct from the new "Confucian-Shinto" position that was reaching its high point with Yamazaki Ansai. In the *Takkyo Domon,* for example, Soko emphasized that the continuity of the imperial line was indissolubly bound up with its divinity and with the instructions of Amaterasu: the eternal existence of the divine line was fixed by divine decree. In addition to the super-

---

[8] For Bushido influence on loyalty to the emperor in the thinking of Yoshida Shoin, see pp. 177–82.

natural aspect, Soko discussed this subject from the standpoint of ethics. In the *Yamaga Gorui* he wrote: "In this realm, of all under heaven, there is *the* legitimate line. From creation until the present day, it has never been broken for one day. Even China could not hope for such *taigi*." [9] Even when unschooled and unlettered men seized the reins of actual power and authority, they never failed to observe the Relationships and Virtues and continually respected the position of the emperor. At all times, "the relationships of father and son, of lord and subject, were correctly observed. This is the *taigi* of this realm." [10]

The refusal to criticize the shoguns' assumption of power, and the insistence that they had always maintained proper respect for the emperor, were closely connected with Soko's theory on the location of sovereignty. Implicit in many of his writings, this theory was spelled out most clearly in the *Buke Jiki*, which dealt specifically with Japanese history under the rule of the various shogunates. Although he condemned the excesses of the Ashikaga shoguns in imitating court nobles and raising themselves to high court ranks, Soko considered shogunal government to be administered on the basis of the imperial mandate and to be legitimate for that reason. With regard to the Tokugawa authority of his own day, he wrote:

The Imperial Court is the Forbidden Precinct. Happily, the line descended from Amaterasu has possessed hereditary authority for countless generations. Accordingly, even though a military general has grasped the power and directs government and letters within the four seas, this is nevertheless for the reason that he has been commanded to oversee all state affairs on behalf of the Imperial Court, and his serving of the Imperial Court diligently, without the slightest negligence, is in accordance with the Great Propriety obtaining between lord and subject. . . .

For the subject to follow the Way of the subject; with military generals in their turn protecting Kyoto, reverencing the Imperial Court, and respecting the Imperial officials—thus causing the Imperial

---

[9] *Yamaga Gorui*, IV, Book XXXV (Tokyo: Kokusho Kankokai, 1910–11), 132. It is interesting to note that in this passage, Soko himself referred to China as *Chuka*, something to which he was strenuously objecting a few years later.

[10] *Ibid.*, p. 133.

Court to be the Imperial Court, and preserving the true principles of lord and subject, superior and inferior: this, which makes up the Great Propriety and Supreme Duty [*taigi*] of the military family [i.e., Tokugawa], is the nature of the custom of this land, its fundamental Way, excelling those of foreign lands.[11]

Such an argument, unequivocally making the shogun the subject and appointed deputy of the emperor, demonstrated a simultaneous acceptance of basic Shinto and Confucian principles. It was one of the clearest statements of this kind of theory enunciated in the first century of the Tokugawa period.

Soko's assertion that Japan, rather than China, should be designated as the Central Realm of the civilized world was another main element in his interpretation of history. This idea was based on the Chinese principle that a civilized country is "central," barbarian lands "peripheral." China, it was true, had originated the Way of the Sages, but its history proved that its people were unable to follow it. Japan, on the other hand, where the *taigi* of sovereign and subject had never been broken, was the perfect example of the Way, and was therefore superior to China even on China's own terms. Soko did not go so far as to call China barbarian, but of the two countries, he believed Japan had the only real claim on the title of "civilized."

The proposition that Japan is the true *Chuka* may be found in the *Yamaga Gorui*,[12] completed while he was teaching in Edo, but Soko did not begin to make an issue of the point until after his banishment. During the years he spent in Ako, it occupied much of his attention, and, in a passage of the *Haisho Zampitsu*, he presented three reasons to justify his stand. First, the imperial line was continuous: "In this realm, from the Age of the Gods until the present day, the blood-line of Amaterasu, the true lineage, has never varied even for one generation."[13] Second, Japan's military strength, as shown by expeditions to Korea, had in an-

---

[11] *Buke Jiki*, Book XLV. Quoted in Maki Kenji, "Buke Seiji no Taisei ni Kan-suru Edo Jidai Gakusha no Kenkai," *Hogaku Ronso*, XXXV (1936), 1243–44.

[12] *Yamaga Gorui*, I, Book XI, section on "Distinction between Civilized and Barbarian (*Ka-i no Ben*)," 491.

[13] *Haisho Zampitsu*, in Tsukamoto, *Yamaga Soko Bunshu*, p. 482.

cient times resulted in the exacting of tribute and the establishment of Japanese government offices on foreign soil; furthermore,

While the valor of this realm is feared even in foreign countries, as for attempts by foreign countries to invade this one, not even one spot has ever been taken by them. This shows that foreign countries can not match our use of military equipment, cavalry, or weapons; nor the excellence of our troops, tactics, or strategy. Does this military prowess not excel all within the four seas? [14]

Third, in exemplifying the virtues of the sages, based on the *Mean,* Japan was not to be surpassed:

Wisdom, Benevolence, and Courage are the three virtues of the sages. Of these three virtues, if even one is lacking, it is not the Way of the Sages. Now, with regard to these three virtues, if we compare this land with foreign lands, minutely noting each item of evidence, this country is far superior.[15]

Therefore, Soko concluded, "Its culture is such that truly it must rightfully be called *Chugoku.*" [16]

Chucho Jijitsu

Among Soko's writings, the one pre-eminently devoted to demonstrating the superiority of Japan is the *Chucho Jijitsu* ("Actual Facts about the Central Realm"). This work, written in 1669, more than any other established his enduring reputation in the field of political thinking.

The *Chucho Jijitsu* purports to be a historical study of ancient Japan; in fact, it is Soko's commentary on history. Its stated purpose is to awaken the China-worshipping scholars of Japan to the true beauty and significance of their own country. The text consists of brief statements of historical facts as then understood, usually followed by quotations from ancient records or historical works; these in turn are followed by Soko's comments, which vary from a few lines to several pages in length. The comments make up approximately one-half to three-quarters of the

[14] *Ibid.*   [15] *Ibid.*   [16] *Ibid.*, p. 483.

whole book. The work is not arranged in chronological sequence, but according to subject. The events and quotations are chosen by the author as bearing on the subjects and demonstrating the points he wishes to emphasize. His research apparently included all historical materials then extant, as he quotes from the *Kojiki, Nihon Shoki, Kogo Shui,* and *Kuji Hongi,* as well as from many other sources including the *Shinto Gobusho* and Kitabatake Chikafusa's *Jin-no Shoto-ki.* The work is divided into two books —the first of which is more important from the ideological viewpoint—and an appendix.

In the introduction, Soko first confesses the error of his own early viewpoint, then states his absolute faith in the mission of Japan:

> This foolish one, although born on the soil of *Chuka* culture, had not yet perceived its beauty; but, cultivating an exclusive taste for the classics of China, puffed himself up while fawning over foreign personalities.
> How could he have been so heedless! How could he have so lost his aspiration! Is one to prefer the odd, or revere the strange? The water and soil of *Chugoku* excel those of all other countries, and the qualities of its people are supreme throughout the eight corners of the earth. For this reason, the boundless eternity of its gods and the endlessness of the reign of its sacred line, its splendid works of literature and glorious feats of arms, shall be as enduring as heaven and earth.[17]

The first chapter of Book I deals with the meaning of creation as recorded in the ancient traditions of Japan. Soko makes no distinction between the basic principles of Confucianism and Shinto, and derives Confucian virtues from the story of Izanagi and Izanami:

> Male and female are the foundation of *yin* and *yang,* the commencement of the Five Relationships. Given the existence of male and female, afterwards the Ways of husband and wife, father and son, and lord and subject, arise.[18]

[17] *Chucho Jijitsu,* Introduction, in Tsukamoto, *Yamaga Soko Bunshu,* p. 207.

[18] *Ibid.,* Book I, chap. i, in Tsukamoto, *Yamaga Soko Bunshu,* p. 211.

From his treatment of this material, it is clear that Soko considered the basic philosophy of the Way to be a universal truth, having no exclusive connection with China.

Chapter 2 opens by taking up the special nature of Japan's water and soil. These differ from those of all other lands because of the manner of Japan's creation, through the action of Izanagi and Izanami and the agency of their heavenly jeweled spear. Accordingly, the very existence of Japan is a gift of the gods; Japan and its imperial line alike are coeval with heaven and earth. Many countries consider themselves to be the center of the world, but from the standpoint of climate—the change of seasons, the proper balance of wind, rain, cold, and heat—only Japan and China merit such a title. Of the two, Japan's rank is evidently superior because of the manner of Japan's creation: "The fact that this realm is *Chugoku* is inherent in the nature of heaven and earth." [19]

The third chapter, devoted to the significance of the imperial line, is perhaps the most important from the standpoint of political thought. It covers the origin of the imperial family, the *shinchoku* (promise of Amaterasu),[20] the consequent eternity of the imperial line, and Jimmu's assumption of office. Soko emphasizes that although the divine line was carried on by humans, it never lost its divine nature. Regarding Jimmu's assumption of power, he says:

The meaning was that a human sovereign established his authority in succession to Heaven, to rule over all lands, and to be reverenced by the people; so that all within the four seas knew for the first time that they must worship the Son of Heaven, and *illustrious virtue was exemplified* in the Central Land.[21]

[19] *Ibid.,* Book I, chap. ii, in Tsukamoto, *Yamaga Soko Bunshu,* p. 218.

[20] The word *shinchoku* literally means any divine decree, promise, or oracle. However, as used in the Shinto and loyalist writings of the Tokugawa period, this word refers almost exclusively to Amaterasu's promise to her grandson, Ninigi no Mikoto, that the line of his descendants, and the flourishing of the imperial throne of Japan, which they were to occupy, would be coeval with heaven and earth.

[21] *Chucho Jijitsu,* Book I, chap. iii, in Tsukamoto, *Yamaga Soko Bunshu,* p. 243. Italics supplied; a well-known quotation from the *Great Learning.*

As emperor, Jimmu established the pattern of civilization, which apparently included Confucian principles:

Therefore, the Imperial line once being established, it is succeeded to without change for myriads of generations; the populace one and all receive the fundamental law without thought of disobedience; all lands accept the sovereign's decree and give up their vulgar customs; the Three Relationships [22] never sink into obscurity; moral influence never falls into confusion: how could any foreign country hope for this? [23]

Soko then contrasts the tranquil and praiseworthy condition of Japan (which, it goes without saying, is highly idealized) with the frightful record of China and Korea, filled with bloody revolutions and the frequent assassinations of rulers:

In *Chugoku* alone, although from the time of creation until the first human Emperor, some two million years—and from the first human Emperor until the present day, two thousand three hundred years—have elapsed, the Imperial line of the heavenly gods has never changed.[24]

He also points out, although not in such detail as he did later in the *Buke Jiki,* that even though military families had held power for five hundred years at the time of his writing, they had never failed to respect the imperial house. Accordingly, "Throughout the vastness of the eight corners of the earth, and the breadth of foreign lands, there is nothing to be compared with *Chushu.*[25]

At the end of this chapter, Soko remarks that while individual emperors die as humans, the mystical eternity of the line itself is inseparably connected with the Three Sacred Treasures.

In the fourth chapter, dealing with the history and significance of these treasures, Soko calls attention to the special character

[22] That is, the first three, or most fundamental, of the Five Relationships.

[23] *Chucho Jijitsu,* Book I, chap. iii, in Tsukamoto, *Yamaga Soko Bunshu,* pp. 244–45.

[24] *Ibid.,* p. 245.

[25] *Ibid.,* p. 246. *Chushu* ("Central Land") was used by Soko interchangeably with *Chuka, Chugoku,* and *Chucho.*

of Japan's military power. Due to the country's origin in the jeweled spear, its arms must be ever victorious; but in that the spear was jeweled, the might of Japan cannot be applied to wanton killing: it is intended only for subduing evil and extirpating vicious brigands. He then shows how the nature of government is derived from the Three Sacred Treasures:

The jewel is to represent the virtue of warm Benevolence; the mirror is to represent supreme Wisdom; the sword is to represent unflinching Courage. That which they symbolize and give form to, is in each case the absolute virtue of the heavenly gods.[26]

These three virtues are completely sufficient for the emperor: "When the Holy Lord applies these, then within he will have regard for his perspicacious mind, and without he will shape his educative rule."[27] Amaterasu commanded that her descendants should always keep the mirror in their actual dwelling place —meaning that wisdom is a fundamental necessity for the emperor. Thus, from the beginning, the importance of the mirror has been far greater than that of the sword and jewel. This was recognized by the early emperors, who kept the mirror in the imperial palace shrine, worshipping morning and evening.

In closing the chapter, Soko gives another symbolic interpretation distinct from the previous one: "The treasure-mirror is the body of the goddess; the divine jewel is the body of the human sovereign; the treasure-sword is the rule over the subjects."[28]

Chapter 5 deals with education. Soko indicates that it originated with Izanagi and Izanami, who first demonstrated the necessity for following the Way, just as now the emperor is an example for the people. It was further developed during the Age of the Gods, and summed up for the emperor in the bestowal of the mirror. On this occasion Amaterasu made the important promise

[26] *Chucho Jijitsu,* Book I, chap. iv., in Tsukamoto, *Yamaga Soko Bunshu,* p. 249. The term here translated as "absolute virtue" is *shisei* (Chinese *chih ch'eng*), a word often used in Confucian texts to mean "sincerity," but the complete connotation of which does not correspond to any single English word.

[27] *Ibid.*

[28] *Ibid.,* p. 255.

that for her descendants to gaze into the mirror would be the same as gazing upon her.

Soko next takes up the introduction into Japan of Chinese learning,[29] to which he has no objection, inasmuch as it does not disagree with the original Way. The instructions of the gods, he says, were based on disciplining the self before ruling others; in later ages, this principle became the origin of Confucianism.

The sixth chapter is concerned with the technique and purpose of government, which had its source in the *shinchoku* of Amaterasu. The chapter includes two significant points, the first being Soko's approval of the feudal system. He writes that feudalism began with the divine protection given Ninigi no Mikoto, when vassals were assigned to accompany him on his trip to earth; and that it was continued by the policy of Emperor Keiko (supposed to have ruled A.D. 71–131), who assigned territories to his many sons. Feudalism, then, is a normal element of Japanese administration.

The second important point in this chapter is Soko's wholehearted adoption of the principle that "the state is based on the people," which he attributes to Amaterasu. In describing the importance of the people's livelihood and the emperor's duty to foster agriculture and the abundant production of all useful things, he explains the teaching of Amaterasu in words that seem very similar to the ideas of Mencius: "The body of the nation is made up of the people. When the people suffer, the nation declines; when the people are at ease, the nation flourishes. . . . The people are the foundation of the state." [30]

Book II of the *Chucho Jijitsu*, concerned mainly with the origins of laws and ceremonies, is less important from the theoretical viewpoint. However, in the fourth chapter, there is

[29] Confucianism was introduced into Japan by the scholar Wani, from the Korean kingdom of Paekche, in the 16th year of Emperor Ojin, corresponding to A.D. 285 by the standard chronology. (George B. Sansom suggests that 405 would be more accurate. See *Japan: A Short Cultural History* [2nd ed.; New York: Appleton-Century-Crofts, 1943], p. 36.) The entry of Buddhism was later, probably in 552.

[30] *Chucho Jijitsu*, Book I, chap. vi, in Tsukamoto, *Yamaga Soko Bunshu*, p. 288.

an interesting passage on the relationship between military prowess and the Japanese national character:

It goes without saying that the origin of *Chugoku* was the jeweled spear . . . and then there was bestowed upon the heavenly offspring the treasure sword. . . . Thus, it is not necessary to explain further how the arms of *Chuka* are distinct from all in the wide world within the four seas.[31]

The Appendix is made up of a variety of questions concerned with Japanese history, each followed by Soko's answer. It is here that one of his clearest statements is to be found on Confucianism and Buddhism in their relation to Japan. Confucianism, he says, does not differ from the Way:

The great and sacred Way is but one and not two. It is modeled after the body of heaven and earth; it is based on human feelings. The dissimilarities in the details of its teaching are all due to the differences of water and soil, and to peculiarities of custom and tradition. The people of the five directions all have their own nature; they are not alike.[32]

But of them all, Japan excels, and has been especially blessed by the gods. Buddhism, on the other hand, is an entirely different matter. In Soko's opinion, Buddha was a great sage; his teachings were suited to the needs of his own country, but they are in no way applicable to Japan and should not be followed by the Japanese.

[31] *Ibid.*, Book II, chap. iv, in Tsukamoto, *Yamaga Soko Bunshu*, p. 419.
[32] *Ibid.*, Appendix, in Tsukamoto, *Yamaga Soko Bunshu*, p. 447.

4

Yamazaki Ansai and the Emphasis on the Emperor

YAMAZAKI Ansai occupies a unique place in the history of Japanese thought: he is renowned both as a Confucianist and as a Shinto scholar. Into both aspects of his belief he put a fervent patriotism; the result was a new approach to Shushigaku in which the emperor replaced the shogun as the object of loyal devotion. Ansai was phenomenally successful in stimulating others to accept and propagate his ideas; during his lifetime, his pupils were said to have numbered over six thousand, and many of them became famous teachers who kept his influence alive almost to the end of the eighteenth century.

Ansai as a Confucianist

Early in life Yamazaki Ansai (1618–82) intended to become a Zen priest, and as a boy he entered a temple in Kyoto for train-

52

ing. Later he transferred to a temple in Tosa, on the island of Shikoku, where he came under the influence of Tani Jichu (1598–1649), a Chu Hsi scholar who had formerly been a priest. At the age of twenty-five Ansai gave up the clerical life in favor of Confucian studies; he became interested in Shinto at the same time and five years later rejected Buddhism entirely.

A few years after this, Ansai returned to his native Kyoto, where in 1655 he opened a school and began lecturing on Shushigaku. Even while making his name as a Confucianist, he continued his Shinto studies. During this period, he was receiving instruction from Watarai Nobuyoshi, the famous scholar of Ise Shinto. In the year that he began his lectures on Chu Hsi's thought, Ansai wrote the *Ise Dai Jingu Gishiki Jo* ("Introduction to the Ceremonies of the Grand Shrines of Ise"), in which he argued for the unity of Confucianism and Shinto.

Ansai's influence as a Confucianist resulted from his forceful personality, teaching methods, and example, rather than from extensive writing or philosophical speculation. He discouraged wide study of the classics and Chinese literature, advocating instead concentration on Chu Hsi's commentaries and other works such as the *Hsiao-hsueh;* he constantly warned against obsession with words and neglect of meaning.

His teaching was intensely patriotic, interpreting and applying morality in a specifically Japanese context. He made a sharp distinction between Japan and foreign countries, including China; like his contemporary, Yamaga Soko, he protested against calling China by such names as *Chuka* or *Chugoku*. In his teaching, the concepts of Loyalty and Duty were directed toward the emperor, not toward the Tokugawa family. Ansai did not challenge the Bakufu power in so many words, but he implicitly questioned it by rejecting the Mandate of Heaven theory, and by teaching that T'ang and Wu had violated their duty as subjects when they overthrew their lords.

The proper meaning of *taigi meibun* for the Japanese was brought out by Ansai in a statement that has been frequently quoted because of its bearing on the relation between Confucianism and patriotism. A pupil once asked him what his duty would be, as a student of the Way of Confucius and Mencius, if Confucius as general and Mencius as his lieutenant should lead an army of several hundred thousand invading Japan. Ansai replied:

At a time such as that, I should fasten on strong armor, choose skilled soldiers, and, doing battle with them, take Confucius and Mencius captive; thus repaying my obligation to my country. Such, indeed, is the Way of Confucius and Mencius.[1]

Within ten years after his return to Kyoto, Ansai had gained such a reputation that he was employed as scholar and adviser to the powerful lord of Aizu-*han,* Hoshina Masayuki—a half-brother of the third shogun, Iemitsu, and *tairo*[2] for several years during the reign of the fourth shogun, Ietsuna. At about this time, Ansai began studying under Yoshikawa Koretari, another leading Confucian Shintoist. In 1671, at an initiation ceremony, he was given the name of Suika Reisha[3] by his teacher. After this, on the basis of his conviction that Shinto and Confucianism were one, Ansai gradually created his own eclectic school of Confucian Shinto, eventually devoting all his efforts to its propagation. Thus, in Ansai's life as a teacher, only about ten years were devoted primarily to Shushigaku; following this, he tended more and more to emphasize Shinto.

Suika Shinto

Whereas his teachers, Watarai Nobuyoshi and Yoshikawa Koretari, had been Shinto scholars who accepted Confucian ideas, Ansai, in developing a third important school of Confucian Shinto, moved from Confucianism into Shinto thought.

[1] *Ansai Sensei Gyojo Zukai.* Quoted in Tokushige Asakichi, *Ishin Seishin Shi Kenkyu* (Kyoto: Ritsumeikan Shuppambu, 1934), p. 23.

[2] See Appendix B.

[3] The name "Suika" is based on a quotation from the *Shinto Gobusho,* which Ansai had used in his *Ise Dai Jingu Gishiki Jo.* It is taken from an oracle of Yamato-hime no Mikoto to the effect that the first duty of man is to pray for the blessing of the gods; then to walk in uprightness with divine assistance. The first character, *sui* (blessing), recalls the first half of the statement; the second, *ka* (assistance), indicates the second half. The pertinent passage is quoted in Muraoka Tsunetsugu, "Suika Shinto no Shiso," *Riso,* X (1936–37), 1137.

The resultant philosophy, which came to be called Suika Shinto after Ansai's Shinto name, drew not only on Japanese classics such as the *Nihon Shoki* but on Confucianism and the *Book of Changes* as well. Hayashi Razan's viewpoint was accepted in general, but his theory on the origin of the imperial family [4] was given no credence by Ansai. The new faith also involved an unconditional rejection of Buddhism and all Buddhist connection or influence. As compared to the teachings of Nobuyoshi and Koretari, it put less stress on intellectualism and strongly emphasized practical ethics.

The essence of Suika belief involved the unity of heaven, earth, and man, and the indissoluble connection of morality with the nature of the universe:

> The gods are the spirit of heaven and earth; human beings are the gods of creation. In sum, Heaven and Man are one; and the essence of their Way is found exclusively in the teaching of Reverence. . . . The reason for the distinction of heaven and earth; the reason for the functioning of *yin* and *yang;* the reason for the existence of the Way of Man [i.e., ethics]; all proceed from this.[5]

This quotation contains the two fundamental principles of Suika Shinto—one metaphysical, the other ethical. The metaphysical aspect was usually expressed as *ten-jin yuiitsu*—"Heaven and man, one and only one." The meaning is that the gods were the original body of the universe and of all created things; they were likewise the original pattern for morality. Heaven and earth (i.e., nature, the universe) and man are completely one; the Way of Heaven and the Way of Man are identical—the "One and Only One Way of Heaven and Man." Their appearance of being two is phenomenal, not essential; thus the record of the Age of the Gods (in the *Nihon Shoki*) describes nature in human terms, and human affairs as aspects of nature, the unknown being explained in terms of the known in either case.

---

[4] On the basis of a comparative study of Japanese and Chinese history, Razan had suggested that Ninigi no Mikoto, the great-grandfather of the first emperor, Jimmu, might have been Count T'ai of the Chinese state of Wu (Wu T'ai Po).

[5] *Kamiyo no Maki Fuyoshu.* Quoted in Akaoka Shigeki, "Yamagata Daini no Kokutai Kan," *Denki,* II (1935), 23.

The ethical aspect of Suika Shinto was summed up in the term "reverence," which Ansai considered to be the source of all moral principles. The concepts of reverence and the unity of heaven and earth affected his explanation of the emperor's station.

The Three Sacred Treasures, according to Suika belief, possess a certain spiritual power. Their symbolic meanings are borrowed from Watarai Nobuyoshi: the jewel represents the divine spirit; the mirror, the wisdom of that spirit; and the sword, its sternness. The jewel ranks first,[6] being equivalent to the heart or mind of Amaterasu. All three Sacred Treasures can be reduced to this one, which also represents the commission of appointment to the imperial office. However, the essential meaning, Ansai taught, is deeper than this superficial symbolism. It goes back to the chaos preceding creation, which contained within itself the power of generating all living things. After creation, this divine virtue passed to Amaterasu; and, in accordance with the theory of the identity of heaven and man, it was this power that she bestowed on her descendants forever. This is what the jewel actually represents; and because of this, the emperor rules.

The power, however, is inherent not in the emperor but in the Treasures. Here Chinese theory is reversed: instead of the most virtuous man being chosen for emperor, the emperor is made to possess absolute virtue; and the Three Sacred Treasures are the agency through which this comes about. If the emperor is virtuous before assuming office, well and good; but if not, when he succeeds to the throne and receives the Treasures, his actions are brought into accordance with the Way, and from that time forward he is the same as a virtuous sovereign. Thus, the Three Sacred Treasures, rather than being symbols of the emperor's virtue, in a certain sense are his virtue.

The emperor, then, as the descendant of Amaterasu and the possessor of the Treasures, is in himself the highest expression of the identity of heaven and man; he is heaven and man in one body and is to be afforded absolute and unconditional reverence. Whereas in Chinese theory, the emperor was the Son of Heaven and subject to Heaven's command, in Suika Shinto,

[6] Other thinkers usually ranked the mirror first. *Cf.* the opinion of Yamaga Soko, p. 49.

the emperor is Heaven, and all others are subject to his command.

As a Confucianist, Ansai had taught that Supreme Duty (*taigi*) must be directed toward the emperor; as a Shintoist, he made Duty also include worship of the gods. In other words, reverence for the emperor and worship of the gods were merely two aspects of the same thing. In this way, the Suika teachings operated to unify and vivify Ansai's Japan-centered political views, giving a special emotional fervor to loyalty and patriotism.

Ansai himself pointed out that faith was a prerequisite of his doctrine. The records of the Age of the Gods were not to be comprehended through intellectual processes, as logical propositions; they were their own proof, like the sun and moon, heaven and earth. Faith in the divine blessing and assistance—*sui-ka*—was particularly essential. Thus, while Ansai's system was the outcome of scholarship, research, and thorough familiarity with the advanced philosophy of Chu Hsi, it was still basically mystical.

The Confucian Approach to Loyalty

Ansai's personal disciples and posthumous followers were known collectively as the Kimon school.[7] While this group as a whole was noted for its special emphasis on loyalty to the emperor, its members as individuals generally laid particular stress on either the Confucian or the religious aspect of Ansai's thought. Among those who followed the Confucian approach, Ansai's outstanding pupil was Asami Keisai. Due to his work, more than to that of any other, the prestige and influence of Kimongaku continued to increase even after the death of its founder.

Asami Keisai (1652–1711) was born in the province of Omi, near Kyoto. He began the study of medicine, but abandoned this career in order to enter Ansai's school. After his reputation was established, he opened his own school, and, like Ansai, numbered his pupils in the thousands. He spent his entire life in the vicinity of Kyoto, and refused to take any employment,

---

[7] The word "Kimon" is a two-character abbreviation connoting "Disciples (or, School) of Yamazaki Ansai."

feeling that by keeping himself free to write and teach in accordance with his beliefs he was serving the country as a whole:

> People in general believe that when one is not serving for a stipend, he is ignorant of the Duty of lord and subject; but such is not the case. My being a *ronin* is a service to the country; it is for the purpose of teaching the knowledge of ethics and human relationships. I am one who devotes his efforts to his country.[8]

Keisai's life and teachings were summed up in the words "loyalty" and "patriotism," which he had engraved on the two sides of his *habaki* (fastener for the sword guard).

So far as scholarship was concerned, Keisai excelled in the Chinese classics and literature, but his blast against those who let scholarship come before duty to their country might well have been written by Yamaga Soko:

> Those who read Confucian texts—they are the ones who call China *Chugoku* and consider our own country barbarian; who grieve and lament over the frightful fact that they were born on this barbarian soil. Frightful indeed!—that those who read Confucian texts should have lost the ability to read, and are ignorant of the truth of *meibun taigi*.[9]

While Keisai did not personally accept Suika Shinto, his viewpoint on the emperor was identical with that of Ansai:

> As, from Amaterasu down to the present, the bloodline has continued without a break, truly it is not of human seed. When it is said that one's attitude [toward the Emperor] should be that of reverencing a god, this indeed is absolutely correct. The point in which our country excels all other countries and can justifiably pride itself is precisely this.[10]

It must be noted that during Keisai's lifetime, loyalty to the emperor did not necessarily mean advocating a change in the

---

[8] Quoted by Gokyu Yasujiro in his introduction to the *Seiken Igen* (Tokyo: Iwanami Shoten, 1939), p. 8.

[9] *Chugoku Ben.* Quoted in Takeoka Katsuya, *Son-no Shiso no Hattatsu* (Tokyo: Iwanami Shoten, 1934), p. 39.

[10] *Zatsuwa Hikki,* Book II. Quoted in Takeoka, *Son-no Shiso,* p. 39.

form of government. Keisai identified loyalty to the shogunate with loyalty to the Court, believing, like Yamaga Soko, that the shogun was the appointed deputy of the emperor.

Of Keisai's many writings, by far the best known was the *Seiken Igen,* published in 1689. The purpose of the book was expressed in its title, based on a passage from the *Book of History,*[11] which extols the importance of Duty and recommends a calm fidelity to principle as the sole ambition. This title may be rendered as "Eternal Messages of Sacrificial Dedication."

Keisai's reason for writing the book was to uphold the ideal of *taigi* (Supreme Duty). He felt that this could best be accomplished through presenting actual historical examples, instead of by admonitions or precepts. For this purpose he chose the lives of eight heroes of Chinese history. In making his selection, Keisai was influenced not only by Ansai's principle of reverence, but also by Chu Hsi's interpretation of legitimacy in Chinese history; he is supposed to have read the *T'ung-chien Kang-mu*[12] forty-two times.

[11] The pertinent section is: "By tranquilizing himself [i.e., by being completely willing to make any sacrifice necessary for the sake of Duty], man may dedicate himself to the ancient sage-kings." The two characters Keisai selected from this quotation, *sei* and *ken* (Chinese *ching* and *hsien*), refer, respectively, to tranquilizing (in this special sense) and to dedication. The term *igen* means "words left by one who has passed on"; in this case, the stories of the undying examples of heroic men.

[12] Chu Hsi's great historical work, the *T'ung-chien Kang-mu,* completed in 1172, was a digest of the *Tzu-chih T'ung-chien,* written by Ssu-ma Kuang in 1085. In condensing the original work, Chu Hsi followed what he believed to have been the method of Confucius in writing the *Spring and Autumn Annals:* utilizing history as a means for teaching ethics, by employing terminology that would indicate to the reader whether the actions described were to be praised or blamed. Modern scholarship questions whether the *Spring and Autumn Annals* actually followed such a method; but there is no doubt that Chu Hsi, in writing the *T'ung-chien Kang-mu,* did so. For this reason, his work became the model for "praise-and-blame" writing, and the *T'ung-chien Kang-mu* was considered by scholars of the Chu Hsi school to rank almost equally with the *Spring and Autumn Annals.* In particular, Chu Hsi's emphasis on loyalty to the sovereign and on the importance of recognizing the legitimate imperial line (in determining the location of which he sometimes disagreed with other writers on Chinese history), had a strong effect on Tokugawa attitudes toward shogun and emperor.

Keisai did not merely intend to teach sacrifice and devotion in general; he hoped specifically to strengthen the feeling of loyalty to the imperial house. For this reason, all the examples he chose demonstrated sacrifice for either sovereign or country: some of his heroes were relentlessly opposed to the seizure of power by military men or ministers; others repelled foreign invasion, or refused to yield territory or make dishonorable peace under foreign pressure. Some of the eight heroes were taken from as far back as the Chou dynasty; others, from late Sung and Ming, were themselves followers of Chu Hsi's philosophy, and had been affected by its teaching of loyalty.

Mindful of the punishment meted out to a man like Yamaga Soko, even though he had not shown any disloyalty to the Bakufu, Keisai was keenly aware that any book displeasing to the Edo authorities would be speedily banned. He hoped to avoid any possible criticism by choosing Chinese examples and mentioning nothing whatever related to Japan. However, his intent was that the lessons of the book should be applied at home; he was said to have had "his eyes in the southwest but his mind in the northeast." At the same time, regardless of Keisai's personal feeling toward the Tokugawa family, it is obvious that a book of this sort could help to create opposition to the Bakufu as easily as it could promote loyalty to the emperor.

The Religious Approach to Loyalty

While the pupils who stressed Ansai's religious teachings over his Confucianism were in the minority, this branch of his thought was also a significant element of the Kimon tradition. The eventual vigorous flowering of Suika Shinto was due chiefly to the teaching and writing of Tamaki Shoei, a second-generation disciple. By the end of Shoei's lifetime the number of Suika followers had reached several thousand, and they were spread practically throughout the country.

Tamaki Shoei (Isai) (1670–1736) compiled the *Gyokusenshu,* the authoritative and standard collection of Yamazaki Ansai's Suika teachings. In his own writings as well, Shoei faithfully followed and expounded the Suika philosophy. In the *Kamiyo no*

Maki Soenso, for example, while discussing the essential nature of Amaterasu, he stated that she was both the sun goddess and the actual progenitor of the imperial family, to be understood literally in both senses. The same argument also applied to each successive emperor:

In other countries, above the sovereign there is the Supreme Deity. Above the ruler's decree, there is the decree of Heaven. As for our country, we may say that the sovereign *is* the Supreme Deity. The ruler's decree must be considered to be the decree of Heaven.[13]

Shoei's statement regarding the Three Sacred Treasures was equally positive: "The essential foundation of the Land of the Gods, the mystical essence of the Way of the Gods, even the *li* of Heaven and Earth, and the Way of human morality arise from no other source than these Three Treasures." [14]

This type of thinking, of which Tamaki Shoei was the leading representative, was not restricted to those who specialized in Suika Shinto. It was widely accepted among Asami Keisai's pupils as well, and eventually became characteristic of the Kimon school in general.

First Hints of Restoration

While neither Ansai nor his first-generation pupils seem to have realized the possible political implications of their loyalist viewpoint, the idea of an imperial restoration was discussed by later members of the Kimon school. Of these, the best-known are Takeuchi Shikibu and Yamagata Daini.

Takeuchi Shikibu (1712–67) was born in the province of Echigo, in a family with the hereditary profession of physician. As a youth he went to Kyoto for study and associated with the Kimon

[13] *Kamiyo no Maki Soenso.* Quoted in Fujiwara Hirotatsu, *Kindai Nippon Seiji Shiso Shi Josetsu* (Kyoto: Sanwa Shobo, 1952), p. 34. The word here translated as "Supreme Deity" is *tentei* (Chinese *T'ien Ti*), one of the terms used in the ancient classics to denote a personalized supreme being.

[14] *Ibid.* Quoted in Tanaka Yoshito, *Nippon Shiso Shi Gaisetsu* (rev. ed.; Tokyo: Meiji Shoin, 1943), p. 151 note.

group. Eventually, as a pupil of Tamaki Shoei, he was imbued with a strong Suika faith.

Shikibu opened his own school in Kyoto and became a respected teacher. Although he had several hundred pupils of all ranks drawn from various parts of the country, he concentrated his attention on a group of Court nobles. His desire to raise the intellectual level at the Court, which he felt as a sort of personal mission, was an essential outgrowth of his attitude toward the emperor.

Shikibu took particular pains to instruct those among the Court nobles who were personally close to Emperor Momozono (reigned 1747–62), and to see that they presented his ideas to the young Emperor.[15] In a short work written especially for their benefit, he began in typical loyalist fashion, discussing the position of the imperial family and the duty of loyalty: "Should there be one who turns against this Sovereign, even if it be one's own brother, to punish him with death in utter devotion to the Sovereign is the Supreme Duty [*taigi*] of our country." [16] Then he pointed out the special position of the Court nobles: since the Age of the Gods their ancestors had been hereditary attendants and courtiers; they owed everything they possessed, down to a sheet of paper or a piece of thread, to the benefaction of the emperor. The privilege of serving in his presence was due to the divine assistance of Amaterasu and the blessings conferred by their ancestors; they should never forget its true significance:

. . . if one is treated with reserve by the Sovereign, should he feel even the slightest trace of resentment toward his Lord, know that this would be an impious thing. One must be aware only that he is serving a heavenly god; and with careful consideration to his own conduct, redouble his diligent devotion.[17]

The heart of Shikibu's instruction to the nobles then followed: the reason why the power of the emperor had declined

[15] Emperor Momozono acceded to the throne at the age of six and died at twenty-one.

[16] *Hokoshin Densho.* Quoted in Inobe Shigeo, "Son-no Ronsha to shite no Takeuchi Shikibu no Chii," *Kokugakuin Zasshi,* XLI (1935), 6.

[17] *Ibid.* Quoted in Muraoka, "Suika Shinto no Shiso," p. 1147.

to a point where the general public knew respect for the Bakufu but ignored the Court was that many successive generations of emperors had been lacking in scholarship, hence in virtue; the courtiers likewise were untaught and untalented. If the stimulation of scholarship could be initiated by the emperor and Court, it would extend to the entire nation; the people would unfailingly put their whole trust in the emperor, and as a natural consequence the shogun would return the administration to him. This could be accomplished by the united efforts of the emperor and the Court nobles. Therefore, the courtiers' first duty was to insure that the emperor should receive only useful instruction in the Ancient Way, and be surrounded by those who would have a beneficial influence on him.

Two points are outstanding in this theory of Shikibu. First, he openly discussed the restoration of imperial government; he is considered to be the first thinker who definitely made support of the Bakufu inconsistent with patriotic duty. Second, his theory neither intended nor implied an armed revolt, but, in an interesting persistence of Chinese thought, it was based on implicit faith in the efficacy of the precepts of the *Great Learning*. According to Shikibu's application of these precepts, the right of the emperor to rule was guaranteed by his divine heredity, but the implementation of the right depended on his own development of virtue through scholarship.

Shikibu was highly successful in indoctrinating his noble pupils, and in the summer of 1757 a group of them began to lecture to Emperor Momozono on the *Nihon Shoki,* emphasizing the ancient form of government and anticipating the possibility of its restoration. Many of the older nobles of high rank opposed these ideas as dangerous, and in response to their criticism the lectures were discontinued. However, in the spring of the following year the lectures were resumed, owing to the keen interest of the seventeen-year-old Momozono. This time the Bakufu took action: twenty or so of the nobles were deprived of their offices or sentenced to house arrest, and Shikibu was banished from Kyoto, forbidden ever to return.

With Takeuchi Shikibu, Japanese political thinking and the official reaction to it both entered a new stage. The point at issue was not that of reverence for the emperor; Shikibu's statements on that subject were no different from those of Yamazaki Ansai, Asami Keisai, or Tamaki Shoei. But Shikibu's interpretation of the implication of that reverence went one step beyond previous thinkers and envisaged the eventual abdication of the shogun. It is not at all clear how soon he expected this event to occur, whether within the lifetime of Momozono, or two or three generations later. Nevertheless, his ideas did inject a new element into loyalist theory, and it was this new element the Bakufu recognized as a threat to its hegemony. At the same time, the potentially incendiary nature of the *Seiken Igen* was coming to the fore; the use of this book in his lectures was one of the offenses with which Shikibu was charged.

The new trend was further exemplified by Yamagata Daini (1725–67), an Edo scholar who was never exposed to the loyalist atmosphere of Kyoto. Born in the province of Kai, a short distance west of Edo, after studying the Kimon philosophy he opened his own school in the city, where he taught Confucianism, military science, and etiquette. His viewpoint—like that of Shikibu, impregnated with loyalty to the emperor and the possibility of restoration—is evident in his major work, the *Ryushi Shinron*. In the first part, entitled "Rectification of Names," he wrote that the divine emperors were the foundation of the country, that they had created the Way for the prosperity and welfare of the people and had established civilization and order. Their government had continued for over two thousand years; their virtue had permeated the hearts of the people; no one remained unaffected by their influence. Their power was temporarily in a state of decline, but "if the efforts of one or two loyal subjects could be obtained, it is probable that their position could easily be restored." [18] In thus hinting at the possibility of revolt, Daini went slightly beyond Shikibu theoretically, although Shikibu had done more to put his theory into practice.

Among the pupils of Yamagata Daini was the *karo* (prime minister) of Obata, a small *han* in the province of Kozuke. In connection with internal politics of the *han,* some of his enemies reported to the government that this man's teacher, Yamagata

---

[18] *Ryushi Shinron,* Book I. Quoted in Akaoka, "Yamagata Daini," p. 26.

Daini, was plotting the overthrow of the Bakufu. While there appears to be no substantiation for the charge, which would have been militarily absurd for anyone as unimportant as Daini in the feudal hierarchy, his published advocacy of imperial restoration had rendered him open to suspicion. On this basis, he was arrested and executed.

There was no close personal relationship between Takeuchi Shikibu and Yamagata Daini, and Shikibu was not involved in the alleged plot; but both were members of the Kimon school, and they had mutual friends.[19] For such reasons, and also perhaps because of the similarity in their viewpoints, on the day that Daini received the death sentence, Shikibu was sentenced to deportation to the lonely island of Hachijojima. En route he fell sick, and died without reaching his destination.

[19] For example, Fujii Umon (1720–67), who was a pupil of Takeuchi Shikibu. After fleeing Kyoto at the time of Shikibu's arrest, he made his home with Yamagata Daini; but being implicated in Daini's supposed plot, he was then arrested and sentenced to death.

5

Kokugaku: The Reaction Against Chinese Thought

KOKUGAKU ("National Learning") represented a reaction against the dominance of Chinese classics and Chinese philosophy. It was based on an awakening awareness of Japan itself as a significant entity and as the proper object of study for the Japanese. Thus, in opposition to the Way of the Sages and the Confucian virtues, Kokugaku was characterized by a desire to derive all necessary ethical and spiritual guidance from Japanese historical records, and a zeal to purify Japanese customs and institutions of all corrupting influences, thus re-establishing the Ancient Way.

66

Origin and Intent of Kokugaku

Kokugaku was created mainly by the successive efforts of four scholars, whose activities extended over a span of some one hundred and fifty years, from the beginning of the eighteenth to the middle of the nineteenth centuries. The concept originated with Kada no Azumamaro (1669–1736), who proposed (a) that scholars should clarify the meaning of the ancient words; (b) that on the basis of this knowledge they should make new studies of the ancient manuscripts; and (c) that when the ancient wisdom was thus rediscovered, they should restore the Ancient Way.[1] Azumamaro's pupil, Kamo Mabuchi (1697–1769), devoted his life to the first of these three points, using the *Manyoshu* as his source material. Mabuchi's disciple, Motoori Norinaga, made the requisite study of the ancient records. On this basis the fourth of the scholars, Hirata Atsutane, created what he confidently asserted to be "pure Shinto," and lived to see his teaching sweep away Suika, Yuiitsu, and the remaining vestiges of the Ryobu doctrine.[2] The entire project was viewed as one connected whole, bringing Azumamaro's hope to fruition.

This Kokugaku program was based on the assumption that the Japanese character was naturally pure, requiring only the removal of besmirching foreign influences to permit it once more to shine forth in splendor. These influences, deriving from Buddhism as well as Confucianism, resulted in a "Chinese heart" (*Kara-gokoro*),[3] which was to be distinguished from the "true heart" (*magokoro*) or "Japanese heart" (*Yamato-gokoro*). It was claimed that because of *Kara-gokoro,* the true Way of the Gods had been entirely forgotten for almost a thousand years; and that not only the decline of the Imperial Court but all of Japan's difficulties grew out of this fact.

[1] The plan was outlined in Azumamaro's memorial, the *So-gakko-kei.* For a German translation, with introduction and notes, see Heinrich Dumoulin, "Sô-gakkô-kei," *Monumenta Nipponica,* III (1940), 590–609.

[2] See Appendix C.

[3] The connotation here is broader than "heart" alone, including such concepts as "mind" and "will."

In a sense, the roots of Kokugaku went back to the beginning of the Tokugawa period, when Hayashi Razan abandoned Buddhism and praised the teachings of ancient Shinto. Following him, it had become the fashion of Confucianists to blame the decline of Shinto on the rise of Buddhism. With the addition of enthusiastic patriotism, this had been the viewpoint of the Kimon school. Kokugaku merely went further, denouncing Confucianism along with Buddhism.

While Kokugaku was intended as a moral and spiritual movement for the reform of the national character, the study of the Ancient Way necessarily included study of the position of the emperor, the organization of the state, and the duties of the subjects. Since research in the Japanese classics was used to prove that the Way of Japan was the Way of the Gods, "Shinto" became less the name of a religion than an all-embracing term for Japanese culture. With the spread of the teachings of Kokugaku, the word *Shinshu* ("Land of the Gods") came into common use along with *Nihon,* as a term referring to Japan. As Shinto belief was purified, reverence for the emperor became more widespread; as Japan's unique character was stressed, national consciousness became stronger.

These results, which were to have a profound effect on the development of patriotic and political attitudes, were due largely to the research, writing, and teaching of the third and fourth of Kokugaku's famous scholars, Motoori Norinaga and Hirata Atsutane.

Norinaga's Life and Thought

Motoori Norinaga (Suzunoya) (1730–1801) was born in Matsuzaka, in the province of Ise. At the age of twenty-one he became head of his family, which was engaged in the cotton wholesale business; but, having no interest in trade, in 1752 he went to Kyoto to further his education. After studying Shushigaku and medicine, Norinaga returned to his home and began to practice as a physician. However, the Japanese classics gradually absorbed his attention; in 1761 he arranged to meet Kamo Mabuchi, and two years later enrolled as his pupil. With Mabuchi's assistance and encouragement, he embarked in 1764 on an analysis of the *Kojiki,* the great project completed only three years before his death. For the last ten years of his life, Norinaga was employed by Tokugawa Harusada, the lord of Kii, as his private physician, a sinecure that did not interfere with research and teaching.

Although coming from what was theoretically the lowest class of the feudal hierarchy, Norinaga eventually broke the class barrier to scholarship. Similarly, his nearly five hundred pupils represented an unusual cross section, including persons of merchant and peasant origin as well as Buddhist and Shinto priests, samurai, and court nobles; of the sixty-six provinces (*kuni*) of Japan, it was said that only two were not represented among them. The geographical distribution of his pupils and the fact that his teachings did not depend on the samurai class alone for their propagation were probably among the factors that gave Norinaga's Kokugaku popular, as well as scholastic, appeal.

Among Norinaga's many writings, the one of outstanding repute was the *Kojiki Den* ("Commentary on the *Kojiki*"), in forty-eight books. In opposition to the prevailing attitude of his time, which valued the *Nihon Shoki* and *Kuji Hongi* more highly, Norinaga chose the *Kojiki* as the object of his study because he believed it to be the least affected by *Kara-gokoro*. His commentary expounded in detail exactly what he considered to have been the "Ancient Way," with strong emphasis on the emperor's inviolable position and absolute, divine authority. Another work significant for its clear presentation of Norinaga's views on government was the *Tama-kushige* ("Jewel-casket"), which he is supposed to have written for his lord, Harusada.

Norinaga's various works are consistently devoted to elucidating the Ancient Way; they include frequent attacks on Confucianism and are based on a conviction that Japan is inherently and intrinsically superior to all other countries. This fundamental attitude is clearly stated in the *Kuzubana:*

The august Imperial Land is the august original land where Amaterasu took birth, the august land that is ruled by her descendants;

and for this reason the fact that it excels all the myriad other countries is too obvious to deserve mention.[4]

In summarized form, Norinaga's argument was as follows: the Way of the Gods is the source of existence of the Japanese nation; land and people came into being through the agency of Izanagi and Izanami; Amaterasu was established as ruler to the end of time. Therefore, the ancient and eternal Way of Japan can be nothing else but the Way of the Gods. This is not to be taken in the narrow sense of religious worship alone, but rather as the fundamental source of government and of all moral and social relations: as the unchanging character of the Japanese nation is fixed for all ages, it must be expressed in the daily life of the people. There is no reason whatsoever for the Japanese to be influenced by inferior foreign doctrines such as Confucianism and Buddhism.

When Norinaga explained the meaning of the Way in terms of its practical application to the life of the individual, he made it consist chiefly of submission to superior forces or powers. The highest forces were the gods, whom he conceived of as primal entities, outside of creation and transcending human understanding in their actions. Accordingly, a human being had no alternative but to acquiesce in the will of the gods.

After the gods, and participating with them in absolute authority because of his descent from the Sun Goddess, was the emperor, to whom Norinaga demanded unquestioning obedience, without considering his personality or moral character. An example of this attitude is found in the *Kojiki Den,* in the section on Emperor Buretsu (reigned 499–507)—who was noted for his cruelty:

It is not for the subject to determine whether the sovereign is "virtuous" or "evil"; this indeed is the point of superiority in the Ancient Way, keeping intact eternally the relation of sovereign and subject, so that the Way suffers neither ruin nor abandonment. Suppose the sovereign to be evil: to consider the subject's making of such a decision

---

[4] *Kuzubana.* Quoted in Tokushige Asakichi, *Ishin Seishin Shi Kenkyu* (Kyoto: Ritsumeikan Shuppambu, 1934), p. 786.

as a proper thing is the Way of foreign lands; truly it is a rebellious act, easily becoming the source of disturbances. . . .

The sovereign's evil deeds do not extend beyond his own lifetime; the suffering of the people is therefore limited, for only a brief space of time. But the violation of the Way of Sovereign and Subject carries on into future ages; the resultant damage is without limit.[5]

Again, in the *Tama-kushige,* Norinaga wrote:

The people of the present day must have no intention other than that of performing such actions as are needful of being performed at the present time, by faithfully observing the commands of the emperor of the present day and avoiding any action at variance with this which proceeds out of their own private thinking. This, in short, has been the purport of the true Way since the Age of the Gods.[6]

Following the emperor in rank was the shogun. Norinaga went further than such writers as Yamaga Soko and Asami Keisai, not only regarding the shogun as the emperor's deputy, but identifying the feudal system completely with the Way of Japan and the original instructions of Amaterasu. Furthermore, he insisted that the nation formed one indivisible unit:

Speaking of the present [i.e., Tokugawa] reign, in the first place it is a reign in which according to the intention of Amaterasu and the charge assigned by the Imperial Court, successive generations of the shogunal family following Ieyasu, the Founding Lord, have established and administered the government of the realm. Furthermore, this government is one that has been accomplished by setting up the various territorial divisions, and entrusting them each to a daimyo.

For this reason, the inhabitants of the various domains are positively not the possession of a private individual; nor is a *han* the possession of a private individual; the people of the whole realm are those people who have in their own day been entrusted by Amaterasu to Ieyasu, the Founding Lord, and to successive generations of the shogunal family; the country also is that country which has been given in trust by Amaterasu.

This being so, since the institutions of the divine Founding Lord, and the ordinances of the successive generations of the shogunal fam-

---

[5] *Kojiki Den,* Book XLIII. Quoted in Muraoka Tsunetsugu, "Suika Shinto no Shiso," *Riso,* X (1936–37), 1149–50.

[6] Tama-kushige (Together with *Hihon Tama-kushige* [Tokyo: Iwanami Shoten, 1934]), p. 36.

ily, are indeed the institutions and ordinances of Amaterasu, they must be regarded with particular consideration; these institutions and ordinances must not be violated or destroyed, but faithfully observed. The administration of the various *han,* as well, since it is an administration that has been given in trust in an orderly manner by Amaterasu, must be effected with extreme care. The necessity of tenderly nurturing the people, never forgetting that they are those people who have been entrusted to him by Amaterasu, and so ruling them with special devotion, is of vital importance to the daimyo. Consequently, while firmly impressing this fact also on his subordinates engaged in the actual administration of affairs, it is something that he himself must perpetually bear in mind with no misunderstanding.[7]

Finally, Norinaga advocated universal submission to those of higher rank: "For all inferiors, whether for better or for worse, to conduct themselves in perfect accordance with the commands of the superiors of their age: this was the intent of the Ancient Way." [8] Thus, the ultimate significance of the Way as taught by Norinaga became reverence for all authority at every level, and the unconditional submission of those who lacked authority.

Norinaga did not take his own teaching so literally as to withhold comment on the evils of his time, but he believed strongly that where evil existed, it was to be righted by action of the gods, not of men. For him, "restoration" of the Ancient Way must take place within men's hearts, not primarily by changing the forms of the external world. These forms in any case were artificial and largely affected by *Kara-gokoro;* the pure *magokoro,* once freed of alien influence, would submit to the will of the gods, and follow the Way of the Emperor, without forms or regulations, simply because of its inherent nature.

Naobi no Mitama

Of all Norinaga's writings, the brief essay, *Naobi no Mitama* ("Spirit of Purification"),[9] is generally considered the best presen-

[7] *Ibid.,* pp. 28–29.

[8] *Uiyamajumi* (Together with *Suzunoya Tomonroku* [Tokyo: Iwanami Shoten, 1943]), p. 29.

[9] A German translation by Hans Stolte has been published. See "Naobi no Mitama, Geist der Erneuerung," *Monumenta Nipponica,* II (1939), 193–211.

tation of the essence of his thought and one of the major works of political theory of the Tokugawa period. Written in 1771, and actually the closing chapter of the first book of the *Kojiki Den*, it epitomizes the philosophy of the entire work. In it, Norinaga discusses the unique character of the Japanese state and people, based on the foreordained rule of one imperial house for all ages; his faith in the revival of the Ancient Way; and the patent falsity of Confucianism. The following is a summary of those parts dealing particularly with Norinaga's attitudes toward Japan and the emperor:

Japan is the country where Amaterasu came into existence and is therefore superior to all other countries, although they also enjoy her favors. Amaterasu bestowed the Three Sacred Treasures upon her grandson, Ninigi no Mikoto, and proclaimed him sovereign of Japan forever, his descendants to reign so long as heaven and earth exist. Thus, to the end of time, every emperor is the son of Amaterasu—his spirit, mind, and will in perfect harmony with hers. He makes no new precedents, but governs in accordance with the traditions handed down from the Age of the Gods. If doubts occur, he has recourse to divination in order to clarify the intent of Amaterasu.

Thus, for the reign to be carried on just as it was in the Age of the Gods, with the Way of the Gods automatically coming into play; its source could not be sought elsewhere—of this it naturally came to be said that "There is a Way of the Gods." . . . The rule of the emperors, generation after generation, is in essence no less than the rule of gods. . . . In the glorious times of antiquity, there was no such expression at all as "the Way." [10]

As foreign countries—China in particular—are not the domain of Amaterasu, they have no fixed rulers, and the forces of evil have corrupted them. Any low fellow powerful enough can become sovereign; those who were successful in ancient times were revered as sages:

Those who, great in power and keen in intelligence, gained control over people, seized the territory of others and skillfully managed not

[10] *Naobi no Mitama* (Together with *Tamahoko Hyakushu* [Tokyo: Iwanami Shoten, 1939]), pp. 16–17.

to be plundered by others, who administered the country well for a time and afterward even established laws—such men in China came to be called "sages." . . . The system that the "sages" created, constructed, fixed and established—that system, indeed, came to be called "the Way."

Accordingly, what is called "the Way" in China, if we investigate its fundamental import, is essentially but these two points, and no more: a method for seizing the territory of others; and a defense against being plundered by others. . . .

From the very beginning, "the Way" was constructed with filthy hearts for the deceiving of others.[11]

Even in China, the Way has not functioned well: "The Way of the Sages, constructed for the purpose of controlling the country, has on the contrary provided the seeds for its demoralization." [12] Ancient Japan on the other hand enjoyed a tranquil existence; there was no disturbance by inferiors, no interruption in the Heavenly Sun Succession. "Because in truth it had the Way, there was no such word as 'Way'; although there was no such word as 'Way,' it had the reality of the Way." [13] It was only after studying Chinese teachings that the Japanese began to envy the Chinese for their possession of a "Way"; like men who, because of their lack of hair, feel inferior to monkeys and try to show that at least they have a little, the Japanese began to use the term "Way of the Gods."

With regard to the matter of sovereign authority,

The "Mandate of Heaven" is a term invented and handed down from ancient times in their country by the sages, after annihilating their sovereigns and seizing the country, for the purpose of avoiding responsibility for their crimes. As a matter of fact, heaven and earth are not entities which possess a mind, and thus they cannot issue commands. If Heaven truly had a mind, it would also possess reason; then, entrusting the state to a virtuous man, it would insure a good administration.[14]

The history of China shows that the opposite has occurred; this cannot reasonably be attributed to the will of Heaven. Usurpa-

11 *Ibid.*, pp. 17–18. 12 *Ibid.*, p. 20.
13 *Ibid.*, p. 20. 14 *Ibid.*, p. 23.

tion started as far back as Shun and Yu,[15] who invented the theory of "voluntary cession" to deceive the people. All the ills of the world—the misfortunes of the good and the prosperity of the wicked—are due to the actions of evil gods, which are sometimes too strong for even Amaterasu to overcome; but the Chinese, having no correct knowledge of the Age of the Gods, attribute these happenings to the will of Heaven.

In countries like China, there is no fixed ruler:

. . . an ordinary man suddenly becomes king; and the king, again, suddenly becomes an ordinary man. . . . One who plots to seize the country but is unsuccessful is despised and hated as a traitor; while the one who is successful is venerated and reverenced as a sage. Consequently, the so-called sages themselves were merely rebels who succeeded in their designs.[16]

The position of Japan's emperor is completely different; the imperial family has been appointed to this office since the beginning of creation, according to the intent of Izanagi and Izanami. Amaterasu gave no permission to disobey the emperor under any circumstances:

. . . consequently, for another person to investigate or consider whether he is virtuous or evil, is impossible. So long as heaven and earth exist, while the sun and moon give light, for countless tens of thousands of generations, he is the Undisplaced, the Sovereign Lord. In the ancient language, the reigning emperor in each generation was termed a god, and in truth he is one. Consequently, abandoning discussion as to whether the sovereign is virtuous or evil, simply to obey, venerate, and serve him is the true Way.[17]

The disrespect shown to the emperors from the Middle Ages on, and the violence done to them by such "filthy scoundrels" as the Hojo and Ashikaga families, was the direct effect of studying the Chinese classics; it resulted from "taking the deranged customs of that land to be wisdom, and being unable to comprehend the proper Way of the Imperial Land." [18] During the

[15] The legendary founder of the Hsia dynasty.
[16] *Naobi no Mitama*, p. 25.
[17] *Ibid.*, p. 25.
[18] *Ibid.*, p. 26.

same period, the final proof of the faultiness of the Chinese Way came when China was conquered by barbarians and had to acknowledge their leader as the Son of Heaven!

Therefore:

> After cleansing and purifying his thoughts from the defilement of the Chinese classics, one should with a resplendent heart devoted to his glorious country make a thorough study of the ancient records. By so doing, he will of his own accord come to know that there is no "Way" that must be accepted and practiced. To know this fact is indeed to accept and practice the Way of the Gods.[19]

Atsutane's Life and Thought

In the nineteenth century, the Kokugaku school was effectively divided into two branches. Norinaga's teaching was continued, with emphasis on literary and linguistic study, by his eldest son, Haruniwa (1763–1828), and his adopted successor as head of the family and school, Motoori Ohira (1756–1833). The school at Matsuzaka continued to flourish and to extend Norinaga's influence throughout the country; Ohira alone had over a thousand pupils. The further expansion of Norinaga's philosophy was carried on independently by Hirata Atsutane, and it was chiefly this branch of the school that explored the political possibilities latent in Kokugaku thought. Atsutane assumed the duty of bringing Kada no Azumamaro's original plan to fulfillment; he was personally little concerned with the political implications involved in re-establishing the original purity of the Way of the Gods, and is known primarily as a Shinto reformer. However, the exaggerated stress he placed on Japan's superiority over all other nations, at a time when patriotism was fast becoming synonymous with the slogan of *son-no* (revere the emperor), was eventually to encourage anti-Bakufu sentiment and action among some of his disciples.

Hirata Atsutane (1776–1843) was born in Kubota (modern Akita), the son of a samurai of Satake-*han*. At the age of seven, he began to study the classics under Nakayama Seiga, a follower of the Kimon school, and an ardent imperial loyalist. He also

19 *Ibid.*, p. 35.

received medical training from his uncle and independently developed an interest in Japanese literature. At nineteen he went to Edo to continue his studies. While there, he was befriended and finally adopted by a samurai of Matsuyama-*han* (Bichu), a teacher of the Yamaga school of military science, after whom he took the name of Hirata.

In the summer of 1801, Atsutane investigated the writings of Motoori Norinaga for the first time. Almost immediately he applied for admission to the Matsuzaka school. However, it was just prior to Norinaga's death, so that he was actually enrolled as a "posthumous pupil," and had no opportunity to study under Norinaga personally. Nevertheless, this was the turning point in Atsutane's intellectual life; henceforth he devoted himself to the study and propagation of the Ancient Way, and was eventually recognized as Norinaga's leading disciple.

By 1808, Atsutane's doctrine was accepted as orthodox. His fame had become so great that he was invited by the Jingi Haku (Chief of the Imperial Bureau of Shinto Affairs, the Jingi-kan) to instruct all the priests under his jurisdiction in the teachings of the Ancient Way. This officially terminated the observance of Ryobu (or Hakke) Shinto.

Atsutane's greatest triumph, which he considered the culmination of the plan of Azumamaro, occurred in 1823, when the Yoshida family (subordinates in the Imperial Shinto bureau) also expressed their acceptance of his theories, and invited him to instruct the priests of Yuiitsu Shinto. This meant not only the end of the propagation of that doctrine but also the healing of the breach between the Shirakawa and Yoshida families, which had existed since the fifteenth century. From this time on, all priests supervised by the Jingi-kan taught the same Shinto belief.[20]

Atsutane's efforts brought praise from the Imperial Court and gifts from many daimyos. In 1838, at the age of sixty-two, he was appointed to the service of his native *han*. At the same time,

---

[20] This doctrine, laid down by Hirata Atsutane, forty-five years later became the official state religion of Japan, when the Jingi-kan was made the highest-ranking branch of the Meiji government, and the separation of Shinto and Buddhism was rigidly enforced.

however, opposition to his writings was increasing, due to their stimulation of patriotism and loyalty to the Court. In 1840 he was banished from Edo and ordered to cease writing. He spent the remaining few years of his life in Akita, in seclusion but still enjoying the favor of his own *hanshu.*

The theory of Kokugaku had been perfected by Norinaga; Atsutane broadened its scope and application. He emphasized the value of the *Nihon Shoki* in addition to the *Kojiki;* in addition to historical records, he placed a high value on such material as ancient Shinto prayers (*norito*) and the words for traditional sacred dances (*kagura*). Thus, his studies and writings were based on wider research and more thorough knowledge of ancient history and conditions than were Norinaga's. Atsutane was also familiar with Chinese and Indian Buddhism, Taoism, and Confucianism, and he had some knowledge of Western science and Christianity; he used all this material in his commentaries and lectures, but only as a supplement to the Ancient Learning.

Atsutane insisted that before beginning the study of the Ancient Learning, it was absolutely essential to purify one's *Yamato-gokoro;* the establishment of criteria for knowing what should be venerated and what condemned depended on this. In other words, a true Japanese heart and soul was the only valid foundation for discerning truth and error. Thus, despite the breadth of his knowledge and scholarship, Atsutane essentially followed the tradition of patriotism based on faith.

Atsutane himself never ceased to emphasize the religious purpose of his teachings. In the *Koshi-cho,* he wrote that the Ancient Way was not merely a matter of government; it must also bring tranquillity to the spirit and repose to the heart. But Atsutane's Ancient Way taught that the emperor as the descendant of Amaterasu was to be worshipped as a god manifest in man (*arahitogami*); that the land and people owed their existence to Amaterasu, and that government must be according to her command. The further he was able to go in purifying Shinto of Confucian and Buddhist elements, the more Atsutane was stimulating the fundamentally political attitude of loyalty to the emperor. While, like Norinaga, he accepted those virtues that

Confucianism emphasized, considering them to be the inborn ethical impulses of the Japanese soul, he made the devotion of subject to sovereign the supreme virtue: in effect, like Yamazaki Ansai, he considered Duty equivalent to worship.

Atsutane carried the absolute superiority and supremacy of Japan to its highest possible point of expression, going far beyond the arguments of Yamaga Soko and the essentially poetic patriotism of Norinaga. For example, in the *Nyugaku Mondo* ("Questions and Answers for Beginning Students") he wrote that the traditions of Japan had naturally influenced foreign countries; thus, the Imperial Generative Deity had in China been called Higher Emperor (Shang Ti), Heavenly Emperor (T'ien Ti), etc., and in India had been given the name of Brahma. Even countries far to the west of India, he pointed out, believe that heaven and earth, mankind, and all things were created by a great god. Accordingly, Japan is the original ancestor of all countries, the main or root country of the world. The emperor is the sole true Son of Heaven and sovereign of the world, destined to rule all within the four seas as lord and master. Shinto is the original source of all Ways and all learning; therefore, the true Way must be found in the actual facts of Japanese ancient history, before the traditions were clouded by any foreign influence.

Atsutane's *Kodo Taii* ("Essentials of the Ancient Way") was especially intended to instruct the Japanese people in the true nature of their country and its tradition. In this work, he pointed out that the difference between Japan and other lands is physical as well as spiritual: other countries developed from the small islands that came into being through the congealing of seafoam during the process of creation. Their growth into lands and continents, involving the slow and gradual accretion of soil, obviously was not completed until long after the creation of Japan through the direct agency of Izanagi and Izanami.

Although it is undeniable that they, too, were all produced through the creative power of the Imperial Generative Deity [Taka-mi-musubi no Kami], still, since the foreign countries were not given birth to by Izanagi and Izanami, nor are they the particular homeland of the Sun Goddess, from this there may be readily understood that distinction of reverence and contempt, of virtue and evil, which has existed from the very beginning between the August Land and them. Giving this further consideration, we may properly appreciate that the Imperial Land is the root source of heaven and earth, so that its affairs are one and all superior to those of all other countries, and consequently anything whatever pertaining to the various foreign countries must be inferior to that of the Imperial Land.[21]

In the *Tama-dasuki* ("Jewel-cord"), a compilation of lecture notes and answers to students' questions, Atsutane argued that not only the emperor and certain noble families (as generally understood) but all Japanese, were the descendants of the gods:

This, our glorious land, is the land in which the gods have their origin, and we are one and all descended from them. For this reason, if we go back from the parents who gave us life and being, beyond the grandparents and great-grandparents, and consider the ancestors of ancient times, then the original ancestors of those must necessarily have been the gods.[22]

Atsutane justified filial piety and ancestor worship on the basis of this connection with the gods.

It was in the *Tama-dasuki* also that Atsutane recorded his evaluation of some of the leading figures of recent Japanese history. He praised both Toyotomi Hideyoshi, for respecting the emperor and making Japan feared in foreign countries, and Tokugawa Ieyasu, for establishing peace and enforcing reverence for the emperor among the daimyos.

Atsutane's denunciation of Shinto as he found it being practiced was presented in the *Zoku Shinto Taii* ("Essentials of Vulgar Shinto"). His opinions on Suika Shinto—similar to Kokugaku in its attitude toward the emperor—are of particular interest. Atsutane wrote that Yoshida (Yuiitsu) Shinto, the teachings of Watarai Nobuyoshi, and Suika Shinto, were then the most widely accepted. The Yoshida thought, he said, was strongly affected by Buddhist influence; Watarai Nobuyoshi had made

---

[21] *Kodo Taii.* Quoted in Tokushige, *Ishin Seishin,* p. 787.

[22] *Tama-dasuki,* Book I. Quoted in Hisamatsu Senichi, *Kokugaku to Tama-dasuki* (Tokyo: Naikaku Insatsu-kyoku, 1943), p. 37.

strained analogies with the *Book of Changes,* explaining every detail of the Age of the Gods in that way:

. . . then, as for the teaching of Yamazaki Suika [Ansai], in addition to utilizing the foregoing theories, it is forced into agreement with the Sung Confucian study of *li.* All these schools take *yin* and *yang* and the Five Elements as their basis; but among them, the Suika school is by far the worst.[23]

Nevertheless, while attacking Ansai's method of presentation, Atsutane had nothing but praise for his motives. He wrote that despite Ansai's farfetched analogies and actual misrepresentations of the Way, he was completely patriotic and did not show the uncomplimentary attitude toward Japan so common in Confucian scholars. Rather, it was because of Ansai's great love for Japan that he desired to give it a Way equal in validity to Buddhism or Confucianism; and his mistakes grew only out of his zeal.

[23] *Zoku Shinto Taii.* Quoted in Nomura Hachiro, *Kokugaku Shiso Shi* (Tokyo: Meiseido Shoten, 1943), p. 196.

6

Mito: The Acceptable Synthesis

THE POLITICAL philosophy that was to represent the final stage of Tokugawa thinking on emperor and nation originated in Mito-*han*, the seat of one of the three main houses of the Tokugawa family. Mitsukuni, the second lord of the *han*, who was Ieyasu's grandson, had conceived the idea of hiring outstanding scholars to prepare a new and complete compilation of the history of Japan on the model of Ssu-ma Ch'ien's *Shih Chi*, one of the outstanding historical records of ancient China. To this he gave the name of *Dai Nihon Shi* ("Great History of Japan"). The research was begun in 1657, but not all of Mitsukuni's successors were so zealous as he in its support, so that the entire work required almost two hundred and fifty years, and was not completed until early in the twentieth century. The reasons why the compilation of such a scholarly treatise eventually produced a new emperor-centered patriotic theory lie in a combination of Chu Hsi influence, the general Tokugawa intellectual environment, and the strong personality of Mitsukuni himself, which dominated the early years of the project.

The Mito Tradition

Tokugawa Mitsukuni (Mito Mitsukuni; Giko) (1628–1700) combined administrative ability with scholarly interests to an unusual degree. Not only did he encourage Confucian studies—as, for example, by employing the famous Chinese exile scholar, Chu Shun-shui—he also patronized the study of Japanese literature, and he was on friendly terms with the leading Shinto scholars of the day, Watarai Nobuyoshi and Yoshikawa Koretari. Furthermore, his main purpose in initiating work on the *Dai Nihon Shi* was to advance a cause to which he was personally devoted— that of loyalty to the emperor. The idea for a new Japanese history bringing out this theme is supposed to have first occurred to him at the age of seventeen, when he read the biography of Po-i [1] in the *Shih Chi*.[2]

In later years, the direct influence of the *Dai Nihon Shi* would be felt mainly in educated and scholarly circles; but Mitsukuni also took a step to demonstrate the meaning of loyalty in a concrete way that would appeal to the masses. Having great admiration for the exemplary devotion of Emperor Go-Daigo's famous general, Kusunoki Masashige (Nanko),[3] he was shocked to discover that Masashige's grave on the battlefield of Minatogawa was neglected and unhonored. In 1692 Mitsukuni remedied this situation by erecting a monument at the site, bearing an eight-character inscription in his own calligraphy, and on the back of the stone, a tribute to Nanko written some years before by Chu Shun-shui.

[1] The brothers Po-i and Shu-ch'i were the traditional examples of loyalty in Chinese history. They felt their obligation to Chou, the last king of Shang, so strongly that they refused to eat grain produced under King Wu, preferring to starve to death while trying to live on bracken in the wilderness.

[2] This statement is made in the introduction to the *Dai Nihon Shi*, written in 1715 by Mitsukuni's adopted son, Tsunaeda.

[3] For Emperor Go-Daigo, see note 16, Chapter 1.

The Minatogawa monument, situated in an easily accessible spot near one of the main highways of feudal days, became an object of renown that could not fail to impress its lesson on even the most ignorant passerby. As the first objective sign of respect for the "lost cause" of the Southern Court, something that by implication signified loyalty to the emperor and to legitimacy in the imperial line, it had an incalculable effect in stimulating such ideas among later generations.[4]

The type of scholars whom Mitsukuni chose for his historical enterprise is also significant. Chu Shun-shui (Chu Chih-yu; known in Japan as Shu Shunsui) (1600–82) left China because of his unwillingness to live under the Manchu government and never gave up hope of a Ming restoration; Ugai Rensai (1633–93) was a pupil of Yamazaki Ansai; Kuriyama Sempo (1671–1706) was another member of the Kimon school; and Miyake Kanran (1674–1718) was a pupil of Asami Keisai. All were noted for their devotion to the twin ideals of loyalty and legitimacy.

One of the novel approaches in the *Dai Nihon Shi* was that of effecting certain changes in the listing of ruling emperors. Of these, the change of greatest ideological importance was the recognition of the Southern Court established by Go-Daigo at Yoshino as the true location of sovereignty, while the emperors of the "Northern Court" at Kyoto were regarded as usurpers.[5]

[4] While the *Dai Nihon Shi* is little read now except by specialists, the tomb of Nanko is still a flourishing center of pilgrimage and worship. The ancient battlefield has become the heart of the modern city of Kobe. Here, in a quiet grove of camphor trees (alluding to the fact that the name *Kusunoki* signifies "camphor tree"), one may still see the stone dedicated by Mitsukuni, now on a granite pedestal and sheltered by a roof dating from the Meiji period. Nearby, a life-size statue of Mitsukuni has recently been erected, showing him in the common dress he often wore so as to be indistinguishable from his people. Standing in the same grounds is a shrine to the spirit of Nanko, rebuilt in luxurious style after its destruction in World War II, which testifies to the power Masashige still exerts over the thinking of the people and to the accuracy of Mitsukuni's judgment in choosing him as a symbol of patriotism. (Personal observation, summer, 1956.)

[5] Strictly speaking, this was not a new proposal, as Kitabatake Chikafusa had also argued in favor of the Southern Court. However, since his time it had been an open question, on which the *Dai Nihon Shi* scholars were forced to come to a decision.

This decision was based on a definite criterion of legitimacy proposed by Kuriyama Sempo, and adopted as the official position of the Mito school. Sempo argued that in accordance with the intent of Amaterasu, physical possession of the Three Sacred Treasures was the only incontrovertible proof of the right to be emperor; that the Treasures could not be separated from the position of emperor; and that a person who did not possess them *ipso facto* had no claim to possess them. According to this interpretation, the Southern Court, because it held the Three Sacred Treasures, was the legitimate center of authority from the time of Go-Daigo (reigned 1318–39) until its last emperor, Go-Kameyama, voluntarily surrendered the Treasures to Go-Komatsu of the Northern Court in 1392.

By thus giving scholarly sanction to what had originally been a myth, the compilers of the *Dai Nihon Shi* lent considerable encouragement to the amalgamation of Shinto belief and national patriotism. In later years, their position was generally accepted, and after the Meiji Restoration it became the orthodox viewpoint of Japanese historians. The scholars of Mito themselves considered their theory as an important contribution to Japanese thought. In the introduction to the work, Mitsukuni's successor, Tokugawa Tsunaeda (Shukko) (1656–1718), the third lord of Mito, wrote:

Since the beginning of emperors in the shape of men, for more than two thousand years, the descendants of the gods in succession have continued the direct and sacred line; the traitor has never effected his usurping intention. The location of the Sacred Treasures is as radiant as the sun and moon. How noble! How magnificent! If we seek for the basic reason, in truth it is due to the fact that the benevolent influence of the Ancestral Head has solidified the popular will and has become the mighty rock foundation of the state.[6]

It must, however, be pointed out that neither Mitsukuni nor the scholars who completed the first two sections of the *Dai Nihon Shi*—the major part of the work—had any intention of attacking the Bakufu. In their concept of the Japanese state the

---

[6] *Dai Nihon Shi,* I, Introduction (Tokyo: Dai Nippon Yubenkai, 1928), 3–4.

emperor was supreme and the shogun acted as his loyal minister; but this involved no sense of antagonism toward the Tokugawa regime. The importance of the *Dai Nihon Shi* was that it set the standards upon which later attitudes were based: by stressing legitimacy in the imperial line and providing an easily understandable criterion for its determination, *taigi* was clarified; by placing the accounts of the shoguns in the "Biographies" rather than the "Main Annals," *meibun* was illustrated. Out of this soil grew the philosophy of the later Mito school.

Nineteenth-Century Renaissance

From about 1740 to 1800, work on the *Dai Nihon Shi* was practically at a standstill. Then, as part of a general intellectual revival in Mito-*han* encouraged by the sixth lord, Tokugawa Harumori (Bunko) (1751–1805), compilation and writing began once more in earnest. However, by this time, both the intellectual climate of Japan and political conditions had changed radically. Shushigaku had been attacked by such iconoclasts as Ogyu Sorai and Motoori Norinaga; at the same time the Kimon school and Kokugaku had reinforced the religious sanctions behind the *Dai Nihon Shi*'s interpretation of legitimacy, and had added the factor of national pride. Recurring economic crises had weakened the power as well as the prestige of the Bakufu, and its internal difficulties were soon to be heightened by the new problem of foreign relations.

Developing at such a time and in such an atmosphere, the new Mitogaku was more active in its practical application of theory (*jitsugaku*), more ardent in its loyalty, and more conscious of Japan and its sublimity than the old. By the middle of the nineteenth century, this new Mito thought was dominating imperial loyalist circles, and the increasing tension between Edo and Kyoto was being reflected in tension between Mito and Edo.

The way in which this later phase differed from early Mito thought is illustrated, for example, by their respective treatments of the Age of the Gods. In the "Main Annals," it is dismissed in a few lines at the beginning of the account of Emperor Jimmu. In the "Monographs," on the other hand, it is recorded in great detail and treated as the source of *kokutai* (a word that had not yet come into use in the early period), the foundation of national law and institutions—its study indispensable to the Japanese subject.[7]

The scholar credited with giving the new direction to the Mito school was Fujita Yukoku (1773–1826), who was put in charge of the historiographical work early in 1803. Yukoku was a man of broad interests who admired the writings of Kumazawa Banzan, found much good in Ogyu Sorai, and was a personal friend of Ota Kinjo (1765–1825), one of the leaders of the Setchu ("Eclectic" or "Compromise") school that had developed out of Sorai's teachings. Nevertheless, in his feeling for *taigi meibun,* which had been so emphasized by Chu Hsi, Yukoku yielded to none. The nature of his thought is exemplified in the following statement:

In majestic Japan, from the time the land was founded by the Imperial ancestors, with Heaven as their father and Earth as their mother, the holy offspring, the descendants of the gods, by continuing in virtue generation after generation, have ruled all within the four seas in splendor.

All within the four seas, reverencing them, call them "Emperor." Throughout the breadth of the Eight Islands, among all the countless people, from ancient times down to the very present, there has never been a commoner, even if he possessed unrivaled strength or matchless wisdom, who attempted even for one day to seize Imperial rank. The titles of lord and subject, the social position of superior and inferior, in their correctness and solemnity are as unchangeable as heaven and earth.

By virtue of these facts, there has never yet been a land comparable to ours in the eternity of its Imperial line, and the permanence of its

[7] The "Monograph on the Gods" (*Jingi-shi*) is the opening one of the section, and was the first to be written. In its original form, it was completed and circulated among the historians working on the project before the end of 1803. See Kurita Tsutomu, *Sui-han Shushi Jiryaku* (Tokyo: Ookayama Shoten, 1928), p. 122.

[8] The two phrases referring to ships or vehicles and to human strength have been borrowed by Yukoku from the *Mean* (chap. xxxi, 3), where they form part of a eulogy of Confucius.

national Throne, so far as ships or vehicles can travel, or so far as can be reached by human strength,[8] or even in the furthest reaches of the Eastern Paradise.[9]

While a viewpoint of this sort would not necessarily be inconsistent with support of the Bakufu, Yukoku also denied the validity for Japan of the *tenka no tenka* theory. In his *Shigi Taisaku,* he argued that Japanese government must be based on Japanese principles, that the emperor must take a personal interest in the problems and living conditions of the people, and that "the realm is the realm of His Majesty."[10]

In addition to stressing the emperor-directed aspect of patriotism, Mito, in its nineteenth-century-renaissance period, was characterized by a new, aggressive attitude that demanded the use of force in repelling foreign encroachment and in making Japan respected by other nations as well as by its own people. This way of thinking eventually came to be called *"jo-i";* and Yukoku pioneered in its development also. He was the first scholar of Mito to emphasize clearly the need for national defense as an essential element of loyalty and patriotism; as early as the 1790's, he was instrumental in arousing his lord, Harumori, to the danger of Russian penetration from the North. In 1824, when a group of English sailors landed on the Mito coast at Ozuhama, Yukoku warned his son Toko of their probable motives, advising him that if they were set free by the Bakufu, Toko should attempt to kill them. If war with England were to result, he suggested, it should be fought, not avoided; the temporizing policy of the Bakufu was in error, and the martial spirit of the nation must be awakened.

Even more significant than Yukoku was the thinker who succeeded in integrating the Mito viewpoint on Confucianism, Shinto, *taigi meibun,* and the essentials of patriotism. This was Aizawa Yasushi, known as the most eminent scholar of Mito in his generation.

Aizawa Yasushi (Seishisai; Hakumin; Kozo) (1782–1863) was

[9] *Seimei Ron.* Quoted in Fujiwara Hirotatsu, *Kindai Nippon Seiji Shiso Shi Josetsu* (Kyoto: Sanwa Shobo, 1952), p. 32.

[10] *Shigi Taisaku.* Quoted in Ono Hisato, *Meiji Ishin Zengo ni okeru Seiji Shiso no Tenkai* (Tokyo: Shibundo, 1944), p. 169.

born in Mito, the son of a samurai who held a minor administrative post. At the age of nine he began studying under Fujita Yukoku, who was still a youth himself. After continuing his studies in Edo, Yasushi was appointed tutor to the children of the seventh lord, Harutoshi (Buko), among whom were the future eighth and ninth lords, Narinaga and Nariaki. Later, he held various administrative offices in the *han,* and, especially after Nariaki's accession in 1829, was highly respected as a counsellor. He succeeded Yukoku as head of the historical research project; and when Nariaki founded a new *han* school, the Kodokan, Yasushi became its first principal. Outliving not only Yukoku but even Nariaki and Fujita Toko, he continued to be regarded as the dean of Mito thought until he died on the eve of the Meiji Restoration.

In many ways, Yasushi's thinking resembled that of previous scholars. In the *Tekiihen,* for example, where he summarized the basic Mito philosophy, he explained the spiritual superiority of Japan to all other countries in terms of its eternal Heavenly Sun Succession, in which the emperor, representing the gods to the people, functioned as both ruler and teacher. The themes of the distinction between superior and inferior, and of reverence for the Three Sacred Treasures, recur throughout his writings. Yet there were new elements in Yasushi's thought, reflecting the Mito tradition and the conditions of the times. One of these was the theory of *kokutai,*[11] viewing the Japanese people as one great family of a particular and distinctive nature, whose emperor was father as well as lord. Those born in the Land of the Gods, Yasushi said, had no excuse for being ignorant of *kokutai*. Another new element was Yasushi's preoccupation with the danger of foreign aggression and the proper methods of forestalling it in order to preserve the essential nature of the Land of the Gods.

This latter problem was of course recognized not only in Mito; a general debate was then going on in administrative and educated circles over the relative merits of "closed country" vs. "open country" as a national policy. This had started out as a matter affecting economics and defense rather than politics, but

[11] See Appendix D.

it soon became entangled with the question of loyalty to emperor and shogun. By midcentury, when the Bakufu was signing treaties with foreign countries in defiance of the Emperor's command, it seemed superficially that "open country" could be equated with "support the Bakufu" and that "closed country" corresponded to "revere the Emperor" (*son-no*).

This appearance, however, was misleading. As the Mito scholars pointed out, "closed country" was not a traditional imperial policy, but an expedient initiated under Tokugawa rule; "open country" and the consequent enhancement of Japan's international authority and prestige would be the only policy consonant with its history and *kokutai*. Even a cursory reading of Japanese history would show that "reverence for the Emperor" could not mean "closing the country." What Mito proposed in place of closing the country was *"jo-i."* This term, which apparently came into use in the 1830's, may be translated as "repel the barbarian"; [12] superficially again, it seems equivalent to "closed country," and was so understood by many who adopted it as a slogan. Its inner meaning, however, was rather the opposite.

The *jo-i* thought of Mito was based on a fear that the moral fiber of the people was weakening. Relations with foreign nations must be prevented, or postponed, while the national spirit was aroused and national strength built up; they would then be established on Japan's own terms, advantageous to its own interests. If this policy meant fighting a war in the meantime, well and good; the important point was that nothing should be yielded to foreigners under their threats of force.

The germ of *jo-i* thought had been present in Fujita Yukoku's teaching, but Aizawa Yasushi's *Shinron* brought it before the

---

[12] For additional details on the origin of the term, see p. 105. It is sometimes translated as "expel the barbarian"; but the inaccuracy of this translation should be clear from the fact that foreigners had not yet been admitted to Japan when the slogan came into use. Rather than intending the physical expulsion of foreigners, *jo-i* connoted the repelling of foreign aggression. It is obvious that repelling aggression is not necessarily inconsistent with maintaining foreign relations; the Mito thinkers were prepared to accept foreign relations if they could be carried on under conditions that did not prejudice Japan's interests or *kokutai*.

public. As envisioned in this book, which became the basic Mito text on the subject, *jo-i* was a means, not an end; its goal was the preservation of *kokutai* both spiritually and materially, a return to the days of ancient glory when barbarians felt respect and fear for the might of divine emperors. It was not only completely different from the theory of "closed country"; it was in fact a more far reaching and aggressive plan than that of the Bakufu's "open country."

The presentation of this plan was one of the purposes of the *Shinron;* the *kokutai* theory with which the book opened was the essential premise. Since *jo-i,* like *son-no,* was thus closely related to *kokutai,* the concept made a place for itself as an integral part of loyal and patriotic attitudes, and the two terms were soon linked together as *"son-no jo-i."*

Shinron

Aizawa Yasushi's *Shinron,* the first piece of writing to attract general attention to the new Mito thought, was eventually to outrank even the *Dai Nihon Shi* as Mito's most significant contribution to political philosophy. It was the pioneer work on the theory of *kokutai;* furthermore, it presented a definite, carefully thought-out program for unifying and strengthening the nation. It was to this aspect that its title ("A New Proposal") referred. As an integral part of his program, Yasushi had included a carefully-phrased but unmistakable call for the Emperor to assert his authority and assume control as the natural, divinely ordained leader of the nation.

The book was completed in 1825; it circulated in manuscript and quickly gained popularity. Unauthorized editions were printed in various places as early as 1830, and it became a favorite text in *han* schools throughout the country. The fame of the *Shinron* was so great, and its connection with patriotic sentiment was so intimate, that in the 1850's and 1860's it was said no one deserved the name of *shishi* (imperial loyalist) unless he possessed a personal copy.[13]

[13] See notes to Iwanami edition, by Tsukamoto Katsuyoshi, *Shinron* and *Tekiihen* (combined ed.; Tokyo: Iwanami Shoten, 1941) p. 293.

The entire work is significant. Beginning with the fundamental theory of *kokutai,* which takes up the major part of Book I, it shows the danger threatening the Japanese nation and its *kokutai* because of foreign aggression; this is followed by suggestions for defense, or the counterattack, which compose most of Book II. The part summarized here consists of the first chapter of Book I, in which Yasushi presents a skilful synthesis of Confucian ideals with Shinto beliefs and derives the political aspects of *kokutai* from examples in Japanese history, thus demonstrating the close relationship in Mito thought between Confucianism, historical research, and patriotic theory. That the general principles of *kokutai* are in harmony with the thinking of Yamaga Soko, the Kimon school, and Kokugaku, is clearly shown by the opening words of the introduction:

I would respectfully state regarding the Land of the Gods, that being the source from which the sun rises, and the place where vital energy originates; and with the acceding of the Heavenly Sun Succession to its Throne generation after generation being changeless throughout eternity; it is by its very nature the chief country of the earth, providing law and order for all lands.[14]

The new element added to this by Yasushi's *kokutai* thought, the unity of sovereign and people, appears at the beginning of Chapter 1:

By the grace of the Imperial Sovereign all within the four seas are protected, and in eternal tranquillity under an everlasting reign, the land is free from disturbance. These things are not due to his subjugating the people through terror and seizing control for his time. They are indeed, rather, necessarily due to the fact that the whole nation with one accord looks up to him affectionately, and could not bear separation.[15]

Thus, the continuity of the imperial line, aside from the fact that it was ordained by Amaterasu, means also that no other family would ever dare to consider assuming this position. For this

[14] *Shinron,* Book I, Iwanami ed. pp. 8 and 9. (This notation signifies: Chinese text, p. 8; Japanese text, p. 9.)
[15] *Ibid.,* pp. 12 and 13.

reason, Japan since its inception has been the model of "Righteousness between sovereign and subject," of "Affection between parent and child." [16]

Following a fairly standard interpretation of the Three Sacred Treasures, Yasushi introduces an original theory concerning the physical identity of each successive emperor with Amaterasu:

At the time when the Heavenly Ancestress bestowed the Sacred Treasures, particularly blessing the Treasure-Mirror, she declared: "When you gaze into this, it shall be even as gazing upon me." Thus, countless generations, by worshipping this, become the Heavenly Ancestral Deity: when the holy son, the divine descendant, worshipping the Treasure-Mirror, sees the reflection therein, that which he sees is the bequeathed body of the Heavenly Ancestress; seeing which is even as seeing the Heavenly Ancestress.[17]

As the emperor is both divine and human, from this dual nature proceeds the unity of worship and administration that is the fundamental characteristic of Japanese government. There is a further corollary: for the people to fulfill their duty to their ancestors, it is necessary that they follow the example of the ancestors in serving the imperial household. Filial Piety, therefore, is equivalent to Loyalty; they are not two separate obligations, but one and the same. The emperor, being the supreme object of both, is father as well as lord; the unity of Loyalty and Filial Piety, which makes the nation one family, is the foundation of society and state. On the one hand, worship is administration, and on the other, administration is the original source of education.

Following this section, Yasushi admits that despite the imperial family's heavenly lineage certain disorders have occurred in Japanese history. These have arisen, he believes, from two main causes: changes wrought by time, and the penetration of false doctrines from other lands. In explaining what he means by the "changes of time," the author presents a historical interpretation of *kokutai* that leads him to a revolutionary conclusion—namely,

[16] These are the basic two of the Confucian relationships, which are to be characterized (from the standpoint of subject and child) by the virtues of Loyalty and Filial Piety, respectively.

[17] *Shinron*, Book I, Iwanami ed. pp. 14 and 15.

that the time in which he is living offers the ideal opportunity for the emperor to resume personal rule. While the entire *Shinron* supports the same thesis, this one section stands out as giving an ideological justification for restoration. The argument runs as follows:

The archetype or ideal example of Japanese government was the administration of the first emperor, Jimmu: he tranquilized the nation and established the state; land and people were directly controlled by the Imperial Court. Time made changes in the system he had established, but the administration was reformed and the power of the Court restored by Emperor Sujin (supposed to have ruled 97–29 B.C.). As centuries passed, the nobles gradually succeeded again in taking the land for their own; but once more the imperial authority was asserted, and the Taika Reform (645) was carried out.

Private lands and private serfs were abolished; these one and all were returned to the Imperial Court. The realm was united; there was no place that was not the sovereign's land, none who was not the sovereign's subject; and the realm was again well ruled.[18]

With the seizure of power by the military class and the founding of shogunal governments in the Middle Ages, the true culture of Japan was once more threatened with extinction; *taigi* and *meibun* were ignored, and the distinction of domestic and foreign—that is, consciousness of Japan's superiority over all other countries—was lost:

---

[18] *Ibid.*, pp. 34 and 35. This passage includes a paraphrase of a verse from the *Book of Odes* (Book II, chap. vi, Ode 1, 2), which is quoted in *Mencius, Book* V, Part I, chap. iv, 2. In Legge's translation it reads:

Under the whole heaven,
Every spot is the sovereign's ground;
To the borders of the land,
Every individual is the sovereign's minister.

The character translated by Legge as "minister" may bear that connotation in Japanese also, but is more commonly understood as "subject" or "vassal." Derk Bodde translates the original Chinese as "subject" rather than "minister." See Fung Yu-lan, *A History of Chinese Philosophy,* I (Princeton: Princeton University Press, 1952–53), 11.

When land and people can not be united under one authority, Administration and Education can not be effected. Then, as a climax, Loyalty and Filial Piety are together abandoned, and the Great Way of Heaven and Man [19] falls to the ground.[20]

The efforts of Ieyasu were praiseworthy; by making Loyalty and Filial Piety his foundation, he was able to establish two hundred years of peace; his descendants have been rewarded with honors and office by the Imperial Court. Nevertheless, abuses have again arisen: great lords are living in luxury with no thought for the famine or distress of the people; wickedness abounds and there is no effort to curb it; barbarians are spying on Japan and none shows anxiety. Samurai and people alike think only of their own profit; none exerts himself in loyalty or concern for the nation. "When high and low alike are so oblivious and neglectful, how shall the land and people be united, and how shall *kokutai* be sustained? . . . truly we are moving toward a bottomless abyss." [21]

However, there is a brighter side; the changes of the times have created a rare opportunity: "At the present time [22] the Bakufu in a decisive step has given a clear command to the country, that if barbarians are discovered they are unfailingly to be crushed." [23] Officials and people alike are firmly determined to carry out this order; popular feeling has been unified and solidified to an unusual degree and cannot be effaced.

The fact that at the present time, the feudal system is in effect throughout the land, is obviously due to the Great Ancestor's having established his rule. The fact that Ieyasu built upon the foundation of Loyalty and Filial Piety is due to the Heavenly Ancestress' having bestowed her instructions.

If now, taking these for precedents, and relying on the ineffaceability of the popular will, the Divine Holy One, determining to rule the realm, should govern the land and control the people, should rec-

[19] Note the use of Suika Shinto terminology.

[20] *Shinron*, Book I, Iwanami ed. pp. 36 and 37.

[21] *Ibid.*, pp. 38 and 39.

[22] A reference to the Bakufu order of 1825 (Bunsei 8. 2), to the effect that foreign ships appearing in Japanese waters were to be driven away unconditionally. The *Shinron* was written just after this order was issued.

[23] *Shinron, Book* I, Iwanami ed. pp. 40 and 41.

tify the Duty [*gi*] of lord and subject and strengthen the affection between parent and child; and, bringing the entire realm under his sway, should make it his personal affair—how should this prove so difficult to accomplish? This is indeed the one moment in a thousand years, the opportunity which positively must not be lost.[24]

In this daring statement we see the kernel of the new Mito thought: all the forces of history point to the fact that the time for restoration is at hand; for if Duty (*gi*) is rectified, it must unfailingly, like Loyalty and Filial Piety, point to the emperor alone.

Having led up to this proposal by means of the slow and careful arguments summarized above, Yasushi devotes the remainder of his book to the detailed problems connected with promoting a national renaissance. He discusses such subjects as the importance of arms in Japanese history, the possibility of making foreign alliances, the clever stratagems by which the barbarians are attempting to weaken Japan, the necessity of reforming the administration and developing a more public-spirited attitude in the people, and plans for a modern coastal defense system. He closes the final chapter with a reminder to his readers that the traditions fixed since the founding of the nation are being threatened by foreign aggression. The only hope lies in returning to the instructions of Amaterasu, restoring reverence for the gods, confirming the people in Loyalty and Filial Piety and in their desire to offer themselves in the service of the emperor; and in this way, unifying the country and enhancing the national power.

Nariaki and Toko

The new philosophy of the Mito school, having been given its theoretical foundation by Aizawa Yasushi, was cast into its final form in the 1830's and 1840's. Many participated in this process, but dominating them were the figures of the *hanshu*, Nariaki, and of Fujita Yukoku's son, Toko. These two presented a unique example of a daimyo and a scholar who worked so closely together that the most famous brief statement of Mito beliefs, the

24 *Ibid.*

Kodokan-ki, is attributed sometimes to one and sometimes to the other; and one of Toko's main works, the *Hitachi Obi,* has as its sole purpose the explanation and defense of Nariaki's opinions. To Nariaki and Toko jointly, the definitive statement of Mito thought must be credited.

Tokugawa Nariaki (Mito Nariaki; Rekko) (1800–60), the ninth lord of Mito, acceded as *hanshu* in 1829. An energetic administrator who made every effort to put the suggestions of the *Shinron* into effect locally and who urged their adoption nationally, he encouraged such innovations as smallpox vaccination and military drill, and melted temple bells into cannon for coastal defense. Nevertheless, he held that the only valid use of Western astronomy, geography, ships, and guns was for guarding the ethics and spirit of Japan from foreign encroachment. Nariaki was an active participant in the Edo politics of his time, but his policies and proposals frequently conflicted with the purposes of the Bakufu. He was forced to retire from the position of *hanshu* in 1844, and except for a few years beginning in 1853, when he was given duties in connection with coastal defense, from this time on Nariaki was generally out of favor with Edo. On two occasions he was placed under "warning" or house arrest; his advisers and assistants, including Yasushi and Toko, also received similar punishment.

As early as 1838, Nariaki's concern over national problems was revealed in a memorial he submitted to the Bakufu, presenting several concrete suggestions based largely on the program of the *Shinron,* and completely opposing trade or diplomatic relations with the West.[25] In 1845, as recorded by Fujita Toko in the *Hitachi Obi,* his viewpoint was similar: trade could benefit only foreign countries, bringing nothing useful into Japan; the people must unite to keep Christianity out and protect the Land of the Gods.

Even when confronted by Commodore Perry's arrival and demand for treaty relations, Nariaki saw no reason to change his attitude; if anything, it was stiffened. In a memorial to the

[25] Memorial of Tempo 9. 8. 1, in *Mito-han Shiryo Bekki,* III. Summarized in Nakamura Toshikatsu, "Mito Rekko no Ichi-Kensaku," *Keizai Shi Kenkyu,* XVII (1937), 757–58.

Bakufu on August 14, 1853, he urgently advised preparation for war, saying:

When we consider the respective advantages and disadvantages of war and peace, we find that if we put our trust in war the whole country's morale will be increased and even if we sustain an initial defeat we will in the end expel the foreigner; while if we put our trust in peace, even though things may seem tranquil for a time, the morale of the country will be greatly lowered and we will come in the end to complete collapse.[26]

This argument was followed by ten reasons for not choosing peace, including a repetition of many points from his 1838 memorial. The following year, on the occasion of Perry's return, Nariaki wrote again to the Bakufu to urge a militant rejection of the American demands.[27]

In 1857, shortly after he had been relieved of his duties as military counsellor in charge of coastal defense, Nariaki wrote directly to Emperor Komei, in a bitter condemnation of Bakufu foreign policy. On Perry's first visit, he said, when diplomatic correspondence was accepted at Kurihama, ". . . all samurai of loyal spirit ground their teeth in anger at this defilement of *kokutai*." Furthermore, when Perry was received with honors at Yokohama the following year, Japan had "incurred the greatest humiliation since the founding of our nation." [28]

Citing the example of England, which, although smaller than Japan, was able to rule the ocean and seize a country as vast as India, Nariaki stated his conviction that the strength of a country depended not on its size, but on its administrative methods and traditional customs. As far as the latter were concerned, there was nothing to fear: "The customs of our land,

[26] W. G. Beasley (trans. and ed.), *Select Documents in Japanese Foreign Policy: 1853–1868* (London: Oxford University Press, 1955), p. 103.

[27] This memorial is included in *Genji Yume Monogatari,* translated by Ernest M. Satow as *Japan: 1853–1864* (Tokyo: Naigai Shuppan Kyokai, 1905), pp. 5–6.

[28] Memorial of Ansei 4. 7. 23, in Katsu Yasuyoshi (ed.), *Kaikoku Kigen,* III (Tokyo: Kunaisho-zo, 1893), 2267.

which from ancient times, according to the profound intent of the Imperial Goddess, have reverenced Arms and made Loyalty and Duty paramount, truly are not to be found in other countries." [29] But as for the former, the policies of the Bakufu were solely for the benefit of one man or one family and would be disastrous to the nation as a whole.

Then, showing that he identified himself primarily with the interests of the Court rather than with those of the Tokugawa family, Nariaki wrote that Bakufu policy was not generally supported by officials and daimyos and that a real opportunity was at hand for the "rebirth of the Imperial Land." Just as Yasushi had done thirty years before, Nariaki called on the Emperor to take command and immediately order the Bakufu to alter its policy. If this were done, he said, daimyos and other leading samurai (*shomyo*) alike would unite behind him. If the order were disobeyed, the blame for the result would be on the Bakufu alone; but if the Emperor should fail to act,

. . . the disgrace of the Imperial Land will be exposed before all nations; the *kokutai* will be unable to maintain its prestige; and furthermore, future generations looking back at this time will find the crimes of the Bakufu officials in truth too many to count.[30]

The following year, when the Edo authorities defied Emperor Komei's instructions and signed a "provisional treaty" of amity and commerce with the United States, Nariaki wrote to the *tairo* (Ii Naosuke) and the *roju* [31] to denounce the government's action as a violation of Loyalty and Filial Piety, and a negation of the *taigi* of shogun to emperor ordained by Ieyasu: to sign a

[29] *Ibid.*, 2270.

[30] *Ibid.*, 2272. This argument shows how easily the principle of *jo-i* could merge into that of *son-no*. There is no doubt that Nariaki was using *jo-i* partly as a political weapon, out of personal pique because of the treatment he and his son, Yoshinobu, had received at the hands of the shogunate government. W. G. Beasley suggests also that Nariaki's *jo-i* was primarily a way of asserting Japan's equality with foreign countries rather than a sincere proposal for a foreign policy. See Beasley, *Select Documents,* pp. 11–18.

[31] See Appendix B.

treaty without the approval of the emperor was impossible.[32]

Contemporary with Nariaki, and slightly younger, was Fujita Toko (1806–55), Yukoku's only son. While somewhat overshadowed by Aizawa Yasushi, Toko was famous in his own right as a teacher with a warm, human personality, an apostle of practical scholarship in action (*jitsugaku*), and an expounder and defender of the new Mito philosophy.[33]

Toko's ability was recognized even during the reign of the eighth lord, Narinaga; but his chief role in *han* affairs came when he was appointed Nariaki's private secretary in 1840. Completely in sympathy with his lord's program, his fortunes followed those of the *hanshu,* and in 1844 Toko was placed under house arrest lasting several years.

During this period of seclusion some of his best-known works were written—the *Hitachi Obi,* a defense of Nariaki's opinions and actions; the *Kodokan-ki Jutsugi,* which he considered his masterpiece; and the *Seiki no Uta.* This last, the "Song of the Spirit of Righteousness," was a fervently patriotic essay praising the glories of Japan, showing how at every crisis in the national history the Spirit of Righteousness had provided a deliverer, and suggesting that in his time that role might well be destined for Nariaki. Unfortunately for Toko's hopes, Nariaki did not live to participate in the Meiji Restoration. Toko himself was killed in the great earthquake of 1855.

Throughout Toko's writings, the practical proposals of the later Mito school were presented and defended—return of political authority to the emperor, reorganization of the armed forces with the inclusion of peasant militia, defense of Ezo (Hokkaido), removal of the ban on large ships, and so on. In the fashion that had become typical of Mito, Toko made all these plans corollary to the great central theory of *kokutai.* The *Dai Nihon Shi*

[32] Letter of Ansei 5. 6. 20, in Katsu, *Kaikoku Kigen,* III, 2303–5. For details on the signing of the treaty, see note 30, Chapter 11, of the present volume.

[33] Toko's best-known pupil was Saigo Takamori (1827–77), of Satsuma, who, although not distinguished in the intellectual field, actively plotted against the shogunate and became the leading general of the Restoration armies in 1867–68.

continued to be regarded with pride and reverence; this great historical work, Toko said,

. . . makes clear first of all that the Land of the Rich Reed Plains excels and is to be reverenced above all other countries beyond the seas; and that the Heavenly Sun Succession's continuing on and on to rule over the realm for all time, from the Age of the Omnipotent Gods so long as heaven and earth shall last, is the fundamental reason why the positions [*meibun*] of sovereign and subject can never be altered.[34]

In the *Hitachi Obi*, Toko also clarified the meaning of the term "Shinto" as used by the Mito school. Attributing the Mito viewpoint to Nariaki, he wrote:

What my Lord means by Shinto is not what people know as a Shinto sect based on personal teachings, making strained analogies with *yin, yang,* and the Five Elements; nor is it a Shinto surreptitiously compounded by taking Confucian and Buddhist ideas.

It must be exclusively the Way of the Imperial Court, precisely as it was from the beginning of heaven and earth until the reign of Emperor Ojin, before the teachings of foreign lands had yet crossed over;[35] it is what they practiced generation after generation that he regards as Shinto. . . .

Even though we call it Shinto [the Way of the Gods], we are not limited to this. It is possible also to designate it as the Way of the Imperial Court, the Way of Yamato, the Imperial Way [*Kodo*],[36] or the Great Way.[37]

Kodokan-ki Jutsugi

Soon after assuming his duties as ruler of Mito-*han*, Nariaki began to plan the founding of a new school that would perpetuate

[34] *Hitachi Obi*, Book II, in Takasu Yoshijiro (ed.), *Mitogaku Zenshu*, I (Tokyo: Nitto Shoin, 1933), 350.

[35] Crossed over, that is, from the mainland to Japan. See note 29, Chapter 3.

[36] Although the word *Kodo* ("Imperial Way") had occasionally been used before by Hayashi Razan and others, in the sense of *Odo*, its special application as "Way of the Land of the Gods" was initiated by Toko. Like the term *kokutai,* the word *Kodo* quickly came into general use as Mito writings circulated throughout Japan. Cf. the document of 1869 cited on p. 237.

[37] *Hitachi Obi*, Book II, in Takasu, *Mitogaku Zenshu*, I, 357–58.

the ideals connected with the name of Mito and bring together the best in both Japanese and Chinese learning. To this school he gave the name of the Kodokan. In order to clarify its purpose, he had a brief statement prepared, which came to be known as the *Kodokan-ki* ("Record of the Kodokan"). The importance Nariaki attached to this statement is indicated by the effort that went into its preparation. The first draft was written in Japanese by Nariaki himself; it was then put into Chinese, and handed to Toko with instructions to revise it. Toko, adding many of his own ideas, prepared a new Chinese draft, which was subjected to thorough study and criticism by a committee of three, including Aizawa Yasushi, each of whom independently made suggestions for changes. Their proposals and arguments were submitted to Nariaki, and in 1837 he made the final decision on the exact wording of the text. This text, only 491 characters in length, was eventually carved on a rock erected in the garden of the school.

Because of the unusual care and effort that had gone into its preparation, the *Kodokan-ki* was regarded as an official statement epitomizing the principles of Mito; but due to its brevity and difficult classical style, Nariaki felt that a commentary was urgently needed. The result of his request was Toko's *Kodokan-ki Jutsugi* ("Commentary on the *Kodokan-ki*"). Upon its completion, Toko requested criticisms from some of the other scholars of Mito, such as his lifelong friend, Toyoda Tenko,[38] who wrote the introduction to the book; but not including Yasushi, who was strictly incommunicado at the time. After making a few changes, Toko finally released the manuscript in 1849. The work represents the individual scholarship of Fujita Toko; however, because the original *Kodokan-ki* was itself the cooperative product of the best minds of the Mito school, this commentary also stands as the finest complete exposition of Mitogaku in its ultimate stage of development.

The *Jutsugi* begins with the Chinese idea that the Way of Man originates in, or is based on, the will of Heaven. Just as the Way of Heaven and Earth is a unifying factor in the world of nature,

---

[38] Toyoda Tenko (1805–64), a pupil of Fujita Yukoku, was a member of the research staff and later became its director. Known chiefly as a historian, he wrote several of the "Monographs" in the *Dai Nihon Shi*.

the Way of Man must be a source of unity in the world of mankind.

But the Way of Japan is a special, particularized Way, not possessed by any other country. It is this special Way to which the Kodokan is dedicated. In order to understand this Way, absolute faith in the ancient Japanese story of creation is essential; the tendency to disbelieve, which has become increasingly pronounced since the Middle Ages, is deplorable. The analogies some persons make between Japanese records and the *Book of Changes,* involving *yin, yang,* and the Five Elements, are completely baseless; but on the other hand, the scholars of Kokugaku go too far, and include purely personal ideas in their explanations. The Way of Japan actually originates in the fundamental obligation of Filial Piety, applying both to living parents and to ancestors, to rulers as well as to subjects, and having worship as its highest expression.

Toko then shows how the Chinese worship of Heaven, while corresponding to the worship of Amaterasu, does not have the same basic validity. The result of his argument is to give Amaterasu the place in Japanese belief that Heaven occupies in Chinese philosophy, but with the distinction that the vague and abstract Chinese concept is replaced by a concrete, physical interpretation. Thus, Toko continues:

The Way of worship in the Land of the Gods originated in the distant Age of the Gods; in ancient times nothing was heard of such matters as "Heaven" or "Shang Ti." . . .

Above, the Heavenly Ancestress is in body the same as the heavenly [i.e., phenomenal] sun; below, her spirit resides in the Treasure-Mirror. This being so, the radiant Orb, and the lofty Shrine of Ise, being in truth the dwelling places of the spirit of the Heavenly Ancestress, successive generations of emperors worship and serve them. Thus have the obligations of worshipping Heaven and of serving the ancestors been simultaneously preserved.[39]

In this way, under the guidance and instructions of Amaterasu, there developed the Way of the Japanese people. This Way means: for the emperor, to reverence the gods and love the

---

[39] *Kodokan-ki Jutsugi,* Book I, in Takasu, *Mitogaku Zenshu,* I, 11.

people; for the people, to show their devotion to the nation in the form of pure loyalty to the imperial family. In accordance with this Way, generation after generation of the Heavenly Sun Succession, possessing the Three Sacred Treasures, reigns over all; while the descendants of the ancillary gods who accompanied Ninigi no Mikoto on his descent to earth perform their duties in support of the imperial family; this is the foundation of the Land of the Gods.

This land of the sun's source is the point of origin of the *yang* force; its earth spiritual; its men heroic; its food abundant; its arms sufficient. The superiors apply virtue in nurturing life and loving the people; the inferiors with one accord devote their wills to serving the superiors. Their valor in war originates in their natural constitution. These are the reasons why the *kokutai* is august.

And when we speak of military valor, it does not signify the mere flaunting of authority by means of force and violence alone; beyond this, it must necessarily originate in the essence of loyalty and love.[40]

In explaining the desirability of accepting useful ideas from China, Toko carefully points out that these must supplement, or promote the development of, the Imperial Way; and that only those ideas consistent with Japanese principles can be admitted. Chief among these are the Five Relationships and Five Virtues; the *Kodokan-ki* specifically mentioned the most ancient period of Yao, Shun, and the Three Dynasties as a model. Yet even here, the change of mandate theory, whether accomplished by "voluntary cession" or by the use of force, must be rejected as the complete antithesis of *kokutai*. As a praiseworthy example of the proper attitude, Toko cites the Taika Reform (645). Although, he says, it was clearly based on knowledge of the actions of Chou Kung,[41] its most significant point was the restoration of worship to the dominant place in government; to accept the knowledge of China was to reinforce the traditions of Japan.

In such terms, the *Kodokan-ki Jutsugi* presents Mito's final views on the nature of the Japanese state. In addition, two other passages are worthy of note.

[40] *Ibid.*, pp. 15–16.
[41] See note 37, Chapter 2.

In describing the pious and benign policy of Ieyasu, the *Kodokan-ki* stated that, among other actions, he had "revered the sovereign" (*son-no*) and "repelled the barbarians" (*jo-i*). These were two separate quotations from the *Shih Chi* of Ssu-ma Ch'ien.[42] Although both had already come into use in the Japanese vocabulary, they were permanently welded into one phrase by Toko's commentary. In a single paragraph, he not only creates the rallying cry for the imperial loyalists, but he also sets the seal of approval on their use of the word *shishi* [43] to describe themselves:

In this majestic Land of the Gods, the Heavenly Sun Succession generation after generation, with reverence for the Three Sacred Treasures, reigns over all creation. The distinction between superior and inferior, between internal and external, is as unchanging as heaven and earth. For this reason, then, *son-no jo-i* is in truth the Supreme Duty [*taigi*] of the *shishi jinjin* in devoting his loyalty to the service of his country.[44]

[42] Both occur in Ssu-ma Ch'ien's personal preface to this work: (a) "Foster learning, *revere the sovereign*"; (b) "Externally, *repel the barbarians;* internally, provide for laws."

[43] The term *shishi* (Chinese *chih-shih*) was used by both Confucius and Mencius, with a meaning that may be rendered as variously as "gentleman of aspiration" and—Legge's translation—"determined officer." In general, it may be taken as "brave man of virtue." It is often combined with the word *jinjin* (Chinese *jen-jen*), "benevolent man." Thus, in the *Analects,* Confucius said, "The *chih-shih jen-jen* [*shishi jinjin*] does not violate Benevolence in order to get life; but sacrifices life in order to carry out Benevolence." According to *Mencius,* "The determined officer [*shishi*] never forgets that his end may be in a ditch or a stream." (Legge's translation, Book III, Part II, chap. i, 2.)

With the connotations of bravery and virtue, Yamaga Soko used the terms *shishi* and *shishi jinjin* throughout his *Bukyo Shogaku,* as a Japanese equivalent for, and replacement of, the Confucian term *chun-tzu* (Japanese *kunshi:* "superior man"). Probably through this channel, as well as through familiarity with the original texts of Confucius and Mencius, the word *shishi* entered the samurai vocabulary, but in the late Tokugawa period it acquired the special significance of intense loyalty to *kokutai* and a desire to display devotion in service to the imperial cause. It is in this sense that Fujita Toko is using it.

[44] *Kodokan-ki Jutsugi,* Book II, in Takasu, *Mitogaku Zenshu,* I, 50.

Concerning the essential identity of Loyalty and Filial Piety, Toko writes:

Although their roads are different, the point they reach is the same. With regard to one's father, it is called Filial Piety; with regard to one's lord, it is called Loyalty. So far as the application of one's sincere devotion is concerned, they are one. . . .

To advance and serve one's lord, fulfilling *taigi,* is the expression of Filial Piety to one's parents. . . . To retire and see to the needs of one's parents, contributing to the improvement of society, is the expression of Loyalty to one's lord. Fundamentally, Loyalty and Filial Piety are not two; the distinction lies solely in their application.[45]

[45] *Ibid.,* pp. 92–94.

Part Two

The Application of Loyalist and Patriotic Theories in the Mid-Nineteenth Century

The Example of Yoshida Shoin

7

Life of Yoshida Shoin

W E H A V E seen how renewed faith in the stories of antiquity, as developed by thinkers of various schools, affected attitudes toward emperor and nation, and how the synthesis of Shinto traditions and Confucian principles finally became a Japanese theory of the state.

So long as a theory remains within the covers of a book, it is powerless to influence events. Only by convincing minds and hearts to act, serve, and sacrifice can such a theory truly fulfill its objective. One of the peculiar characteristics of the late Tokugawa period was the swift spread of the new-old theory throughout the country:

From one man to two, from two to four or ten, from ten to a hundred or a thousand, from a thousand to ten thousand, this conceptual impulse completely permeated the hearts of the Japanese people: . . . a spirit of awakening to the essential principles on which the nation was founded, of reverence for the glory of *kokutai*.[1]

[1] Kumura Toshio, *Yoshida Shoin no Shiso to Kyoiku* (Tokyo: Iwanami Shoten, 1942), p. 3.

What did this awakening reverence for *kokutai* mean in the life of an individual? In order to examine the subject of loyalty to emperor and nation from the side of the man whom the theoretician hoped to inspire, Yoshida Shoin (1830–59), a samurai of Choshu-*han* (the far western end of the main island of Japan), has been selected as typical of his time.

Shoin is considered the best single representative of late Tokugawa thought because, in his own person, he gathered together the influences of the preceding two hundred years. His viewpoint on the relation of shogun to emperor, arising from his belief in the overriding duty of each Japanese to serve his nation rather than any lesser loyalty, was in itself the culmination of Tokugawa thought trends, a distillation from the teachings of many groups and many writers. Priding himself on his adherence to no one school, Shoin studied and compared the ideas, compatible and incompatible, which abounded in his intellectual world; from them he charted his own course with confidence and faith, and on this basis sacrificed his life with no regret.

It is possible to trace the evolution of Shoin's thinking from absorption with the purely military problems of defense to comprehension of the reason for defense, in preserving *kokutai;* and ultimately, to the realization that there was no duty higher than that of serving the cause of the emperor, regardless of the cost to the individual or potential danger to the nation. In the mental and emotional conflicts experienced by Yoshida Shoin, during the period from 1851 to 1859, it is possible to see why and how the thinking of the entire nation evolved from unquestioning acceptance of the shogunate to fervent emperor-centered patriotism, during the half-century from 1850 to 1900. For this reason, the correspondence, essays, memorials, occasional writings, and one or two major works that Shoin left constitute an invaluable documentary record of the way in which this "conceptual impulse" permeated the hearts of his generation.[2]

[2] Yoshida Shoin's collected works have been published in two editions, both bearing the title *Yoshida Shoin Zenshu,* compiled under the auspices of the Yamaguchi-ken Kyoikukai (Educational Association), and published by Iwanami Shoten. The first edition, in ten volumes, was released in 1934–36; the second edition, twelve volumes, in 1938–40. The first edition contains some useful collateral material, not written by Shoin, which was

omitted from the second; the second edition has the advantage that all material originally written in *kambun* (Chinese or Japanese-Chinese) has been rearranged into Japanese word order—a normal practice when Tokugawa writings are reprinted in modern Japan. In the present study, the second edition was used, and is referred to as *YSZ.*

Because Shoin has been made into something of a national idol, an immense quantity of secondary literature on his life and thought has been produced for popular consumption: broadly speaking, in the late nineteenth century he was treated as a Restoration hero; in the 1930's and 1940's, as an apostle of overseas expansion and antiforeignism. While research was of course involved in the preparation of some of these works, the possibility of an objective and scholarly appraisal was greatly increased after the collected works were published, as the committee in charge made strenuous efforts to obtain and collate all extant writings of Shoin, preserved in various parts of Japan by public institutions as well as by private families.

Aside from the *Zenshu* itself, the most authoritative material on Shoin consists of the studies made by two members of the *Zenshu* compilation committee: Hirose Yutaka and Kumura Toshio. As a supplement and guide to the *Zenshu,* I have relied chiefly on the following: Hirose Yutaka, *Yoshida Shoin no Kenkyu* (2nd rev. ed.; Tokyo: Shibundo, 1944); Kumura Toshio, *Yoshida Shoin* (Tokyo: Iwanami Shoten, 1941); and Kumura Toshio, *Yoshida Shoin no Shiso to Kyoiku.*

A word may be in order concerning Western-language materials on Shoin.

Robert Louis Stevenson's "Yoshida Torajiro," in *Familiar Studies of Men and Books,* is perhaps the earliest account, but is based only on hearsay.

Horace E. Coleman's abridged translation of the life of Shoin by the famous writer Tokutomi Iichiro (Soho), published as "The Life of Shōin Yoshida," *Transactions of the Asiatic Society of Japan,* XLV (1917), Part I, 119–88, suffers from the idol-worshipping approach of the original. If this is discounted, Coleman's translation contains useful information, although in some cases the interpretations are misleading.

Probably the best introduction to Shoin is Heinrich Dumoulin's "Yoshida Shōin (1830–1859)," *Monumenta Nipponica,* I (1938), 350–77. The author mentions the existence of the *Zenshu,* but has relied for source material mostly on an older collection of Shoin's letters. Unfortunately, he tends to overemphasize the element of "imperial restoration," and to ignore the significant factor of evolutionary changes in Shoin's viewpoint.

The article by H. J. Timperley, "Yoshida Shōin—Martyred Prophet of Japanese Expansionism," *Far Eastern Quarterly,* I (1942), 337–47, is based entirely on Western-language sources. It contains many misleading statements and a few factual errors, but has some value in demonstrating Shoin's importance in the expansionist movement.

Shoin's Early Years

Yoshida Shoin [3] was born September 20, 1830, in Matsumoto, on the outskirts of Hagi, the administrative seat of Choshu-*han*. He was the second son of Sugi Yurinosuke, a samurai of lowly rank who engaged in farming. At the age of five, Shoin was adopted by his father's younger brother, Yoshida Daisuke, who had the hereditary duty of teaching Yamaga military science [4]

The most recent publication on Shoin is by far the most detailed: H. J. J. M. Van Straelen, *Yoshida Shōin, Forerunner of the Meiji Restoration* (T'oung Pao, Monographie II [Leiden: E. J. Brill, 1952]). It is based on the *Zenshu* as well as on secondary material and treats Shoin in various aspects—as teacher, writer, etc. Even this, however, must be used with care. The writer has apparently leaned too heavily on secondary material for his interpretations, which leads him sometimes to make statements that can not be borne out by Shoin's own writings. (For example, on p. 15, where he suggests that Shoin's antiforeignism resulted from hatred of the Bakufu; precisely the reverse is true.) There are also several minor factual errors in this work, notably in the conversion of dates from the Japanese to the Western calendar.

The material presented herein differs from all of the foregoing. It is narrower in scope, concentrating on Shoin's political attitudes and their origins; it is far more detailed in its treatment; and particular stress is laid on the evolutionary factor, which is one of the most significant elements in Shoin's thought if we are to use it as a key to understanding the rise of a new ideology. I have drawn upon all the books of the *Zenshu*, using Shoin's most important work, the *Komo Yowa*, and his diaries, memorials, essays, and lectures, as well as his correspondence; and to the greatest degree possible, I have followed the policy of letting Shoin speak for himself by abridging, paraphrasing, or translating his own writing.

In every instance where a quotation used by Dumoulin or Van Straelen appears in the present study, I have retranslated it directly from the original.

[3] His boyhood name was Toranosuke. Later he used several other names, of which the best known, other than Shoin, was Torajiro; but for purposes of clarity, he is herein called Shoin consistently.

[4] The relationship went back to Shoin's ancestor, Yoshida Tomonosuke, who was a pupil of Yamaga Soko's son, Takamoto. In this way, the Yoshida family became teachers of the Yamaga school, a profession Shoin was expected to continue in his generation.

at the Meirinkan.[5] When Daisuke died a year later, Shoin succeeded to his responsibility, and it became necessary to accelerate his education. He continued living in the Sugi family home; and as another uncle, Tamaki Bunnoshin, was also a part of the family group,[6] Shoin's earliest studies were supervised jointly by his father and uncle.

At the age of seven, early in 1838, Shoin entered the Meirinkan to begin his military education. Shortly after this, his uncle Bunnoshin set up his own home, and for the next few years, Shoin lived alternately with parents and uncle. His intellectual progress was so rapid that soon after his ninth birthday, he gave his first lectures at the Meirinkan, and in the following year (1840) he lectured before the *hanshu* on a chapter from Yamaga Soko's writings. However, in this case at least, the lecture was prepared for him by Bunnoshin.

Shoin continued simultaneously to study and teach under supervision until 1848, when his tutelage was completed and he became an independent teacher on the staff of the Meirinkan. His education up to this time had included (in addition to the Four Books and Five Classics) the seven military classics of China, the *Bukyo Zensho*,[7] and the study of other schools of military science in addition to his own specialty. This type of education involved not merely tactics and strategy, but a broad knowledge of ethics, government, and Chinese history. He had also studied Shushigaku with his uncle Bunnoshin. Under one of his Meirinkan teachers, Yamada Uemon, he had been aroused to the dangers of foreign invasion, and he was already becoming

[5] The Meirinkan, established by Choshu-*han* at Hagi in 1719, was one of the oldest *han* schools in Japan. Originally upholding Ogyu Sorai's viewpoint, in Shoin's day it was dominated by Shushigaku.

[6] The Sugi, Yoshida, and Tamaki families were closely interrelated by adoption and marriage. Yurinosuke's great-grandfather was a Yoshida, adopted into the Sugi family. Yurinosuke's uncle had been adopted into the Tamaki family, and as he had no heir, Bunnoshin (Yurinosuke's second younger brother) was adopted as his son. In the next generation, the Tamaki and Yoshida families were both carried on by children of Shoin's elder brother, Umetaro, through marriages and adoption, respectively. See genealogical charts in *YSZ*, I, 69–74.

[7] A collection of Yamaga Soko's writings on military subjects, used as a text in the Yamaga school.

interested in the problems of coastal defense. However, so far as actual knowledge of the world was concerned, Shoin had not yet been outside the borders of Choshu-*han*.

Broadening Horizons

The *hanshu,* Mori Yoshichika (Takachika), gradually became impressed with Shoin's ability, and after hearing one of his lectures in 1850, decided that he, too, would study the Yamaga school. Due to his favor and interest, Shoin was permitted shortly after this to leave the *han* for the first time for a trip to Kyushu. His chief purpose was to study at the headquarters of the Yamaga school in Hirado, but as he traveled by way of Nagasaki, by chance Shoin visited the only two places in Japan that had been exposed to foreign influence.

At Hirado, Shoin attended the lectures of Yamaga Bansuke, the then head of the family, but no close relationship developed. The person who took the greatest interest in him was Hayama Sanai, one of the leading samurai of Hirado-*han,* who had studied in Edo. Sanai had a great wealth of books which he generously made available to Shoin. Shoin remained in Hirado almost two months studying under Sanai, during which time he read or looked through about eighty volumes, including several works on Yomeigaku, Miyake Kanran's *Chuko Kangen,* Aizawa Yasushi's *Shinron,* and other writings of the Mito school, as well as a variety of books on the classics, history, and military science. Sanai was also better informed on world conditions and European aggression in China than anyone Shoin had met before. Through his influence, the Hirado trip proved to be a great intellectual stimulation to the youthful Shoin.

After leaving Hirado, Shoin spent about a month in Nagasaki observing conditions in an "open port." He called at the official residences of the Chinese and Dutch, was entertained on board a Dutch ship, received instruction in spoken Chinese, and studied gunnery. His interest in Western technology, with particular emphasis on its military aspects, dated from this time. Before returning home, he visited other places in Kyushu, meeting scholars and persons of interests similar to his own, in an endeavor to increase his store of knowledge. In Kumamoto, he met Miyabe Teizo, a fellow-teacher of the Yamaga school, who was to become a lifelong friend. After four months, he arrived back in Hagi in time for New Year's, with a broadened viewpoint that was to affect the remainder of his life.

The following spring (1851), after the *hanshu* received his diploma—completing his studies of the Yamaga school under Shoin—it was decided that Shoin should spend some time in Edo. This trip was made as a member of the daimyo's retinue. One of its high points for Shoin was passing the tomb of Nanko at Minatogawa,[8] where he stopped to make obeisance. Three days later, when one day was spent resting at Fushimi in the outskirts of Kyoto, Shoin wrote a poem in praise of Nanko, lauding him for thinking only of Duty and the Way, not of fame.[9]

Arriving in Edo on May 9, Shoin determined at once to improve his knowledge of military science, the classics, and Western learning. His first step was to become a pupil of Yamaga Sosui, head of the Edo branch of the Yamaga school. He attended Sosui's lectures twelve times a month, and, together with Miyabe Teizo and another friend, soon became one of his three favorite pupils. When Sosui wrote a book, the *Rempei Setsuryaku,* he asked these three to check its contents and each to write a preface for it. However, Shoin did not care much for his personality, and as he found Sosui was not particularly respected in Edo, he gradually put more emphasis on his other studies.

Among these, the most important were Chinese literature and the classics. Almost immediately upon his arrival in Edo, Shoin had enrolled as a pupil of Asaka Konsai,[10] who, in addition to

[8] See pp. 83–84.
[9] Recorded in Shoin's diary of the trip, the *Toyu Nikki,* in *YSZ,* X, 135–36.
[10] Asaka Konsai (1785–1860) was the last outstanding teacher at the Shoheiko. He advocated an open-minded search for learning, using not only the works of Chu Hsi and Wang Yang-ming, but those of Ogyu Sorai and the Han and T'ang dynasty writers; he also found good in Taoism and Buddhism. Although he considered the message of the sages to be of eternal validity, he said, "The Way of scholarship demands that we should take the good from many sources." (*Konsai Kanwa,* I.

his duties as a professor at the Shoheiko, was in charge of the literary division at the Choshu-*han* school in Edo. Shoin attended his lectures regularly—in a building on the grounds of the *han* mansion—and was also a frequent visitor at his home.

During 1851, Western technology was still subordinate to military science and classical studies among Shoin's interests, but he was nevertheless affected by what he had seen in Nagasaki. He paid a social call on Sakuma Zozan,[11] one of the outstanding scholars of his time in Dutch and Western science, on the same day that he enrolled under Yamaga Sosui; and two months later, formally enrolled as Zozan's pupil as well. However, his attendance at Zozan's lectures was somewhat irregular, and it was only after the arrival of Commodore Perry in 1853 that this contact took on real significance for Shoin.

During his first summer in Edo, Shoin took up fencing, and continued with Dutch, which he had begun in Hagi; but he does not appear to have made much progress in the latter study. He also gave his own lectures twice a month at the *han* school. In July, he made a ten-day trip with Miyabe Teizo, inspecting the coast of Sagami Bay on both the Sagami and Awa sides, as an exercise in planning coastal defense.

Perhaps the most important new element to enter Shoin's thinking at this period, as a result of associating with other young samurai from various parts of the country and hearing the lectures of famous scholars, was an appreciation of history. He wrote to his brother that he realized as never before the vast range of historical knowledge and his own ignorance of it.[12] This factor probably contributed to his decision to include Mito among the places to be visited on the lengthy tour of the Northeast that he undertook during the winter of 1851–52.

Plans for this trip were under discussion for several months in the fall of 1851; it was to be made with Miyabe Teizo and a third friend, Ebata Goro. Shoin had received the verbal permission of his *hanshu,* and the three friends decided to set

Quoted in Inoue Tetsujiro, *Nippon Shushigakuha no Tetsugaku* [14th printing; Tokyo: Fuzambo, 1924], p. 544.)

[11] For a survey of Sakuma Zozan's life and viewpoint, see pp. 149–53.
[12] Letter to Sugi Umetaro (Kaei 4. 8. 17), in *YSZ,* VIII, 65–70.

out on the fourteenth day of the twelfth month (January 5, 1852). While Shoin and Teizo were interested primarily in broadening their knowledge of Japan,[13] Ebata Goro intended in the course of the trip to avenge himself against an enemy of his brother; and the specific date chosen was the anniversary of the vengeance taken by the forty-seven samurai of Ako.[14] In the meantime, Shoin's lord had returned to Hagi, but the essential written permission to travel had not arrived. Faced with the conflict between keeping his promise to his friends and obeying the law, Shoin for the first time took the bold step he was to repeat more than once and in more serious contexts: that of placing personal duty above law.

Because of the necessity for secrecy, Shoin left alone, but the three friends met according to plan in Mito a few days later. One month was spent in this stimulating atmosphere, discussing and absorbing the theories of Mitogaku. During this period, Shoin was treated very cordially by Aizawa Yasushi (then almost seventy years of age), being permitted to visit his home six times. He also received the personal advice of Toyoda Tenko [15] as to the proper method of studying the national history and met others of the Mito group.[16]

After leaving Mito, Ebata Goro separated from his friends; Shoin and Teizo continued their circuit of the Northeast, by way of Aizu, Niigata, Akita, Aomori, Morioka, and Sendai, returning to Edo on May 23. Their chief interest in these remote regions was the possibility of Russian invasion from the North. However, the developing trend of Shoin's thought is shown by their making a side trip to the island of Sado to visit the grave of Emperor Juntoku, who died there in exile (1242) under the

---

[13] It was the current custom for young samurai who were interested in national problems to leave their *han,* often secretly, to travel throughout the country. On these trips, they made new friends and observed the conditions of other *han:* this was called "investigating the state of the nation." Shoin's great antagonist, Yamagata Taika, refers to such activities of the *shishi* group in a passage cited on p. 155.

[14] See note 2, Chapter 3.

[15] See note 38, Chapter 6.

[16] He was unable to call on Fujita Toko, due to the fact that Toko was under strict house arrest at the time.

Kamakura shogunate. At the straits of Tsugaru, Shoin recorded his anger over the insolence of foreign ships, passing through "pretentiously" from time to time. On the same occasion, he wrote of his interest in finding five villages in this vicinity composed of Ainus who had become completely Japanized. The germ of his future thinking may be seen in his comment:

At the present time, there is no difference between them and ordinary people. So the barbarians too are equally men, and if by training they can be transformed in this way, Chishima [the Kuriles] and Karafuto [Sakhalin] as well must become the same as these five villages.[17]

The trip to the Northeast was one of the turning points in Shoin's life; in addition to the stimulus he received at Mito, it gave him a far broader knowledge of the geography and conditions of Japan and began the strengthening of his character that later impelled him to follow his conception of the right, regardless of personal sacrifice.

First House Arrest

A few days after returning to Edo, Shoin surrendered himself at the *han* mansion and requested punishment. He was ordered to return to his home in Hagi and there await the decision of the *hanshu*. This period of house arrest lasted approximately seven months. It was during this time that he first began referring to himself as "Shoin."[18]

The intense activity of the past two years, which had taken Shoin from Nagasaki to Aomori and had exposed his mind to the arguments of the leading scholars in classical learning, military science, Western knowledge, and the Mito school, was exchanged for an equally intense inactivity, during which he could digest and integrate what he had seen and heard. His first thought was to repair his ignorance of Japanese history; on the basis of this new study he decided that it was the strong, ag-

---

[17] *Tohokuyu Nikki,* in *YSZ,* X, 285.

[18] *Sho (matsu)* refers to his home in *Matsu*moto; *in,* to seclusion or inactivity.

gressive foreign policy of the ancient period that had "made the Imperial Land the Imperial Land." At the same time, his reading included Chinese history, world geography, and general information on foreign countries.

A letter Shoin wrote to Yamada Uemon [19]—one of his old, respected teachers at the Meirinkan—during this period of house arrest is significant in revealing how his newly developing patriotic consciousness was combined with a strong but unorthodox interest in Chinese learning.[20] Although he had found pleasure in studying the history and conditions of European countries (being particularly impressed by the history of Russia), he felt that the study of Japanese history was equally useful; how desirable it would be, he said, to see the ancient power of Japan, and its policy of foreign conquest, revived. Then, in discussing the policy of the Meirinkan, he suggested broadening its curriculum so as not to emphasize Chu Hsi alone, but to include the Ming and Ch'ing dynasty Investigatory school, Wang Yang-ming and his forerunner Lu Hsiang-shan, Ito Jinsai,[21] Ogyu Sorai, and even non-Confucian writers such as Lao Tzu.

Near the end of the year (January 18, 1853), Shoin received his sentence: he was dismissed from the Mori service and from his hereditary position at the Meirinkan; his name was removed from the samurai register; and he was placed in the custody of his father, Yurinosuke. From this time to the end of his life, Shoin remained legally a *ronin* and was never free from custody, either technical or actual. It goes without saying that his changed legal status had no effect on his personal loyalty to his lord. It did, however, place him in financial difficulties, since his independent income (57 *koku* [22] as compared to Yurinosuke's 26) was discontinued.

The *hanshu* retained a feeling of respect for Shoin, and, simultaneously with his sentence, granted him free permission to travel and study during a ten-year period. Taking advantage

[19] See p. 113.

[20] Letter to Yamada Uemon (Kaei 5. 8. 26), in *YSZ*, VII, 363 ff.

[21] Ito Jinsai (1627–1705) was a well-known Confucian scholar who, like Yamaga Soko and Ogyu Sorai, refused to follow the orthodox Chu Hsi teaching.

[22] See Appendix B for definitions of *ronin* and *koku*.

of his lord's liberality, Shoin left Hagi the following month to return to Edo. On this trip, in order to familiarize himself further with the various sections of Japan, he avoided the regular route he had traveled before, and after stopping on Shikoku, visited Nara and the shrines at Ise for the first time, then proceeded through the interior by way of Gifu and Gumma. He reached Edo on June 30, just eight days before the arrival of Perry's ships at Uraga.

Black Ships

Shoin heard of the arrival of the "black ships" the day after they anchored. Hurrying immediately to Zozan's house, he found his teacher had already received the news and had left for Uraga with a group of other pupils. The next day he joined them; Zozan, by observation from the shore, was checking the size and type of the ships and, so far as possible, their guns.

After the delivery of President Fillmore's message, it was obvious that the danger to the country was even more acute than had been thought, and Shoin began to study much more seriously than before under Zozan. At the same time, Zozan took more interest in him than previously, because of his earnestness and unfortunate experience, so that a close understanding developed between them. Zozan was now surrounded by hosts of eager pupils, anxious to prepare for the war that was expected the following spring,[23] but Shoin became one of his favorites.

Spending long hours with Zozan and other friends discussing

[23] The reasons for expecting war ran as follows: If the Bakufu agreed to sign a treaty under threat of force, thus reversing one of its most fundamental laws because of foreign pressure, it would reveal its inability to perform its original and basic function, that of national defense. Rather than undergo such a humiliation, it would refuse to negotiate; in answer to this insult, the United States would declare war.

The reasoning of the Bakufu was similar, but believing the dangers of foreign invasion to be worse than humiliation, it signed the treaty. However, this only resulted in strengthening domestic opposition and was an important factor in the collapse of the shogunate a few years later. These crosscurrents were reflected in Shoin's thinking from 1853 to 1859.

the national crisis, Shoin once again came to feel that he must act, regardless of the consequences. Although already in disgrace and with no right whatsoever to present his views, and even though he knew that his father, now responsible for his actions, might be punished as a result, Shoin decided that his lord must be given advice that could, he believed, save the nation. Accordingly, he prepared a lengthy memorial, the *Shokyu Shigen* ("An Absolutely Necessary Private Opinion"), and took it to the *han* mansion for transmittal to the daimyo. The officials, although abusing Shoin soundly for his impertinence, were prevailed upon to accept it, and it eventually reached Mori Yoshichika. While the major part of the text repeated some of Zozan's suggestions, this memorial also contained original thought, and from this standpoint it was the earliest of Shoin's more important writings. It was followed by other detailed recommendations, not all of which reached the *hanshu*.

A little over a month after Perry's squadron had left, the Russian Admiral Putiatin entered Nagasaki harbor with four warships. By the time this news reached Edo, Zozan was convinced the time was at hand for someone to take the step of leaving Japan for study abroad. Although he had long been proposing this, the Bakufu had refused to alter its regulations; but Zozan felt the coming of the foreign ships offered an opportunity that should be seized. As Shoin was willing and anxious to be the first to make the attempt, Zozan gave him money for expenses and a poem of encouragement, and on October 20, Shoin set out for Nagasaki.

Loyalty to the emperor had always been an element in Shoin's thinking, but from about this time it began to take on a more personal aspect than previously. In all his travels, he had never entered the city of Kyoto; now, believing that he was leaving his native land for an unknown future, he stopped at the ancient capital in order to bow in respect at the Imperial Palace. Here in Kyoto, Shoin was deeply moved by what he learned of Emperor Komei's grief and anxiety over the political and international situation of Japan, and he expressed his newly aroused feelings of reverence and sympathy for the Emperor in the famous poem *Hoketsu wo Hai-shi-tatematsuru* ("On Worshipfully Venerating the Imperial Palace").[24] He also made the acquaintance of Yanagawa Seigan (1789–1858), a friend of Zozan's, who, as an ardent loyalist, was acting as a sort of elder adviser to the *shishi* group in the Kyoto area. This contact was to prove of great importance to Shoin in later years.

From Osaka, Shoin took a boat to Bungo in northeastern Kyushu, then proceeded to Kumamoto for a week's visit with Miyabe Teizo. Through Teizo, he met Yokoi Shonan[25] at this time. When he reached Nagasaki, he found that Putiatin had left a few days previously.[26]

After a brief visit in Hagi with his parents, whom he had not seen for almost a year, Shoin, joined by Miyabe Teizo and another friend, returned to Edo. On the way, Shoin spent several days in Kyoto, calling on Yanagawa Seigan, and becoming friendly with many imperial loyalists, including Rai Mikisaburo and Umeda Umpin (Genjiro). From this time on, Shoin began more and more consciously to identify himself with the *shishi* group.

He arrived in Edo just before New Year's (January 25, 1854).

---

[24] In *YSZ*, X, 405–6. A German translation appears in Dumoulin, "Yoshida Shôin," pp. 358–59. An English translation prepared from this German version is included in Timperley, "Yoshida Shōin—Martyred Prophet," pp. 342–43.

Shoin made several revisions of this, which was to become one of his best-known poetic works. Many years after the Meiji Restoration, the original manuscript of the 1856 version was presented to the Imperial Household. In 1908, on the fiftieth anniversary of Shoin's death (forty-ninth by the Western manner of counting), a stone some ten or twelve feet high, carved with an enlarged reproduction of this manuscript, was erected in Kyoto to Shoin's memory. This stone may be seen today, in the grounds of the Kyoto-*fu* Public Library, near the *torii* of the Heian Shrine. (Personal observation, summer, 1959.)

[25] Yokoi Shonan (1810–69) was an outstanding thinker, influential in political affairs during the late Tokugawa and early Meiji periods.

[26] Putiatin was in Nagasaki from August 22 to November 23, 1853. Shoin arrived November 27 and left December 1. Putiatin returned January 3, 1854, to spend another month there, but Shoin, who of course had no way of knowing his plans, was then already back in Kyoto.

Failure at Shimoda

Two and a half weeks after Shoin's return to Edo, Commodore Perry's ships made their second appearance, this time anchoring off Yokohama (Kanagawa). For the next six weeks, Shoin and his friends were extremely busy preparing for war. Shoin submitted another urgent memorial to his lord, outlining the measures that might be taken immediately even though the nation was unprepared. Various personal plots and plans were discussed with Teizo and other friends, including one to assassinate Perry; this was abandoned when they decided it would do more harm than good. When, contrary to their expectations, the Bakufu signed the Treaty of Kanagawa on March 31, their activity came to an abrupt halt.

With Zozan's approval, Shoin decided to make a second attempt to go abroad. Included in his plans this time was another young samurai of Choshu, Kaneko Shigenosuke, whom he had met since returning from Nagasaki and whose zeal to serve the nation matched his own. On April 2, Shoin and Shigenosuke went to Hodogaya, a short distance inland from Yokohama. There they wrote a letter, which they called the *To-i-sho* ("Application for Joining the Barbarians"),[27] and discussed ways and means of getting it into the hands of the Americans. The letter described their sincere desire to go abroad for study despite the laws of their country, requested assistance, and stressed that the matter should be handled with the utmost secrecy. While at Hodogaya, Shoin maintained close contact with Zozan, then on duty at Yokohama in connection with coastal-defense respon-

[27] A copy dated Kaei 7. 3. 11 (April 8, 1854) is included as an appendix to the *Kaikoroku,* in *YSZ,* X, 469–71. An English translation of the copy actually delivered, which may have differed in minor details, appears in the official report of the Perry expedition: Francis L. Hawks, *Narrative of the Expedition of an American Squadron to the China Seas and Japan* (Washington, D.C.: A. O. P. Nicholson, 1856), p. 420 note. Variants of this translation may be found in S. Wells Williams, "A Journal of the Perry Expedition to Japan (1853–1854)," *Transactions of the Asiatic Society of Japan,* XXXVII (1910), Part II, 172–74; and in J. W. Spalding, *Japan and Around the World* (New York: J. S. Redfield, 1855), pp. 284–85.

sibilities.[28] However, before an opportunity could be found for delivering the letter, Perry's ships moved to Shimoda.

Shoin and Shigenosuke followed suit, arriving at Shimoda on April 15. They spent several days studying the ships and observing the movements of the Americans when they came ashore; on one occasion they started out in a small boat, but the waves were too high for them. Finally, on April 24, they were able to approach one of the officers who had come ashore near Shimoda and was standing alone, waiting for friends. While admiring his watch chain, Shoin slipped the letter inside his coat. It now also contained a postscript added at Shimoda, mentioning the difficulty they had had in making contact, and requesting the Americans to send a boat for them that evening.

That night, as no one came to meet them, they rowed out themselves, reaching the ships about 2 A.M. on April 25. Permitted to board the flagship, the U.S.S. *Powhatan,* they were interviewed by Commodore Perry's interpreter, the Rev. S. Wells Williams. The *To-i-sho* was in Williams' possession, and he identified them as its authors by having them sign their names.[29] Perry refused their request as a violation of Japanese law, which, in view of the very delicate nature of the newly established treaty relations between the United States and Japan, he could not condone. Shoin realized that his case was hopeless, but tried to prolong the conversation until dawn, feeling certain that the Commodore would not force him to go ashore in broad daylight, and that he could obtain valuable information by spending even one entire day on board the ship.[30] However, this proved impossible to arrange. As their boat, containing their swords and a few other possessions, had been washed away by high waves while they were boarding the *Powhatan,*[31] Perry had the two men put ashore

[28] See p. 151.

[29] That is, the aliases they were using. Shoin called himself Kanouchi Manji; Shigenosuke, Ichigi Kota.

[30] This information as to Shoin's inner motivation is from his own account, *Sangatsu Nijushichi-ya no Ki* ("Chronicle of the Night of 3rd Month 27th Day"), in *YSZ*, X, 459–66.

[31] The official American report implies a strong possibility that they had let their boat go adrift intentionally. See Hawks, *Narrative of the Expedition,* p. 421. But as Shoin and Shigenosuke were inexperienced in

by American sailors, and made sure they would be landed while it was still dark.

After a few hours of vain search along the shore for their boat, Shoin and Shigenosuke gave themselves up to the authorities. The boat was found later; in it, besides a copy of the *To-i-sho*, there was discovered the poem Zozan had written when Shoin started for Nagasaki. Thus, Zozan's complicity was clearly established, and he also was arrested.

After this, his second attempt to go abroad, had ended in failure, Shoin abandoned any further hope of personally studying Western learning; and at the same time, his fundamentally anti-foreign sentiment, which he had managed to hold in abeyance temporarily, again asserted itself. While confined with Shigenosuke in the Shimoda jail, he read books borrowed from the official in charge. According to his own account,

Day and night I explained aloud the reason why the Imperial Land is the Imperial Land, the essential nature of human ethics, and why we should hate the barbarians. The prison guard, although rude and ignorant, was still possessed of a human heart, and could not help shedding tears in lamenting our aspirations.[32]

At one of his interrogations, when accused of planning to betray the secrets of Japan to foreigners, Shoin replied: "For the sake of the nation I desired to investigate conditions in foreign lands; then how should I intend to reveal the affairs of the nation to them?"[33]

After about two weeks of confinement and questioning at Shimoda, Shoin and Shigenosuke were transferred to Demma-cho prison in Edo, where Shoin was assigned a room adjoining that of Zozan. During this time, Shoin and Shigenosuke attempted to model their actions on those of the forty-seven samurai. In a letter to his brother from Demma-cho prison, Shoin wrote:

At a former time when Ako was grievously injured, there were the forty-seven loyal samurai, who sacrificed themselves to take revenge

handling boats, Shoin's own statement that the loss of the boat was accidental is more likely to be correct. See *YSZ*, X, 461.

[32] *Kaikoroku*, in *YSZ*, X, 436.

[33] *Ibid.*, p. 437.

on the enemy; even to the present day their renown remains gloriously in the public attention. . . . The samurai of Ako, taking revenge on the enemy for the sake of their lord, willingly defied the law against fighting within the castle; Norikata [Shoin], exerting his efforts for the sake of the nation, willingly defied the law against going overseas.[34]

After six months of confinement in Demma-cho prison, Shoin and Zozan were sentenced to house arrest and turned over to their respective *han* governments. While they never saw each other again, they maintained close touch by correspondence for the rest of Shoin's life.

In Shoin's case, the sentence of house arrest was changed by the Choshu-*han* administration to one of imprisonment. He and Shigenosuke were transported to Hagi as criminals; on arrival, Shoin was confined in Noyama prison, reserved for upper-class samurai. Shigenosuke, of lower rank, entered Iwakura prison, where he died of illness less than three months later.

Noyama Prison

Shoin's imprisonment at Noyama lasted a little over one year, from December 13, 1854, to January 22, 1856. During this time he received support and encouragement from his father and brother, as well as from men of influence in the *han,* so that he was able to devote himself uninterruptedly to scholarly pursuits. His brother Umetaro scoured the entire region obtaining literature for him to read; Shoin spent his time studying, writing, and teaching. His pupils were drawn from among the other prisoners,[35] all of whom were older than he.

It was Shoin's custom when he read to keep a writing brush in his hand, and to copy for future reference any passages he particularly admired. He was amazingly quick in both reading and writing: according to his meticulous records, during this year in prison and the ensuing one at home, he read over one thousand pieces of literature; while the material he copied simultaneously would amount in modern print to about three thou-

---

[34] Letter to Sugi Umetaro (Ansei 1. 4. 24), in *YSZ,* I, 388.
[35] There were eleven prisoners beside Shoin.

sand pages.[36] In addition to the classics, military classics, and older histories, some of the Tokugawa-period titles to be found in his prison reading list are: Miyake Kanran's *Chuko Kangen,* Rai Sanyo's *Nihon Gaishi* and *Nihon Seiki,*[37] Asami Keisai's *Seiken Igen,* Aizawa Yasushi's *Tekiihen* and *Kagaku Jigen,* and Fujita Toko's *Hitachi Obi* and *Kodokan-ki Jutsugi.*

Soon after his return to Hagi, Shoin wrote the *Kaikoroku,* a detailed account of all events connected with his attempt to go to America. At this time, he also produced his first work long enough to be considered as a book, the *Yushuroku* ("Record of Confinement"). This manuscript, consisting mainly of plans by which the nation could deal with the conditions immediately facing it, shows the strong influence of Zozan's thought, but basically it is a presentation of Shoin's own thought, which was then in a transitional stage. It reveals Shoin as still thinking from the standpoint of a military man, and at the same time with a growing appreciation for the importance of *kokutai.* For example, he suggests that as Fushimi's location near Kyoto commands the heart of Japan's land and water communications, a great European-style fort should be built there to protect the emperor and the capital. His continuing belief in the importance of Western studies is shown by the suggestion that a military school should be connected with the fort, its curriculum to include foreign languages and the study of Dutch, Russian, American, and English books.

[36] This estimate is given in Kumura, *Yoshida Shoin no Shiso to Kyoiku,* p. 79.

[37] Rai Sanyo (1780–1832) was renowned both as historian and as poet. His education—at the hands of his father, Rai Shunsui, and two famous professors of the Shoheiko, Bito Jishu (who was his uncle) and Shibano Ritsuzan—was according to orthodox Shushigaku. Sanyo's two best-known works, the *Nihon Gaishi* and *Nihon Seiki,* were noted for their *taigi meibun* approach to Japanese history, and contributed greatly to arousing sentiment for imperial loyalty. The *Gaishi* especially may be included with the *Seiken Igen* and *Shinron* among the most influential books in the late Tokugawa period. Sanyo's poetry, written in the same spirit, was also extremely popular.

Shoin's friend, Rai Mikisaburo, was Sanyo's son. Executed for his loyalist activities in 1859, Mikisaburo was eventually buried adjacent to Shoin's grave in Tokyo.

The latter part of the *Yushuroku* is devoted to proposals for the future expansion of Japan, and the demonstration that a strong, aggressive foreign policy is inherent in *kokutai*. Shoin reinforces this argument by an appendix, in which he cites and comments upon illustrative examples from ancient Japanese history. In his selection of material, he emphasizes that the ancient, and therefore normal or correct, policy of Japan toward foreign countries was characterized by stern but kindly justice and willingness to accept foreign learning. This work was written at Zozan's request and with his encouragement; after completing it, Shoin sent it to his teacher for criticism.

Early in his confinement at Noyama—or possibly while at Demma-cho [38]—Shoin had a dream that affected the remaining years of his life. In this dream, a supernatural figure appeared, who showed him a new name: Niju-ikkai Moshi ("Twenty-one Times Courageous Samurai"). Shoin awoke immediately, knowing that this referred to him—that he must be more courageous if he wished to be a true samurai. Up to this point in his life, he reflected, there had been but three courageous acts: leaving Edo without permission for the trip to Mito; submitting the *Shokyu Shigen;* and making the attempt at Shimoda. From this time on, in addition to the other names he used, Shoin frequently signed himself as Niju-ikkai Moshi; he made this one of the themes of his life, and endeavored to prepare himself for the eighteen additional proofs of courage that he believed would be necessary to fulfill his destiny.

This year in prison also saw the beginning of Shoin's friendships with two Buddhist priests—Gessho [39] and Mokurin.[40] Early

[38] Shoin wrote an account of the dream the week after arriving in Hagi, but did not specify the date of the dream itself, beyond saying that it was while in prison. See *Yushuroku,* Appendix, in *YSZ,* I, 389–90.

[39] Not to be confused with the priest Gessho 月照 (1813–58) of the Kiyomizu temple in Kyoto, who was associated with Saigo Takamori. Shoin's friend Gessho 月性 (1817–58), known as the "coastal-defense priest" because of his zeal, devoted most of his efforts to preaching the need for military preparedness to the people of Choshu.

The way in which Buddhism, too, could serve the purposes of patriotism in this period is shown by Gessho's *Buppo Gokoku Ron* ("On Buddhism for the Protection of the Country"), written in 1856, which Shoin prized

in the year, Shoin sent four poems to Gessho, saying he had known his name for ten years. In April, Gessho came to Hagi and held a discussion meeting in Umetaro's home. Shoin disagreed completely with Gessho's thesis that loyalty to the emperor demanded opposition to the Bakufu, and there was much correspondence between them on the subject. In the fall, when Mokurin visited Hagi, he initiated correspondence with Shoin in a similar vein, probably at Gessho's suggestion. Shoin was so impressed with his patriotism that he sent Mokurin a copy of the *Yushuroku* for criticism, and a close sympathy developed. Although priests, both Gessho and Mokurin belonged to the *shishi* faction and had contacts in other parts of the country; Gessho was an associate of Yanagawa Seigan, Umeda Umpin, and Rai Mikisaburo.

Shoin's longest and best-known work, the *Komo Yowa* ("Additional Remarks while Lecturing on *Mencius*"), was begun during this year. Among the courses he had organized for the benefit of the other prisoners, Shoin's lectures on *Mencius* were so well received that he was asked to repeat them. He took the opportunity to formalize and record them, this book being the result. The lectures follow the outline of *Mencius* and include much useful explanation of the text. Their chief importance,

highly and recommended to his pupils. Strangely enough, in this work Gessho spoke of Japan as "Land of the Gods," a term popularized by Kokugaku and the Mito school. Discussing the duty of defending the nation, he said:

> To repel the foreign invasion for the sake of the nation and thus to protect the country: this is public duty, a righteous war. . . . Living, as loyal and devoted subjects of the Emperor, your names will be resplendent for a thousand years; dying, you will be reborn in the Pure Land as Buddhas, endowed with life for immeasurable eternity. [Quoted in Ogawa Goro, "Choshu-han ni okeru Shomin Kin-no Undo no Tenkai to sono Shisoteki Haikei," *Kenkyu Ronso*, No. 8 (1953) p. 16.]

[40] Mokurin (1824–97) was from near Hiroshima, in the province of Aki. As he was deaf because of childhood illness and could not carry on the regular duties of a priest, he spent most of his time in study and travel. His contribution to Shoin's thought went beyond mere support or encouragement, and effected a fundamental change in attitude toward the emperor, which fixed Shoin's course for the remaining years of his life. (See pp. 190–91.)

however, is as a vehicle through which Shoin was able to express his personal opinions on a wide variety of subjects—the relation between emperor and shogun, the conduct of foreign affairs, the purposes of education, and so forth. His care in recording them and in sending them to Yamagata Taika for criticism [41] indicates that he had in mind a much wider audience than the half-dozen prisoners and guards who formed his regular class. Only a little more than half completed when Shoin was released from prison, the *Komo Yowa* was finished at the urgent request of his father and brother, after he returned home. Although not arranged in any logical sequence other than chapter and verse of *Mencius,* it forms the best single source of material on Shoin's thinking.

The Shoka Sonjuku

When Shoin's *han*-imposed prison sentence was cancelled, he was permitted to return to his parental home in accordance with the prior Bakufu order of house arrest. Theoretically, he was not allowed to see anyone outside his immediate family, but this rule was not enforced strictly, and before long the boys of the neighborhood began coming to request help in their studies. After a few months, Shoin started regular lectures for them, on Yamaga Soko's *Bukyo Shogaku,* and the number of pupils increased.

During this summer (1856), Shoin's uncle, Kubo Gorozaemon, decided to open a small school and to call it the Shoka Sonjuku,[42] the name that had been used for a school taught by Tamaki Bunnoshin during Shoin's boyhood. Shoin was enthusiastic over the plan; and, visualizing the effect that a school might have, not only on Hagi but even on the entire nation, if it were based on correct principles, he wrote his opinion in a brief essay entitled the *Shoka Sonjuku-ki.* In it, Shoin's ideas on the purpose of education, reflecting his experiences during the past three years, were clearly expressed. He was later to put these ideas into effect himself when he took over the school:

[41] See pp. 153 ff.
[42] Signifying "Matsumoto Village School"; however, one character in the name of Matsumoto has been altered to make it more elegant.

Study means the learning of that which makes one a man. This school bears the name of the village. If it shall cause the people of the village to enter in Filial Piety and Brotherly Devotion, and to depart in Loyalty and Faithfulness, then in truth it will bring no shame upon the name of the village. . . .

That which has by far the greatest import for a man is *kun-shin no gi* [Duty of lord and subject]. That which has by far the greatest significance for a nation is *ka-i no ben* [discrimination of civilized and barbarian].[43] But what sort of times are prevailing throughout the land? *Kun-shin no gi* has not been considered for some six hundred years; and now, in the present day, *ka-i no ben* has been discarded along with it. . . .

If those born on the soil of the Land of the Gods and favored with the benefactions of the Imperial household, within should lose *kunshin no gi*, and without should forget *ka-i no ben*, wherein could be found the purpose of learning, or that which makes a man a man? [44]

As Shoin had such a deep interest in his uncle's school from its inception, and as most of the school's pupils were receiving informal instruction from him at the same time, it was mutually agreed about a year later to turn the teaching responsibility entirely over to Shoin. A small building on the Sugi family property was remodeled for the purpose, and, with the permission of the *han* government, a new Shoka Sonjuku was opened on December 20, 1857. Because Shoin was still under house arrest, his uncle Gorozaemon remained nominally in charge, and he, as well as Bunnoshin, assisted in the instruction from time to time; but it was recognized by all as being Shoin's school.

The Shoka Sonjuku operated under Shoin's supervision for about one year, corresponding almost exactly with the calendar year 1858. The number of boarding pupils varied from two to nine; including the day pupils, the total enrollment reached about thirty at times, with considerable turnover. Shoin's instruction gained such favorable attention that, beginning in August, he was permitted to add the Yamaga school's courses to his curriculum, and the students soon began military drill and gunnery lessons.

The lectures at the Shoka Sonjuku covered a broad range. More important than subject matter, however, was the spirit

---

[43] For a fuller explanation of this term, see pp. 165–66.
[44] *Shoka Sonjuku-ki*, in YSZ, IV, 178–79.

Shoin infused into his teaching. His main purpose, in accordance with what he had written in the *Shoka Sonjuku-ki*, was to inculcate samurai ideals and arouse loyalty to emperor and nation. Thus, in a letter to Majima Hosen, a pupil whom he left in charge of instruction when he was returned to prison early in 1859, he wrote: "Courage and integrity, the application of Duty —these are the basic principles of the Sonjuku; not merely the reading of books alone." [45]

Just as his material was not limited to books, so Shoin's teaching method was not limited to formal lectures. In place of a professorial attitude, he followed a policy of close intimacy and companionship with his students. Not much older than some of the students, and unprepossessing at first glance, Shoin was frequently mistaken for one of his pupils by those who did not know him, but young and old were immediately impressed and attracted when he spoke.

On the basis of a curriculum planned by himself, and through the application of his own teaching methods, Shoin achieved results little short of incredible. In this entire four-year period, covering one year in prison, two of informal teaching at home, and one of the Shoka Sonjuku, the number receiving instruction from him totaled nearly eighty. Almost every one of these was active in bringing about the Meiji Restoration or in political affairs after the new government was established. His best pupils, those recognized as the leaders of the school, in most cases died before the Restoration. [46] Of those who lived—chiefly the younger ones—between thirty and forty eventually received honors ranging from titles of nobility to court rank. Among them were two prime ministers, Prince Ito Hirobumi and Prince Yamagata Aritomo; a councillor, Kido Koin; [47] and cabinet ministers and ambassadors, such as Count Yamada Akiyoshi, Viscount Shinagawa Yajiro, and Viscount Nomura Yasushi. Since there is no reason to assume that the people of the Hagi area were intrin-

[45] Letter to Majima Hosen (Ansei 6. 1. 4), in *YSZ*, VI, 65–66.

[46] These included Kusaka Genzui, Irie Sugizo, and Yoshida Eitaro, who were killed or committed suicide in connection with skirmishes in Kyoto in 1864; and Takasugi Shinsaku, who died of illness in 1867.

[47] Kido Koin died before the orders of nobility were established, but his family was later ennobled in recognition of his services.

sically more talented than those of other regions, the only possible conclusion is that Shoin possessed a remarkable ability to evoke or instill those traits of character on which he placed chief importance.

During this three-year period of house arrest, Shoin was becoming increasingly anxious and concerned over the trend of national affairs. In September, 1856, through correspondence with Mokurin, he was finally convinced that loyalty to the emperor was the supreme duty, overriding even the obligation of national defense. His acceptance of this opinion, against which he had long argued, was an emotional experience similar to a religious conversion and can best be described as his "illumination." [48] In January, 1857, Umeda Umpin came to visit him. As Shoin's relations with the group around Yanagawa Seigan in Kyoto became more and more intimate, *son-no jo-i* became the topic of greatest interest in his conversations and discussions with friends in Hagi. From this time on, observing the relations between Court and Bakufu from the purely *kokutai* standpoint and without considering the factors of strengthening or weakening the nation strategically, as he had previously, it was easy for Shoin to advance into the active anti-Bakufu sentiment already held by many of his associates. Because of his personality and methods of teaching, it was inevitable that his thinking on national problems should be reflected in the instruction at the Shoka Sonjuku.

The year during which Shoin was operating the school happened to be the same year in which the *tairo*, Ii Naosuke, signed new commercial treaties with the United States, Netherlands, Russia, England, and France, in spite of the Emperor's refusal to grant approval. Shoin wrote a succession of strongly worded memorials and other statements of opinion opposing Bakufu policy, calling for the protection of *kokutai* and a refusal to accept foreign insults. Some of these were submitted to the *hanshu;* some, which he sent to Yanagawa Seigan, reached the attention

[48] Shoin's reading around this time included Yamaga Soko's *Yamaga Gorui, Seikyo Yoroku,* and *Haisho Zampitsu;* Amenomori Hoshu's *Kokuo Shogo Ron;* Yamagata Daini's *Ryushi Shinron;* Motoori Norinaga's *Kojiki Den;* Hirata Atsutane's *Tama-dasuki;* Aizawa Yasushi's *Shinron* and *Kagaku Jigen;* and Fujita Toko's *Kodokan-ki Jutsugi.* For Amenomori Hoshu, see note 16, Chapter 11.

of the Emperor. In the *Taigi wo Gi-su,* addressed to Mori Yoshi-chika on August 21, 1858, Shoin definitely recognized that the shogun had violated the imperial command, and for the first time expressed definite anti-Bakufu sentiment. It was the week after this, when the Shoka Sonjuku was permeated with an atmosphere of patriotic indignation and with Shoin's loyalty to the Emperor, that the military drill and gunnery lessons were inaugurated.

During this year also, Shoin was sending his trusted disciples on more or less secret errands: Katsura Kogoro (later known as Kido Koin) went to Edo; and Kusaka Genzui, to Kyoto. Plans and plots filled the air. A few days after the *Taigi wo Gi-su,* Shoin wrote the *Jigi Ryakuron* ("Brief Discussion of the Duty of the Times"), arguing that if the shogun continued to defy the Emperor, it would become necessary to take up arms in the Emperor's defense. In September, six pupils, including Ito Hirobumi and Yamagata Aritomo, went to Kyoto, and made new contacts. Plans to assassinate Bakufu officials were discussed. A group of samurai from Mito were already attempting to get support for their plot to kill the *tairo*,[49] but Shoin felt Choshu should act on its own, rather than participating in the plans of another *han.*

It was finally decided that the men of Choshu would select as their victim Manabe Akikatsu, a member of the *roju,* who had been sent to Kyoto in October to stamp out loyalist activities and had imprisoned many of Shoin's friends, including Umeda Umpin and Rai Mikisaburo. On December 10, Shoin, with seventeen friends and pupils, took an oath for the assassination of Akikatsu, and Shoin wrote a farewell letter addressed jointly to his father, uncle Bunnoshin, and brother.[50] Plans were completed, and the conspirators decided to leave for Kyoto on January 18. Whereas in other cases such plots were private affairs,

[49] Successfully consummated a year and a half later, March 24, 1860: the Sakurada-mon incident.

[50] The original copy of this letter is one of the objects now composing the *shintai* or *mitama-shiro* (spirit-substitute, or object of worship) at the Shoin shrine in Hagi.

Shoin wrote to one of the *han* officials, requesting assistance. As a result, he was returned to Noyama prison on January 8, 1859, and many of his accomplices were also imprisoned or placed under house arrest.

Shoin considered this plot as the fourth in his series of courageous acts.

Final Imprisonment and Execution

During this second imprisonment at Noyama, which lasted about six months, Shoin continued to encourage his pupils to carry out various schemes and, without success, urged his lord Yoshichika openly to support the Emperor. In May, Sakuma Zozan's nephew, Kitayama Yasuyo, came to Hagi and was able to meet Shoin secretly at night on two occasions. Finally, an official message from the Bakufu arrived, ordering Shoin to Edo for trial. He was permitted to spend the last night before his departure at home with his parents; returning to prison and leaving for Edo on June 25 he considered to be his fifth act of courage. His attitude still remained as he had expressed it in February, in a letter to his brother-in-law: "Have I not told [my friends and pupils] how one should die for his country, neither shunning misfortune and failure nor considering whether he is wise or foolish? Now it is such a case." [51]

After several months at Demma-cho prison, in the course of which he was often questioned by officials but was never given the opportunity to discuss what to him were the significant issues, Shoin was informed in November that he had only a few days to live. On November 19 and 20, he wrote the *Ryukonroku* ("Record of an Everlasting Soul"), his last will and testament, giving his views on the inadequacy of the Bakufu trial procedure, regretting his failure to impress the officials either with his sincerity or with the urgent needs of the times, and expressing the hope that his friends would carry on: "My fervent prayer is that you, the friends who share my aspirations, heroically taking over

---

[51] Letter to Odamura Inosuke (Ansei 6. 1. 12), in *YSZ*, VI, 79.

my purpose, may indeed render distinguished services in the cause of *sonjo*." [52, 53]

On November 21, 1859, Shoin was executed. Two days later, his body was buried by a group of pupils including Ito Hirobumi and Katsura Kogoro (Kido Koin).

[52] Shoin's personal abbreviation of *son-no jo-i, sonjo,* was used frequently in his later writings. The meaning is approximately "loyalty and patriotism in action."

[53] *Ryukonroku,* in *YSZ,* VII, 326.

8

Formative Influences on Shoin's Thought

THE ALL-CONSUMING patriotism that became the most compelling ideal in Shoin's life grew out of his familiarity with a variety of philosophies and opinions. In attempting to analyze his thought, or to break it down into the original sources on which it was based, we are aided by the fact that for almost one year, Shoin had responsible direction over the Shoka Sonjuku. We may reasonably assume that the curriculum he established and taught there included the elements he considered to be of fundamental importance.

According to the account of his pupil Amano Gomin,[1] written in 1897, the instruction at Shoin's school could be classified under three main headings:

[1] *Shoka Sonjuku Reiwa,* in *Yoshida Shoin Zenshu* (hereafter cited as YSZ), XII (Tokyo: Iwanami Shoten, 1938–40), 187–200.

(1) Classical: Here, Shoin's frame of reference was basically Chu Hsi, but he used many other materials, including Wang Yang-ming, Ito Jinsai, and Ogyu Sorai, and mixed them with his own observations and comments, accepting and rejecting elements in each.

(2) National and Historical: In Japanese studies, he relied chiefly on Motoori Norinaga's *Kojiki Den,* but he also used the writings of the Mito school and unofficial histories such as those of Rai Sanyo.

(3) Information on the West: He used all Western works then available in translation, as well as Chinese books on world geography.

This broad selection of material resulted partly from Shoin's own intellectual curiosity and integrity, which did not permit him to be bound by any one school of thought, and partly from the wide number of stimuli and scholastic experiences to which he had been exposed. These influences, which formed the foundation for his political philosophy, also exemplify the strangely confused crosscurrents of the late Tokugawa intellectual world.

Classical and Confucian Influence

Shoin's basic—as distinguished from military—education was dominated by the influence of his father, Sugi Yurinosuke, and his uncle, Tamaki Bunnoshin. His father taught him the Four Books and Five Classics; his uncle grounded him in Shushigaku. He learned the importance of *taigi meibun* from both; and, in his father's teaching especially, loyalty to the imperial household was stressed. Among the Four Books, his favorite, which he began to study at the age of seven, was *Mencius.*

In later years when he himself taught the classics, Shoin relied chiefly on Chu Hsi's commentaries, using them as a starting point for either criticism or supplementation. This is very clear in the *Komo Yowa,* the series of lectures on *Mencius* that he gave in 1855–56. Although occasionally saying that Chu Hsi should not be accepted, sometimes quoting other writers to correct or add to Chu Hsi's explanation, it is obvious that the Chu Hsi commentary is the base from which he is working. But while Shoin may be considered as essentially a follower of Shushigaku, it was in no sense a slavish acceptance; his opinion on the classics was perhaps 70 to 80 per cent in accordance with Chu Hsi.[2]

Shoin's views on the orthodox transmission of Confucianism display his own unorthodox tendency. After explaining that the orthodox line ran from Yao and Shun, via Chou Kung and Confucius, to Mencius, where it was broken, he names various writers of the Sung period, including Chu Hsi, and suggests: "But since among them, Master Ming-tao was pre-eminent in virtue, it is not impossible to consider that he continued the line of Confucius and Mencius."[3]

In thus ranking the elder of the Ch'eng brothers above Chu Hsi, Shoin revealed the independence of thought that made it impossible for him to be a complete follower of Shushigaku, regardless of the predominant influence it exerted on him.

Shoin was familiar with some writings of the Yomei school at least from the age of eighteen or nineteen, and on his trip to Hirado in 1850, he read Wang Yang-ming's *Ch'uan-hsi Lu*. As Hayama Sanai had been a pupil of Sato Issai,[4] he had an appreciation for Yomeigaku that he was able to pass on to the young Shoin. Shoin was particularly susceptible to Yomei influence because of similarities between his own background and personality and those of Wang Yang-ming. Like Wang Yang-ming, he was interested in military affairs, favored the practical application of learning, concerned himself with current national problems, and tended to introspective, subjective thinking. It was not strange that the "unity of knowledge and action" should appeal to him.

In any case, Shoin did not feel that Shushi and Yomei thought were mutually exclusive; rather, taking Chu Hsi's teaching of

[2] This estimate is given in Kumura, *Yoshida Shoin no Shiso to Kyoiku* (Tokyo: Iwanami Shoten, 1942), p. 55.

[3] *Komo Yowa*, Book IV, Part III, in *YSZ*, III, 511. The reference is to Ch'eng Ming-tao (Ch'eng Hao), one of Chu Hsi's forerunners in the Neo-Confucian school.

[4] See below, note 27.

self-development for his basis, he freely used Yomei theory as a supplement. He made his stand clear in a letter written during the last year of his life:

> I once read Wang Yang-ming's *Ch'uan-hsi Lu,* and I feel it is full of significance. . . . [He also mentions other Yomei works he has studied.] Nevertheless, I have not made a concentrated study of Yomeigaku only. It is merely that what that school holds to be true not infrequently agrees with my own conception of truth.[5]

Shoin was, in fact, not interested in upholding one school of thought as against another; he preferred to apply the teachings of the sages to the environment in which he found himself. Above all, he prized the instructions from the *Great Learning:* "exemplify illustrious virtue" and "fashion a new people." Interpreting these maxims as demanding respectively the training of the self and the training of others, Shoin considered them the twin foundations of scholarship.

Tested by such criteria, the sages themselves were not necessarily ideal examples. When starting his lectures on *Mencius,* his first words were:

> In reading the classics, the point of fundamental importance is not to adulate the sages. If one feels even the slightest trace of adulation, the Way will not become clear; and even though one studies, in place of profit he will receive harm.[6]

As an example, he pointed out that both Confucius and Mencius had committed unpardonable crimes against loyalty by leaving the lands of their birth to serve other rulers. Later in the same work, returning to this theme, he condemned Shun for having married without his parents' consent, and Mencius for having excused Shun's action. As the sages themselves did not measure up to the ideals they taught, their actions could not be taken as models.

Beyond this, Shoin constantly warned against worship of China. Like many others, from Yamazaki Ansai down to the

---

[5] Letter to Irie Sugizo (Ansei 6. 1. 27), in *YSZ,* VI, 122.
[6] *Komo Yowa,* Book I, in *YSZ,* III, 18.

Mito school, he believed that a true understanding of Chinese thought must necessarily lead to patriotism for one's own country. In his lectures on Yamaga Soko's *Bukyo Shogaku*, after explaining that a true investigation of *li* would lead one to distinguish between domestic and foreign, he said:

If, for example, because of reading Chinese books, one should yearn for China and forget his own land, or should revere the ancient sage-kings of China and neglect the Divine Holy Ones of his own land, all such results represent the evil of not thoroughly investigating *li*.[7]

On the other hand, even when patriotism overshadowed all else in his thinking, Shoin never abandoned the Confucian foundation. In a letter written from prison in Edo one week before his execution, he said:

While it is indeed essential to investigate the legitimacy of scholarly theories, it is completely useless to take sides either with Shushigaku or Yomeigaku. Making the four characters *"son-no jo-i"* our objective, we must take the good points from the writings, or from the school of thought, of anyone whatsoever. The school of Motoori [Norinaga] and the Mito school are quite dissimilar, but in the two words *son* and *jo* both are identical. Hirata [Atsutane], again, differs from Motoori; while he also has many defects, works such as the *Shutsujo Shogo* and *Tama-dasuki* are excellent. Among the Kanto [Edo] scholars, from Doshun [Hayashi Razan] on, Arai [Hakuseki], Muro [Kyuso], [Ogyu] Sorai, [Dazai] Shundai, and others all flattered the Bakufu, yet in them there are still a few points worth taking. And even though a man like Ito Jinsai was not distinguished for his *son-no*, his scholarship is profitable to a person, not harmful.[8]

National and Historical Influence

Shoin's gradual awakening to the importance of history as a factor in patriotism has already been mentioned. His familiarity with the works of the Kokugaku school, at least in the later years of his life, may be judged from the quotation just cited. He also knew of Rai Sanyo's *Nihon Gaishi* from boyhood. However, Shoin's earliest interest in this field, rather than being

---

[7] *Bukyo Zensho Koroku*, in YSZ, IV, 213.
[8] Letter to Irie Sugizo (Ansei 6. 10. 20), in YSZ, IX, 488.

strictly historical, lay in analyzing accounts of battles from the standpoint of military theory. At the same time, the Bushido aspect of Yamaga Soko's teachings appealed strongly to him, so that Soko may be viewed as the first great influence in shaping his character.

Although Shoin paid little attention to Soko as a Confucianist, he eventually came to have a strong appreciation for such writings as the *Chucho Jijitsu* and *Haisho Zampitsu*. Thus, his admiration for Soko, whom he always called his "departed master," was based partly on Soko's teaching of Bushido and partly on his role as a patriotic historian. In the opening remarks of his lectures on the *Bukyo Shogaku* Shoin explains why he places particular faith in the writings of his departed master. He cites Soko's ideal of "constant preparedness"; mentions the inspiration that his teaching gave Oishi Yoshio, the leader of the forty-seven loyal samurai of Ako; and, as his third point, says:

> My departed master, born into a world of vulgar Confucianists who adored a foreign country and despised their own land, alone rose above them, rejected heretical arguments, investigated the divine and holy Way of antiquity, and wrote the *Chucho Jijitsu*.[9]

In his own teaching of Bushido, Shoin, like Soko, emphasized that the ultimate duty of the samurai was to the emperor, and he added much material on *kokutai* when lecturing on Soko's principles.

The term *kokutai* was known to Shoin and had appeared in his writings even before he first left Choshu-*han,* and he had been trained by his father in loyalty and patriotism from his earliest years; but his real appreciation for the special characteristics of Japan and the importance of its national history was the direct result of his trip to Mito. For this reason, his personal exposure to Mito thought and argument marked a definite turning point in Shoin's intellectual development and must be ranked, after Yamaga Soko, as the second great influence in his life. Shoin described the impact of his Mito experience as follows:

[9] *Bukyo Zensho Koroku,* in *YSZ,* IV, 208.

Last winter when I visited Mito, I met Aizawa [Yasushi] and Toyoda [Tenko] for the first time. As I listened to them speak, I said miserably: "Born in the Imperial Land, if I am ignorant of that which makes it the Imperial Land, how can I face Heaven or Earth?" [10] On my return home, I immediately took up the *Rik-kokushi* [11] and read them.[12]

Thus motivated to study anew the national history, Shoin was especially impressed by the contrast between the dominant and aggressive policy of ancient Japan and the current attitude of the Bakufu. The indignation that this discovery aroused in him was to form an integral part of his outlook. History became for him a source of patriotic inspiration, its practical importance greater than that of the classics.

In a letter of early 1855 to his brother Umetaro, written from Noyama prison after the failure of his attempts to go abroad, Shoin discussed the relative merits of history and the classics:

I do not completely disagree with your suggestion that what is not based on the classics should not be called scholarship. [Sakuma] Zozan is a classical scholar, and when I was formerly studying under him, he told me time after time that I must read the *Analects* thoroughly. At that time I disagreed strongly. When I would say that for the rapid awakening of loyal spirit, nothing compared with the reading of history and knowing the deeds of those who excelled in wisdom, Zozan would reply, "Error may result from that." [13]

He had also received similar advice from Yokoi Shonan when he was in Kumamoto, Shoin continued; and he had a fair knowledge of Shushigaku:

Nevertheless, I cannot help feeling that its value can not be compared with that found in studying history. Long ago, Confucius himself, considering that actual occurrences were more pleasant and clear

[10] An obvious reflection of one of Yasushi's arguments. See p. 89.

[11] The "Six National Histories"—the official records of the most ancient period, beginning with the *Nihon Shoki*.

[12] Letter to Kurihara Ryozo (Kaei 5, about 6th or 7th month), in *YSZ*, VII, 352.

[13] Letter to Sugi Umetaro (Ansei 2. 1. x), in *YSZ*, VIII, 403–4.

than mere words, wrote the *Spring and Autumn Annals*. . . . This being so, for quickening the heart and nurturing the spirit, in the final analysis there is nothing comparable to the actual facts concerning those who excel in wisdom.[14]

Eventually, Japanese history took on such significance for Shoin that he even regretted the excessive amount of time he had spent on Chinese literature. In 1859, he wrote: "As a child, being completely and exclusively immersed in Chinese works, I was extremely negligent with regard to the august Imperial Land; . . . I feel a good deal of shame on this account."[15] However, his interest in Japanese history did not mean that he ignored Chinese; nor did he ever go so far as to say that the study of the classics was unnecessary. In closing the letter of 1855 to his brother, Shoin wrote that he had recently been very busy, reading not only Rai Sanyo's *Nihon Gaishi* (Japanese history), but Asami Keisai's *Seiken Igen* (heroic examples taken from Chinese history), and the *Mean* and *Great Learning* as well.

After visiting Mito, Shoin's newly aroused interest in history extended beyond history itself, and included a desire to familiarize himself with the specific teachings of the Mito school, as set forth in such works as the *Shinron* and the *Kodokan-ki Jutsugi*. For example, during December, 1853, while traveling by boat from Choshu to Osaka with Miyabe Teizo and another friend, he took a copy of the *Shinron* with him to read and discuss on the voyage. Gradually, Shoin's viewpoint came more and more to resemble that of the Mito school. While he always reserved his own freedom of thought—particularly his inability to accept the extreme anti-Buddhist opinions of the Mito scholars—it does not seem out of character for him to have remarked: "I agree strongly with the teachings of Mito. In my opinion, the Way of the Land of the Gods lies therein."[16] During the last two or three years of Shoin's life, the *Shinron* was the book probably mentioned most frequently in his voluminous correspondence.

[14] *Ibid.*, pp. 404–5.
[15] *Zagoku Nichiroku*, in *YSZ*, VII, 257.
[16] *Komo Yowa*, Book IV, Part III, in *YSZ*, III, 479.

Attitude Toward Buddhism

Opposition to Buddhism had been an element of Tokugawa political thought from the time of Hayashi Razan; it was especially noticeable in the writings of Kokugaku and the Mito school. One of the chief reasons for this was the close connection between loyalty to the emperor and Shinto belief. Buddhism, because of its weakening or reinterpreting pure faith in the emperor as the lineal descendant of Amaterasu, was thought to be fundamentally unpatriotic. Furthermore, from the Confucian standpoint Buddhism was mistrusted because it denied the importance of the physical life and minimized or negated the responsibilities involved in the Five Relationships.

For such reasons, Shoin, in accepting Confucianism as well as Japanese tradition, necessarily displayed disapproval toward Buddhism, but his attitude was much milder than that of Kokugaku or the Mito school. His condemnation of the effects of Buddhism did not extend to its followers: his favorite sister, Chiyo, was an ardent Buddhist, and Shoin remained on good terms with an uncle on his mother's side, a priest by the name of Chikuin. His lack of intolerance was shown also in his close friendship with the two priests Gessho and Mokurin.

In an 1854 letter to Chiyo, after explaining the importance of believing in the gods, he wrote: "Furthermore, there is no necessity for believing in Buddha. But neither is it entirely desirable to go contrary to others and revile Buddha." [17] Five years later, writing to his sister again on the same subject, he discussed basic Buddhist beliefs with sympathy and understanding; he stated that he had read the Lotus Sutra and he appreciated her faith in Kannon (Avalokitesvara) but that absolute faith in the gods of Japan was more desirable.[18]

Shoin's chief objection to Buddhism was its deleterious effect on the popular understanding of *kokutai*. An early illustration of this viewpoint occurred in March, 1853. Traveling by boat through the Inland Sea, Shoin went ashore on Shikoku near

[17] Letter to Kodama Chiyo (Ansei 1. 12. 3), in *YSZ*, VIII, 322.
[18] Letter to Kodama Chiyo (Ansei 6. 4. 13), in *YSZ*, IX, 337–43.

the present city of Kotohira. This is famed as the birthplace of Kobo Daishi, while in the same vicinity is the grave of Emperor Sutoku (reigned 1123–41). Shoin was saddened to find that although everyone he spoke to knew of Kobo Daishi, many did not know the name of the emperor buried there. A poem he wrote on this occasion included the line: "The rise of Buddhism was the decline of the Imperial Way." [19]

In the following year, when compiling the appendix of the *Yushuroku,* Shoin included a comment on Buddhism's entering Japan in 552:

The damage caused to us by Buddhism is obviously very great. However, the scriptures, for example, should not be indiscriminately discarded. What is to be deplored is only the failure to be informed on topics of current importance and the not knowing how to make a selection. If, because an evil doctrine leads the masses astray, we should commit the error of becoming intimate with foreign countries, this would be a mistake.[20]

That the useful elements of Buddhism should be distinguished from the harmful was mentioned again in the *Komo Yowa.* After remarking that he could not accept the anti-Buddhist position of the Mito school, since, after thirteen hundred years in Japan, Buddhist belief had a definite hold on the hearts of the people, Shoin said:

I should like to write an essay on the harm done by Buddhism, citing in evidence the cases of damage caused by it in ancient and modern times in itemized sequence, and showing that if these harmful elements were completely eliminated, as a result Buddhism would naturally be profitable to the country. But as yet I have not had the leisure.[21]

In the last year of his life, Shoin went so far as to give a qualified assent to Buddhism. When one of his favorite pupils wrote that he was planning to become a Buddhist priest, Shoin ap-

[19] *Kichu Yureki Nichiroku,* in *YSZ,* X, 351. For the connection this had with Kobo Daishi, see Appendix C.

[20] *Yushuroku,* in *YSZ,* I, 361.

[21] *Komo Yowa,* Book IV, Part III, in *YSZ,* III, 479.

proved his intention, saying that even among priests, "there are those who feel reverence for the emperor. In the teaching of Zen also, there is something which serves to fix the resolution of the heart; this too is profitable." [22]

Shoin's attitude toward Buddhism was not typical of the nationalistic scholars whose theories he followed in general. It is probable that his opinion was closer to that of the people, so that in a sense his position was more representative than that of the scholars. The failure of the official anti-Buddhist policy followed by the early Meiji government would seem to bear this out.

Influence of Sakuma Zozan

During the course of his lectures on *Mencius,* in 1855, Shoin said:

In studying the learning of Europe and America, to adore and idolize the barbarians . . . must be rejected absolutely. But the barbarians' artillery and shipbuilding, their knowledge of medicine, and of physical sciences, can all be of use to us—these should properly be adopted. . . .

When I was desirous of going to America, my teacher Zozan said to me: "If this duty were to be undertaken by one who was not possessed of a firm aspiration for loyalty, one who did not recognize the obligation resulting from the benefactions [*on*] of the nation, it would unfailingly lead to great harm. Truly you are fitted for this responsibility." [23]

Shoin's approval of the adoption of Western technology and science and his refusal to admit anything that might alter the Japanese spirit were, of course, harmonious with Mitogaku. However, in their fear of Christianity, Nariaki and Fujita Toko eventually recommended prohibiting even the study of science; and Shoin could never accept such an extreme position. In this regard, his thinking was shaped by Sakuma Zozan, whose teaching must be considered as the third great influence in the formation of Shoin's philosophy. As Shoin himself wrote, "I took Taira

[22] Letter to Irie Sugizo (Ansei 6. 1. 27), in *YSZ,* VI, 120.
[23] *Komo Yowa,* Book II, in *YSZ,* III, 136–37.

[Sakuma] Zozan for my teacher, thoroughly accepted his special theories, and made my decisions in all things accordingly." [24]

Shoin had originally enrolled in Zozan's school during the summer of 1851, but at that time Zozan was only one of three teachers from whom he was receiving instruction, and Zozan's "special theories" were by no means his chief interest. It was not until Commodore Perry forced the Bakufu to accept diplomatic correspondence at Kurihama, and the weakness of Japan's military situation suddenly became apparent, that Shoin turned decisively to Zozan's teachings as the only salvation for Japan. The intensity of his feeling and the radical change in his outlook occasioned by the demands of the United States were reflected in a letter to his brother:

Sakuma Zozan is the hero of the present day; he is the one man of all in the capital. . . . Along with patriotic indignation, spirit and principle, he is possessed of scholarship and discernment. Men like Fujimori, Shiodani, and Hagura all know *kokutai;* but Zozan is the man above all others who comprehends *taigi.*

[Asaka] Konsai [25] is a vulgar Confucianist; I detest him exceedingly; I will positively never enter his door again. Men like Hayashi [Fukusai],[26] [Sato] Issai,[27] and Tsutsui [Masanori] [28] are all vulgar

[24] *Yushuroku,* in *YSZ,* I, 340.

[25] At this time, Asaka Konsai was one of the most respected teachers of Edo (see note 10, Chapter 7). Only two years previously, Shoin had written: "Konsai is a distinguished scholar, who excels in the classics and literature. He leads his pupils on with great patience." (Letter to Nakamura Michitaro, Kaei 4. 6. x, in *YSZ,* II, 125.)

[26] Hayashi Fukusai (1800–59), the head of the Shoheiko, was appointed by the Bakufu the following year as a special diplomatic agent in charge of the negotiations that eventuated in the Treaty of Kanagawa. Due to Perry's insistence that he would treat with none but the highest authorities, Fukusai was represented as holding a rank only one degree lower than that of the shogun. The Americans, misinterpreting his title "Head of the University," believed him to be the "prince of Daigaku." See Francis L. Hawks, *Narrative of the Expedition of an American Squadron to the China Seas and Japan* (Washington, D.C.: A. O. P. Nicholson, 1856), pp. 335, 342.

[27] Sato Issai (1772–1859) had taught for many years at the Shoheiko, and Asaka Konsai and Sakuma Zozan were both among his students. While he was officially classified as a follower of Shushigaku because of the regulations, his inward adherence to Yomei thought was an open

Confucianists advocating a conciliatory policy; Konsai too is necessarily of the same sort.[29]

From this time on, Shoin frequented Zozan's home day and night, and their relation became like that of father and son. In order to understand Shoin's thought and actions after 1853, it is essential to know something of Zozan.

Sakuma Zozan (Shuri) (1811–64), a samurai of Matsushiro-*han* in Shinano province, northwest of Edo, received a standard literary education, the last three years of which were under Sato Issai. In 1839, he opened a school of classical studies, in which he emphasized Shushi over Yomei, although remaining on friendly terms with his teacher, Issai. Within a short time he had established a reputation as one of the leading younger scholars of Edo.

Not content with classical learning, Zozan determined to master Western science and technology, which were then being studied through the medium of the Dutch language. In the fall of 1842, he entered the school of Egawa Tarozaemon, the leading exponent of Western military science and gunnery. Almost at the same time, his *hanshu,* Sanada Yukitsura, was given a coastal-defense assignment by the Bakufu. As his personal adviser, Zozan prepared a memorial of detailed proposals for defense, which he submitted to the daimyo at the end of 1842.[30] This document significantly demonstrates that the advanced nature of Zozan's views did not entail abandoning fundamental principles.

Zozan opened the memorial by pointing out that a foreign invasion would endanger not merely the position of the Tokugawa family but that of the imperial house itself, unique among all

secret, and most of his pupils were more or less affected by the Yomei viewpoint.

[28] Tsutsui Masanori (1778–1859) was an important Bakufu official, for many years one of the two *machi-bugyo* (governors) of Edo. Later in this same year (1853), he was one of the two ministers plenipotentiary sent by the Bakufu to Nagasaki to negotiate with the Russian Admiral Putiatin.

[29] Letter to Sugi Umetaro (Kaei 6. 9. 15), in *YSZ,* VIII, 215–16.

[30] Memorial of Tempo 13. 11, in Tokushige Asakichi, *Ishin Seishin Shi Kenkyu* (Kyoto: Ritsumeikan Shuppambu, 1934), pp. 166–68.

the countries of the world, having continued without interruption for a hundred generations; and that the problem was therefore a matter of concern to the whole nation. He then made eight proposals:

(1) Fortify and set up gun emplacements at the coastal points of greatest danger throughout the country.

(2) Temporarily suspend the export of copper to the Netherlands; manufacture large cannon.

(3) Build large Western-style ships to insure the shipment of rice to Edo without loss from shipwrecks.

(4) Appoint marine shipping inspectors to check on foreign ship movements and prevent piracy.

(5) Build Western-style warships and practice naval maneuvers.

(6) Establish schools in all parts of the country to teach Loyalty, Filial Piety, and Duty.

(7) Introduce governmental reforms, to obtain popular support by clarifying reward and punishment.

(8) Provide for the promotion of talented and capable men to positions where they can be of service to the nation.

The importance of this memorial lies in the fact that the ideas contained therein were the foundation of Zozan's teaching in later years, when he had thousands of pupils. Similar or identical proposals are found throughout Shoin's writings of the 1850's.

Zozan received his diploma from Egawa Tarozaemon in 1843 and in the summer of 1844 took up residence in the home of Kurokawa Ryoan, a leading scholar of Dutch and Western science. Within less than a year, he was able to read and explain Dutch texts on natural and applied sciences, military science, and gunnery. During the next few years he continued to study Dutch, and performed technical and scientific experiments, in all of which he showed amazing proficiency. For example, following instructions in Dutch texts, he constructed a camera and all necessary photographic equipment, mixed the required chemicals, and, with the help of a servant he had trained, took his own photograph.[31] In 1849, he compiled a new Japanese-

[31] Zozan's photographic self-portrait has been frequently reproduced, and may be seen in almost any book on his life or thought.

Dutch dictionary. He experimented with the casting of cannon; starting with small sizes in 1848, in the spring of 1851 he first successfully fired a fifty-pounder. It was later in this year that Shoin enrolled as his pupil.

Prior to this time, Zozan had opened a new school in Edo, with a curriculum based jointly on the classics and Western science, both of which he insisted were essential. With regard to the way in which his own knowledge had gradually broadened, he later wrote:

By the time I was twenty, I knew that men were joined together in one province; by the time I was thirty, I knew that they were joined together in the nation; by the time I was forty, I knew that they were joined together in the five continents.[32]

The popularity of Zozan's curriculum in the critical period of the 1850's was such that he is said to have enrolled fifteen thousand pupils, although it is questionable how many of these could have received his personal attention.

With the arrival of Perry in 1853, Zozan was appointed military adviser for Matsushiro-*han*. Shortly afterwards, he submitted a memorial of urgent proposals; the most important new suggestion was that regardless of whether peace or war was to result from the talks with the American representatives, young men of talent should be sent abroad immediately to investigate conditions in foreign countries, purchase large ships through the good offices of the Dutch, and learn navigation. If this proposal were to be accepted, Shoin naturally hoped to be among those chosen.

On Perry's return early in 1854, Matsushiro-*han*—together with Kokura-*han*—was assigned to coastal-defense duty in the Yokohama area, and Zozan took up residence there in connection with his supervisory duties. During this time, it was decided to open Shimoda as a treaty port. Zozan strenuously opposed this: in his opinion, Shimoda was the Cape of Good Hope of Japan—much too valuable to run the risk of foreign seizure. If it should be occupied by foreign troops, it would be very difficult

---

[32] *Seikenroku.* Quoted in Tokushige, *Ishin Seishin,* p. 166.

to recapture. He recommended Yokohama as far superior in every way: as it was close to Edo, keeping watch on the foreigners' activities there would be simple; it would be convenient for trade; and, if the foreigners should attempt an attack on Edo from the sea, it would make little difference whether their ships were based on Shimoda or Yokohama. Zozan's patriotism was no less than that of Nariaki and Fujita Toko; but because he advocated the opening of ports, he became labeled in the popular mind as a proponent of *kaikoku* (open country), a term applied by the *shishi* faction to what they considered the weak, conciliatory policy of the Bakufu.[33]

When it was discovered that he was implicated in Shoin's attempt to go abroad, Zozan's responsible position did not help him, and he was arrested immediately. Like Shoin, sentenced to house arrest and placed in the custody of his *hanshu* in November, 1854, it was nine years later before Zozan regained his freedom.

Although invited to enter the employment of both Choshu and Tosa early in 1863, Zozan refused; the following year, he was appointed military and naval adviser to the Emperor, and he moved to Kyoto. He had several personal audiences with Emperor Komei and continued to argue for introducing Western technology, opening ports, and improving coastal defense. He had been in Kyoto only a little over three months when he was murdered by two samurai of Choshu because of his allegedly unpatriotic *kaikoku* views.

In short, Zozan proposed using Western techniques to build up the strength of Japan and make it one of the great powers of the world. His goal was not distinguishably different from that of the Mito school, but his methods were radical while theirs were conservative. It was his hope to unite "Eastern ethics" with "Western arts"; he interpreted Chu Hsi's instruction to "investigate *li*" as meaning the study of natural philosophy, not metaphysics. Thus, where Mito united Confucianism with Shinto, Zozan united it with science: this was the fundamental distinction between their *jo-i* and his *kaikoku*. Zozan had little interest in

---

[33] Shoin's detailed account of Zozan's arguments may be found in the *Yushuroku*. See *YSZ*, I, 335-37.

history and had no use for Kokugaku. Shoin, by accepting Zozan's ideas without abandoning Mito or Kokugaku, had to bridge the gap between the national-historical viewpoint and that of Western science as interpreted by Japanese scholars.

Opposition of Yamagata Taika

In considering the many and varied influences on Shoin's thought, it would be a serious error to suppose that he developed a nationalist, patriotic philosophy because he was not exposed to any other viewpoint. As a matter of fact, he was thoroughly familiar with the Hayashi-official school and its support of the Bakufu. In Choshu, this was represented by Yamagata Taika, the former head of the Meirinkan. Taika had retired because of old age before Shoin developed his personal philosophy, but he was still intellectually vigorous and continued to dominate the atmosphere of the school. Taika had studied at the Shoeheiko and had a wide reputation, not limited to Choshu, as a true Shushi scholar. Taika and Shoin felt a reciprocal respect for each other's personality, and completely refused to accept each other's thinking; students at the Meirinkan were forbidden to read Shoin's writings until 1863, four years after his execution.

Despite, or perhaps because of, their fundamental differences, Shoin sent his *Komo Yowa* to Taika for criticism, section by section, as it was completed; after receiving Taika's replies, in many cases he wrote rebuttals. The comments on both sides were so extensive that this debate takes up almost one hundred pages in the *Yoshida Shoin Zenshu*. Thus there can be no doubt whatsoever that Shoin knew Taika's viewpoint as well as he did his own. Both wrote frankly and even pungently, without attempting superficial politeness. For example, in deriding Shoin's attachment to Mito, Taika brought up the statements in the *Shinron* to the effect that Japan is the place of the sun's origin, the source of vital force, and so forth; he continued:

As I have mentioned previously, the sun is considerably larger than the earth; it makes the circuit of the outer heavens once every day and night, and without the slightest pause illumines every country of the world. How then should it come forth from our land? If one is to say it comes forth from the east, to the east of our country lies the continent of America. East of America are the various countries of the Western world. Heaven and earth are spherical in form; how shall East and West be fixed points? . . . Furthermore, to say that the earth is like a body, of which our country corresponds to the head—this is an excessively childish opinion, laughable in the extreme.[34]

Without attempting to enter into the details of Taika's and Shoin's mutual disagreement, Taika's position on three major topics is presented below in his own words, to indicate the sort of thinking that Shoin knowingly and purposefully opposed. The bulk of this material is taken from an unpublished manuscript apparently written between the middle of 1856 and the middle of 1859, made available to the present writer through the kindness of Dr. Kumura Toshio. This manuscript, *Ima no Sho-Ko O-Shin ni Arazaru no Ben* ("That the Present Daimyos are not Vassals of the Emperor"), summarized Taika's position on the relationship between emperor and shogun, with theoretical and historical arguments.

According to Taika, there was no doubt that the shogun, rather than the emperor, possessed sovereignty over Japan. Stating that the shogun's authority could not be explained by the Chinese "Way of the Overlord" theory, he said:

The shogun of our land is in no sense similar to this. He is not the ruler of one province. He is the lord of all the territory and people within the four seas. Thus, whereas by the power of the emperor not one foot or inch of land can be bestowed or withdrawn, the shogun by his own free will bestows land upon those who are meritorious and deprives of their domains those who transgress. Furthermore, the power to bestow favors upon all the people of the land according to his own desire is completely in his own hands. From the Imperial Court down, within the four seas one and all obey his ordinances [*hatto*]; there is no refusal whatsoever. . . .

The officials of Ming China designated the Ashikaga shoguns as *Nihon Kokuo*; again, in correspondence with Korea, the shogun was styled sometimes *Nihon Kokuo* and sometimes *Nihon Koku Taikun*. The significance of this is, that in all these cases the using of such titles accorded with the facts.[35]

[34] *Komo Yowa*, Appendix, in *YSZ*, III, 607.

[35] *Ima no Sho-Ko O-Shin ni Arazaru no Ben* (Manuscript book; copy dated 1859).

The shogun's right to rule was based by Taika squarely on the Mandate of Heaven:

A certain person [i.e., Shoin] says: "But then, who gave him this power?"

Did the emperor grant this power? I reply, No! Or if one says, Did the daimyos grant this power?—again I reply, No! The emperor did not grant it; the daimyos did not grant it; but it was just as Mencius said: "That which is done without man's doing it is from Heaven." [36] —and without any person to grant it, this power of its own accord is in his hands. The emperor himself can not deprive him of this power; and when we consider that not only can he not deprive him of it, but that furthermore, from the emperor down, within the four seas one and all obey his law with absolutely no objection—if Heaven did not bestow this power, then who did? What Heaven has bestowed, not even the Son of Heaven can take away.[37]

In addition to thus using the Mandate of Heaven theory to justify the original assumption of power by the shogun, at other times Taika used it in a corollary sense, to argue against any change in the *status quo*. In his criticism of the *Komo Yowa,* he voiced strong objection to the activities of the *shishi* group—going from village to village, making personal contacts, arousing a military spirit, as if preparing some kind of a plot:

Thus it appears that now, making an occasion of insults from the Americans, they are plotting suddenly to raise troops, and taking advantage of this disturbance, to inflame kindred spirits and achieve the exploit of a Restoration. If so, this is ignorance of the Mandate of Heaven. In heaven and earth the force of time brings various changes and alterations; which is to say that Heaven is beyond the influence of human power. For this reason, there is no possible course other than that of resignation to the Mandate of Heaven. If one is not resigned to the Mandate of Heaven and attempts to win against it by human strength, he may instead bring about an overwhelming calamity. This we may know from the cases of Emperors Go-Toba and Go-Daigo.[38]

On the question of loyalty, and whether shogun or emperor was the proper object of Duty, Taika's explanation uninten-

[36] *Mencius,* Book V, Part I, chap. vi, 2. This quotation is according to Legge's translation.

[37] *Ima no Sho-Ko.*

[38] *Komo Yowa,* Appendix, in *YSZ,* III, 592–93.

tionally illustrates the curious dilemma faced by supporters of the Bakufu in the mid-nineteenth century, when the theory of *kokutai* was rapidly gaining strength:

As the emperor is the Great Lord of our country, it goes without saying that not only the various daimyos, but everyone, from the shogun above to the officials and people of the many *han* below, must hold him in reverence and awe.

But if one is to speak of Duty between lord and subject: Since the establishment of feudalism there are vassals of the emperor; there are vassals of the shogun; there are vassals of the daimyos; and there are vassals of the leading samurai. Each devotes himself in loyalty to his own lord, and it cannot be that any has two hearts [i.e., serves two masters]. Thus, supposing that there is such a thing as responsibility to the Imperial family, this is to be known only by the emperor's own vassals [i.e., court nobles], and it must also be carried out by the exertions of those daimyos who have already been assigned to the defense of the Imperial Court by the orders of the Bakufu. It is not the responsibility of any other daimyos, nor of their retainers, unless they receive the order of the Bakufu; in which case they must serve the interests of the emperor in obedience to the Bakufu's command.

But when the vassals of the shogun exert themselves in loyal service only to the shogun, and the vassals of the daimyos demonstrate their loyalty only to their own lords, the Way of Loyalty and Filial Piety is fulfilled. For the land in this way to be governed without effort, and for the emperor thus tranquilly to maintain his exalted position—this must be considered also as loyalty to the emperor.[39]

Shoin's Philosophy

With Shoin's unquestioning acceptance of Confucianism and its Five Relationships as the normal basis of society, his belief in Bushido as the standard of personal character, his absolute faith in the promise of Amaterasu and in the ancient traditions of Japan, and his conviction that Western technology and science must be adopted without delay, his thinking possessed a complexity that makes it impossible of simple definition. In his short and troubled life, he himself was never able to give it thorough or precise exposition. For this very reason he may be considered a typical example of his time; the inherent conflicts between the various elements of his philosophy were all present in late Toku-

[39] *Ima no Sho-Ko.*

gawa Japan, and it would be difficult to say that they have yet been resolved one hundred years later. The glory and the tragedy of Japan's participation in the modern world were both foreshadowed in Yoshida Shoin.

While the general outlines of his thought were fixed from an early age, Shoin's detailed ideas on the state, the emperor, and national problems changed and developed according to his personal contacts and the conditions of the times. Nevertheless, the personal contacts that affected him the most were those he selected for himself: he voluntarily went to Mito, he took Zozan for his teacher, he requested Taika's criticisms. Shoin was firm in his purpose to investigate truth: he listened to the opinions of others; he eagerly studied ancient and modern books; he then decided the way he must go on his own responsibility. Knowing Shinto and Buddhism, he chose Shinto; knowing the ideologies of the Bakufu and Mito, he chose the Way of the Imperial Land. Shoin's personal decision for Amaterasu and Emperor was an expression of the spirit that made possible the Meiji Restoration less than a decade after his death. His teacher, Zozan, and his antagonist, Taika, were both greater scholars than he; but, one too radical and the other too conservative, neither caught and expressed the spirit of the age as Shoin did.

If there was any outside element influencing Shoin's thought, it was the power politics of nineteenth-century Europe and America. The sudden revelation of Asia's helplessness made a deep impression on his militarily trained mind. In his lectures on the *Bukyo Zensho* in 1850, he referred to the Opium War and the ineptitude of Chinese diplomacy, which started by calling the English barbarians and ended by honoring them as equals. In his *Shokyu Shigen,* written in 1853 shortly after Perry's arrival, he alluded to these facts again. Citing the example of the British on the coast of China, he wrote that if action should start against Japan, the foreigners would undoubtedly seize the Izu islands, which control the entrance to Sagami Bay, and from which point they could not only ravage the coast but prevent Japanese provision ships from entering Uraga. In the *Yushuroku* (1854–55), he mentioned that although the English claimed all of Australia, they had developed hardly one-tenth of its area, and added: "I often feel that if we had taken it first, it would necessarily have been of great advantage." [40] In the same passage, he described the danger Japan faced from the United States: Washington, he said, was the largest country in America; situated in the eastern part, it had been encroaching on its neighbors and forming a union with them; recently it had added western parts to the union, including California; it was now separated from Japan only by the ocean.

There is no doubt that the catalytic agent bringing Shoin's *son-no* and *jo-i* thought to a head was the arrival of Perry, to which his reactions were the same as those of Tokugawa Nariaki.[41] In the *Shokyu Shigen,* he wrote:

The afflictions caused by foreign barbarians date back a long time, and obviously they are not something that started today. Nevertheless, at the present time the matter of the American barbarians is actually before our eyes in its urgency; it is the greatest affliction of all ages. Since 6th month 3rd day [July 8], when the barbarian ships entered Uraga harbor, day and night they have been scurrying around examining the situation of a land that is not their own; their contempt and insults are truly something one can bear neither to see nor to hear about.[42]

His reaction to this, based on his faith in the *shinchoku* of Amaterasu and his study of ancient Japanese history, was that the Western countries were following what should have been Japan's policy, as the use of military force for overseas expansion was an integral element of *kokutai*. While the Westerners held a temporary advantage due to the failure of Japan to pursue its proper course, Japan had only to adopt their techniques in order to regain its rightful place in world affairs, and to insure the achievement of its destiny as the source of civilization and center of an eternal world empire.[43]

With regard to the duty of the individual, unchanging regardless of personal danger or the confusion of the times, Shoin wrote:

[40] *Yushuroku,* in YSZ, I, 349.
[41] See p. 98.
[42] *Shokyu Shigen,* in YSZ, I, 297.
[43] These ideas are discussed in Chapter 9.

People in general, when discussing the duty of serving one's lord, have the opinion that if great exploits are not achieved there is no profit to the nation. This is a serious error. The very concept of exemplifying the Way means to be oblivious of worldly achievement; and when one's concept of Duty is correct he can not consider profit.[44] In serving his lord, if there is disagreement, for having admonished his lord he may be put to death, he may be imprisoned, he may undergo starvation. If he meets with such experiences, even though he appears to have achieved neither exploits nor honor, in that he has not lost the Way of the subject, he is an eternal example to later generations, and unfailingly the tone of their customs will be stimulated and improved. Finally the standards of that country will be fixed, and it will come to be that wise and foolish, noble and base, together laud and respect the ideal of fidelity. In such a case, even though that person appeared to achieve neither exploits nor honor, how may we count the hundreds and thousands of years that his loyalty will endure? This is to be called the greatest of loyalties.[45]

The sincerity with which Shoin held to this ideal was such that, putting it into complete effect, he persisted in actions that led to his own death some four years after this passage was written.

On his philosophy in general, the following extract is probably the best explanation that Shoin gave in a single place:

If one is to discuss the basic principles of the Way, it means that born as a man, one should know that which makes him a man, and exemplify the Five Relationships; dwelling in the Imperial Land, he should know the essential nature of the Imperial Land; serving his own *han,* he should know the essential nature of his own *han;* on these elements he should establish his foundation.

Then, beyond this, each individual should perform his own particular office. The Confucian scholar should thoroughly and exhaustively study the classics and history; the astronomer, astronomy; the geographer, geography; the physician, the art of medicine; the artist, painting; and the same with bow, horse, sword, lance, and gun—each and every one skillfully following the specialized profession of his family, bringing it ever nearer to perfection; and, in addition, the samurai as samurai, the peasant as peasant, the artisan as artisan, the merchant as merchant—each must perform his proper office.

On the basis of such a general outline, proceeding in an orderly and

---

[44] This is based on Yamaga Soko's teaching in the *Shido.* See pp. 41–42, this volume.

[45] *Komo Yowa,* Book I, in *YSZ,* III, 19.

settled way, obviously such knowledge as Western physical science is not to be discarded; and on the other hand, there is no necessity to revile the sages over trifling matters. This indeed is the ultimate achievement of Benevolence and Wisdom.[46]

[46] *Ibid.*, Book IV, Part II, in *YSZ*, III, 441.

9

Attitude Toward the Nation

IN THIS and the following two chapters, Shoin's attitudes toward the nation, the emperor, and the Bakufu, respectively, will be discussed. As his thinking matured in the light of the critical national problems of the 1850's, the changes in Shoin's viewpoint were naturally reflected in differing and sometimes conflicting statements on the same subject. This is most noticeable in connection with the Bakufu and the Tokugawa family. Even where actual change of viewpoint is not a factor, a certain difference of emphasis may be observed. For example, stress on the nation as an object of loyalty was greater in his earlier writings; in his later years, the emperor took on greater importance. The rapid evolution of his thinking in the brief nine years of his adult life is another of the reasons that makes Shoin's writings the key to an understanding of late Tokugawa political thought.

Kokutai

In later years, the word *kokutai* became familiar as expressing the fundamental Japanese attitude toward the state, but it must be remembered that this term was just coming into use during Shoin's lifetime. The various ways in which he applied it—first as a synonym for "face" or honor, then as phenomenon, and finally as noumenon—not only represent a change in his use of a word but are more important as indications of Shoin's gradually developing appreciation for the "essential nature" of Japan.

In one of his early lectures on the *Bukyo Zensho,* given in 1850, Shoin was clearly using *kokutai* in the sense of honor, or the avoidance of disgrace. The loss of *kokutai* because of yielding to barbarians must be distressing to the ancestors, he said, but "if the *kokutai* handed down from the time of the ancestors is preserved steadfast and unshaken; that is to say, even should there occur a war which it is impossible to win, if sovereign and subjects together one and all meet their end and die in battle, so that not the slightest disgrace is incurred," [1] then the ancestors can not be disappointed even though the result is the extinction of the nation.

Three years later, at the time of Perry's arrival, Shoin was still using the word in a similar sense; in a letter to his brother, he reported that:

The circumstances under which the barbarian documents were accepted at Kurihama on the 9th [July 14], with two *bugyo* [2] officiating, and the naval and military forces of four *han* in attendance, represented an excessive loss of *kokutai.* [3]

However, in this case it is also possible to understand the meaning of "dignity" or "prestige." This was after Shoin's visit to Mito; that he was thinking of a further patriotic connotation is

[1] *Bukyo Zensho Kosho,* in *Yoshida Shoin Zenshu* (hereafter cited as YSZ), I (Tokyo: Iwanami Shoten, 1938–40), 100.

[2] See Appendix B.

[3] Letter to Sugi Umetaro (Kaei 6. 6. 20), in *YSZ,* VIII, 178.

indicated by his comment that the events at Kurihama reminded him of a picture he had seen, of a British officer negotiating with a disloyal Chinese official at Canton.

Near the end of the same year (1853), in one of his urgent memorials on the needs of the times, Shoin used the term in its phenomenal sense as "power, influence, or authority in action." The position of the Imperial Court from the earliest times was based on military strength, he wrote; on subjugating barbarians in all directions—this was *kokutai* from its inception. But in the Middle Ages the power to make war was stolen by vassals: "The Imperial Way was not clear; *kokutai* was not maintained." [4] Finally, the nation was even humiliated by "pirates":

> The affair of the past summer at Uraga was in truth an insult to the nation unparalleled since the founding of the Empire; and shortly after, there was the affair at Nagasaki. Can there be any person born in the Imperial Land, no matter who he may be, who does not hope for the restoration to its former state of the emperor's military power? [5]

It is only when the defenses of Kyoto, Edo, and the whole country have been made secure against the pirates, that "the Imperial Way will be clear, *kokutai* will be maintained, and the military power of the emperor will be restored to its former state." [6]

Kokutai in this sense could be subject to cyclical variations, flourishing and declining; and Shoin so used the term throughout the *Yushuroku*. But by the summer of 1856, when he was completing the *Komo Yowa,* he made a clear distinction between the phenomenal sense, to which he now gave the name of "national customs," and the noumenal, for which he reserved the designation of *kokutai:* that fundamental and unchanging ideal, growing out of the national history and therefore of a distinct character for each country, which by its operation gives rise to the phenomenal appearance. He also distinguished both "national customs" and *kokutai* from the Way:

---

[4] *Kyumusaku Is-soku,* in YSZ, I, 323.
[5] *Ibid.* [6] *Ibid.,* p. 325.

The Way, as it is the common Way of all under heaven, may be called "universal." *Kokutai,* as it is the essence of one country, may be called "unique." The Five Relationships of lord and subject, father and son, husband and wife, older and younger, friend and friend, are the universal characteristics of all under heaven. Something that excels all other nations, as *kun-shin no gi* toward the Imperial Court, is the unique characteristic of one country. . . .

National customs and *kokutai* are of course distinct. In general, the customs of a country develop naturally. When sages appear, they select the good from these, cleanse them of evil, and create a definite shape; this is called *kokutai.* . . . Although *kokutai* and national customs are obviously distinct, they are derived from one and the same source. . . .

In the family, one observes the family regulations; in the village or district, one follows the traditional customs of the village or district; living in a *han,* one obeys the laws of the *han;* living in the Imperial Land, one reveres the *kokutai* of the Imperial Land. Then, afterwards, one should also study the Way of the sages of China and inquire into the teachings of the Buddha of India.[7]

Although not clearly stated, the above passage implies that the *kokutai* of Japan, as distinguished from that of other countries, depends on the emperors—since they took the place of sages in Japanese history; this was brought out more clearly in one of Shoin's replies to Yamagata Taika's criticism: "In China, there were people and later there was an emperor; in the Imperial Land, there were the Divine Holy Ones and later there was a populace; the *kokutai* is fundamentally dissimilar."[8]

From this time on, Shoin ordinarily employed the term in its noumenal sense. For example, in the fall of 1856, in his lectures on the *Bukyo Shogaku,* he said:

The evil prevalent among scholars, that when they read the books of another country, they not only think the affairs of that country alone are praiseworthy, but even look upon their own country with all the more contempt, developing a longing for foreign lands—this is the result of not knowing that the *kokutai* of the Land of the Gods differs from the *kokutai* of other countries.[9]

This gradually maturing appreciation for the significance that

[7] *Komo Yowa,* Book IV, Part III, in *YSZ,* III, 498–99.
[8] *Ibid.,* Appendix, in *YSZ,* III, 551.
[9] *Bukyo Zensho Koroku,* in *YSZ,* IV, 210.

the Mito school had given to the term *kokutai* was an important factor in Shoin's ideological development.

Ka-i no ben

One of the phrases frequently encountered in Shoin's writings, especially after the Bakufu made its start in the conduct of foreign relations, is *ka-i no ben*. This term, literally "discrimination between civilized and barbarian," and the concept expressed by it were derived from the Chinese belief that their culture was superior to that of all other countries; its import is the same as the designation of China by such names as *Chung-kuo* (*Chugoku*) and *Chung-hua* (*Chuka*). Just as these names were taken over by Tokugawa-period patriots from Yamaga Soko on, and applied to Japan rather than to China, the term *ka-i no ben* was also employed as a convenient expression signifying "Japan's superiority to all other countries." However, even in this patriotic usage, it did not necessarily include the concept of hatred or contempt for foreigners: as sometimes argued during the Tokugawa period, to respect one's own parents does not demand despising others'.

In Shoin's application of the term, on the other hand, *ka-i no ben* became the minor premise that, following the major premise of *kokutai*, led to the conclusion of implacable antiforeignism. Since he believed that the spiritual and ethical values of Japan were destined eventually to bring enlightenment to the entire world, he felt it mandatory to preserve them free of foreign influence; and as the best protection against psychological invasion would be a psychological defense, he insistently taught hatred of the foreigners in order to prevent the development of admiration for the West. He once explained his reasoning by analogy with Chinese thought: "Hatred for the barbarians, in the *Spring and Autumn Annals,* was not primarily hatred for the barbarians themselves. It was hatred of China's imitating and entering into barbarian ways." [10]

Shoin's feeling that the root of the trouble between Asia and

[10] *Komo Yowa,* Book II, in *YSZ,* III, 136.

the West lay in this "distinction between civilized and barbarian," and that the foreigners' inexcusable actions originated in their ignorance of common ethics, went back at least to the time of Perry's arrival. The Americans' refusal to go to Nagasaki as requested made a strongly unfavorable impression on him: "The barbarians said: 'We know only to serve the commands of our own country. How should we know the laws of Japan?' Their arrogance was increasingly immoderate."[11] With regard to Perry's policy on the occasion of his return trip, Shoin wrote in February, 1854:

Recently, seven of the American barbarians' warships have been anchored in close proximity to Edo. Their attitude is obviously crafty; their appearance, extremely violent. Therefore it is proper that the righteousness of the nation be extended and the crime of the recalcitrant barbarians be punished. . . . At the present juncture, other than discussing the great significance of *Chugoku* and "barbarian," nothing else is worthy of mention.[12]

Later, when Yamagata Taika objected to his teaching of hatred on this basis, remarking that the Westerners too knew ethics and had charitable and philanthropic institutions in their own countries, Shoin agreed there was some truth to his argument, but refused to yield the main point: "My opposition to America and Russia, designating them as mean and despicable, is in connection with their senseless invasions, and the insatiability of their sinister intentions."[13]

One significant point in connection with Shoin's *ka-i no ben* is that he restricted it solely to the area of ethical and moral values, so that it had no bearing on the adoption of Western science and technology. In the *Yushuroku,* he wrote: "In mechanical instruments and practical arts, changes occur year after year; but in the ability to start with reflection and end in demonstration, obviously there is no *ka* [civilized] nor *i* [barbarian]."[14]

[11] *Yushuroku,* in YSZ, I, 333.
[12] *Kaisensaku,* in YSZ, I, 318.
[13] *Komo Yowa,* Appendix, in YSZ, III, 551.
[14] *Yushuroku,* in YSZ, I, 345.

The Meaning of Defense

In his early adult years, Shoin's patriotism for Japan was based on, and closely bound up with, his training as a teacher of military science. His awareness of the aggressive intentions of Europe and America—aroused by Yamada Uemon while Shoin was still a youth and given concrete proof in his mind by the policy of Commodore Perry—inflamed his love of country and aroused his faith in the destiny of Japan. Based on his knowledge of tactics and strategy, Shoin prepared and submitted large numbers of plans and suggestions for strengthening land and naval defenses. His advice on strictly military subjects is outside the scope of the present study, but his estimate of the reasons why defense was necessary has a definite bearing on the question of loyalty and patriotism, since it ran through all his writings on duty to the nation and was a contributing factor in his eventual repudiation of the Bakufu. The contrast between the self-seeking motives of Europe and America and Japan's civilizing mission was also one aspect of *ka-i no ben*.

One of the best examples of Shoin's opinion on Western policy is the *Bokushi Moshitate no Omomuki Rompaku Joken* ("An Itemized Refutation of the Contents of the American Official's Statement"), written in 1858. In this essay, Shoin took up and answered one by one the arguments Townsend Harris had used in his conference of December 12, 1857, with Hotta Masayoshi (the member of the *roju* in charge of foreign affairs), which had paved the way for the new 1858 treaties of amity and commerce.[15]

[15] The references are naturally to Shoin's indirect quotation of Townsend Harris, rather than to Harris himself. Shoin's source of information was probably based on the Japanese record of the Hotta-Harris conversation, in which the two statements mentioned here appear as follows:

a) "The United States have no possessions in the east and do not desire to have any, as other countries do."

b) "It is the uniform custom of the United States, while frequently making treaties with other countries, not to annex any country merely by force of arms."

(In W. G. Beasley (trans. and ed.), *Select Documents in Japanese Foreign Policy 1853–1868* [London: Oxford University Press, 1955], p. 160.)

In reply to Harris' statement that the United States differed from other countries, and desired no territory in the Orient, Shoin wrote:

> That the American barbarians have in truth not yet been able to get one inch of ground or one foot of land in the Orient is for the reason that so far, their strength is insufficient. If their strength were only adequate, would they not hope to emulate Spain in Luzon, Holland in Java, and the English barbarians in Ceylon? Merely because they are without power, for them to mouth the words of Benevolence and Righteousness instead, is detestable.[16]

With regard to Harris' saying that not one mile had ever been added to United States territory by force of arms, Shoin answered:

> This is a complete falsehood. Aside from the events of bygone times, when the American official Perry came in 1854, among the books he presented to the Bakufu there was such a thing as a picture of the military victory over Mexico. . . . Again, a drunken barbarian at the Yokohama Club, drawing his sword, showed how the victory over Mexico was won, and was bragging of his own exploits—this I have heard directly from an eyewitness. When New Mexico was added to the United States, is it possible that this was done without the force of arms? Such is the duplicity of this statement.
>
> From the foregoing, it appears that the general behavior of the United States is a means for getting us to lick their candy. Who can be ignorant of the fact that they have placed poison in the candy? [17]

In addition to being greedy, crafty, and cunning, the enemy, as Shoin realized, possessed great material strength. On the actual danger to Japan involved in treaties of "amity and commerce," Shoin wrote in 1857:

> In the Keicho and Genna periods,[18] since the persons with whom we dealt were all from small islands, or were insignificant foreigners,

---

[16] *Bokushi Moshitate no Omomuki Rompaku Joken,* in YSZ, V, 278.

[17] *Ibid.,* 279–80.

[18] In Keicho (1596–1615) and Genna (1615–24), before the closing of the country in 1636, the Bakufu maintained relations with various foreign countries.

the situation was such that we could easily wield the power of life and death over them. The countries with which we are concerned at present are hardly of this sort.[19]

The measures Shoin proposed to cope with such an enemy fell into two main categories: military and psychological. Under the military heading, as shown for example in the *Shokyu Shigen,* he wrote in detail of the urgent need for adopting Western artillery and cavalry and building or purchasing warships. Nor did he overlook the role of an austerity program: in the same memorial, emphasizing the importance of concentrating on the immediate necessity, he wrote that parties for the enjoyment of poetry and sake, or for flower and moon viewing, must be abandoned. Deploring the weakness and ineptitude of the samurai class in general, he also proposed discontinuing unearned stipends and several times suggested organizing a peasant conscript army.

In the final analysis, however, Shoin recognized that even more important than the physical aspects of war was the mental and spiritual outlook of the people. With this in view, in many of the memorials on military preparedness he also suggested governmental reforms. Writing on this subject while in prison in 1855, he lamented the fact that the treaties with foreign countries had been signed, but said that the matter of immediate importance was to look after the welfare of the people, so that having a good life they would not regret dying, and having affection for their superiors they would not hesitate to sacrifice their lives. Acquiring guns and ships while neglecting the spirit of the people was the surest way to failure.[20]

In Shoin's view, duty to the nation was not the special prerogative of any one group, but transcended class division and the local loyalties of the *han* system. In the *Komo Yowa,* he wrote:

The matter of the nation in its relationship to the barbarians is of course the responsibility of the ruler and his ministers, but at the same time, for those who have been born in the Land of the Gods, all the

[19] *Gaiban Tsuryaku,* in YSZ, XII, 112.
[20] *Gokusha Mondo,* in YSZ, II, 270.

myriad people "under the whole heaven, to the borders of the land" [21] must make it their personal responsibility.[22]

And again, in the same work:

For barbarians, mutually competing, to come in large numbers, although it is indeed a serious matter for the nation, is not a real basis for profound apprehension. What must be a matter for profound apprehension is the fact that men's hearts are not righteous. If men's hearts were only righteous, they would die a hundred deaths to protect their country. . . .

In recent years, not infrequently *kokutai*[23] has been violated by the coming of foreigners. The continuation of these incidents down to the present is due to the fact—I am sorry to say—that the Bakufu and the samurai, high and low, in the various *han,* all being unrighteous of heart, are unable to die loyally for the sake of their country.[24]

Once it is thoroughly realized that patriotism has no relation to the class structure, and when loyalty to the nation replaces that to the *han,* the defenses of Japan will be truly safeguarded:

If we shape our course by making our zeal strong and our plans valiant, and if we employ our troops with a clear awareness both of our strength and of favorable openings, even without ships and guns we will still be able to overrun the five continents with power to spare —then what do we have to fear from Russia or America? And if we lack such a spirit, what use do we have for ships and guns? [25]

Destiny of Japan

While Shoin frequently expressed anxiety and concern over the handling of current problems, there was no doubt in his mind as to the ultimate outcome:

It goes without saying that for the Imperial Land to reign in all directions is as unending as the Heavenly Sun Succession, as boundlessly

[21] A quotation from the *Book of Odes* and *Mencius.* See note 4, Chapter 10.

[22] *Komo Yowa,* Book IV, Part II, in *YSZ,* III, 378.

[23] Phenomenal *kokutai.*

[24] *Komo Yowa,* Book II, in *YSZ,* III, 162–63.

[25] Letter to Yamada Uemon (Ansei 2. 8. 1), in *YSZ,* II, 284.

eternal as heaven and earth; then, if it should decline for a time, is there any possibility but that it should flourish again? . . . The gods of Heaven, blessing and protecting our land, will unfailingly bring forth an excellent ruler, a talented sovereign; the situation will take a new turn, and the nation will again flourish as of old.[26]

Shoin did not, however, believe that this could come about entirely automatically, without exertion and struggle. Japan was destined to be supreme, but it must make itself worthy of its destiny by following the standard Confucian method laid down in the Eight Precepts: only by purifying itself would it be entitled to rule others. On the other hand, since its ultimate right to rule was guaranteed, there was no objection to the use of arms where necessary in enforcing this right.

It is a mistake to overlook the ethical basis in Shoin's thinking and to see in him only a fanatic expansionist; but it is equally a mistake to ignore his complete acceptance of the thesis of Yamaga Soko and the Mito school that "the Imperial Court established the state by force of arms." [27] In other words, he held that force must be used only for purposes of righteousness and that Japan's cause was righteous. These ideas are brought out in the following quotations from the *Komo Yowa:*

If the sovereign is possessed of a sincere heart, if men of wisdom and talent are raised to office, and if good government is effected, what difficulty will there be in extending the authority of the nation over the four seas and routing the foreign barbarians? [28]

At present, to establish the magnificence of the Land of the Gods and rout all barbarians is the Way of Benevolence. Those who would hinder this are without Benevolence. How shall Benevolence not triumph over non-Benevolence? [29]

Thus, even when Shoin's thought encompassed the hegemony of the world, he assumed that Japan represented Benevolence, the fundamental Confucian virtue.

[26] *Yushuroku,* in *YSZ,* I, 331–32.

[27] Letter to Kurihara Ryozo (Kaei 5, about 6th or 7th month), in *YSZ,* VII, 353.

[28] *Komo Yowa,* Book III, Part I, in *YSZ,* III, 191.

[29] *Ibid.,* Book IV, Part I, in *YSZ,* III, 319.

Japan's obligation to the world, he felt, should start with the nearby regions:

In relations with neighboring countries, friendship should be made the keynote. Therefore, power, virtue, and righteousness—being the three points in which we excel—must obviously be applied and observed. . . . If, for example, we extend loving protection to a small country, we must prevent its invasion by another.[30]

Just as the kings of the Chou dynasty had used force to bring the benefits of civilization to the barbarians of their day, Japan must face the task of civilizing the nineteenth-century barbarians of the West:

When King Wen and King Wu, under unavoidable circumstances, displayed their courage and made war against countries that denied the Way, who would attempt to prevent them? Yet this is not a thing in which to take pleasure; and furthermore, without ruling oneself, to struggle for supremacy over others is no more than foolishly to open the door to one's own defeat.

Now, indeed, the outer barbarians from all directions are seeking a quarrel with us! In response to such an occasion, it is my ardent hope that the hearts of all in the sixty provinces may become as one piece of rock, so that in this way the worthlessness and meanness of the barbarians may be chastened, and the waves of the sea be cleansed.[31]

So far as actual recommendations were concerned, Shoin accepted the immediate necessity of Mito's *jo-i* theory, but considered that it must be limited to an extremely brief period. At the earliest possible moment, Japan should return to its ancient foreign policy, which he designated as one of "enterprise." After the signing of the Treaty of Kanagawa, when the term "amity" had come into use in connection with Japanese foreign relations, Shoin expressed his views on amity in this way:

When it is clearly understood that we are unable to destroy them, and that they are unable to annex us, then "amity" is possible. . . . But this is a temporary expedient; it is not a policy to be relied on and followed permanently. . . . If, however, it is clearly understood that

[30] *Ibid.*, Book I, in *YSZ*, III, 49.
[31] *Ibid.*, pp. 49–50.

we as leaders and masters are spurring them on, and that they are entirely devoted and faithful to us, then "amity" is truly possible. If it is otherwise, "amity" is actually impossible.

By closing the country and sealing up the barriers, to prepare for the use of force; by conserving our strength and building up our energy, to plan for enterprising action; and to do this immediately— if we understand these three points, the meaning of "amity" is completely expressed; in this way we are to control the barbarians.[32]

Shoin's interpretation of the ancient foreign policy, based on an enterprising spirit, in terms of nineteenth-century conditions, was spelled out in the closing pages of the *Yushuroku:*

If the sun is not ascending, it is descending. If the moon is not waxing, it is waning. If the country is not flourishing, it is declining. Therefore to protect the country well is not merely to prevent it from losing the position it holds, but to add to it the positions which it does not hold. At the present time, it is immediately necessary to make military preparations: when we have a few ships and the guns are sufficient we may well develop Ezo [Hokkaido] and assign it to several lords in fief; taking advantage of the right opportunity we should seize Kamchatka and Okhotsk; admonishing Ryukyu, we should put it on exactly the same footing as that of the various lords within the country who join in paying homage to the shogun; calling Korea to account, we should require it to submit hostages and pay tribute as in the flourishing days of old; in the north obtaining the cession of Manchuria, in the south taking Taiwan and the islands of Luzon; gradually, we must display the vigor of an enterprising spirit. . . .

For the outer barbarians to enter by force and press us, angrily assuming authority—for us, on our part, to hang our heads and hold our breath, establishing communications and trade exactly on the terms they demand, fearing to oppose them on any point—this is what the craftiness of flatterers would equate with the righteousness of our Holy Emperors.[33] Under such conditions, how could we admit their evil theory?

The running of water is a running by its own accord; the standing of a tree is a standing by its own accord; the existence of a nation is an existence by its own accord. How could we be dependent on foreign countries? We will not be dependent on them. How could we be con-

---

[32] *Sokyoku Zuihitsu,* in YSZ, II, 425.

[33] A reference to the argument of the Bakufu, that their entering into relations with foreign countries was actually a return to the ancient policy of Japan.

trolled by foreign countries? We will not be controlled by them. Accordingly, we must control them firmly.[34]

Soon after the first treaties were signed, Shoin seems to have hoped that the early stages of the enterprising policy might be accomplished without objection from the West. In 1855, he wrote:

As we have already established amicable relations with Russia and America, no untoward event whatever must occur on our side. Carefully respecting the regulations and with attention to our promise, we must give them no cause for arrogance. Taking advantage of favorable opportunities, we will seize Manchuria, thus coming face to face with Russia; regaining Korea, we will keep a watch on China; taking the islands of the South, we will advance on India. Planning on all three, we must determine which is the easiest, and put that into effect first. This is an enterprise which must continue eternally so long as the earth shall last.[35]

Three years later, when the Bakufu proposed to sign new treaties, Shoin was strongly against the idea. In the *Taisaku Ichido* ("One Method of Counterattack"),[36] he outlined a detailed plan for meeting the problem as it stood in 1858. The first step was to remove all foreigners from Japan; the treaty relations could be terminated honorably by asking Townsend Harris to leave and explaining that Japan did not need the good offices of other countries. Once freed of the foreigners' presence, Japan could prepare to open foreign relations on its own terms and in its own way. Ships would be constructed, and military expeditions sent overseas. Government offices and military stations would be established in such places as Canton, Java, South Africa, and Australia. This program would naturally cause some conflict with the foreigners, and for that reason they could not be allowed residence in Japan while it was being effected. However, as soon as Japan had made itself a recognized world power, it would send representatives to California, sign a treaty of amity there, and from that time on, engage in foreign relations. The

---

[34] *Yushuroku*, in YSZ, I, 350–51, 353–54.
[35] Letter to Yamada Uemon (Ansei 2. 8. 1), in YSZ, II, 284.
[36] In YSZ, V, 136–43.

entire project, Shoin estimated, should require no more than three years.

By the time he had been returned to Noyama prison, in 1859, Shoin was convinced that it was too late even for such a plan; there was no other course than once more to prepare for war. In a letter to Ohara Shigenori, a councillor (*sangi*) at the Imperial Court who was then taking the lead in organizing loyalist sentiment, he wrote: "For the people 'under the whole heaven, to the borders of the land,' death is preferable to respecting the treaty with the Americans." [37] The death of the individual, in any case, could not affect the glorious destiny of Japan: "The final outcome will be to crush America, Russia, England, and France, to extend the sway of the Imperial authority over all nations, and to establish the foundation of the state for all ages." [38]

[37] Letter to Ohara Shigenori (Ansei 6. 2. 14), in *YSZ*, VI, 151.
[38] *Ibid.*, p. 152.

10

Attitude Toward the Emperor

SHOIN's basic loyalty to the emperor was taught him in boyhood by his father. However, the intensity of his feeling and his estimate of the relative importance of loyalty to the emperor as compared with the urgent necessity of national defense were subject to a developmental process. During the first part of his life, defense, including *jo-i* and the future *kaikoku* based on an enterprising spirit, composed the main element in his thought; loyalty to the emperor was corollary. But as Shoin became more and more imbued with the spirit of *kokutai*, his feeling of personal devotion to the emperor was strengthened to such a degree that ultimately the emperor became "main" and foreign relations were "corollary." On the basis of his writings, it is possible to date his final acceptance of this reversed viewpoint precisely in the month of September, 1856. Naturally, a great deal of thought led up to this "illumination," so that 1856 as a whole may properly be considered a critical year in the evolution of Shoin's philosophy.

176

At the same time, it must be remembered that the change was one only of emphasis or degree and not a reversal in the sense of rejecting something previously accepted. Just as Shoin's loyalty for the emperor was a part of his outlook from childhood, so his deep anxiety over foreign relations continued until his death. Thus, the year 1856 should in no sense be taken as an arbitrary date setting off a period of "patriotism" from one of "loyalty to the emperor." Both currents were continuing, integral parts of his thinking from first to last.

In analyzing Shoin's attitude toward the emperor, two elements may be distinguished: those originating in Bushido, and those based on faith in Shinto. The Bushido influence was stronger in Shoin's early years, arising, as it did, out of his training in the Yamaga school. As his thinking matured, particularly under the stimulus of Mitogaku, he added to this a strong and unquestioning faith in the ancient traditions; and it is quite possible to interpret his "illumination" as resulting from the triumph of the religious influence over that of Bushido. Here again, however, both were interwoven, and Shoin's strong personal faith in Amaterasu reinforced his Bushido ideals. These two influences are treated separately below because they are diverse in origin, not because they are mutually exclusive or chronologically distinguishable.

Bushido Influence

Bushido loyalty to the emperor may be distinguished from loyalty stemming from religious faith in that Bushido loyalty necessarily includes some of the other obligations derived from the Five Relationships. On the one hand, the theoretical distinction between *hanshu* and emperor may become blurred, as both alike are "one's lord"; and on the other, the duty of Filial Piety, ideally to be made equal to Loyalty, must be fitted into the scheme. These factors are illustrated in Shoin's *Komo Yowa* remarks on the duty of subject to sovereign:

Toward lord and toward father, it may be said that the obligation is the same. Calling one's lord foolish and unenlightened, and leaving one's native land to seek a lord elsewhere, is the same as calling one's father stupid and obstinate, and leaving one's family to take a neighbor as father. . . .

The subjects of China are like servants hired for half a season. Naturally they have the right to shift about, choosing their lords according to good or ill. The subjects of our land are hereditary subjects, and for this reason they share equally with their lord in death or life, in joy or sorrow; and even if it leads to death, their Way can positively not permit the forsaking and abandonment of their lord. . . .

In recent times, the barbarians from overseas . . . are rapidly heaping insults upon the Superior Land. How are we to control them? There is no other course than to clarify the great significance, which I have just explained, of how our *kokutai* differs from that of foreign countries—then let the people of the nation die for the nation, let the people of the *han* die for the *han*, let the subject die for his lord, let the son die for his father—if such a zeal becomes adamant, what shall we have to fear from the barbarians? [1]

Another point to be remembered in connection with Bushido loyalty is that, rigid as its demands may seem, the ultimate criterion is always internal: the individual must decide for himself where his duty lies in any given case. If his duty, as he sees it, happens to conflict with law, the law must be ignored. (This is a most significant factor in the example of the forty-seven samurai of Ako, to whom Shoin often referred in glowing terms.) When his brother chided him for breaking the law at Shimoda, Shoin replied: "That prohibition pertains to the Tokugawa era alone; this matter would have concerned the three-thousand-year-old Imperial Land. How should I have leisure to think of *that?*" [2]

Again, during his last imprisonment at Noyama, Shoin wrote:

Chu Hsi says: ". . . Whether one is guilty or not guilty lies only within himself. This is why the ancients sacrificed themselves for the sake of Benevolence." Chu Hsi's words are rather similar to the position which I take. However, the question of being guilty or not guilty must be left to the general opinion of later generations. My intention is solely to exert my efforts in right action.[3]

[1] *Komo Yowa,* Book I, in *Yoshida Shoin Zenshu* (hereafter cited as YSZ), III (Tokyo: Iwanami Shoten, 1938–40), 18–20.

[2] Comments in answer to a letter from Sugi Umetaro (Ansei 1. 12. 5), in *YSZ*, VIII, 331.

[3] *Zagoku Nichiroku,* in *YSZ*, VII, 258.

In his earliest writing of ideological significance, the *Shokyu Shigen,* Shoin opened with a discussion of *taigi.* At this time he had no intention whatsoever of opposing the Bakufu, but he had already accepted the *kokutai* theory that emperor and people form one unit. In order to make his point that all without exception owed their primary loyalty to the emperor, he quoted *Mencius* and the *tenka no tenka* theory. This theory had, of course, been one of the main supports of the Bakufu, but by giving it a *kokutai* interpretation, Shoin was able to use it in the opposite sense. His reasoning ran as follows: "The realm is the realm of the nation; it is not the realm of one man. Therefore, it is not the property of the shogun. The emperor is identical with the nation. Therefore, it is the realm of the emperor." He developed his argument in this way:

> *"Under the whole heaven,*
> *Every spot is the sovereign's ground;*
> *To the borders of the sea [land],*
> *Every individual is the sovereign's subject [minister]."* [4]

This *taigi* is the clear instruction of the holy classics; who could be ignorant of it? Nevertheless in recent times, there is a sort of detestable vulgar theory, which runs as follows: Since Edo is the seat of the Bakufu, it is the *hatamoto,*[5] the *fudai*[5] lords, and the branches of the Tokugawa family alone who should exert their strength in its defense; as the lords of the various other *han* must give primary consideration each to his own *han,* they are not necessarily obliged to make efforts for the defense of Edo. Alas! Such people are not only failing to render due honor to the shogun, but in truth they must be called uninformed regarding the *taigi* of the realm. It goes without saying that one must honor his own *han.* But the realm is the realm of the emperor; that is to say, it is the realm of the nation; it is not the private property of the shogun.

---

[4] In using this quotation from *Mencius* (Book V, Part I, chap. iv, 2), which Mencius had taken from the *Book of Odes,* Shoin was undoubtedly also alluding to Aizawa Yasushi's use of the same material in the *Shinron.* (See note 18, Chapter 6.) The translation given here is Legge's, with two alterations: (a) Shoin wrote "sea" in place of "land"; (b) the character that Legge construed as "minister" was normally used by Shoin in the sense of "subject."

[5] See Appendix B.

Therefore, if anyone whosoever in the entire realm is insulted by the foreign barbarians, it is a matter of course that the shogun, naturally leading all the lords of the realm, must wipe out this disgrace to the nation and bring tranquillity to the mind of the emperor. At such a time, how could it be said that the people "under the whole heaven, to the borders of the land" are not obliged to pour out their exertions? And how should there be leisure to decide whether it is one's own *han* or another *han*? [6]

Often cited as the epitome of Shoin's Bushido thought is his *Shiki Shichi-soku* ("Seven Principles for the Samurai"), which he wrote early in 1855 to honor the attainment of majority by his cousin, Tamaki Hikosuke, and which was afterwards used at the Shoka Sonjuku and circulated widely throughout Choshu-*han*. Of the seven principles, the first three all relate to the question of loyalty: first, as a member of the human race; second, as a member of the Japanese nation; and third, as a samurai:

1. Anyone born as a man must know well that which distinguishes man from the birds and beasts. In the final analysis, it is that man has the Five Relationships; of which the most important are those of lord-subject and father-son. Therefore, that which makes a man a man has Loyalty and Filial Piety as its foundation.

2. Anyone born in the Imperial Land must know well that which makes us superior to the entire world. In the final analysis, it is that the Imperial Court is of one line for ten thousand ages, and that the samurai of our land inherit salary and rank generation after generation. The emperor nurtures the people, thus continuing the great enterprise of his ancestors; the subject-people show loyalty to their lord, thus carrying on the desire of their forefathers. That lord and subject are one body; that Loyalty and Filial Piety are united; only of our country is this true.

3. In the Way of the samurai, nothing is more important than Duty. Duty is effected by means of courage; and courage grows by means of Duty.[7]

---

[6] *Shokyu Shigen*, in YSZ, I, 298–99.

[7] *Shiki Shichi-soku*, in YSZ, IV, 20. The second part of paragraph 2 (beginning "The emperor nurtures the people . . .") was quoted approvingly in the *Kokutai no Hongi* (see Appendix D), trans. John O. Gauntlett, ed. Robert K. Hall (Cambridge: Harvard University Press, 1949), p. 90.

The theme of such a Confucian-Bushido loyalty to the Emperor ran through all of Shoin's discussions of contemporary issues, and some of his bitterest criticisms were directed against those who did not recognize it. In the *Jiseiron* (1858), he said:

At the present moment, the two hundred and sixty lords [i.e., of the various *han,* large and small] . . . heedless of the current problems of realm and nation, anxious only for themselves and their families, truckling to the times . . . never consider even in a dream the Supreme Duty [*taigi*] of service to the emperor.[8]

One of the most fundamental elements of Bushido thought is the obligation to repay favors received, expressed in the term *on,* which may mean either the benefaction or the duty arising out of its acceptance. Shoin felt this obligation with great keenness, not only toward the house of Mori, the rulers of Choshu, but in an additional idealized way, which he made the wellspring of his action. One case where he mentioned this was in explaining his reason for attempting to go abroad in order to investigate conditions in foreign countries:

Although of humble station, I too am a man of the Imperial Land. . . . While thinking of my parental home with regret because of Duty, it became unendurable for me to sit by, idle and silent, neglecting the repayment of my *on* to the nation.[9]

Again, speaking of this as a general principle, he said:

As both you and I were born in the august Imperial Land, and in particular as we are samurai following the profession of arms, that we must serve in that office, the Way of Arms, and repay the great benefactions [*on*] of the Imperial Land, is something that goes without saying.[10]

Later, Shoin defined his concept of *on* with great clarity; its repayment demanded one's best efforts. In February, 1859, he wrote:

[8] *Jiseiron,* in YSZ, V, 251–52.   [9] *Yushuroku,* in YSZ, I, 332.
[10] *Bukyo Zensho Koroku,* in YSZ, IV, 207–8.

The obligations [*on*] that we should properly repay are seven in number. The favor [*on*] of Amaterasu . . . the favor of the Heavenly Descendants [i.e., emperors] . . . the favor of the departed lords [i.e., of the Mori family], the favor of the present lord . . . the favor of the ancestors, the favor of the parents, must be repaid. The knowledge of these six obligations results from knowledge of the Way. The favor of knowing the Way—although diffused among books, sages and wise men, teachers and friends, it can be reduced to one—must be repaid. All told, this makes seven great obligations. Nevertheless, our body is but one; our heart is but one. By means of one to repay seven; is this not beyond the capacity of the individual? Ah! the Way is one; requitement is also one; how then should it be difficult? . . . In truth, if one exemplifies the Way well, either in living to repay the debt to the Heavenly Descendants, or in dying to repay the debt to the Heavenly Ancestress; by this he will expunge the guilt of the past and discharge the obligation of the present.[11]

This is the key to understanding Shoin's Bushido: the obligations recognized are those to Amaterasu, the emperor, the *hanshu*, and the parents. In a manner that was entirely illogical from the standpoint of actual feudal relationships, the shogun was ignored, and the emperor was inserted as lord of the *hanshu*. Thus, in Shoin's thinking, all the force of Bushido teaching, which made *kun-shin no gi* the supreme ideal, was directed toward the emperor as apex of the feudal hierarchy rather than toward the shogun. For this reason, the exemplification of the Way itself was found by Shoin in service to the emperor; and it was in this sense that he called *kun-shin no gi* the essence of the Five Relationships, or that which makes a man a man.[12]

Influence of Religious Faith

The second basic element in Shoin's attitude toward the emperor, completely distinct from the Five Relationships of Confucianism, stemmed directly from his faith in the gods of Japan. As he expressed this fundamental belief in a letter to his sister:

[11] *Noyama Nikki*, in *YSZ*, VI, 116–17.
[12] See p. 131.

One must worship and revere the gods. The country of Yamato is called the Land of the Gods; it is the honorable country which was founded by the lordly gods. This being so, for those who were born within this august and honorable land, without distinction as to whether noble or base, to neglect the lordly gods is an unpardonable thing.[13]

Shoin's faith was not merely an abstract belief in the existence of the gods; it applied literally to the story of the Age of the Gods as recorded in the *Kojiki* and *Nihon Shoki*. He rejected the "Confucian Shinto" type of interpretation, following instead Kokugaku and the Mito school in demanding implicit acceptance of the ancient traditions. In the *Komo Yowa,* he wrote:

In our favored land, after Kuni-no-toko-tachi no Mikoto, through generation following generation of gods, there finally came into being Izanagi and Izanami. These gave birth to the Land of the Great Eight Islands, to mountains, rivers, plants, trees, and people; and then gave birth to the Possessor of all under heaven, the Imperial Ancestress, Amaterasu.

After her, the successive Holy Ones have continued one after another; and the prosperity of the Imperial Throne, as unchanging as heaven and earth, is to be passed on to ten thousand times ten thousand generations; in this way, the land, mountains, rivers, plants, trees, and people, have all been guarded and protected from the time of the Imperial Ancestress on.[14]

In reply to Taika's criticism, Shoin insisted firmly: "It is not possible to argue this matter. To doubt it is completely impossible. The Way of the Imperial Land in its entirety has its origin in the Age of the Gods." [15]

This unquestioning faith also gave Shoin complete trust in the *shinchoku* as the eternal protection of Japan:

According to the *shinchoku* of Amaterasu, "the increasing prosperity of the Heavenly Sun Succession shall be as unending as heaven and earth." Thus, so long as there is perfect confidence in the *shinchoku*, Japan can never perish. And if Japan can never perish,

---

[13] Letter to Kodama Chiyo (Ansei 1. 12. 3), in *YSZ*, VIII, 321.
[14] *Komo Yowa*, Book IV, Part III, in *YSZ*, III, 463.
[15] *Ibid.,* Appendix, in *YSZ*, III, 552.

its righteous spirit shall be redoubled and a time of regeneration must unfailingly arrive.[16]

To this faith in Amaterasu as Possessor, Ruler, and Protector of the nation, Shoin added a faith in Amaterasu as a deity interested in his personal spiritual well-being. Upon his return to prison in 1859, not hearing from his friends and not knowing that they were unable to communicate with him, completely discouraged, he wrote:

> The *kunshi*[17] have cut off relations with me. Is my Way at fault? If my Way is at fault, obviously I can expect only to die. If my Way is not at fault, even though the *kunshi* cut off relations with me, can I be cut off by the heavenly goddess Amaterasu, the departed lords, and the ancestors?[18]

And, later in the same day: "Now I am calmly leaving the question of life or death for Heaven to decide; still within myself I expect that by my death I shall repay my debt to Amaterasu."[19]

It was an Amaterasu in whom he had this sort of faith that Shoin considered the Ancestress of the Imperial family, and it was this Amaterasu whose love and guidance were continued by each successive generation of emperors:

> The establishment of the foundation of the Land of the Gods was deep and ancient. When the two Primeval Deities [i.e., Izanagi and Izanami] had given birth to the Eight Islands, and then to mountains, rivers, plants, and trees, subsequently they gave birth to the Sun Goddess, and made her the Possessor of all under heaven. . . . By this, the foundation of the Land of the Gods was first established.
>
> When the Sun Goddess had become the Possessor of all under heaven, subsequently she became the Ancestress of the Heavenly Sun Succession, enduring for ten thousand generations. Down to the present day, anyone who receives birth in the Eight Islands . . . is a recipient of the blessings of the two Deities; and in this regard, how

---

[16] Letter to Horie Yoshinosuke (Ansei 6. 10. 11), in *YSZ*, IX, 470.

[17] A common Confucian term (Chinese *chun-tzu*), usually translated as "superior man." Here, merely a courteous reference to his friends and pupils.

[18] *Noyama Nikki*, in *YSZ*, VI, 110.

[19] *Ibid.*, p. 117.

does [the emperors'] continuing the succession of the Sun Goddess differ from the Age of the Gods? [20]

For such reasons, Shoin could say in the *Komo Yowa*, expressing the standard concept of the *kokutai* theory:

From the viewpoint of the nation, there is none to be revered more than the emperor. From the viewpoint of the emperor, there is nothing to be respected more than the people. This Lord and this people, since the time of creation, have never been separated for even one day. Therefore, if the Lord exists, there are people; and if there were no Lord, there would be no people. In the same way, if the people exist, there is a Lord; and if there were no people, there would be no Lord.[21]

It is obvious that when Shoin viewed the emperor in this light, the duty of serving him in loyal devotion was entirely different in nature from the duty of serving the *hanshu,* even though the distinction might superficially appear to be obscured through calling them both by the same title of "lord."

While Shoin did not go into details concerning the theory of the emperor as a "manifest god" (*arahitogami*), he did recognize both divine and human elements in his nature. Basically, Shoin considered him as a human:

The idea that the emperor is actually a being above the clouds, and not of human seed, is entirely contrary to the Ancient Way. After the decline of the Imperial Court, this concept developed; and furthermore, after it developed, the Imperial Court declined more and more.[22]

Setting the emperor apart from the people was a violation of his true nature, Shoin explained; and making him nothing more than a religious symbol merely suited the purposes of the feudal lords. Originally, the emperor had governed in person, appearing in the audience hall, receiving the advice and suggestions of his

---

[20] *Kofusangetsu Shoro-ki,* in YSZ, IV, 173.
[21] *Komo Yowa,* Book IV, Part III, in YSZ, III, 463.
[22] *Ibid.,* Book III, Part II, in YSZ, III, 261.

ministers and the complaints of the people. But later, a change had come about:

The sovereign remained deep within the palace; in the audience hall only the ministers and officials consulted and deliberated, and only after the decision had been reached did it come to the ear of the sovereign. . . . From that time on, no matter how wise the sovereign might be, there was not the slightest possibility for him to take a personal part in the affairs of state; finally it reached the point where he gave away his authority and bestowed it on powerful families.[23]

In 1855, while lecturing on *Mencius,* Shoin stated that in some cases the emperors themselves had been responsible for their loss of power, due to the fact that their personal virtue had been insufficient to affect the nation and so to control the feudal lords:

With all due respect, it was pointless for Emperors Go-Shirakawa and Go-Toba to feel nothing but hatred and anger toward [Taira no] Kiyomori, [Minamoto] Yoritomo, and [Hojo] Yoshitoki. . . . For them grievously to offend these important families was in truth something that ought never to have occurred.[24]

Nevertheless, such cases could not alter the intrinsic nature of the emperor, nor could they affect the duty of the loyal subject toward him. Especially after 1856, Shoin more and more emphasized the supreme majesty of the emperor and the absolute authority that was his by right of his divine ancestry, if he chose to use it. For example, in the *Taisaku Ichido,* written in 1858, Shoin said:

Whatever place is illumined by the heavenly sun, that place is under the rule of the Imperial Goddess. The command of the Emperor is the will of the Imperial Goddess. That it must be worshipfully obeyed can not be a subject for argument. If one should meet death while obeying his command, that death is even as life. If one should preserve life by rejecting his command, that life is worse than death.[25]

[23] *Shokyu Shigen,* in YSZ, I, 299–300.
[24] *Komo Yowa,* Book III, Part I, in YSZ, III, 173.
[25] *Taisaku Ichido,* in YSZ, V, 143.

Thus, even though Shoin held the emperor to be a human being and admitted that emperors had made mistakes in the past, he made the emperor an object of religious devotion who participated in all the attributes of Amaterasu.

In connection with Shoin's attitude toward the emperor as an object of religious veneration, his opinion on the Three Sacred Treasures is pertinent. In the *Komo Yowa,* when discussing the topic "things which appear to be two but are actually one," he cited four examples, of which the first was the "Sacred Treasures and the legitimate line." [26] For further details he referred to an essay he had written after reading Kuriyama Sempo's *Hoken Taiki,* and which he appended to the *Komo Yowa.* In this, Shoin gave his reasons for accepting Kuriyama Sempo's viewpoint; but he also pointed out that violent seizure of the Treasures could not give anyone a claim on the Throne:

The location of the Sacred Treasures is unfailingly the legitimate line, and where the legitimate line is located, unfailingly the Sacred Treasures are. The Sacred Treasures and the legitimate line cannot be viewed separately. . . .

What I previously mentioned concerning the unity of the Sacred Treasures and the legitimate line was spoken of a proper voluntary transfer. It did not refer to seizure by force. . . .

Since the Sacred Treasures are the subject of voluntary transfer by emperors in the legitimate line, for sovereign and subject, high and low, to guard them absolutely unto death, is a manifest obligation. When this obligation is clearly understood, the unity of the Sacred Treasures and the legitimate line will become increasingly plain and obvious.[27]

As early as 1853 Shoin had felt it was the duty of the subjects to guard the physical symbols of the emperor's divine authority, and he had made this the topic of one of his urgent memorials on national problems. Pointing out that Ise and Atsuta [28] should follow Kyoto in importance from the standpoint of defense—thus ranking them above Edo—he had written:

[26] *Komo Yoma,* Book II, in *YSZ,* III, 140.
[27] *Ibid.,* Appendix, in *YSZ,* III, 515–16.
[28] For the importance of Ise and Atsuta in this connection, see note 17, Chapter 1.

If—what is beyond the bounds of possibility—the unspeakable should happen to the Sacred Treasures of Ise and Atsuta, the Land of the Gods would lose that which makes it the Land of the Gods; heaven and earth would be wrapped in darkness; how could this be? [29]

The Critical Year

The year 1856, which marked the turning point in Shoin's thinking on the emperor's true importance, followed a year in prison, during which he had read and contemplated more than at any previous time. The new intensity of his devotion to both emperor and nation is shown in several writings of this period. Among them, the *Shoka Sonjuku-ki* has been mentioned previously; others included the *Shichi-sho Setsu,* his comments to Saito Eizo, and the *Mata Yomu Shichi-soku.*

The *Shichi-sho Setsu* ("Discussion of Seven Lives"), written in May, 1856, is a tribute to Nanko (Kusunoki Masashige) and an expression of Shoin's hope to be of eternal service to his country.[30] In his opinion, there is one eternal *li* of the universe, which is transmitted by the heart; *ch'i* pertains to the body. Therefore, the body is individual; the heart, general. Using the individual for the benefit of the general, that is, sacrificing the body for an ideal, makes one a great person; the opposite makes one a mean person. Nanko, in dying, hoped to be reborn seven times to vanquish the enemies of the nation; but, Shoin suggests, so long as his spirit is felt in the hearts of others, he will have not only seven lives but eternal life. For his own part, Shoin feels that he, too, participates in the *li* of Nanko. He once attempted to act on his own responsibility for the good of the nation; and—although he failed just as Nanko did—he hopes that his eternal heart may serve to stimulate later generations, and that he also may have seven lives to devote to this purpose.

In 1853, Shoin had used the *tenka no tenka* theory as an argument for loyalty to the emperor. At that time, he had interpreted its reference to "one man" to mean the shogun. However, in 1856, taking the "one man" as indicating the emperor, he re-

29 *Kyumusaku Is-soku,* in *YSZ,* I, 327.
30 In *YSZ,* IV, 127–29.

jected the validity of the theory, and made his rejection the vehicle for stating unequivocally the absolute power of the emperor over the lives of all subjects. In one of the lectures on *Mencius* early in July,[31] he mentioned that this theory had recently been given as a subject for compositions at the Meirinkan, and he pointed out that it was fallacious and not based on the authority of the classics. Quoting the verse "Under the whole heaven . . ." from the *Book of Odes,* he stated that this showed the true intent of the classics, and was the normal practice even in China. Although he did not refer to the fact in this lecture, less than two weeks previously he had read one of these compositions, submitted to him by its writer, Saito Eizo,[32] and had been seriously disturbed by the prevailing Meirinkan tendency to defend the authority of the Bakufu.

In his separately written comments on the young student's essay, Shoin brought out the fundamental areas of difference between Japan and all other countries: not only is a change of dynasty impossible under any conditions whatsoever, but the emperor's slightest wish must be the deepest desire of the subject; moreover, every subject, without distinction of class or position, is obligated to defend his country. The major portion of his criticism is as follows:

That "the realm is not the property [lit., realm] of one man" is a statement of the Chinese. In China it is so, but in the Land of the Gods, it is absolutely not so. I would respectfully point out that our Great Eight Islands, upon being founded by the Imperial Ancestor [i.e., Emperor Jimmu], were transmitted to his descendants for ten thousand generations, as unending as heaven and earth. They are not something to which others can have any pretension. That it is the realm of one man, therefore, is obvious. . . .

Even if the Emperor of our land should be as cruel as Chieh and Chou, the millions of people would have no other course than, hopefully bowing their heads in rows at the Imperial Palace, in lamentation worshipfully to pray for sympathetic understanding from the Emperor. If the Emperor should unfortunately be angered, and should kill the millions of people one and all, within the four seas

[31] *Komo Yowa,* Book IV, Part III, in *YSZ,* III, 463-64.
[32] Saito Eizo later became a pupil at the Shoka Sonjuku and one of Shoin's stanch supporters.

there would be no remnant of the people remaining, and the Land of the Gods would perish.

If there should still be one person left, he would have no other desire than to proceed to the Palace for his death. Such would be a person of the Land of the Gods. If he should not proceed to the Palace for his death, he would not be a person of the Land of the Gods. In such a case, if someone like T'ang and Wu should arise . . . though his heart might be benevolent, though his deeds might be righteous, he would be a Chinese or an Indian, a European or an American; he would positively not be a man of the Land of the Gods. And how should the people of the Land of the Gods make a common cause with *them?* . . .

If, by the remotest chance, there should be such a person as the Chinese speak of, to kill his lord out of sympathy for the people, he would be a wild beast, a jackal or a rhinoceros; but he would positively not be a human.

Accordingly, I say: "The realm is the realm of one man." That it is not the realm of one man is merely the statement of the Chinese. Nevertheless, for the people "under the whole heaven, to the borders of the land" all to make the affairs of the realm their own responsibility, and to serve the Emperor unto death; whether they are noble or base, revered or despised, making this no basis for distinction; this is the Way of the Land of the Gods. Only in this sense, perhaps, may it be said that it is not the realm of one man? [33]

According to this statement, in June and July of 1856 Shoin had already developed a firm conviction that if need be, the entire nation (phenomenal *kokutai*) should be sacrificed to preserve its essential characteristics (noumenal *kokutai*). Whereas previously he had hesitated to oppose the Bakufu because of the resultant weakening of the nation in the face of foreign aggression, now he was ready to make this logical application of his belief despite the danger.

This theme was developed during the summer in correspondence with both Gessho and Mokurin, but Mokurin's arguments were particularly convincing. He despised the Bakufu as based entirely on the Way of the Overlord and pointed out that if even Tokugawa Nariaki could not influence its policy, it was hopeless for others to try. Furthermore, supposing that some great general of a different family should rise to power and drive away the barbarians, what advantage would there be in exchanging one

[33] *Saito Sei no Bun wo Hyo-su,* in YSZ, IV, 139–41.

shogunate for another? What was needed were brave subjects ready to sacrifice themselves for the emperor in whatever way might be required. In other words, up to this time, repelling the barbarians had been Shoin's "main" concern, and loyalty to the emperor had been "corollary"; for Mokurin, loyalty to the emperor was "main" and all else "corollary." Finally, Shoin accepted Mokurin's position.

His firm adherence to this new viewpoint is illustrated in the *Mata Yomu Shichi-soku* ("On Re-reading the [*Shiki*] *Shichi-soku*"), which he wrote in December. In this, he explained the substance of the "main and corollary" problem and confessed that he had been in error throughout his entire life until, with the help of a friend (Mokurin), he had attained illumination the previous September. The tone of his language indicates that his change of heart resulted essentially from a triumph of religious feeling over military training:

If one's heart is not fixed, what sort of decision can there be even in affairs of the moment? If one's heart is fixed, how shall it be shaken even for ten thousand ages? . . . Now, trusting in the promise of the Heavenly Ancestress, and receiving the virtue of the successive Holy Ones, I have determined my heart to this, and will hold it for ten thousand ages.[34]

For the balance of his life, Shoin made sacrificial devotion to the emperor his main objective.[35]

The final harmonious combination of the religious and Bushido attitudes that Shoin achieved is shown in his description of the "Way of the Subject," written in 1859 during his second imprisonment at Noyama:

The continuous transmitting of the Imperial line for thousands and tens of thousands of generations without a change can not be at-

[34] *Mata Yomu Shichi-soku*, in YSZ, IV, 187.

[35] The significance of this decision applied not only to Shoin's own life but also to its effect on his pupils after he took over the Shoka Sonjuku. Even while being taught to uphold the cause of *jo-i*, they knew that it was subordinate to *son-no*; and when the goal of *son-no* had been achieved in the Meiji Restoration, Shoin's own disciples could easily abandon the cruder aspects of *jo-i* as no longer suited to the times.

tributed to chance; which is to say that the foundation of the Imperial Way itself lies in this fact. For at the time when Amaterasu delivered the Sacred Treasures to the Heavenly Grandson, Ninigi no Mikoto, she made this vow: "The increasing prosperity of the Imperial Throne shall be as eternal as heaven and earth."

This being so, the Way of the subject in China or India is unknown to us; we must hold indelibly in mind that in the Imperial Land, since the Imperial Throne is by its very nature eternally existent, the Way of the Subject is likewise eternally existent. . . .

Should one inquire as to what is the Way of the Subject, in the words of Ame-no-oshi-hi no Mikoto: [36] "We will not die peacefully, but will die by the side of our king. If we go to the sea, our bodies shall steep in the water. If we go to the hills, over our corpses the grass shall grow." [37] This truly is the Way of the Subject.[38]

[36] The archer-bodyguard who accompanied Ninigi no Mikoto on his descent to earth.

[37] A quotation from the *Manyoshu*. This translation is given by George B. Sansom, in *Japan: A Short Cultural History* (2nd ed.; New York: Appleton-Century-Crofts, 1943), p. 266.

[38] *Zagoku Nichiroku,* in *YSZ,* VII, 257–58.

11

Attitude Toward the Bakufu

IT HAS been pointed out, in connection with Kokugaku and the early Mito school, that loyalty to the emperor did not necessarily or even ordinarily involve opposition to the Tokugawa shogunate. This was true also of Shoin's position. Conforming to his Bushido principles, he could have no cause to attack the Bakufu so long as it fulfilled the duty of serving the emperor. There was never any question in Shoin's mind that the shogun had the duty of serving the emperor, and even when brought to trial in 1859, he still hoped that the shogun's administration might be made to see its duty. When Shoin finally felt himself required to oppose the Bakufu, he was not opposing either the Tokugawa family as such or its hegemony in the Japanese political sphere, but only its disloyalty to the emperor. If this fact is remembered, the reason for his apparently conflicting statements can be understood.

Shoin's basic attitudes toward the Bakufu may conveniently be classified under the headings of Bakufu-emperor relationships and Bakufu-*han* relationships. The changes in these attitudes, taking shape in the year 1858, must be considered separately, as they represented his reaction to a new situation.

Bakufu-Emperor Relationship

Up to the end of his life, there is no hint in Shoin's writings that he considered it necessary to eliminate the feudal lords, including the Tokugawa family, from the administration. Near the close of the Tokugawa period, proponents of reform spoke frequently of establishing a new form of government on the basis of *kobu-gattai* (union of court nobles and feudal lords); Shoin also accepted this theory and referred to it from time to time. Among the advocates of this plan there were two factions: those who aimed at the preservation and face-saving of the Bakufu and were hoping to broaden its base; and those who desired to restore the power of the emperor, but were willing that the Bakufu should continue if it proved its loyalty. Shoin's adherence was naturally to the latter of these two groups. Although he occasionally made vague mention of "restoration," it should ordinarily be taken in this sense, as is shown in a letter of 1858:

If the Imperial command is carried out in all particulars by the shogun and the various *han;* if the shogun leads the *han* in obedient service to the Imperial Court; and if the various *han* use their influence to mediate between the Imperial Court and the shogun, so that heaven and earth are associated in tranquillity—then will the Imperial Way not be reborn? [1]

Shoin constantly argued against the opinion, or the criticism, that loyalty to the emperor detracted from loyalty to the shogun. In one of the early lectures on *Mencius,* he said:

Among all the *han* of the seven roads,[2] where is there one that does not serve the command of the Emperor and obey the order of the Bakufu? Mutually joining their wills and combining their

[1] Letter to Nakatani Shosuke (Ansei 5. 3. x), in *Yoshida Shoin Zenshu* (hereafter cited as *YSZ*), V (Tokyo: Iwanami Shoten, 1938–40), 133.

[2] The seven roads were the main highways of Japan, leading out of Kyoto in all directions. By extension, the term means "the entire country."

strength, they must obediently serve the Imperial Court and the Bakufu—this is their obvious duty.[3]

Later, in answer to Taika's criticism, he wrote:

To consider that recognizing the importance of the Imperial Court means to belittle the Bakufu is a shallow viewpoint. It is due to the very fact of the Imperial Court's existence that there is also a Bakufu. Therefore, while reverencing the Imperial Court is the great means for tranquilizing the Imperial Land, necessarily the Bakufu also is automatically important. To consider that when one speaks of recognizing the importance of the Imperial Court, he is ignoring the Bakufu, is a distorted outlook. Reverence for the Imperial Court must be accompanied hand in hand by that for the Bakufu.[4]

Even in 1859, Shoin insisted that his attitude was not anti-Bakufu, but that he desired only to see the will of the Emperor enforced. Writing in Noyama prison, he pointed out that an Imperial Rescript of the preceding year had called for *kobu-gattai* and had continued the Emperor's approval of the Bakufu. His own efforts, he said, had always aimed at "Imperial support of the Tokugawa family, *kobu-gattai,* reverent obedience to the Emperor's will, unswerving loyalty to the Emperor, faithfulness to the Bakufu." [5]

If loyalty to the emperor was not incompatible with faithfulness to the shogun, in Shoin's opinion the opposite was also true: even those who were clearly vassals of the shogun were obliged to serve the emperor as well. This point was brought out strongly in one of his replies to Yamagata Taika. The old scholar had written, in words almost identical to those of his *Ima no Sho-Ko O-Shin ni Arazaru no Ben,* that there were vassals of the emperor, vassals of the shogun, vassals of the daimyos, and so forth —intending this as an argument against Shoin.[6] Shoin replied that he was in perfect agreement with this statement,[7] and, a few days later, explained why it did not affect his position:

[3] *Komo Yowa,* Book I, in *YSZ,* III, 49.
[4] *Ibid.,* Appendix, in *YSZ,* III, 569.
[5] *Guan no Omomuki,* in *YSZ,* VI, 300.
[6] *Komo Yowa,* Appendix, in *YSZ,* III, 565.
[7] *Ibid.,* p. 566.

As for saying that the feudal lords are the vassals of the shogun, there is no need for persuasion. They are clearly and distinctly set off from the officials appointed by command of the Imperial Court; I would not argue even one word to the effect that they are not vassals of the shogun. . . . But whether they be vassals of the shogun, or vassals of the emperor, if they revere the Imperial Court, respect the Bakufu, repel the barbarians, and love the common people, nothing more need be said. He who ignores these four duties is a traitor.[8]

While thus upholding the authority of the shogun and in no way questioning his right to administer the government, Shoin also taught that the shogun had no intrinsic or perpetual claim on the office, holding it only at the pleasure of the emperor:

As the Heavenly Sun Succession is to endure eternally, as unending as heaven and earth, these Great Eight Islands, being founded by the Heavenly Sun, are to be eternally protected by the Sun Succession. Accordingly, the millions of people rightfully make the interests of the Heavenly Sun Succession their own, and can have no other thought.

As for the case of the *Sei-i Tai-Shogun,*[9] only a person designated to that responsibility by command of the Imperial Court can occupy that office. For this reason, if the shogun should be similar to the Ashikaga family in his neglect of duty, it is even possible for the office to be immediately abolished.[10]

In making this statement, Shoin was undoubtedly thinking of foreign relations, his great area of disagreement with the Bakufu. A few months after this lecture was given, he pointed out in a letter to Mokurin [11] that while there was no serious impropriety involved in the Bakufu's calling itself "Government of the Japanese Empire" in relations with foreign countries, it was completely impossible to designate the shogun as "Great Lord" (*Taikun;* at that time usually anglicized as "tycoon").

Early in 1857, he wrote again and at greater length on this subject. Reviewing Japanese diplomatic history, he said that in ancient times subjects had not carried on foreign relations in

[8] *Ibid.,* p. 570.

[9] The seldom-used complete official title of the shogun.

[10] *Komo Yowa,* Book I, in *YSZ,* III, 59.

[11] Letter to Mokurin (Ansei 2. 11. 1), in *YSZ,* IV, 81–83.

their own name; this was naturally the prerogative of the emperor. Only after the military class seized control had this custom arisen; Ashikaga Yoshimitsu had even had the perversity to style himself *Kokuo*. The Tokugawa Bakufu had revived many of the Ashikaga forms and procedures; their conduct of foreign relations, in particular, merited severe criticism: they were obliterating *ka-i no ben* and thus repeating the error of the Ashikagas:

There has been a Supreme-Monarch-Ruling-all-under-Heaven [12] of our Great Eight Islands since primeval times. For the shogun to have himself designated as *Kokuo*, domestically is of course disgusting in its presumptuousness; and at the same time, toward foreign countries it is excessively obsequious; [13] in both ways alike it is contrary to our *kokutai*.[14]

By using the title *Taikun* rather than *Kokuo*, the Tokugawa Bakufu took this into account to some extent, he continued, but it was still likely to create misunderstanding:

If it should become the practice of foreign countries in general to refer to the Great Eight Islands of the Supreme-Monarch-Ruling-all-under-Heaven as the "Kingdom of Japan," how could the Bakufu answer to the country?—how apologize to the Emperor? [15]

Less than three months after writing these remarks, Shoin came across a copy of an essay on the subject of the shogun's title,

[12] Shoin here intentionally used an archaic term for emperor.
[13] That is, it is obsequious to hide the fact that Japan is ruled by a Heaven-descended emperor and make it appear to be ruled by a king equal in rank to the king of Korea and lower than the emperor of China. Further light on Shoin's meaning is shed by the statement of Yoshi S. Kuno that in their diplomatic relations,

. . . neither Japan nor Korea recognized the existence of the emperor of Japan or the imperial government of that country. The shogun never used his official titles, such as *Shogun* or *Sei-i Tai-shogun*, or any other official titles or ranks conferred upon him by the emperor of Japan, in the state papers sent to Korea. . . . The Tokugawa shogunate thus kept the existence of the emperor of Japan from the knowledge of Korea. [*Japanese Expansion on the Asiatic Continent*, II (Berkeley: University of California Press, 1940), p. 332.]
[14] *Gaiban Tsuryaku*, in *YSZ*, XII, 86.
[15] *Ibid*.

which had been sent to Arai Hakuseki in 1711 by Amenomori Hoshu,[16] and which strenuously opposed the use of the word *kokuo* for the shogun. Delighted with its contents, Shoin said that Hoshu had expressed his own feelings better than he could himself, and that Hoshu's argument, in its deep feeling for emperor and nation, was a correction of the errors of superiors and a model for inferiors.[17]

From this sort of discussion, the limitations on Shoin's loyalty to the Bakufu become apparent. Compared with his absolute and unquestioning devotion for the emperor, his attitude toward the shogun was a "faithfulness" conditioned on the latter's fulfillment of his own obligations. When Bakufu policy became prejudicial to the interests of emperor or nation, Shoin felt not only free but obligated to criticize or oppose it.

Bakufu-Han Relationship

Shoin's concept of the relation between the Bakufu, or shogun, and the lords of the several *han* was affected by his insistence that the individual samurai's loyalty to his own *han* lord was fundamental. In a sense, this did not differ from the custom,

16 Amenomori Hoshu (1668–1755), as the official scholar of Tsushima-*han*, had duties in connection with the exchange of diplomatic correspondence between Japan and Korea. Being unable to accept Arai Hakuseki's ideas on the question of the shogun's title (see pp. 27–28), he put his opinion in the form of an essay called the *Kokuo Shogo Ron*, and sent Hakuseki a copy. In this, he said that he feared later generations would find Hakuseki at fault in this matter; while the shogun held control of the actual government, the Imperial Court alone controlled the assignment of rank, so that the shogun could not arbitrarily give himself a title:

> The title of *Taikun* is certainly improper, but changing it to *Kokuo* is also improper. Furthermore, I know of no national government at all, superior to the present Imperial household. Under these circumstances, it is incumbent on us, by refraining from openly designating the shogun as king, to appreciate somewhat the great principle of the allegiance of the subject. [Quoted in Yoshida Togo, *Tokugawa Seikyo-ko*, I (Tokyo: Fuzambo Shoten, 1894), p. 156.]

17 *Gaiban Tsuryaku*, Epilogue, in *YSZ*, XII, 113; also *Amenomori Hoshu Sensei no Kokuo Shogo Ron Batsu*, in *YSZ*, IV, 303–5.

universal since the time of Minamoto Yoritomo, according to which a samurai considered as his lord and master that person to whom his services were directly due and from whom he received his stipend. However, Shoin's view diverged from the common one in that he refused to admit the shogun as the direct superior of the *hanshu*. He saw the relationship essentially in terms of a family, where the emperor corresponded to the father and the daimyos to sons. Even though the shogun was the leading daimyo, and therefore entitled to respect as the elder brother, the primary loyalty of each was to the emperor as father, not to the shogun as elder brother. This duty was shared by the subordinate samurai, so that for them, two loyalties existed: to *hanshu* and to emperor. To Shoin, it was inconceivable that these two loyalties could be incompatible. Thus, when Yamagata Taika charged that advocacy of loyalty to the emperor meant ignoring duty to the *hanshu*, Shoin replied:

Were I to be disloyal to my lord, how could I be truly loyal to the Imperial Court? Were I to be disloyal to the Imperial Court, how could I be truly loyal to my lord? To divide the Imperial Court and my lord, and separate them into two, is a commonplace, vulgar view.[18]

Such criticisms apparently continued, as in 1859 Shoin wrote again on this matter, fervently declaring his loyalty to *han* and lord:

My friends have the opinion that my *sonjo* means to forget my lord's province . . . [in my] desire to save the Land of the Gods from the barbarian influence. Ah! were I to die ten thousand deaths, how could I bear to abandon my lord's land! . . . As for my feeling of loyalty to my lord, if I were not to reverence the Land of the Gods and drive out the barbarian influence, what should I set my hand to? . . . From the time of my unauthorized trip and the attempt to go overseas, down to the various recent plans for loyal service to the Emperor . . . my inmost heart has never lessened by even one hairsbreadth in attachment to my lord.[19]

[18] *Komo Yowa*, Appendix, in *YSZ*, III, 566.
[19] *Chiko Nangen*, in *YSZ*, VI, 281–82.

Feeling such an ardent devotion to his lord, it was natural that Shoin, from his study of history, should come to realize that the Tokugawas were basically no more noble than Choshu's house of Mori,[20] and that the difference in their respective stations was due mainly to the fortunes of war, sanctified by the emperor's approval. As he wrote, also in 1859:

> The vassals of our Mori family, too, since fortune was against their arms, because of their defeat at Sekigahara [21] came under the domination of the Tokugawas. But . . . as the Tokugawas have indeed been appointed to the position of shogun by the Imperial Court, it is impermissible to harbor private animosity.[22]

These were the attitudes that formed the basis for Shoin's summation of the relationship between emperor, *hanshu,* and shogun in the *Mata Yomu Shichi-soku:* "Even though because of his favors, the obligation to the shogun is very great, he is not the lord of my lord." [23]

Out of these elements—primary duty to the emperor, recognition of the Tokugawa family's control of the government, and refusal to recognize a feudal relationship between Tokugawa and Mori—Shoin fashioned his original "admonition theory." This theory expressed his view as to what faithfulness to the Bakufu should mean: it would demand sincere and prolonged efforts aimed at persuading the shogun to take the path of service to the emperor, but if those efforts should finally fail, the obligation of "faithfulness" would be terminated.

The first hint of this theory is to be found in the *Shokyu Shigen.* Here, in discussing the necessity for reforming the *han* administration, Shoin suggested the advisability of the *hanshu's* accepting direct admonition from his people: "Should there be one desiring to speak with the lord, even though it be in the

---

[20] The Mori family traced its descent from Emperor Heijo (reigned 806–9). The Tokugawas were descended from Emperor Seiwa (reigned 858–76).

[21] The decisive battle, in 1600, as a result of which Tokugawa Ieyasu later claimed the right to rule all Japan.

[22] Letter to Nomura Yasushi (Ansei 6. 4. 4), in *YSZ,* IX, 321.

[23] *Mata Yomu Shichi-soku,* in *YSZ,* IV, 189.

dead of night, he should unfailingly condescend to come forth, take his seat, and hear the words of that person." [24]

A year and a half later (April, 1855), in his first letter to Gessho,[25] Shoin applied this idea to the Bakufu. Criticizing Gessho's talk of anti-Bakufu action, he said the enemy was external, not internal, and that the country could be united behind the *jo-i* program if the Bakufu were properly admonished and persuaded of its duty.

In the following year, arguing the question of loyalty with Yamagata Taika, Shoin once more mentioned his "admonition theory":

My whole desire is, in company with the Bakufu and the several feudal lords, to serve the Imperial Court. Inasmuch as the shogun is such by appointment of the Imperial Court, I consider him to be a loyal servant of the Imperial Court. If—although it is unthinkable —disloyalty should occur, every person, from the lords on down, must assume the responsibility for admonition.

In Taika's opinion, he views the shogun as a rebel against the Imperial Court: therefore, if one should serve the Imperial Court, he would be disloyal to the Bakufu. This is as much as to say that when one serves the Bakufu, the Imperial Court means no more to him than an unknown stranger.[26]

In the above statement, Shoin implied that the duty of admonishing the shogun was a general one to be carried out by all; in fact, however, he hoped this task would be accepted by his lord, Yoshichika. Aside from the question of basic duty involved, there was good reason for such an expectation. The Mori family had a reputation for loyalty to the emperor antedating Tokugawa rule, and it was related by marriage to some of the highest-ranking families of court nobility. Throughout the Tokugawa period, the daimyo of Choshu had many special privileges in this connection, such as that of stopping in Kyoto on *sankin-kotai*[27] trips in order to visit his friends among these families, including the houses of Arisugawa, Takatsukasa, Konoe, Ichijo, and

---

[24] *Shokyu Shigen,* in YSZ, I, 300.
[25] Letter to Gessho (Ansei 2. 3. 9), in YSZ, IV, 22–26.
[26] *Komo Yowa,* Appendix, in YSZ, III, 595.
[27] See Appendix B.

Saionji. Because of this tradition, it could be argued that the Mori family had a special obligation to uphold the interests of the emperor. Accordingly, if any of the daimyos were actually to admonish the shogun concerning his lack of obedience, Mori Yoshichika would be a logical choice.

With this background in mind Shoin wrote his most detailed exposition of the "admonition theory," to be found in a letter to Mokurin of September, 1856 (the month of his "illumination"). At this time, even though he was ready to accept the possibility that action against the shogun might become necessary, he hoped to avoid it by means of admonition; and he strongly felt that all must share in the shogun's guilt so long as the admonition was not carried out. The main points of his argument were as follows:

I am a vassal of the Mori family, and accordingly it is my place to exert myself day and night in the Mori service. The Mori family are vassals of the Emperor, and accordingly it is their place to serve the Emperor day and night. For us to render loyal service to our lord is the same as rendering loyal service to the Emperor.

Nevertheless, in the past six hundred years, there have been many times when my lord did not exert his efforts in loyal service to the Emperor. Truly, that this is a great crime is self-evident. My sole desire is to cause my lord, in this day, to make up the loyal service of the past six hundred years. However, as I am under confinement, I am unable either to submit memorials or to speak in person. . . .

On a later occasion, when I have obtained a pardon . . . first of all, instructing the chief minister [i.e., of the *han*], I will make him know the guilt of six hundred years, and that it should be compensated for in loyal service today; then I will cause my lord to be informed of this; then others of the same rank as my lord, one and all should be made to know this Duty; after this, the shogun must be made to know his previous faults without exception, and caused to arise in loyal service to the Emperor. . . .

Now, while in confinement, to abuse the shogun is mere idle talk; and furthermore, while I myself do not call attention to the guilt of the shogun I have no right to live. Thus I am equally guilty with him. My lord also is equally guilty. While ignoring my own sin to discuss the sin of another is something I would die before doing. . . . On a later occasion, I will remonstrate with my lord, and if he will not heed, I will continue my admonition even until I am punished by death for it. . . .

If my lord accepts my direct exhortation, when he realizes the great crime of the past six hundred years it will then be his place to effect the admonition of the other daimyos and even of the shogun. Although the shogun is not the lord of my lord, the favors received in the past two hundred years, since he assumed the responsibility of supreme administrator, cannot be ignored; and therefore, three admonitions—nine admonitions—effort after effort must be made. If, when every effort has been exhausted, he still does not appreciate his guilt, then unavoidably, there will be no other course than for my lord, together with those daimyos who realize the crime, to present this matter to the Imperial Court and to carry out the Emperor's command.[28]

Aside from the "admonition theory" itself, an interesting feature of this letter is its advocation of responsibility for serving the emperor on three levels, all of which were eventually put into effect: (1) *Individual:* Shoin's sense of his own responsibility later became increasingly dominant, leading to such steps as the plot against Manabe Akikatsu. (2) *Choshu-han:* While Yoshichika was unwilling to take action at first, after Shoin's death his arguments were instrumental in stiffening *han* policy toward the Bakufu and in bringing about such incidents as the firing on foreign ships by Choshu-*han* coastal-defense units in 1863. (3) *General:* Choshu finally combined with other loyal *han* to force the complete surrender of Tokugawa power.

Final Rejection of the Bakufu

While Shoin's loyalty to the emperor, based on the unchanging essence of *kokutai,* was necessarily idealistic and independent of existing conditions, his faithfulness to the Tokugawas was conditioned on his practical assessment of current Bakufu policy. Thus, his disillusionment with the shogunate was first expressed in strong language at the precise time when he was placing his supreme trust in the emperor. In the *Mata Yomu Shichi-soku,* he wrote:

It is said that the Imperial Court above is august, the Bakufu below is respectful. If it were actually as it is said, then what cause for distress would there be at present? Only the fact that it is not so

[28] Letter to Mokurin (Ansei 3. 8. 18), in *YSZ,* VIII, 518–20.

gives rise to the indignation of the *shishi*. . . . While the one indeed is august, where is the respectfulness of the other?

The untoward events of the past six hundred years are all something that a true subject can not bear to discuss. For a military vassal to establish a government was started by [Minamoto] Yoritomo; for a subordinate vassal to take command began with [Hojo] Yoshitoki; for a rebellious vassal to seize the country originated with [Ashikaga] Takauji. The exploits of these three vassals cannot suffice to compensate for their crimes. . . .

When we come down to the temporizing of the present day, it is unchanged from the former times of Yoritomo, Yoshitoki, and Takauji.[29]

However, for this dissatisfaction to turn to outright opposition, it was necessary that the shogun manifest a wilful violation of the emperor's command, and it was also desirable that the emperor order his punishment. Emperor Komei, for his part, was quite hesitant to oppose the Bakufu, and his failure to take a strong stand or to repudiate his disloyal minister created a problem in ideological consistency that Shoin was never able to solve completely; eventually, he was driven very close to the point of personally admonishing the Emperor. Still, the theory of the situation was clear; and, for many others as well as for Shoin, the *ichoku* question (violation of the Imperial command) was the factor that turned loyalty to the emperor into active opposition to the shogunate.

From the *kokutai* viewpoint, the shogun was no more than an official appointed by the emperor to carry on the details of national administration. From the Confucian viewpoint, even assuming that the shogun held the Mandate of Heaven, there could be little doubt that the emperor was in the position of Heaven. From either viewpoint, if the emperor withdrew his support, the shogun would have no right to office; and according to Confucianism, he would further become a mere common fellow subject to the violent punishment of Heaven, to be meted out through some human agency. Accordingly, pinning the label of *ichoku* on the shogun would be the first step toward the rebirth of the Imperial Way. For this reason, *ichoku* became one of the most useful tools of the *shishi* group in arousing sentiment for a Restoration. The development of this argument is shown by the changes in Shoin's sentiments during a less-than-six-month period in 1858.

As the two sides became clearly distinguished, the Bakufu refused the advice of other important branches of the Tokugawa family and took more and more repressive measures against the pro-emperor group, such as placing Tokugawa Nariaki under house arrest and imprisoning loyalists of lower rank; however, the only case of *ichoku* actually charged during Shoin's lifetime was in connection with foreign relations.[30] Here, the known in-

[30] The historical background was as follows: Since late in 1857, the Bakufu had been intending to negotiate new commercial treaties with the Western powers. Hotta Masayoshi was sent to Kyoto to obtain Emperor Komei's approval, which he expected as a matter of course. However, sentiment at the court was opposed, and due to the urgent representations of a group of eighty-eight court nobles, the Emperor withheld approval. In an Imperial Rescript of May 3, 1858 (Ansei 5. 3. 20), he ordered the Bakufu to consult the daimyos—after which he would make his decision. On June 6, the Bakufu sent out requests for the opinions of the daimyos; but without consulting further either them or the Emperor, it proceeded to sign a treaty with the United States on July 29, followed shortly after by pacts with the Netherlands, Russia, England, and France. Because they were made without the Emperor's approval, these agreements were announced as "provisional treaties" (*kari-joyaku*); but this concession did not mollify anti-Bakufu sentiment; nor, apparently, was it clearly explained to the foreign powers. (For information on the intrigues by which the Emperor was persuaded to defy the Bakufu for the first time in Tokugawa history, see W. G. Beasley [trans. and ed.], *Select Documents in Japanese Foreign Policy 1853–1868* [London: Oxford University Press, 1955], pp. 38–42; the text of the Imperial Rescript of May 3, 1858, appears on pp. 180–81.)

The policy of pushing the treaties through was enforced by Ii Naosuke, who had become *tairo* on June 4. While Shoin's memorandums mention the Tokugawa family, the shogun, and the Bakufu indiscriminately, what he was actually opposing was not the person of the shogun but the fact that the national government should defy the will of the sovereign. This is shown by the fact that one of his strongest attacks, the *Jiseiron*, was written after the thirteenth shogun, Iesada, had died, and had been succeeded by the twelve-year-old Iemochi. (The death of Iesada occurred August 12, 1858. It also preceded by a few days Shoin's *Taigi wo Gi-su* and *Jigi Ryakuron*, but the news had not yet reached Hagi at the time of his writing them.)

tentions of the Bakufu diverged so widely from the desires of the Court that, during the early months of 1858, the possibility of a violation had already become a topic of discussion before it occurred.

When Emperor Komei handed down the rescript of May 3, Shoin was immediately notified by Kusaka Genzui, his brother-in-law and one of his favorite pupils, who was then in Kyoto. In response to the occasion, he wrote the *Taisaku Ichido*.[31] While this dealt mainly with the problem of foreign relations, it also touched on the *ichoku* question: "If—by the remotest possibility —the shogun should disobey the Imperial command, it would be a simple matter for the nation to arise as one man and take his life. But the shogun would never do such a thing." [32]

It was June 22 when the official message arrived in Hagi from the Bakufu, requesting the opinion of the daimyo. Mori Yoshichika was then in Edo, but without waiting for his return, Shoin immediately wrote his own reaction, the *Guron* ("A Fool's Opinion"). Although, he said, "The Bakufu appears to have not the slightest intention of obeying the Imperial command," [33] he could hardly bring himself to consider "the remote possibility that the Bakufu would violate the Imperial command." [34] The main argument of the *Guron* was that if the Emperor gave the order to fight the United States, popular support would be so strong that the Bakufu could not resist acceding to his will. As yet, Shoin had expressed no hint of anti-Bakufu sentiment. A few days later he sent copies of the *Taisaku Ichido* and the *Guron* to Yanagawa Seigan, who eventually, to Shoin's intense happiness, showed them to Emperor Komei.

On August 20, Shoin learned what to him was the astounding news that the Bakufu had signed the treaty with the United States. He blazed up in anger at this outrageous act and immediately wrote a letter to one of the high officials of the *han* government, in which for the first time he proposed a resort to arms against the shogunate:

[31] See pp. 174-75.
[32] *Taisaku Ichido*, in YSZ, V, 143.
[33] *Guron*, in YSZ, V, 152.
[34] *Ibid.*, p. 153.

Now the Bakufu has clearly and definitely violated the Imperial command. Its crime fills up heaven and earth. . . .

Obedient service to the Imperial command is the public duty of the entire realm. If it should happen that the Bakufu does not act accordingly, let our *han,* by applying immediately to the Emperor, bring the matter to a decision. We can never chime in with the flatterers [i.e., supporters of the Bakufu]. Submitting a memorial on this to the Emperor, we will receive his settlement of it; and if as a result the Bakufu rebels and wages unrighteous war, even if our samurai meet their death and our province perishes, how should these things be refused in following the Way? [35]

The next day, Shoin wrote his great outburst against the shogun, the *Taigi wo Gi-su* ("I Argue for *Taigi*"), and submitted it to Yoshichika, who had in the meantime returned to Hagi. In this memorial, he expressed the following sentiments:

Ignoring the distress of the nation, heedless of the shame of the nation, he disobeys the Imperial command. This crime of the shogun's can not be contained in heaven and earth; gods and men, all are enraged. . . .

The shogun is a national criminal. If we now let him go without chastisement, what will the nation say of us for all eternity? . . . To serve the Imperial command is the Way; to chastise rebellion is Duty. . . .

If in this day, our *han* should decisively propose the cause of *taigi* [Supreme Duty] to the nation, as a result of the public wrath of the millions of people, internally, the shogun would as a matter of course be isolated; and furthermore, externally, the American barbarians as well would withdraw in defeat; the renaissance of the Imperial Court awaits only the bending of a finger.[36]

Despite his castigation of the shogun in this memorial, Shoin had still not completely given up the idea of reforming him by admonition; in closing, he expressed the hope that perhaps Choshu might intercede and bring him back to the path of *taigi*.

This was followed three days later by another memorandum of recommendations to the *hanshu,* the *Jigi Ryakuron* ("Brief Discussion of the Duty of the Times"). In this, Shoin made four

---

[35] Letter to Maeda Sonemon (Ansei 5. 7. 12), in *YSZ,* V, 190–91.

[36] *Taigi wo Gi-su,* in *YSZ,* V, 192–94. Cf. the similar reaction of Tokugawa Nariaki, pp. 99–100, this volume.

points: (1) the Bakufu's *ichoku;* (2) the necessity for outspoken remonstrance; (3) the Emperor's anger against the barbarians; and (4) the duty of the Mori family to ease the Emperor's mind by assuring him of their complete support for any command he might give. Facing the possibility that war with the Bakufu might result—"in case an incident should occur, and the Imperial Court should place its confidence in us, the shogun would unfailingly consider us as an enemy" [37]—he then discussed the details of raising loyal troops to fight the shogun and the procuring of assistance from other *han.*

As time went by, and his lord did not seem disposed to act on his advice, Shoin determined to make an appeal directly to the Emperor. This was the *Jiseiron* ("On the Conditions of the Times"), written on November 2 and sent to Ohara Shigenori, his friend at the Imperial Court. After pointing out how the Bakufu was not only signing treaties in defiance of the Emperor's will but punishing those who displayed loyalty to their sovereign, Shoin pleaded for the Emperor to issue a new rescript:

If the Emperor does not take a particularly decisive step, the Land of the Gods must unavoidably become the possession of the barbarians. The *shinchoku* of the Imperial Goddess will be terminated today; the Three Sacred Treasures as well will come to an end today.[38]

Continuing, he wrote that with the foreigners taking over the country, opium and Christianity would not be far behind; the Emperor must act immediately to prevent the Bakufu from carrying its policy further:

The Bakufu apparently has a plan for hastily strengthening its ties of amity with the foreign barbarians, before the various provinces [i.e., *han*] can arise in righteous effort. Under the conditions of the immediate present, no matter how many hundred Imperial commands are handed down from the Throne, no matter how many thousand memorials of righteous argument are submitted by the several lords, the Bakufu makes not even one move toward obedient service, but only hastens the more its amity with the foreign barbarians.[39]

[37] *Jigi Ryakuron,* in *YSZ*, V, 203.
[38] *Jiseiron,* in *YSZ*, V, 250.   [39] *Ibid.,* p. 251.

Then, in a complete reversal of his earlier stand, Shoin demonstrated that loyalty to the emperor was now his sole objective, even at the cost, if necessary, of defying his own lord. He praised the undying inspiration of Emperor Go-Daigo's actions and stated that if Komei would but give the word loyal servants like Nanko would arise from the lower ranks and come to his support regardless of their lords' indifference; but that if the Emperor did not act, it would be unreasonable to expect any glorious achievement:

The Tokugawas are more and more extending the sway of their evil power; the feudal lords one and all are under the thumb of the Tokugawas; not a hand can be lifted in service to the Emperor. In the lower ranks, even among loyal samurai, without exception there is none who is not a vassal either of the shogun or of the lords; and such being the case, it does not happen that any, taking the initiative over his lord, plans righteous undertakings. Finally, even those who have given their hearts to the Imperial Court, cherishing their aspirations will die of old age.[40]

The *Jiseiron* was the high point of Shoin's attacks against the Bakufu. A few weeks after this he was arrested because of the Manabe plot, but even in prison, occupied with plans for his friends to carry out, he found little time for serious writing. The only hint of the direction his ideas were taking occurs in a letter of early March, 1859: "I was on the point of submitting an argument concerning a Restoration, but as I have not yet given it sufficient consideration, I will put it off to some future time." [41]

Later in March and April, he tried to persuade Yoshichika to stop in Kyoto on his spring trip to Edo, in order to visit the Emperor and urge him to take steps against the Bakufu; but this effort, too, was unavailing. Completely discouraged with his lord's failure to accept his suggestions, at the end of May Shoin wrote: *"It is useless to tell* our lord personally that he must act in the spirit of *sonjo. It is better to construct* some kind of an incident which will create *sonjo, and present him with it."* [42]

[40] *Ibid.,* p. 253.
[41] Letter to Irie Sugizo (Ansei 6. 1. 27), in *YSZ,* VI, 121.
[42] Letter to Irie Sugizo (Ansei 6. 4. about 22), in *YSZ,* IX, 351. Emphasis marks (corresponding to italics) in original.

Before he could work out the *fait accompli* that would force the hand of the *hanshu*, Shoin was transferred to Demma-cho prison in Edo.

Even in going to Edo, Shoin had some hope that he could impress the Bakufu officials by his personal admonition: "I was firmly convinced that if Heaven deigned to recognize my trifling amount of sincerity, the officials of the Bakufu would unfailingly approve my argument." [43] But when he tried to discuss the *ichoku* question with the examining magistrate, he was abruptly stopped. In his farewell letter to his father, uncle, and brother, the week before his execution, he said:

The Bakufu is failing completely to administer justice; the barbarians are domineering over the government freely and without restriction. Nevertheless, it cannot be said that the Land of the Gods has yet fallen to the ground; above, there is the Holy Emperor; below, loyal souls and righteous spirits abound. Thus, I pray that the nation will not suffer too great a loss of strength.[44]

His last will and testament was imbued with the feeling that individuals would have to take the responsibility for loyal service to the nation: "The affairs of the nation can be accomplished only through the persons and the resolve of those who desire to serve the nation." [45] As for himself, his work was still unfinished: "Seven times returning to life, my resolve to repel the barbarians—can I forget?" [46]

[43] *Ryukonroku,* in *YSZ,* VII, 319.
[44] Letter to Sugi Yurinosuke, Tamaki Bunnoshin, and Sugi Umetaro (Ansei 6. 10. 20), in *YSZ,* IX, 480–81.
[45] *Ryukonroku,* in *YSZ,* VII, 328.
[46] *Ibid.,* p. 330.

Part Three

Conclusion

12

A Japanese Theory of the State

Our Imperial Ancestors have founded Our Empire on a basis broad and everlasting, and have deeply and firmly implanted virtue; Our subjects ever united in loyalty and filial piety have from generation to generation illustrated the beauty thereof. This is the glory of Our *Kokutai,* and herein also lies the source of Our Education. . . . the prosperity of Our Imperial Throne coeval with heaven and earth. . . .

The Way here set forth is indeed the teaching bequeathed by Our Imperial Ancestors, to be observed alike by Their Descendants and the subjects, infallible for all ages and true in all places. . . .

—*Imperial Rescript on Education,* 1890 [1]

[1] These excerpts follow the official translation as cited in George B. Sansom, *The Western World and Japan* (New York: Alfred A. Knopf, 1950), p. 464, except for the use of the original word *kokutai,* which the translation renders as "the fundamental character of Our Empire."

The Tokugawa Intellectual Environment

IF WE SHOULD attempt to characterize the intellectual environment of the Tokugawa period in one word, perhaps it could best be described as "conservative." It resisted change and yielded but slowly to altered conditions; more importantly, it considered the Golden Age to have been in the past. In political matters, as in others, this was not a time when innovation was favored. Motoori Norinaga spoke for many when he said:

Even things that are profitable, if they are of a new form, are customarily considered to be troublesome; and for this reason, things that are traditional, even though containing slight elements of harm, for the most part should remain as they are.[2]

Political thinking consisted not so much of developing new ideas as it did of skilfully utilizing old ones—either suggesting new interpretations, or choosing particular elements for new emphasis. In the some two hundred and fifty years of the Tokugawa period, Muro Kyuso's social-contract theory was a rare exception to this statement. Much more typical was the way in which Yoshida Shoin used Aizawa Yasushi's quotation of Mencius' citation from the *Book of Odes*. Training in Confucian methodology encouraged this tendency: what was appreciated in a scholar of Shushigaku was not the creation of new concept symbols, but dexterity in manipulating the existing ones. When Confucian standards prevailed, some thinkers then began to apply this method to Shinto research as well, seeking a Golden Age in Japan's own myths and records that would exceed in antiquity even the legendary founding of China. Thus, conservatism eventually affected both the method of scholarship and its choice of subject matter; and the role of the Bakufu came to be judged on how closely it conformed to the ideal standard of some largely imaginary prehistoric epoch. This idealization of the past is one of the noticeable results of Tokugawa political thinking.

[2] *Hihon Tama-kushige* ed. Muraoka Tsunetsugu, Book II (Tokyo: Iwanami Shoten, 1934), p. 82.

Another characteristic of the Tokugawa intellectual world that undoubtedly influenced the nature of political thought was the relative paucity of material for study and discussion. There was, of course, the great body of Chinese literature, but generally speaking this was not accessible to the ordinary person. There were few Japanese writers on a given subject; the available works of each were also few. Yoshida Shoin's experiences help to substantiate these points: he had to travel to Hirado, for example, to find a copy of Wang Yang-ming's best-known work; and when he was in prison his brother went to great lengths to borrow books for him to read. We also find Shoin copying as he read, in order to have the material at hand for future reference, and frequently rereading the same works.

Thus, any Tokugawa-period writer was apt to be familiar to succeeding generations, to be read and reread. In a society that resisted change and continued largely to employ Chinese for scholarly composition, neither his basic frame of reference nor his mode of expressing himself was likely to go out of date. Later writers normally based their proposals on what had gone before, either praising and amplifying it or, if they determined to apply some different criterion, criticizing and opposing it. New ideas tended to be built on the old, and were chiefly new composites of material from various pre-existing sources. Viewed in this way, the current of Tokugawa political thought appears somewhat as a slow, majestic eddying in a pool without inlet or outlet; yet there was a discernible process of development.

Early Tendency of Tokugawa Thought

In the beginning, official support for Shushigaku encouraged the rise of a class new to Japan—the professional Confucian teacher or scholar. Whereas previously the study of Confucianism had been so closely connected with Buddhism that it had been assumed any scholar must be a priest, it now became possible for individuals in the service of the Bakufu or the *han* governments to throw off the form of the priesthood and to stand unequivocally for Confucianism. Under the influence of such teachers, it was to be expected that the newly stabilized and subsidized samurai class would hold attitudes similar to those of China toward government, and that the authority of the Bakufu would be explained in Confucian terms. This tendency was shown by such men as Hayashi Razan and Arai Hakuseki.

However, as the scholars, drawn almost exclusively from the samurai, increased in number and self-confidence, some began to question the justification for relying solely on Chinese history and example, and started to investigate independently the ancient records of Japan. Among the first of those who found Japan more significant than China were Kumazawa Banzan and Yamaga Soko; the latter's *Chucho Jijitsu* discussed many of the points that were to become significant to patriotic writers, while his clarification of the principles of Bushido gave new meaning to the concepts of Loyalty and Duty.

Although the Hayashi school's interpretation of Shushigaku continued to support the authority of the shogunate, after Muro Kyuso this group was devoid of fresh ideas, and the Shoheiko did not seem to produce or attract challenging thinkers. By the end of the seventeenth century, increasing interest in national history and tradition brought about a reaction against the emphasis on China inherent in pure Shushigaku, and even stronger opposition to the antipatriotism displayed by such men as Ogyu Sorai. This meant that for the next hundred years the most vital political thought in Japan would represent a conscious effort to elevate Japanese ideas over Chinese.

In the early part of the eighteenth century, this tendency was evident among the disciples of Yamazaki Ansai. In general, the Kimon school retained the Confucian framework but gave it a Japanese application. One of the best examples of the result was Asami Keisai's *Seiken Igen,* which eventually became one of the major texts of the restoration ideology. Approximately one hundred and fifty years after it was written, the *Seiken Igen* was universally known and respected among the imperial loyalist faction, even though its use in the *han* schools had been prohibited. The famous slogan *son-no jo-i* summed up exactly the moral of this book.

Ansai's Suika Shinto also had its effect, although in the final analysis its particularly mystical and nonrational approach to the emperor stimulated loyalty more than it did pure religious faith. And in Takeuchi Shikibu and Yamagata Daini, the Kimon school was later credited with producing the first martyrs of the imperial restoration movement, unintentional though their sacrifice may have been.

Influence of Kokugaku

Before the end of the eighteenth century, the stress on Japan and its essential superiority had been further invigorated by the efforts of the Kokugaku scholars. Their denial of any validity whatsoever in Chinese thought and their complete rejection of Confucianism as a norm were too extreme to be entirely acceptable in an environment as thoroughly Confucianized as Tokugawa Japan; nevertheless, their scholarship was widely respected.

Both Norinaga and Atsutane contributed to the emerging sense of loyalty to the emperor and patriotism for Japan. With regard to their concept of the emperor, there was no essential difference between Kokugaku and Suika Shinto. Both schools viewed him as a god, to be revered and obeyed unquestioningly; in this, Kokugaku operated to strengthen and sanction a tendency that had already been widely disseminated.

With respect to the nation, however, Kokugaku went further than Ansai or even Yamaga Soko. The fact that Norinaga openly and continuously ridiculed Confucianism, while praising the inherent nature of Japan, stimulated the throwing off of intellectual bondage to China and contributed to a feeling of national pride. Another important factor was Norinaga's emphasis on the fundamental unity of the Japanese state and people, as shown in the *Tama-kushige*. In opposition to the trend fostered by the Tokugawa government—that of considering the several *han* and their lords as the primary objects of devotion and loyalty—Norinaga insisted that the Japanese nation formed one indivisible unit, the *han* being set up merely for convenience in administration. This idea was indispensable for the broadening of emperor-directed loyalty into national patriotism.

It is true that the political viewpoint expressed in Norinaga's writings, characterized by passive acceptance of the status quo, could not by any stretch of the imagination be taken as sanctioning revolt against the Bakufu. But it is also true that he postulated absolute obedience throughout the hierarchy from top to bottom: superiors must be submissive to their superiors. Furthermore, although he denied the right of subjects to question the virtue of the emperor, he did not apply this principle with regard to the motives of the shogun. Thus, when the shogun's government defied the express will of the Emperor (less than sixty years after the death of Norinaga), according to Norinaga's statements there could be no doubt that the Bakufu was in error.

While the teachings of Atsutane were essentially the same as those of Norinaga, the extreme degree to which he carried the principle of patriotism was a characteristic feature of his own viewpoint. Like Norinaga, he ignored the potentially incendiary nature of his ideas: even when the Mito scholars were beginning to propose reforms that would have seriously altered the status of the shogunate,[3] there is no indication that Atsutane believed reverence for the emperor to be inconsistent with approval of the Bakufu. Within a few years of Atsutane's death, however, the widening cleavage between Tokugawa policies and the desires of the Emperor was becoming more obvious. At this time, Atsutane's school developed an activist spirit previously lacking in Kokugaku, and many of its members associated or identified themselves with the imperial loyalist (*shishi*) faction.

Probably the greatest of Atsutane's pupils was Okuni Takamasa (Nonoguchi Takamasa) (1792–1871), an independent thinker who had previously studied Shushigaku at the Shoheiko. In accordance with Atsutane's method, he also investigated Western science. But both while teaching in his own school in Kyoto and subsequently when employed successively by two daimyos, he made loyalty to the emperor and the Imperial Way the heart of his philosophy. In his writings and in his personal relations with the *shishi* group in the Kyoto area, Takamasa encouraged the *son-no* movement. In his *Yamato-damashii,* written about 1850,

[3] Aizawa Yasushi's *Shinron* was written three years before Atsutane's *Tama-dasuki* was published.

he put the case for imperial restoration very strongly. This book aroused opposition among supporters of the Bakufu, and was bitterly condemned by Hayashi Soken, the tenth-generation head of the Shoheiko. On the other hand, when a copy circulating anonymously came to the attention of Nariaki of Mito, he praised it as the "essence of the imperial learning," and, on ascertaining the identity of the author, honored Takamasa by receiving him in personal audience.

Another of Atsutane's pupils was Yano Gendo (1823–87), who played an important role in the new Meiji government. He worked as an adviser to Iwakura Tomomi—one of the few Court nobles who became politically active—and was influential in re-organizing the Jingi-kan (Bureau of Shinto Affairs). Later, he held various official posts concerned with history and records.[4]

The pupils who studied under Atsutane during his lifetime numbered only about five hundred, but his increasing fame, due largely to his success in carrying out the reform of the official Shinto doctrine and ritual, created such a desire for the honor of association with his name that over thirteen hundred were enrolled as "posthumous pupils." His adopted son, Hirata Kane-tane (1801–82), continued as head of the school and carried Atsutane's influence over into the Meiji era.

The followers of both Norinaga and Atsutane went into every part of Japan, establishing themselves as local teachers and spreading the knowledge of the Ancient Learning. The literary tendency that dominated Norinaga's branch was as efficacious in its way as the more active attitude of Atsutane's followers; through poems (*waka*) and songs, even peasants and common city people were gradually awakened to the beauties of the Ancient Way and the Imperial Land. By the middle of the nineteenth century, the patriotic principles of Kokugaku were no longer confined to a cer-

---

[4] On the political results of the official establishment of Shinto as the state religion of the new Meiji government, an excellent source of information is Daniel C. Holtom, *Modern Japan and Shinto Nationalism* (rev. ed.; Chicago: University of Chicago Press, 1947). See especially "The Religious Foundations of the Japanese State," chap. i (pp. 1–27), where the influence of Atsutane is specifically mentioned.

tain group or school, but, like those of Kimongaku, had become widely known throughout the country.[5]

Significance of Mito Thought

When planning the *Dai Nihon Shi,* Mitsukuni had defined the ideal attitude for historical research as being one of complete open-mindedness: "With reverence for the gods and Confucianism, to oppose the gods and Confucianism; worshipping Buddha and Lao Tzu, to reject Buddha and Lao Tzu."[6] Nevertheless, in actual practice the outlook of the Mito school from the beginning was based on a combination of Shushigaku and Shinto. This was due partly to the influence of Chu Shun-shui and other Chu Hsi scholars and partly to Mitsukuni's own partiality: as *hanshu,* his administration was strongly pro-Shinto and anti-Buddhist.

At the same time, it is noteworthy that Mito had no close connection with the Hayashi or official school of Shushigaku. The leading scholars who worked on the *Dai Nihon Shi* during Mitsukuni's lifetime were either trained by Chu Shun-shui or came from the Kimon school. Furthermore, there was a close and cordial relationship between the Mito group and Yamaga Soko; it was Chu Shun-shui who gave him the name of Soko; and Soko's ideas, particularly with regard to Bushido and the nature of the Japanese state, are frequently found in the writings of Mito scholars.

Kokugaku when it developed was entirely independent of the Mito school, and yet there was an essential similarity in their viewpoints. Disagreeing in their evaluations of Confucian doctrine, Mito and Kokugaku were united in asserting that since the time of creation the ideal pattern of government, ethics, and morality had been the peculiar possession of Japan. As these two

[5] On the way in which the imperial-loyalist aspect of Kokugaku was spread, see Fujii Jintaro, *Meiji Ishin Shi Kowa* (4th ed.; Tokyo: Yuzankaku, 1937), pp. 42–43. Also Kinoshita Kaijun, "Kokugaku no Fukyu to Kin-no Undo," *Chuo Shidan,* II (1921), 188–96.

[6] Quoted in Iijima Tadao, *Nippon no Jukyo* (Tokyo: Nippon Bunka Kyokai Shuppambu, 1938), p. 70.

schools relied for authority on the same records, the only real distinction to be made between their respective attitudes toward emperor and nation is that Mito emphasized the historical aspect, while Kokugaku emphasized the religious.

After the flowering of Kokugaku, Aizawa Yasushi was able to transform such religious and poetic impulses into militant patriotism. When he combined the two trends that had developed during the Tokugawa era—acceptance of Confucianism as the basis of society, and faith in the ancient traditions of Japan —he avoided both the China worship of pure Confucianism and the quietist *laissez-faire* aspect of Norinaga's Kokugaku. Consequently, Yasushi presented to his generation a new political theory of extreme attractiveness.

The Mito school's final union of Shushigaku and Shinto did not result in a new form of Confucian Shinto philosophy, as had happened in the case of Yamazaki Ansai, since their essential interest was political rather than religious. Rather, the heart of Chu Hsi's ethical teaching—loyalty resulting from recognition of inherent duty—was reinterpreted in terms of Shinto belief, on the basis of the *shinchoku* of Amaterasu, as demanding undeviating and eternal loyalty to the Heavenly Sun Succession of the imperial house—and this was also equated with Filial Piety. It was, in other words, the theory of *kokutai*.

Thus, Confucianism played a dual role during the Tokugawa period: while in one sense it became an integral part of Japanese culture,[7] in another sense it evoked Japanese self-consciousness and national pride to a degree that had not existed before. In other words, the history of Tokugawa-period attitudes toward emperor and nation shows a gradual acceptance and assimilation of those elements of Chinese thought that seemed to fit the emerging concept of *kokutai*, together with the questioning and ultimate rejection of those elements considered "non-Japanese."

[7] With regard to the continuing influence of Confucian thought in Japan up to World War II, a useful source of information is Warren W. Smith, Jr., *Confucianism in Modern Japan* (Tokyo: Hokuseido Press, 1959). A particularly valuable section is that tracing the origins of the Imperial Rescript on Education, pp. 68–88.

Final Contribution of Mito

By the middle of the nineteenth century, even the highest level of the feudal hierarchy was feeling the results of changing opinion. In 1863, the fourteenth shogun, Iemochi, traveled to Kyoto in order to pay homage to Emperor Komei and to report on his administration. This trip demonstrated that the shogun considered himself a subject of the Emperor, and it was the first visit made by a shogun to an emperor since the days of Iemitsu, over two hundred years earlier.

More impressive and more definitely related to Mito was the case of the fifteenth and last shogun, Tokugawa Yoshinobu (1837–1913). By a strange turn of fortune, Yoshinobu was in fact the seventh son of Nariaki, was educated at the Kodokan, and shared his father's appreciation for the principle of imperial loyalty. After the checkered political situation brought him to the position of shogun in 1867, he faced the impossible task of reconciling loyalty to the emperor with the conflicting demands of the foreign powers and of rebellious *han* lords. Finally unable to maintain his position against an alliance led by Satsuma and Choshu, he terminated the shogunate government by submitting his resignation to the Imperial Court on November 9, 1867.

Even though the timing and manner of his resignation were dictated by outside events, the public announcement shows the application of the Mito historical viewpoint, and the results of Yasushi's and Toko's teaching:

Looking at the various changes through which the Empire has passed, we see that when the monarchical authority became weakened, the power was seized by the Ministers of State, and that afterwards, owing to the civil wars of the periods Hōgen (1156–59) and Heiji (1159–60), it passed into the hands of the military class. Later on again my ancestor received special favour from the Throne (by being appointed Shogun), and his descendants have succeeded him for over 200 years. Though I fill the same office, the laws are often improperly administered, and I confess with shame that the condition of affairs to-day shows my incapacity. Now that foreign intercourse becomes daily more extensive, unless the Government is directed from one central point, the basis of administration will fall to pieces.[8] If, therefore, the old order of things be changed, and the administrative authority be restored to the Imperial Court, if national deliberations be conducted on an extensive scale, and the Imperial decision then invited, and if the Empire be protected with united hearts and combined effort, our country will hold its own with all nations of the world. This is our one duty to our country, but if any persons have other views on the subject they should be stated without reserve.[9]

Yoshinobu's firm adherence to the theory of "emperor as sovereign" was underlined two months later, in an interview of January 8, 1868, with the British minister, Sir Harry Parkes, and the French minister, Léon Roches. Despite his feeling that Satsuma and other *han* were using the authority of the Court to take unfair advantage of him, Yoshinobu stated unequivocally: "As to who is the sovereign of Japan, it is a question on whom [*sic*] no one in Japan can entertain a doubt. The Mikado is the sovereign."[10]

In later years, Yoshinobu preferred to credit his resignation entirely to his boyhood training, and in so doing he showed the continuing effect of the Mito ideology. In 1904, the then Prince Tokugawa Yoshinobu explained his action to a group of friends, including Count Okuma Shigenobu. According to his conversation, as recorded by Count Okuma,

Yoshinobu was once solemnly told by his father, Nariaki, that in the Mito house they had one secret instruction, handed down from generation to generation ever since the time of Mitsukuni. "If," said he, "the Shōgunate should be so unfortunate as to take up arms against the Emperor, our descendants must observe the motto, 'Loyalty knows no blood relationship.' This hereditary instruction has

[8] Note the influence of the *Shinron*. (See this volume, p. 95.)

[9] Manifesto of Keio 3. 10. 14, in Katsu Yasuyoshi (ed.), *Kaikoku Kigen*, III (Tokyo: Kunaisho-zo, 1893), 2930; this translation from John H. Gubbins, *The Progress of Japan: 1853–1871* (Oxford: Clarendon Press, 1911), p. 305.

[10] Quoted in a memorandum by Sir Harry Parkes, in *H. R. Executive Documents*, 3rd Session, 40th Congress, 1868–69, I (Washington, D.C.: Government Printing Office, 1869), 621. At this period, the foreign diplomats customarily designated the shogun as "Taikun" or "Tycoon" and the emperor as "Mikado."

been given to every scion of the Mito house as he reached manhood, and you must be ready at all times to act accordingly." [11]

Later, after becoming shogun, Yoshinobu decided that duty to the emperor demanded the termination of the Bakufu. In his own words, as recorded by Count Okuma:

Deeply conscious of the urgency of the situation, I decided to restore the political power to the Emperor. . . . This I did in obedience to the spirit of the secret injunctions I had received from my father, and which were due to the profound foresight of our ancestor Iyéyasu. [12]

In this statement one hears the echo of the *Shinron* and the *Kodokan-ki Jutsugi;* Ieyasu established the state on the Supreme Duty of Loyalty and Filial Piety. It is somewhat ironic that the founder of the Tokugawa power, having patronized the study of Confucianism as a bulwark for his regime, should three centuries later be lauded by his descendant in the terms of Confucianism for having decreed the dissolution of that power.

The circle was completed. Once Chu Hsi's ethics had been thoroughly assimilated, the Japanese Mandate of Heaven was enforced, and there was no place for the shogunate. When Mito had completed its synthesis of Confucianism and the Way of the Land of the Gods, not only Tokugawa political thought but the Tokugawa age itself had come to a close.

Summation

We have seen how a Japanese theory of the state came into existence during the Tokugawa period. Its effects on the social and political development of the Japanese people are beyond the scope of this study. However, it may be worthwhile to point out a few examples of the remarkable way in which this theory persisted in the Japanese consciousness.

[11] Okuma Shigenobu (ed.), *Fifty Years of New Japan,* I (2nd ed.; London: Smith, Elder, & Co., 1910), 62–63; originally published in Japanese as *Kaikoku Goju-nen Shi.*
[12] *Ibid.,* pp. 67–68.

The formative influence exercised on Japanese ethical and patriotic attitudes by the Imperial Rescript on Education (1890) has been pointed out many times. Its union of the *shinchoku* of Amaterasu with the Confucian virtues of Loyalty and Filial Piety and its stress on *kokutai* were by no means universally accepted among the intelligentsia of the Meiji period. Yet this Rescript and the reverence demanded for it had their effect, as generation after generation of young school children was exposed to its subtle pressure. The effect was even greater after governmental and educational positions began to be filled by persons trained from childhood under its influence.

Forty-five years after the Rescript on Education was promulgated, public opinion had become so thoroughly regimented by this and other means that a respected authority on constitutional law, Professor Minobe Tatsukichi, was publicly censured and forced to resign from the faculty of Tokyo Imperial University because he taught that the emperor was "an organ of the state."

In 1937, further standardization of political attitudes at all levels began through the publication of an official text on *kokutai* by the Bureau of Thought Control of the Ministry of Education.[13] For its authority, this text drew heavily on writers, including those of the Tokugawa period, who had stressed the ancient, unchanging aspects of the Japanese character.

Despite the progress made by modern Japan in technology, science, and military strength, political theory, as applied to the Japanese state, was changing more and more into a matter of unquestioning faith in eternal principles rather than one subject to normal intellectual processes. As inculcated by the Imperial Rescript on Education and as laid down by the Bureau of Thought Control it was an unchanging, crystallized theory; it was a theory that had been produced in the Tokugawa intellectual climate of conservatism and worship of antiquity. Inapplicable as such a theory had been to the problems of the nineteenth century, it is little short of incredible that it could have continued to gain support into the middle of the twentieth.

While it may be justifiably argued that this kind of thinking was encouraged as part of a definite policy for strengthening the

[13] See Appendix D.

power of the central government, the question remains: could such a policy have been followed for more than half a century, could it have met with such unquestioned success, if it had not been acceptable to the Japanese people? In other words, was the acceptance of the *kokutai* theory merely the result of propaganda, or was it an inevitable element in an essentially conservative Japanese society?

Opposition to the theory existed: from Itagaki Taisuke and the antigovernment journalists of early Meiji down to the socialists of the 1920's, there were always nonconformists. Definite attempts were made to introduce the responsible-cabinet system into the Japanese government; and it has been claimed with reason that democracy *could* have evolved under the Meiji constitution—nothing in that document prohibited, for example, the choice of a prime minister in accordance with the will of the lower house. But the fact remains that democracy did not evolve, and that as the years went by the democratic tendencies that had started to develop little by little shriveled away and disappeared.

The final questions suggested by this study are these: Is Japan now, after World War II, at last going to abandon nonrational conservatism and the worship of antiquity as the foundations of its political attitudes? Is Japan willing to open itself to the thought currents prevalent in other parts of the world? Is Japan ready, in other words, to become a *psychologically participating* member of the modern world for the first time? Or is Japanese political thinking after all, like the Heavenly Sun Succession, coeval with heaven and earth? Perhaps we must wait another fifty years for the answers to such questions. As Ogyu Sorai said long ago, "Among the people today there are some who doubt, among the people today there are some who believe."

Appendixes

A: *Table of Tokugawa Shoguns*

1. Ieyasu (Toshogu) (1603–5) (Note: Although nominally in retirement, Ieyasu continued to dominate the administration until his death in 1616.)
2. Hidetada (1605–23) (in retirement 1623–32)
3. Iemitsu (1623–51)
4. Ietsuna (1651–80)
5. Tsunayoshi (1680–1709)
6. Ienobu (1709–12)
7. Ietsugu (1713–16)
8. Yoshimune (1716–45) (in retirement 1745–51)
9. Ieshige (1745–60) (in retirement 1760–61)
10. Ieharu (1760–86)
11. Ienari (1787–1837) (in retirement 1837–41)
12. Ieyoshi (1837–53)
13. Iesada (1853–58)
14. Iemochi (1858–66)
15. Yoshinobu (Keiki) (1867–68) (in retirement 1868–1913)

B: *Glossary of Terms Pertaining to the Tokugawa Administrative System*

Bakufu—the shogunate, or central government of Japan; collective term for the shogun's policy-determining and administrative officials. "Shogun" originally had a military connotation, and the word "Bakufu," literally meaning "tent (or camp) administration," corresponds roughly to the term "GHQ." In the literature of the late Tokugawa period, the word "Bakufu" often refers to the shogun himself, just as "Imperial Court" may mean "Emperor."

Bugyo—a general term for Bakufu officials from the middle to the upper level of the administrative hierarchy, including those charged with such functions as local government, supervision of finance, and—near the close of the Tokugawa period —relations with foreigners.

Fudai—refers specifically to those feudal lords whose ancestors had supported Tokugawa Ieyasu before the battle of Sekigahara. As a general rule, high offices under the Bakufu could be filled only by members of this group, as the descendants of those who submitted after Sekigahara (called *tozama*) were traditionally considered unreliable.

Han—with the exception of a few areas ruled directly by the Bakufu, such as Edo and Osaka, this was the basic unit of local government. The individual *han* varied greatly in area and importance; each was governed semiautonomously by a lord owing feudal allegiance to the shogun, and whose position, rank, and income were fixed by the Bakufu. The word *han* is sometimes translated as "clan," but is closer in meaning to the medieval European "fief."

Hanshu—the ruler, or lord, of a *han*. The position was ordinarily hereditary, but since it was based on a lord-and-vassal relationship with the Tokugawa family, the appointment could be

230

revoked or the incumbent transferred to another *han* at the will of the shogun. (Such cases occurred mainly in the early, formative period of Tokugawa rule.) The word *hanshu* was used interchangeably with "daimyo," and is often so translated.

Hatamoto—direct vassals of the Tokugawa family, lower in rank than the *fudai* lords, but holding the right of audience with the shogun. Many Bakufu officials in the lower ranks were drawn from this class.

Koku—a measure of capacity, approximately five bushels. In terms of rice, this unit was used to measure the productivity (and, consequently, the value to the lord) of the various *han;* it was also the standard unit for computing the stipends of the samurai. Traditionally assumed to represent the amount of rice required to support one man for one year, with the development of a money economy the *koku* underwent wide fluctuations in actual purchasing power.

Roju—highest policy-determining organ of the Bakufu, usually consisting of four or five men, appointed from among the *fudai* lords. In addition to its power of general supervision over the government, the *roju* concerned itself with the activities of the daimyos and with relations between the Bakufu and the Imperial Court. Toward the end of the Tokugawa period its authority as a group became more titular than real, but some members continued to wield influence as individuals.

Ronin—members of the samurai class who were not employed by any lord and thus had no particular duty or allegiance. A samurai might become a *ronin* in a variety of ways, including dismissal, resignation, his lord's loss of the fief, etc.

Sankin-kotai—enforced attendance by daimyos at the shogun's court. As a means of control, each *hanshu* was required to spend four to six months a year in Edo, and to leave his family there at all times. Detailed regulations varied; the general rule was in effect from 1635 to 1862.

Tairo—shogun's regent, an office outranking that of members of the *roju*. This post was filled only in time of crisis, but when appointed, the *tairo* conducted all state affairs at his own discretion.

C: *Main Schools of Shinto Thought*

IN ADDITION TO Yamazaki Ansai's Suika Shinto, which is discussed in the main text of this study, the Shinto sects or schools most important in connection with Tokugawa political thinking were five in number:

1) *Ryobu Shinto* was developed by priests of the Shingon sect of Buddhism during the Heian period; although it is attributed to Kobo Daishi (774–835), the founder of Shingon, there is no definite proof for this. Its chief teaching was that the various Shinto deities represented transmigrations of Bodhisattvas; it was essentially a method by which the forms of Shinto could be preserved by believers in Buddhism. By making Buddhism fundamental and Shinto corollary, Ryobu Shinto decreased the emphasis on pure Shinto belief and thereby lessened the significance of the emperor's position.

For some seven hundred years, this was the standard form of Shinto. During this time, the position of Chief (*Jingi Haku*) of the Imperial Bureau of Shinto Affairs (Jingi-kan) became hereditary in the Shirakawa family; while they preserved the Ryobu teaching, the particular rituals and ceremonies they developed were known as *Hakke Shinto*.[1] As other forms of Shinto arose, the number of shrines under the control of the Shirakawa family lessened. By the end of the Middle Ages, what was left of Ryobu was identical with Hakke, and during the Tokugawa era the two terms were more or less synonymous.

2) *Ise Shinto* (*Watarai Shinto*) was developed by the Watarai family, priests in hereditary charge of the Outer Shrine of Ise, chiefly by Watarai Ieyuki (1266–1351). Its basic scripture was the *Shinto Gobusho,* alleged and then generally believed to be an

---

[1] *Hakke* signifies "family of the (Jingi) Haku," i.e., the Shirakawa family. This family was descended from Emperor Kazan (reigned 984–86).

ancient classic, although actually written some time between the end of the Heian and the middle of the Kamakura period. Ise Shinto also relied on other ancient records, such as the *Kojiki, Nihon Shoki,* and *Kuji Hongi;* in addition, it included elements of Ryobu Shinto, the Chinese creation theory, and Confucian ethics. Even quotations from Neo-Confucian philosophy were included in Ieyuki's writings.

The important contribution made by this teaching was its reversal of the respective places of Shinto and Buddhism. While still retaining the general thesis of Ryobu Shinto, the Watarai theory made Shinto fundamental and Buddhism corollary by considering the Bodhisattvas to be avatars of the Shinto gods. The details of Ise Shinto as elaborated by Watarai Ieyuki are supposed to have influenced the thinking of Kitabatake Chikafusa.

3) *Yuiitsu Shinto (Yoshida Shinto)* was founded by Yoshida Kanetomo (1435–1511). He continued the Japan-centered tendency initiated by Ise Shinto, and elaborated the theory that Japan's Way of the Gods was the fundamental and original Way of all Ways, the basis of Buddhism, Confucianism, and Taoism. According to this theory, Buddha and Confucius, each a holy man in his own country, manifested the eternal truths of Shinto.

Whereas Ise Shinto represented the beliefs of the Watarai family alone and was of interest chiefly to scholars, Yuiitsu Shinto had a popular appeal and soon began to gain adherents. Spreading rapidly in Kyoto, it was accepted by Emperor Go-Tsuchimikado (reigned 1464–1500), and thereafter was the official belief of the Imperial Court. The position of the Yoshida family— a branch of the ancient Urabe family of diviners—had a great deal to do with the propagation of Yuiitsu Shinto, as they had the hereditary duty of assisting the Shirakawa family in the Jingi-kan. The right of appointing priests was divided between these two families; and while the Shirakawas continued to appoint believers in Ryobu Shinto to the shrines under their control, the Yoshida family appointed only adherents of their doctrine to the shrines they supervised. By the beginning of Tokugawa rule, or approximately one hundred years after the founding of Yuiitsu Shinto, the new faith was far stronger than the old, and both Emperor Go-Yozei (reigned 1586–1611) and Tokugawa Ieyasu were initiated into its mysteries. With a few exceptions, such as Ise (directly under the Imperial Court), practically all the shrines of Japan were controlled by either the Shirakawa or the Yoshida families; [2] and as the Yoshidas held a great majority of the shrines, during the Tokugawa period Yuiitsu Shinto became the general belief of the common people throughout the country.

4) The increased interest in Japanese history and tradition at the beginning of the Tokugawa period engendered a corresponding upsurge in Shinto thought; but, because it was accompanied by the widespread study of Confucianism, the result was Confucian Shinto, a new form in which Chinese ideas were freely used to supplement Shinto dogma. Confucian Shinto was necessarily confined to those who could appreciate Chinese literature and did not affect the hold of Yuiitsu Shinto on the people in general.

This trend, exemplified in Hayashi Razan, first made itself felt in the actual Shinto world with Watarai Nobuyoshi (Deguchi Nobuyoshi) (1619–90). Influenced by Razan, Nobuyoshi revised Ise Shinto, removing all Buddhist ideas and connections, replacing them with Confucian, and explaining the events of the Age of the Gods by reference to the *Book of Changes*. His best-known work was the *Yofukki* (1651), in which he expressed ideas very similar to those of Razan: the Way of the ancient sages of China, the Way of the *Book of Changes,* agreed with the Way of the Gods of Japan; it must be the natural Way of heaven and earth. Therefore, he said, those born in the Land of the Gods should follow the Way of the Gods and exemplify the Confucian teaching: the sovereign reigning in accordance with the Way of the Gods manifests Benevolence; the subject who serves his sovereign according to the Way of the Gods is a loyal subject. Also, he pointed out, there is a warning against following Buddhism in the *Yamato-hime no Mikoto Seiki* (one of the five parts of the *Shinto Gobusho*), but no such statement is made regarding Confucianism.

[2] Theoretically, all Shinto priests, like court nobles, were responsible to the emperor. Control over their appointment was never assumed by the Bakufu.

Although Nobuyoshi's teaching was still called Ise Shinto, it was a markedly different doctrine from the original Watarai theory; Shinto remained the fundamental or main element, but the corollary position was now occupied by Confucianism. This was the first Shinto thought since the Heian period to be free from Buddhist influence. In that Confucianism could be used to inculcate loyalty to the emperor, while Buddhism traditionally had been little concerned with such obligations, this new interpretation was a step of real significance to political thinking.

5) *Rigaku Shinto (Yoshikawa Shinto)*—the second school of Confucian Shinto—was propounded by Yoshikawa Koretari (1615–94), who was influenced by Razan's studies and who had been initiated into Yuiitsu Shinto. Koretari felt that Shinto properly had two aspects—the ceremonial, conducted by the priests, and that of general application, which he called Rigaku, the study of *li*.[3] The latter he believed to be more important. As may be seen from the emphasis on *li*, this was almost as much a Neo-Confucian school of thought as it was Shinto.

[3] Rigaku (Chinese Li-hsueh) was an alternate designation for the philosophy of Chu Hsi.

D: *Kokutai*

THE WORD *kokutai* (Chinese *kuo t'i*) is found in Chinese documents even before the Han dynasty, with the meaning of "organ of the state" or "organization of the state," but it was not used in Japan either by scholars or common people until the Mito school gave it a Japanese definition. The term began to find a place in Mito writings as early as the beginning of the nineteenth century, but was publicized particularly by Aizawa Yasushi's *Shinron*. Thus, writing in 1856, Yamagata Taika, the leading scholar of Choshu-*han,* said:

> The term *kokutai* is sometimes found in writings such as those of the Sung period, but I have never come across it in the writings of our country. Was it perhaps advanced first in Mito-*han?* In their *Shinron,* in speaking of *kokutai* they say. . . .[1]

The concept underlying the word *kokutai,* in the basic sense of "the unique characteristics of Japan," had of course long existed and had been expressed by writers from Kitabatake Chikafusa down to Hirata Atsutane, but a simple term to describe the concept had been lacking. Once the term had been introduced, however, it was employed by various writers, or by the same writers at various times, to carry slightly differing connotations. In its deepest sense, the word *kokutai* generally came to indicate what may be called noumenon, an inner essence or mystical force residing in the Japanese nation as a result of Amaterasu's *shinchoku,* and because of which Japan necessarily developed characteristics distinct from those of other lands. In another sense, it might refer to phenomenon, or the outward manifestation of

---

[1] From Yamagata Taika's criticism of Yoshida Shoin's *Komo Yowa,* in *Yoshida Shoin Zenshu,* III (Tokyo: Iwanami Shoten, 1938–40), 606–7.

236

those characteristics. Occasionally, it must be understood simply as national prestige, or "face." [2]

According to *kokutai* thought, Japan is a patriarchal state, in which everyone is related and the imperial house is the main or head family. The emperor is the supreme father, and loyalty to him, or patriotism, becomes the highest form of Filial Piety. Because of the command of Amaterasu, this structure is both sacred and eternal; compliance with its requirements is the obligation and deepest wish of every Japanese.

After being introduced and publicized in the writings of the Mito school, the term and concept of *kokutai* became better known by the middle of the nineteenth century; it received official approval from the time of the Meiji Restoration. An early example of its official use, only thirteen years after Yamagata Taika had complained that the word was unknown to him, is found in a directive of 1869 concerning the curriculum at the Shoheiko:

A school is something that renders practical service to the realm and nation by means of expounding the Way, broadening knowledge, and producing virtue and talent. In the final analysis, the essence of the divine scriptures and the national classics lies in reverence for the Imperial Way [*Kodo*] and a clear understanding of *kokutai*. In other words, to make the Imperial Land their objective must be considered the first duty of scholars.[3]

From this point on, *kokutai* gradually became the keynote of Japanese political thought. Kiyohara Sadao, one of the leading apologists for Japanese nationalism in the twentieth century, has given *kokutai* a modern definition:

In our *kokutai*, sovereign and people form one body. Thus, when we think of the people, we must think simultaneously of the Emperor who is the central point of that people. In the same way, when we think of the Emperor, we must think simultaneously of the

[2] Noumenal and phenomenal *kokutai* as shown in the writings of Yoshida Shoin are further discussed on pp. 162–65.

[3] Directive of Meiji 2. 6. 15, in Mombu-daijin Kambo (Office of the Minister of Education) Hokoku-ka (comp.), *Nippon Kyoiku Shi Shiryo*, VIII (Tokyo: Mombu-daijin Kambo Hokoku-ka, 1890–92), 134.

people who support that Emperor and hold him as their point of unity, of the people who by their intrinsic nature are subordinate to and dependent on that Emperor.

For this reason, to conceive of the Emperor as standing alone without the existence of the people is impossible, while to conceive of the people as separated from the Emperor is likewise impossible. As a chisel requires a mallet, the union of the two elements forms one body. Within the word *Tenno* [Emperor] there is included the concept of *jimmin* [people]; and when we use the word *jimmin*, this presupposes at the same time the concept of the *Tenno* who forms its mainstay. This is the most important part of our *kokutai*.[4]

Shortly after the above statement was written, the viewpoint expressed in it was made the orthodox and mandatory belief of all Japanese subjects, and expanded into a book, the *Kokutai no Hongi* ("Essential Meaning of *Kokutai*"), intellectual compliance with which was enforced through the Bureau of Thought Control of the Ministry of Education. The opening words of this work are as follows:

The unbroken line of Emperors, receiving the Oracle of the Founder of the Nation [i.e., *shinchoku* of Amaterasu], reign eternally over the Japanese Empire. This is our eternal and immutable national entity [i.e., *kokutai*]. Thus, founded on this great principle, all the people, united as one great family nation in heart and obeying the Imperial Will, enhance indeed the beautiful virtues of loyalty and filial piety. This is the glory of our national entity [i.e., *kokutai*]. This national entity is the eternal and unchanging basis of our nation and shines resplendent throughout our history.[5]

Later in the book, the term "one great family nation" is defined:

[4] Kiyohara Sadao, *Kokushi to Nippon Seishin no Kengen* (Tokyo: Fujii Shoten, 1934), p. 38. Cf. Yoshida Shoin's statement, p. 185, this volume.

[5] This translation is taken from the English edition: John O. Gauntlett (trans.), and Robert K. Hall (ed.), *Kokutai no Hongi* (Cambridge: Harvard University Press, 1949), p. 6.

The first Japanese edition was published in 1937. Written by an officially appointed committee of scholars, it cannot be attributed to any one author; but according to Hall's introduction to the English edition, the final revision before publication was by Ito Enkichi, head of the Bureau of Thought Control.

Our country is one great family nation comprising a union [lit., "one body"] of sovereign and subject, having the Imperial Household as the head family, and looking up to the Emperor as the focal point from of old to the present. Accordingly, to contribute to the prosperity of the nation is to serve for the prosperity of the Emperor; and to be loyal to the Emperor means nothing short of loving the country and striving for the welfare of the nation. Without loyalty there is no patriotism, and without patriotism there is no loyalty.[6]

In this book and the enforcement of its dogma in the twentieth century, the *kokutai* theory of the Mito scholars received its ultimate degree of official sanction.

[6] *Ibid.*, p. 83.

Bibliography

MATERIALS IN THE JAPANESE LANGUAGE

Bibliographical Sources

(Including Western-language material dealing with Japanese sources)

Borton, Hugh. "A Survey of Japanese Historiography," *American Historical Review*, XLIII (1938), 489-99.

Elisséev, Serge. "Japon," in *Histoire et historiens depuis cinquante ans*, ed. J. Letaconnoux. Paris: Librairie Félix Alcan, 1927-28. II, chap. v, 560-69.

Hatano Kenichi and Yakichi Mitsunaga. *Kenkyu Chosa Sanko Bunken Soran* ("General Survey of Reference Works for Research and Investigation"). Tokyo: Asahi Shobo, 1934.

Higashiuchi Yoshio. *Literature on Contemporary Japan.* Tokyo: Hoover Institute and Library on War, Revolution, and Peace, 1951.

Moriya Hidesuke. "Meiji Ishin Kenkyu ni Kan-suru Nippon Bunken" ("Japanese Literature Relating to Research on the Meiji Restoration"), in *Meiji Ishin Shi Kenkyu* ("Studies in the History of the Meiji Restoration"), comp. Shigakkai. Tokyo: Fuzambo, 1929. Pp. 795-820.

Numazawa Tatsuo. *Nippon Bungaku Shi Hyoran* ("Guide to the History of Japanese Literature"). Tokyo: Meiji Shoin, 1934.

Otsuka Shigakkai (comp.). *Sogo Kokushi Rombun Yomoku* ("General Syllabus of Works on the National History"). Tokyo: Toko Shoin, 1939.

Shigakkai (comp.). *Shigaku Bunken Mokuroku 1946–1950* ("Catalog of Literature in the Field of History, 1946–1950"). Tokyo: Yamakawa Shuppansha, 1951.

Takaichi Yoshio. *Meiji Bunken Mokuroku* ("Catalog of Meiji Period Literature"). Tokyo: Nippon Hyoron-sha, 1932.

Ward, Robert E. *A Guide to Japanese Reference and Research Materials in the Field of Political Science.* Ann Arbor: University of Michigan Press, 1950.

Yoshida Saburo. *Shiso Shi* ("History of Thought"). Tokyo: Shikai Shobo, 1936.

Primary Sources

Aizawa Yasushi. *Shinron* ("A New Proposal") and *Tekii-hen* ("Compilation on Advancing along the Way"), ed. Tsukamoto Katsuyoshi. (Iwanami Bunko, Nos. 2794–96.) Tokyo: Iwanami Shoten, 1941.

Asami Keisai. *Seiken Igen* ("Eternal Messages of Sacrificial Dedication"), ed. Gokyu Yasujiro. (Iwanami Bunko, Nos. 2019–21.) Tokyo: Iwanami Shoten, 1939.

Dai Nihon Shi ("Great History of Japan"). Tokyo: Dai Nippon Yubenkai, 1928.

Fujita Toko. *Kodokan-ki Jutsugi* ("Commentary on the *Kodokan-ki*), ed. Tsukamoto Katsuyoshi. (Iwanami Bunko, Nos. 2222–23.) Tokyo: Iwanami Shoten, 1942.

Katsu Yasuyoshi (ed.). *Kaikoku Kigen* ("The Commencement of the Opening of the Country"). 3 vols. Tokyo: Kunaisho-zo, 1893.

Kokusho Kankokai (comp.). *Shinto Sosetsu* ("Collected Writings on Shinto Doctrine"). Tokyo: Kokusho Kankokai, 1911.

Mombu-daijin Kambo Hokoku-ka (comp.). *Nippon Kyoiku Shi Shiryo* ("Source Materials on the History of Japanese Education"). 9 vols. Tokyo: Mombu-daijin Kambo Hokoku-ka, 1890–92.

Motoori Norinaga. *Naobi no Mitama* ("Spirit of Purification") and *Tamahoko Hyakushu* ("Poems on the Jeweled Spear"), ed. Muraoka Tsunetsugu. (Iwanami Bunko, No. 1324.) Tokyo: Iwanami Shoten, 1939.

———. *Tama-kushige* ("Jewel-casket") and *Hihon Tama-kushige*

("Secret *Tama-kushige*"), ed. Muraoka Tsunetsugu. (Iwanami Bunko, No. 1065.) Tokyo: Iwanami Shoten, 1934.

―――. *Uiyamafumi* ("First Steps on the Mountain") and *Suzunoya Tomonroku* ("Norinaga's Questions and Answers"), ed. Muraoka Tsunetsugu. (Iwanami Bunko, No. 361.) Tokyo: Iwanami Shoten, 1943.

Sakuma Zozan. *Seikenroku* ("Reflection on Errors"), ed. Iijima Tadao. (Iwanami Bunko, Nos. 3377–78.) Tokyo: Iwanami Shoten, 1944.

Takasu Yoshijiro (ed.). *Mitogaku Zenshu* ("Collected Works of the Mito School"). Tokyo: Nitto Shoin, 1933.

Tsukamoto Tetsuzo (ed.). *Yamaga Soko Bunshu* ("Collected Writings of Yamaga Soko"). (Yuhodo Bunko, Vol. XXII.) Tokyo: Yuhodo Shoten, 1926.

Yamaga Soko. *Seikyo Yoroku* ("Essentials of the Holy Teachings") and *Haisho Zampitsu* ("Writings Bequeathed from a Place of Exile"), ed. Muraoka Tsunetsugu. (Iwanami Bunko, No. 2326.) Tokyo: Iwanami Shoten, 1941.

―――. *Yamaga Gorui* ("Systematized Teachings of Yamaga Soko"). 4 vols. Tokyo: Kokusho Kankokai, 1910–11.

Yamagata Taika. *Ima no Sho-Ko O-Shin ni Arazaru no Ben* ("That the Present Daimyos Are Not Vassals of the Emperor"). Manuscript book (copy dated 1859).

Yamaguchi-ken Kyoiku-kai (comp.). *Yoshida Shoin Zenshu* ("Collected Works of Yoshida Shoin") (2nd ed.). 12 vols. Tokyo: Iwanami Shoten, 1938–40.

Secondary Sources

BOOKS

Asai Kiyoshi. *Meiji Rikken Shiso Shi ni okeru Eikoku Gidai Seido no Eikyo* ("Effects of the British Parliamentary System in the History of Meiji Constitutional Thought"). Tokyo: Ganshodo Shoten, 1935.

Fujii Jintaro. *Meiji Ishin Shi Kowa* ("Lectures on Meiji Restoration History") (4th ed.). Tokyo: Yuzankaku, 1937.

Fujiwara Hirotatsu. *Kindai Nippon Seiji Shiso Shi Josetsu* ("Introduction to the History of Recent Japanese Political Thought"). Kyoto: Sanwa Shobo, 1952.

Hashimoto Yatsuo. *Bakumatsu Shiso Shi* ("History of Late Tokugawa Thought"). Tokyo: Nippon Seiji Bunka Kenkyujo, 1943.

Hirose Yutaka. *Yoshida Shoin Komo Yowa* ("Yoshida Shoin's *Komo Yowa*"). (Mombusho: Nippon Seishin Sosho, No. 52.) Tokyo: Insatsu-kyoku, 1944.

———. *Yoshida Shoin no Kenkyu* ("A Study of Yoshida Shoin") (2nd rev. ed.). Tokyo: Shibundo, 1944.

Hisamatsu Senichi. *Kokugaku to Tama-dasuki* ("Kokugaku and the *Tama-dasuki*"). (Mombusho: Nippon Seishin Sosho, No. 43.) Tokyo: Naikaku Insatsu-kyoku, 1943.

Iijima Tadao. *Nippon no Jukyo* ("Japanese Confucianism"). (Mombusho: Nippon Bunka, No. 16.) Tokyo: Nippon Bunka Kyokai Shuppambu, 1938.

Inoue Tetsujiro. *Nippon Kogakuha no Tetsugaku* ("Philosophy of the Japanese Kogaku School"), (rev. 4th ed.). Tokyo: Fuzambo, 1907.

———. *Nippon Shushigakuha no Tetsugaku* ("Philosophy of the Japanese Chu Hsi School"), (14th printing). Tokyo: Fuzambo, 1924.

———. *Nippon Yomeigakuha no Tetsugaku* ("Philosophy of the Japanese Wang Yang-ming School"), (rev. ed.). Tokyo: Fuzambo, 1928.

Ishii Shusaku. *Nippon Kodai Shiso Kenkyu* ("A Study of Japanese Classical Thought"). Tokyo: Kensetsusha Shuppambu, 1942.

Kada Tetsuji. *Meiji Shoki Shakai Keizai Shiso Shi* ("History of Early Meiji Period Social and Economic Thought"). Tokyo: Iwanami Shoten, 1937.

Kato Toranosuke. *Kodokan-ki to sono Jutsugi* ("The *Kodokan-ki* and the Commentary"). (Mombusho: Nippon Seishin Sosho, No. 49.) Tokyo: Naikaku Insatsu-kyoku, 1943.

Kato Totsudo. *Shuyo Dai Koza* ("Great Edifying Lecture Series"), Vol. VII. *Seiken Igen*. Tokyo: Heibonsha, 1941.

Kiyohara Sadao. *Kokushi to Nippon Seishin no Kengen* ("The National History and the Manifestation of the Japanese Spirit"). Tokyo: Fujii Shoten, 1934.

Kono Seizo. *Nippon Seishin Hattatsu Shi* ("History of the Development of the Japanese Spirit") (rev. ed.). Tokyo: Ookayama Shoten, 1941.

Kumura Toshio. *Onore wo Koeru Mono* ("One Who Transcended Self"). Yamaguchi: Yamaguchi-ken Somubu Bunkyoka, 1955.

———. *Yoshida Shoin*. Tokyo: Iwanami Shoten, 1941.

———. *Yoshida Shoin no Shiso to Kyoiku* ("The Thought and Educational Policy of Yoshida Shoin"). Tokyo: Iwanami Shoten, 1942.

Kumura Toshio and Nishikawa Heikichi. *Komo Yowa no Kenkyu* ("A Study of the *Komo Yowa*"). Osaka: Osaka Shimbun-sha, 1944.

Kurita Tsutomu. *Sui-han Shushi Jiryaku* ("Summarized Account of the Historical Research of Mito-*han*"). Tokyo: Ookayama Shoten, 1928.

Maruyama Masao. *Nippon Seiji Shiso Shi Kenkyu* ("A Study of the History of Japanese Political Thought"). Tokyo: Tokyo Daigaku Shuppankai, 1952.

Mikami Sanji. *Son-no Ron Hattatsu Shi* ("History of the Development of Revere-the-Emperor Thought"). Tokyo: Fuzambo, 1941.

Mori Shigeru. *Bakumatsu Shi-Ketsu* ("Four Heroes of the Late Tokugawa Period"). Tokyo: Kinkei Gakuin, 1929.

Muraoka Tsunetsugu. *Nippon Shinto no Tokushitsu* ("The Characteristics of Japanese Shinto"). (Iwanami Koza: Toyo Shicho.) Tokyo: Iwanami Shoten, 1936.

———. *Nippon Shiso Shi Kenkyu* ("A Study of the History of Japanese Thought"). 4 vols. Tokyo: Iwanami Shoten, 1939–49.

Nakae Ushikichi. *Chugoku Kodai Seiji Shiso* ("Political Thinking of Ancient China"). Tokyo: Iwanami Shoten, 1950.

Nishijima Jun. *Jurin Genryu* ("Main Streams of Confucian Thought"). Tokyo: Toyo Tosho Kankokai, 1934.

Nomura Hachiro. *Kokugaku Shiso Shi* ("History of Kokugaku Thought"). Tokyo: Meiseido Shoten, 1943.

Norihira Masami. *Ko-Shinto* ("Ancient Shinto"). (Iwanami Koza: Tetsugaku.) Tokyo: Iwanami Shoten, 1932.

———. *Yamaga Soko no Haisho Zampitsu* ("Yamaga Soko's *Haisho Zampitsu*"). (Mombusho: Nippon Seishin Sosho.) Tokyo: Nippon Bunka Kyokai Shuppambu, 1937.

Ogawa Goro. *Bocho Seishin Shi Josetsu* ("Introduction to the History of the Choshu Spirit"). Yamaguchi: Bocho Bunka Kenkyukai, 1937.

Oka Fukashi. *Yoshida Shoin*. Tokyo: Dai Nippon Yubenkai Kodansha, 1943.

Ono Hisato. *Meiji Ishin Zengo ni okeru Seiji Shiso no Tenkai* ("Development of Political Thought before and after the Meiji Restoration"). Tokyo: Shibundo, 1944.

Osatake Takeki. *Meiji Ishin* ("The Meiji Restoration"). 3 vols. Tokyo: Hakuyo Shokan, 1946.

Sato Kiyokatsu. *Dai Nippon Seiji Shiso Shi* ("History of Political Thought in Great Japan"). 2 vols. Tokyo: Dai Nippon Horei Shuppan K. K., 1939.

Takaoka Noriyuki. *Nippon Kindai Shicho* ("Recent Thought-Trends in Japan"). Tokyo: Mikasa Shobo, 1941.

Takeoka Katsuya. *Son-no Shiso no Hattatsu* ("The Development of Revere-the-Emperor Thought"). (Iwanami Koza: Nippon Rekishi.) Tokyo: Iwanami Shoten, 1934.

Takigawa Masajiro. *Nippon Hosei Shi* ("History of the Japanese Legal System"). Tokyo: Yuhikaku, 1930.

Tanaka Yoshito. *Nippon Shiso Shi Gaisetsu* ("Outline of the History of Japanese Thought") (rev. ed.). Tokyo: Meiji Shoin, 1943.

Tokugawa Ko Keiso Shichiju-nen Shukuga Kinenkai (comp.). *Kinsei Nippon no Jugaku* ("Confucianism in Modern Japan"). Tokyo: Iwanami Shoten, 1939.

Tokushige Asakichi. *Ishin Seishin Shi Kenkyu* ("A Study of the History of the Restoration Spirit"). Kyoto: Ritsumeikan Shuppambu, 1934.

Uzawa Fusaaki. *Shunju Ronshu* ("Collected Essays of Uzawa Fusaaki"). Tokyo: Shunjusha, 1916.

Yamada Yoshio. *Shinto Shiso Shi* ("History of Shinto Thought"). (Keishin Shiso Fukyu Shiryo, No. 6.) Tokyo: Jingiin Shidoka, 1942.

Yoshida Togo. *Tokugawa Seikyo-ko* ("Studies in Tokugawa Period Government and Learning"). 2 vols. Tokyo: Fuzambo Shoten, 1894.

PERIODICALS

Akaoka Shigeki. "Yamagata Daini no Kokutai Kan" ("Yamagata Daini's Views on *Kokutai*"), *Denki*, II (1935), No. 11, 23–27.

Ashikaga Enjutsu. "Muro Kyuso no Gaku" (The Learning of Muro Kyuso"), *Toyo Tetsugaku*, XI (1904), 391–96, 451–56.

Hayashi Jitsugen. "Hitachi no Gakufu to Yoshida Shoin" ("The Mito School and Yoshida Shoin"), *Rekishi Nippon*, II (1943), No. 8, 17–23.

Higo Kazuo. "Hayashi Razan to Sono Shigaku" ("Hayashi Razan and his Historical Studies"), *Shirin*, XIV (1929), 562–74.

Hitomi Denzo. "Miyake Kanran ni tsuite" ("Concerning Miyake Kanran"), *Shibun*, XIV (1932), No. 10, 34–44.

Inobe Shigeo. "Mito Gakuha no Jo-i Ron" ("The Repel-the-Barbarian Theory of the Mito School"), *Shirin*, V (1920), 125–33.

———. "Son-no Ronsha to shite no Takeuchi Shikibu no Chii" ("The Place of Takeuchi Shikibu as an Advocate of Revering the Emperor"), *Kokugakuin Zasshi*, XLI (1935), No. 9, 1–13.

Inoue Tetsujiro. "Hayashi Razan no Gakumon to Kogyo" ("The

Scholarship and Achievements of Hayashi Razan"), *Shibun*, XV (1933), No. 12, 1–12.

———. "Nippon Shisoka Ron" ("On Japanese Thinkers"), *Riso*, X (1936–37), 1089–1120.

Kinoshita Kaijun. "Kokugaku no Fukyu to Kin-no Undo" ("The Diffusion of Kokugaku and the Movement for Loyalty to the Emperor"), *Chuo Shidan*, II (1921), 188–96, 246–52.

Kiyohara Sadao. "Koki Mito Gakuha no Kokutai Ron" ("The *Kokutai* Theory of the Later Mito School"), *Jinja Kyokai Zasshi*, XIX (1920), No. 10, 1–7; No. 12, 1–9.

Kono Seizo. "Motoori Norinaga no Seiji Ron" ("The Political Theory of Motoori Norinaga"), *Jinja Kyokai Zasshi*, X (1911), No. 1, 16–20.

Kurita Motoji. "Arai Hakuseki no Seiji Shiso" ("The Political Thinking of Arai Hakuseki"), *Rekishi to Chiri*, XV (1925), 553–84.

Kuroita Katsumi. "Ogyu Sorai no Shikan" ("Ogyu Sorai's Attitude toward History"), *Shigaku Zasshi*, XXXVIII (1927), 529–38.

Maki Kenji. "Buke Seiji no Taisei ni Kan-suru Edo Jidai Gakusha no Kenkai" ("Views of Tokugawa-Period Scholars on the Military Government System"), *Hogaku Ronso*, XXXV (1936), 1229–65.

Matsui Kiyoshi. "Moshi no Seiji Shiso ni okeru Ni-Ten no Kosatsu" ("A Study of Two Points in the Political Thinking of Mencius"), *Seikei Ronso*, XXII (1953–54), 374–99.

———. "Shina ni okeru 'Kun'-'Min' Kankei to Tokuji Shiso no Kanken" ("Considerations on the Ruler-and-People Relationship and the Philosophy of Virtuous Rule, in China"), *Seikei Ronso*, XX (1951–52), 490–514.

Mikami Sanji. "Kumazawa Banzan no Chotei ni Tai-suru Kangae" ("Kumazawa Banzan's Thinking with Regard to the Imperial Court"), *Meiji Seitoku Kinen Gakkai Kiyo*, IV (1915), 31–42.

Miura Hiroyuki. "Bungei Fukkoki no Jufu" ("Confucian Schools of the Renaissance Period"), *Shirin*, III (1918), 1–17, 212–31.

Miura Kyo. "Butsu Sorai no Keisei Shiso—oyobi Kumazawa Hakkei to no Hikaku" ("Ogyu Sorai's Thinking on Statecraft, and a Comparison with Kumazawa Banzan"), *Toyo Bunka*, No. 117 (1934), pp. 43–56.

———. "Kumazawa Hakkei no Keisei Ron" ("Kumazawa Banzan's Theory of Statecraft"), *Toyo Bunka*, No. 113 (1933), pp. 34–43.

Muraoka Tsunetsugu. "Suika Shinto no Shiso" ("Suika Shinto Thought"), *Riso*, X (1936–37), 1133–51.

Nakamura Toshikatsu. "Mito Rekko no Ichi-Kensaku" ("A Proposal of Tokugawa Nariaki"), *Keizai Shi Kenkyu,* XVII (1937), 755–63.

Nakayama Kushiro. "Kinsei Shina Gakufu no Kinsei Nippon ni Oyoboshitaru Seiryoku Eikyo—Toku ni Tokugawa Jidai no Kosho Gakufu no Seiritsu ni tsukite" ("The Powerful Effect Exerted on Modern Japan by Recent Chinese Schools of Thought, with Special Reference to the Formation of the Investigatory School in the Tokugawa Period"), *Shinagaku Kenkyu,* II (1931), 107–30.

———. "Yamaga Soko Sensei to sono Shikan no Ip-Pan" ("Master Yamaga Soko and an Element in his Thinking on History"), *Rekishi Kyoiku,* IX (1934), 735–42.

Ogawa Goro. "Choshu-han ni okeru Shomin Kin-no Undo no Tenkai to sono Shisoteki Haikei" ("The Development of the Loyalty-to-the-Emperor Movement among Commoners in Choshu-*han* and Its Ideological Background"), *Kenkyu Ronso,* No. 8 (December, 1953), pp. 3–19.

Oka Fukashi. "Yoshida Shoin no Rekishi Kan" ("Yoshida Shoin's Viewpoint on History"), *Rekishi Nippon,* II (1943), No. 8, 2–9.

Sato Kenji. "Yoshida Shoin no Bushido Seishin" ("The Bushido Spirit of Yoshida Shoin"), *Rekishi Nippon,* II (1943), No. 8, 10–16.

Shigehara Yoshinobu. "Hayashi Razan no Kokutai Kan ni Kan-suru Ichi-Kosatsu" ("A Study of Hayashi Razan's Viewpoint on *Kokutai*"), *Shibun,* XV (1933), No. 6, 26–29.

Takasu Yoshijiro. "Fujita Toko no Jimbutsu oyobi Shiso" ("The Character and Thought of Fujita Toko"), *Riso,* X (1936–37), 1178–90.

Takeda Kanji. "Hito to shite no Shoin" ("Yoshida Shoin as a Person"), *Rekishi Nippon,* II (1943), No. 8, 23–27.

Tojo Yoshi. "Gaikoku Bummei to Shoin" ("Foreign Culture and Yoshida Shoin"), *Yoshida Shoin Zenshu Geppo,* No. 12 (April, 1940), pp. 1–10.

Tsuda Sokichi. "Tokugawa Jidai no Shisoka" ("Thinkers of the Tokugawa Period"), *Riso,* X (1936–37), 1121–32.

MATERIALS IN
WESTERN LANGUAGES

Bibliographical Sources

Borton, Hugh, Serge Eliséeff, and Edwin O. Reischauer. *A Selected List of Books and Articles on Japan.* Washington: American Council of Learned Societies, 1940.

Kokusai Bunka Shinkokai. *A Short Bibliography of English Books on Japan* (3rd ed.). Tokyo: Kokusai Bunka Shinkokai, 1936.

Pritchard, Earl H., *et al.* (eds.). *Bulletin of Far Eastern Bibliography.* Washington: American Council of Learned Societies, 1936——.

Ward, Robert E. "A Survey of Political Science Literature on Japan," *American Political Science Review,* XLVI (1952), 201–13.

Books

Armstrong, Robert C. *Light from the East.* Toronto: University of Toronto Press, 1914.

Beasley, W. G. (trans. and ed.). *Select Documents in Japanese Foreign Policy: 1853–1868.* London: Oxford University Press, 1955.

Fung Yu-lan. *A History of Chinese Philosophy,* trans. Derk Bodde. 2 vols. Princeton: Princeton University Press, 1952–53.

Gauntlett, John O. (trans.), and Robert K. Hall (ed.). *Kokutai no Hongi: Cardinal Principles of the National Entity of Japan.* Cambridge: Harvard University Press, 1949.

Gubbins, John H. *The Progress of Japan: 1853–1871.* Oxford: Clarendon Press, 1911.

Hawks, Francis L. *Narrative of the Expedition of an American Squadron to the China Seas and Japan.* (H.R. Executive Document 97, 33rd Congress, 2nd Session.) Washington: A.O.P. Nicholson, 1856.

Holtom, Daniel C. *Modern Japan and Shinto Nationalism* (rev. ed.). Chicago: University of Chicago Press, 1947.

Kuno, Yoshi S. *Japanese Expansion on the Asiatic Continent.* 3 vols. Berkeley: University of California Press, 1940.

Lanman, Charles. *Leading Men of Japan.* Boston: D. Lothrop & Co., 1882.

Legge, James. *The Chinese Classics.* 5 vols. London: Trübner & Co.; Henry Frowde; 1861–72.

Mazelière, Antoine Rous, Marquis de la. *Le Japon: Histoire et civilisation.* 8 vols. Paris: Plon, 1906–23.

Morris, J. *Makers of Japan.* London: Methuen & Co., 1906.

Needham, Joseph. *Science and Civilisation in China.* 2 vols. Cambridge, Eng.: Cambridge University Press, 1954–56.

Ōkuma Shigenobu (ed.). *Fifty Years of New Japan* (2nd ed.). 2 vols. London: Smith, Elder & Co., 1910.

Sansom, George B. *The First Japanese Constitution.* Tokyo: Asiatic Society of Japan, 1938.

——. *Japan: A Short Cultural History* (2nd ed.). New York: Appleton-Century-Crofts, 1943.

————. *The Western World and Japan.* New York: Alfred A. Knopf, 1950.

Satow, Ernest M. (trans.). *Japan: 1853–1864: Genji Yume Monogatari.* Tokyo: Naigai Shuppan Kyokai, 1905.

Shimonoseki Middle School. *Yoshida Shōin.* Yamaguchi: Yamaguchi Kenritsu Shimonoseki Chugakko, 1937.

Smith, Warren W., Jr. *Confucianism in Modern Japan.* Tokyo: Hokuseido Press, 1959.

Spae, Joseph J. *Itō Jinsai: A Philosopher, Educator, and Sinologist of the Tokugawa Period.* (Monumenta Serica Monograph XII.) Peiping: Catholic University of Peking, 1948.

Spalding, J. W. *Japan and Around the World.* New York: J. S. Redfield, 1855.

United States Government. *H. R. Executive Documents,* 3rd Session, 40th Congress, 1868–69, Vol. I. Washington: Government Printing Office, 1869.

Van Straelen, H. J. J. M. *Yoshida Shōin, Forerunner of the Meiji Restoration.* (T'oung Pao, Monographie II.) Leiden: E. J. Brill, 1952.

Yanaga, Chitoshi. *Japan since Perry.* New York: McGraw-Hill Book Co., 1949.

Periodicals

(Note: *Transactions of the Asiatic Society of Japan* is cited as *TASJ*.)

Arai Hakuseki. "'Hyō-chū-ori-taku-shiba-no-ki': Autobiography of Arai Hakuseki," trans. George W. Knox, *TASJ*, XXX (1902), i–xii, 89–238.

Asakawa Kanichi. "Some of the Contributions of Feudal Japan to the New Japan," *Journal of Race Development*, III (1912), No. 1, 1–32.

Clement, Ernest W. "Chinese Refugees of the Seventeenth Century in Mito," *TASJ*, XXIV (1896), 12–40.

————. "Instructions of a Mito Prince to His Retainers," *TASJ*, XXVI (1898), 115–53.

————. "The Mito Civil War," *TASJ*, XIX (1891), Part II, 393–418.

————. "The Tokugawa Princes of Mito," *TASJ*, XVIII (1890), Part I, 1–24.

Coleman, Horace E. "The Life of Shōin Yoshida," *TASJ*, XLV (1917), Part I, 119–88.

Dening, Walter. "Confucian Philosophy in Japan," *TASJ*, XXXVI (1908), Part II, 101–52.

Dumoulin, Heinrich (trans.). "Sô-gakkô-kei," *Monumenta Nipponica*, III (1940), 590–609.

——. "Yoshida Shôin (1830–1859)," *Monumenta Nipponica*, I (1938), 350–77.

Dumoulin, Heinrich, Hans Stolte, and Wilhelm Schiffer. "Die Entwicklung der Kokugaku dargestelt in ihren Hauptvertretern," *Monumenta Nipponica*, II (1939), 140–236.

Fisher, Galen M. "Kumazawa Banzan, His Life and Ideas," *TASJ* (2nd series), XVI (1938), 221–58.

Haga T. "Note on Japanese Schools of Philosophy," *TASJ*, XX (1892), Part I, 134–47.

Hammitzsch, Horst. "Aizawa Seishisai (1782–1863) und sein Werk Shinron," *Monumenta Nipponica*, III (1940), 61–74.

——. "Hirata Atsutane, ein Geistiger Kämpfer Japans," *Mitteilungen der Deutschen Gesellschaft für Natür- und Völkerkunde Ostasiens*, XXVIII (1936), Part E, 1–27.

——. "Kangaku und Kokugaku," *Monumenta Nipponica*, II (1939), 1–23.

Knox, George W. "A Japanese Philosopher," *TASJ*, XX (1892), Part I, 1–133.

Koyama Matsukichi. "Yamaga-Sokō and His *Bukyō-Shōgaku*," *Cultural Nippon*, VIII (1940), No. 4, 67–87.

Kumazawa Banzan. "Dai Gaku Wakumon: A Discussion of Public Questions in the Light of the Great Learning," trans. Galen M. Fisher, *TASJ* (2nd series), XVI (1938), 259–356.

Lloyd, Arthur. "Historical Development of the Shushi Philosophy in Japan," *TASJ*, XXXIV (1906–7), Part IV, 1–80.

Satow, Ernest M. "The Revival of Pure Shiñ-tau," *TASJ*, III (1875), Appendix, 1–87. (Rev. ed., 1905.)

Timperley, H. J. "Yoshida Shōin—Martyred Prophet of Japanese Expansionism," *Far Eastern Quarterly*, I (1942), 337–47.

Uzawa Fusaaki. "Comparative Study of Wang-Tao and Pa-Tao," *Ex-Oriente*, 1925. (Pamphlet reprint.)

Williams, S. Wells. "A Journal of the Perry Expedition to Japan (1853–1854)," *TASJ*, XXXVII (1910), Part II, i–ix, 1–259.

Index

military adviser, 151–52; significance, 152–53

Sakurada-mon incident, 134n

Sanada Yukitsura, 149

Sangatsu Nijushichi-ya no Ki (Yoshida Shoin), 124

Sankin-kotai, 231

Sato Issai: Yoshida Shoin on, 148, 148n–49n; mentioned, 139, 149

Seidan (Ogyu Sorai), 35

Seiken Igen (Asami Keisai): significance, 59, 64, 216; influence on Yoshida Shoin, 127, 144

Seikenroku (Sakuma Zozan), 151

Seiki no Uta (Fujita Toko), 100

Seikyo Yoroku (Yamaga Soko), 39, 133n

Seimei Ron (Fujita Yukoku), 87–88

Seiwa, emperor, 200n

Sempo. *See* Kuriyama Sempo

Setchu school, 87

Shang (Yin) dynasty, 30n

Shibano Ritsuzan, 127n

Shichi-sho Setsu (Yoshida Shoin), 188

Shido (Yamaga Soko): significance, 40, 41–42; influence on Yoshida Shoin, 159n

Shigi Taisaku (Fujita Yukoku), 88

Shih Chi (Ssu-ma Ch'ien): influence on Mito school, 82, 83; origin of terms *son-no* and *jo-i,* 105, 105n

Shikibu. *See* Takeuchi Shikibu

Shiki Shichi-soku (Yoshida Shoin), 180

Shinagawa Yajiro, 132

Shinchoku of Amaterasu: Yamaga Soko on, 47, 50; defined, 47n; Yoshida Shoin's faith in, 156, 158, 183, 191, 208; and *kokutai* theory, 221, 236, 238; in Imperial Rescript on Education, 225

Shinron (Aizawa Yasushi): significance, 90–92, 218n, 236; first chapter summarized, 92–96; Toku-

gawa Nariaki on, 97; influence on Yoshida Shoin, 114, 133n, 144; Yamagata Taika on, 153–54, 236

Shinto: influence on Tokugawa-period thought, 13–14, 14n, 19, 68; relation to Confucianism, 14–15, 18, 21–22, 23; in thinking of Hayashi Razan, 18, 21–22; in thinking of Kumazawa Banzan, 23; in thinking of Muro Kyuso, 30; in thinking of Ogyu Sorai, 33, 34, 35; in thinking of Yamaga Soko, 38, 42, 44, 46; in thinking of Yamazaki Ansai, 52, 53, 54; reformed by Hirata Atsutane, 67, 76, 77, 79, 80–81, 219, 219n; as element in Japanese theory of the state, 85, 109; as element of Mito thought, 88, 101, 220, 221; in thinking of Aizawa Yasushi, 92; in thinking of Yoshida Shoin, 157, 182–88; main schools of thought, 232–35. *See also* Way of the Gods

Shinto Affairs, Imperial Bureau of. *See* Jingi-kan

Shinto Denju (Hayashi Razan), 21–22

Shinto Gobusho, 46, 54n, 232–33, 234

Shirakawa family, 77, 232, 232n, 233–34

Shishi group: origin of term, 105, 105n; activities, 117n, 155; and Yoshida Shoin, 122, 129, 203–4; and *ichoku* question, 204–5; and Okuni Takamasa, 218; mentioned, 91, 152. *See also* Imperial loyalists

Shoei. *See* Tamaki Shoei

Shogun, position of: in Chinese theory, 15–16, 19, 204; Bakufu ideology on, 16; Tokugawa-period theories on, 16–17; Kumazawa Banzan on, 16, 24, 25, 26; Arai Hakuseki on, 16, 27–29; Yamaga Soko on, 16, 43–44, 48; Asami